D1024536

Reuben the Rhino

Tales of the
Alley of Eleven Twists

A Novel By

Simon Sion Ebrahimi

Published by:

Red Brick Corp.

Credits

Cover painting by: **Haleh Mashian**

Cover design: **Armen**

ISBN-10: 0-692-65945-5
ISBN-13: 978-0-692-65945-8

Visit: SimonEbrahimi.com to order additional
copies Email: SimonEbrahimi@gmail.com

Acknowledgement

I thank my wife, Nahid, my daughters, Mitra and Maryam, their spouses and my grandchildren for their support and encouragement in writing this multi-generational family saga.

Although Ruben the Rhino is based on some true events, all persons appearing in this book are fictitious and any resemblance of its characters to real people, living or dead, is entirely coincidental.

This novel would not be in your hands were it not for the generous support of my philanthropist friend Younes Nazarian, his wife Soraya, and their daughter Sharon who sponsored this endeavor through the "Younes and Soraya Nazarian Foundation" with the conviction that the life stories of the Persian Jews must be preserved.

I am further indebted to Rabbi David Shofet, Jack Mahfar, Sion Mahfar, Solomon Rastegar, Hooshang Hamid, Isaac Shemoilia, Daryoush Dayan, Mike Nazarian , Yoel Neman, Parviz Bina and Bijan Bina for their unyielding support on this journey.

Last but not least, I am grateful for the guidance of my friends and critics, Guitta Karuban, Alan Ullman, Benjamin Behin, Nasrin Frahmand, Mojgan Samimi Tosi, Violet Sassooni and Saeed Sassooni.

Prologue

My father's skill in telling stories from memory was exceptional. Night after night *Mani*, as we called our mothers, my siblings and I sat waiting for my father to finish his dinner, drink his tea and then continue his unfinished story from the night before or perhaps begin a new episode.

Telling the legend, he began by slowly raising his hands. Then, as the tale went on, he opened his palms, widened his fingers, gradually stretched his arms, took us up to the crisis, and suddenly brought his hands down and snapped, "*As the nomad pulled out the blade, the Rhino roared with excruciating pain.*"

And we felt the nomad's dagger piercing our own flesh. My mother brushed aside her long black hair, widening her large brown eyes and slapped the back of her hand. I, the little man my father called Cyrus the Great, held my breath and sat straight, hiding the thrilling sensation that had made me shudder.

We could never get enough of Baba's tales, which were like lost images in the mirrors of time, reclaimed by words and passed from one generation to the next.

Chapter 1
Ruben the Rhino and the Nomad

On a rainy night in the late winter of 1834, Ruben the Rhino, the son of Naphtali the Tailor, was returning home after his daily expedition to nearby villages, where he had hoped to obtain provisions for the starving people of Jewbareh, the Jewish ghetto of Esfahan, once again in the grip of famine, when suddenly he heard the gasps of a man begging for his life. As he neared the source of the voice, he saw Abe the Fishmonger lying supine on the ground with a stout nomad sitting on his chest and pushing his thick thumbs into the old fishmonger's throat. The nomad's long robe was soiled in the dirt of the alley, and his trousers sank into the muck. He shouted, "Give me your money, you filthy Jew!" Rain droplets splashed from the predator's turban onto his face and his thick black beard, where the spray sparkled from the dim light coming from the windows of neighboring houses. Ruben ran up to the assailant and grabbed him by the shoulders with his large, strong hands, trying to pull him off the old man. But the nomad was able to resist and only pressed harder on Abe's throat, shouting at Ruben, "Take your *najes* – filthy, untouchable – hands off me or I'll kill you when I'm done with this piece of shit!"

In a sudden whirl of energy, Ruben hoisted the nomad up into the air. "Run! Run!" Ruben ordered the Fishmonger. The grateful old man quickly rose and scurried away. Had he looked back, he would have seen the angry nomad throwing punches, not one of which landed on the Rhino, whose frame was too tall and massive for the nomad's sinewy but short arms. "Put me down or I swear I'll kill you," he screamed.

"You're no match for me, young man," Ruben said calmly as he firmly planted the assailant on the ground. "Please curse Satan,

1

calm down and leave."

Now released from Ruben's grip, the nomad charged towards a basket of fish, kicking it. The fish went flying into the alley and floated over the stream of mud. The furious man ran into the Fishmonger's shop, broke its small set of shelves, tossed the planks out and came back into the alley to attack Ruben again. This time, Ruben grabbed the back of his opponent's coat and pushed him away. The man skidded on the mud and landed on his back. He struggled to stand up, but the ground was slippery with fish, and he fell again. Ruben, grinning, walked up to him and offered his hand.

"Here, brother. Get up and then, please, just leave."

"You dare to touch me, you filthy Jew?" bellowed the nomad as he tottered to his feet and stood on his own.

"What is it that you want? Here," Ruben exclaimed, scooping a handful of coins out of his pocket. "Take everything I have."

"What do you think I am? A beggar?" yelled the nomad. Out of the sheath on his belt, he suddenly pulled a dagger and made the mistake of approaching Ruben, who instantly twisted the man's wrist and forced his hand open. The dagger dropped into the dirt. Ruben bent down, picked it up, and calmly handed it back to his adversary, saying, "In the name of Allah and all His sacred prophets, would you please just GO!"

Taking the dagger, the nomad retrieved his wet and soiled turban, put it on and cursed Ruben, who was trying hard not to laugh at the man's wet and dirty appearance. Then he straightened up and was about to leave when a harsh voice cried out in the night.

"I've been watching you, Zain!"

The nomad turned his face towards the voice and froze. "Oh *salam arbab!*" — greetings my master — he stammered. A tall, bulky man, followed by two other sturdy but shorter figures, emerged out of the darkness. The three men were dressed in black robes and turbans similar to those worn by Ruben's attacker. Seeing their comrade subdued by Ruben, the two men behind their master pulled their daggers and waved them in the air.

"Arbab, please allow us to take revenge on this najes Jew who has the audacity to hurt our Muslim brother!" one of them hollered.

The master rubbed his long moustache with the palm of his hand and shook his head. "Zain has been beaten by *this* Jew," he said to the men, pointing at Ruben. "Let Zain, our capable man, fight his own battle." And then to the nomad, "Go ahead, Brother Zain and squash this filthy Jew!"

With the veins bulging on his mud stained forehead, the little nomad once again took his dagger out of its sheath, turned around, and practically hurled himself at Ruben, crying, "*Allah Akbar*," – God is Great. The dagger pierced Ruben's shoulder. As the nomad pulled out the blade, the Rhino roared with excruciating pain.

"Go for his heart," the master instructed.

Seeing Zain's arm lifted for another blow, Ruben made a quick sidestep, ditching the attacker and the dagger landed in a soft space between the tightly packed bricks of the wall. As Zain hurriedly struggled to pull the dagger out, Ruben grabbed him by the cloak, turned him around, pointed to his bleeding shoulder with his head and panted, "You see what you've done? Please...". But before he could finish what he was saying, Zain clawed Ruben's face with his nails. Reacting to the piercing pain, Ruben spontaneously stretched his arms wide open and with his whole huge body slammed the nomad's small head against the brick wall behind him. Zain's skull sickeningly exploded and blood shot out of his mouth and nose. The would-be murderer had just been murdered. An instant later, Ruben had disappeared into the dark of night as the other three nomads stood there stunned.

A Jew had killed a Muslim...

Chapter 2
Naphtali the Tailor

It was a Friday night in the autumn of 1809, a week before *Rosh Hashanah*, the Jewish New Year, and Rabbi Shimon's Synagogue was almost packed. Halfway through the service, the rabbi stopped reciting prayers and began beckoning the attendants to solicit donations for the needy as well as for the upkeep of the almost three-century old temple, which was in desperate need of repair. Men who had been accompanying Rabbi Shimon, reading from their prayer books as they stood up, bowed, sat down and stood up again, now sighed in relief and seated themselves, cross-legged on threadbare carpets. The gypsum plastered walls of the synagogue were adorned with Persian miniature paintings of flowers, their colors faded with age. About six feet from the ground, the wall was tiled. These tiles, which belonged to the early Islamic period, were also designed with interwoven flowers, mostly a mix of red and pink with dark blue branches, surrounding Hebrew inscriptions from the Torah. Placed in the center of the synagogue was the *mishkan*, a raised platform with a slightly slanted table where the rabbi and other community leaders stood to pray. The mishkan faced the *hekhal*, a cabinet built in the Eastern Wall and decorated on the inside with colorful satin and on the outside with velvet curtains behind which the Torah scrolls were kept within closed doors. Separated from the men, the women sat upstairs on a balcony in the shape of a shoehorn that also faced the Eastern Wall. They were covered head to toe in their chadors as required by the prevailing Islamic laws.

Although at times, within Jewbareh, rabbis were addressed as *"raav"* or *"hakham,"* they had, in accordance with the Muslim majority, come to be referred to as "mullah." In his fifties, Mullah Shimon was thin and small. His long black beard, which almost covered his entire face except for his protruding cheekbones and came down to his chest, gave him an imposing expression. Summer or winter, he wore a *tallit* – prayer shawl – over his black robe and a black felt *kippah*. At the time, there were three other smaller synagogues in Jewbareh with younger rabbis, but because of his seniority and the length of his service to the community, Rabbi Shimon had been elected as the ghetto's senior rabbi and the largest synagogue in Jewbareh had been named after him.

"Ladies, please!" he hollered in his imposing but unavailing voice at the women who were always busy exchanging gossip on the balcony. Shrugging his shoulders in disappointment, the rabbi turned to the men: "This sacred place is falling apart," he pleaded. "Look at the tiles behind you. They're old and are crying for mercy."

"*Dah gheran,*" said Naphtali the Tailor, the *kadkhoda,* governor of Jewbareh, who was the first to stand up and announce his donation of ten silver coins. In his thirties, the kadkhoda was tall and muscular. His full, jet-black beard hung down to his neck. Serene, polite, generous, well dressed, articulate, caring and handsome – these were some of the qualities Jewbarites attributed to their tall and bulky governor. But more than anything else, they said, it was the vibrations of his voice – rough and powerful – that gripped the crowd.

"May *Hashem* reward your generosity in both worlds," said Mullah Shimon, acknowledging the generous contribution.

"*Dah gheran!*" whispered the women upstairs as they stretched their necks to look at their benefactor. He had a mysterious appeal to women, who found him somehow enigmatic. As always, Naphtali's lead was followed by many other donations – although not as big as his. It was at this point that the sexton walked up to Naphtali the Tailor and whispered something in his ear. Naphtali, hastily closed his prayer book, put it back inside his green velvet bag, which was embroidered with the Star of David, and rushed out. A chilly breeze, heralding the arrival of a cold fall, was crawling through the alleys of Jewbareh. Moonlight washed over the thick brick walls of the old houses before disappearing into the dust on the ground. Lightheaded, in a state of ecstasy, with his heart beating vigorously against the walls of his chest and his eyes watering in the cold wind, Naphtali sprinted along the turns and swerves of the Alley of Eleven Twist that run through Jewbareh like a snake, counting each one he passed. The pathway stretched under his feet. It seemed as though his house had run away from him.

"Can somebody tell me why these alleys have never been so long?" he cried aloud.

A dog barked in the distance.

The ghetto was almost empty, except for a few women who had stayed home from the synagogue. They had gathered, wrapped in blankets and warm clothing, in front of the house of Talat the Seamstress. Here they sat on the cold brick porch cracking roasted watermelon seeds, eating the flesh, and spitting the tiny shells into the air and, every now and then, warming their chilled hands under their armpits, as if hugging themselves. Talat hadn't gone to the synagogue that night because she'd had to look after her baby and her elderly father-in-law. Shamsi the Radish needed to stay home and clean up after her family. The Wartfaced Monir had excused herself because of her numerous ailments: "May you never suffer even a tip of the needle of knee pain I am suffering. *Really*, I just couldn't go!"

After commiserating with each other's problems, they got down to serious business, prodding each other for the latest news, gabbing about things of enormous interest and little consequence.

"What's new, what's new?" said Talat the Seamstress. She had the habit of raising her eyebrows up and down as she repeated herself.

"Don't tell me you haven't heard the latest about Rana the Coyote and her husband Joshua the Goat?" asked the Wartfaced Monir.

"No, no. Tell us, tell us!" begged Talat.

"Well, let's see. Where do you want me to start?" asked Monir, suddenly bashful.

"Anywhere, anywhere!"

"All right," said Monir as she took a deep breath and exhaled. "Rana badmouths Tuti the Exfoliator, her husband's mother. Naturally, her husband, the Bearded Mordechai, gets mad and throws a heavy frying pan at her. Are you with me so far?"

"We are, we are!"

"Will you keep quiet and let her talk?" Tannaz the Barrel protested to Talat, and then, turning her heavy body towards Monir, admonished her, "And will you stop being coy and just tell the whole story, for God's mercy?"

7

Monir said gently, "Calm down, Tannaz *jaan*—dear Tannaz. What's the hurry? You know the longer a story takes the better it is. Now," she continued, "where were we? Yes. So the pan hits Rana the Coyote in the head and she passes out. And who do you think just happens to walk in at that moment? You guessed right. Rana's brother, Noori the Scavenger."

"Woe is me, woe is me!"

"Noori finds his sister all bloodied and out cold on the kitchen floor. Seeing the Scavenger, Joshua the Goat takes off, but Noori chases him and catches up with him before he's even out of the backyard. Would you believe that two bonesetters are working as I speak on Joshua's broken bones and…"

"Wait a minute, wait a minute. Look, look!" Talat interr-uptted her, pointing in the direction of a passerby. "Who can that possibly be? It's too soon for the service to have finished! And why is he walking in such a hurry?"

The curious faces all turned to look.

Monir said: "It's… Yes, it *is* Naphtali the Tailor!"

Talat announced: "Oh my God! Oh my God! Maybe his wife…"

"Good news, Agha Naphtali?" Tannaz the Barrel called out loudly.

Monir yelled: "Is the long awaited prince on his way?"

Naphtali passed by hastily, too preoccupied to hear.

"Well! It seems that he's in no mood to tell us what's going on. That's fine. We'll know soon enough. Now back to Rana's story…"

"Here is your Godgiven Rosh Hashanah gift," announced Henna the Midwife, the only Jewish midwife in the ghetto, as she handed the wriggling and kicking newborn to his anxious father, Naphtali. "His mother screamed so loudly the walls of her house trembled." Then she turned to the crowd of women—family, friends, and neighbors that had gathered to help and started by reciting all the customary incantations she knew in *Jidi,* the dialect of the Jewbarites which was a mix of ancient Persian and Hebrew. *"Cheshmeh bad koor"*—May evil eyes go blind. *"Barokh Hashem,"*— God bless—"the boy marched out of his mother like a rhino, tearing her flesh. Blessed be His name, exceptional children like this come into this world once in a hundred years. This beautiful boy will grow to be somebody! Somebody who will bring pride to us all."

The name "Rhino" stuck and this is how Ruben the Rhino, the

child who would become one of the legendary men in the history of Jewbareh, came into the world.

Two years after Naphtali married Ruth, she gave birth to their first child, Rachel. Their second child, Debra, came as a disappointment to her parents who were determined to have a son. Naphtali didn't give up, but his third and fourth children were also girls— Mohtaram, meaning "respectable" and implying "respectfully, no more girls," and Kafi, meaning "enough" and thus implying 'enough girls.' Although they didn't have the means to support their already large family, Ruth and Naphtali decided to try one more time, and when Ruth gave birth to their first son, Ruben, they were delighted to find that they had gotten their wish. Now Naphtali had a son who would not only inherit his house and his business, but would also succeed to his social position, become the kadkhoda of Jewbareh and carry on the family's ancestral legacy of public service.

The rank of kadkhoda of Jewbareh had always been determined by the unanimous vote of the existing leaders. However, in the memory of Jewbareh, the title of kadkhoda had for generations been bestowed upon all of the firstborn sons in the Naphtali family, for it was common belief that each and every one of them had proven himself to be an outstanding leader, mainly owing to the experience his forefathers had handed down.

Chapter 3
The Magic of Wine

Naphtali's shop was in Meat Market Alley, on the sixth turn of the Alley of Eleven Twists. Although his line of work was tailoring for men, he rarely made new suits. The bulk of his business came from repairs and "reversing"--a viable economic solution the Jewbarites had devised to clothe their adolescent sons. If you had no money to buy the cloth for a suit for your fast growing son, the solution was to have your own threadbare suit reversed to the less worn-out side and then have it sized down for him. Although making a suit out of the reverse side of used, shrunken and patched material was a cumbersome job that Naphtali had mastered, the finished products were inevitably hideous outfits with visible flaws, as when breast pocket and buttonholes were shifted from left to right and thus clearly on the wrong side. Moreover, the money Naphtali made from tailoring was so skimpy that, had it not been for his mastery in winemaking, he could never have made ends meet.

Because consumption of alcoholic drinks was forbidden in Islam, Jewbarites brewed their own homemade wine. In mid-autumn, near the end of the grape season, heads of households formed groups and rented wagons from Haji Ghazi's caravansary and drove out about ten miles until they arrived at the vineyards in Julfa, an Armenian enclave. By now, all the edible grapes had been sold to fresh fruit bazaars, and only wine-grade grapes that had turned slightly brown were left on the vines. Dealing with the Armenians of Julfa was hassle free, for the Muslims who considered both Jews and Christians najes, left them free to deal with each other as they liked. So, they examined different vineyards, selected those they wanted, negotiated with

11

and paid the owners, and got down to work, picking the grapes and filling their baskets.

Back from Julfa, they went down to the basements of their houses and emptied the baskets into large clay pots and the process of winemaking began. With the help of his four young daughters and little Ruben, Naphtali started the tedious job of separating the grapes from their stems. Then they hand-squeezed the grapes until they were half-squashed and poured them into large glazed earthenware jars called *boolooni*. In a few weeks' time, the fermented contents of the jars were returned into the clay pots, hand-squeezed again, and poured back—this time the fermented grape juice only— into the boolooni through rough cotton filters to gather the dregs. A few months later, the clear wine was poured into large bottles called *kope* with a width and a height of three feet and a long neck, all covered with a thick straw mesh for protection. Then the tops of the kopes were given an additional covering with a thick piece of cotton cloth and sealed with gypsum. Over time, wine tasting contests had become a tradition in Jewbareh. About a year after each winemaking season, on a Saturday set especially aside, Jewbarite men brought samples of their wines to the synagogue, and after the service, they tasted and praised each other's vintages. Come next day, as they saw each other on the famous Alley of Eleven Twists, they would exchange opinions.

"Joseph managed to make some decent vinegar. No?"

"And how about Shokri's? That potion tasted like carrot soup!"

The only wine no one ever criticized was Naphtali's, because his was always the best. In fact, it was so good that most of it was sold to very rich Muslims whose agents came secretly to Naphtali's house—always in the dark of night so as not to betray their bosses—and paid handsomely for what had come to be known as "Abram's Magic." Rumor had it that Naphtali's biggest customer was the governor of Esfahan. Other Jewbarites occasionally sold much smaller quantities to middleclass Muslims who, despite religious prohibition, nevertheless from time to time enjoyed the fruits of the vine.

While the grapes came from the same vineyard and were fermented by the same process, no one else's wine came close to Tailor's. It was common knowledge in Jewbareh that Naphtali's famous Abram's Magic was the product of a winemaking formula that had been handed down in his family for many generations.

Apparently, in the dim and distant past, an ancestor of Naphtali's called Abram, came up with this secret recipe. Jewbarites had spied on their tailor and his forefathers and found nothing different in the way they brewed their own wine. Many tried to imitate him. Isaiah the Exfoliator swore that he could trace a tang of red apple and saffron in Abram's Magic, added them to his own mixture and ruined it. Nehemiah the Baker put in some sweet pomegranate and red raisins, so that his wine came out potent but tasteless.

And so, no one was ever able to crack the secret of Abram's Magic.

Although it was almost certain that the title of kadkhoda would remain in Naphtali's family, nevertheless Ruben capabilities were to be assessed for the position of governor of Jewbareh. So when he turned sixteen, and was therefore of age, Naphtali took him along to meetings with the other two community leaders--Rabbi Shimon and Mayor Haskell. During these meetings, which took place in Rabbi Shimon's Synagogue mostly on Tuesdays before the evening service, young Ruben became familiar with the community's problems and the customary ways of dealing with them. In fact, the main purpose of his attendance was for him to become familiar with his future responsibilities, and learn from the leadership of the community the virtues of selfless service and respect for the poor and the helpless.

By the time he was eighteen, Ruben was the tallest man in the ghetto — even taller than his father — and powerfully built, just like a rhinoceros. His supple, dark brown hair fell down to his forehead and touched the edges of his full eyebrows. The color of his eyes had remained unchanged since his infancy — light oak-brown with a touch of green. His soft and shiny beard, the same color as his hair, was evenly trimmed. In the first two years of his apprenticeship as kadkhoda, Ruben became familiar with the problems in the ghetto and came up with novel ideas that impressed the leaders. They found him to be not only an intelligent young man of talent, but one dedicated to his people. He became known for his devotion to the needy and his willingness to risk his own safety while confronting hostile nomads. Thus the leadership of the community concluded that Ruben the Rhino, the son of Kadkhoda Naphtali the Tailor, though still young, was nevertheless a man with a good heart, qualified to succeed his father and become the next governor of

Jewbareh.

Soon after Ruben was born, another hungry mouth was added to Naphtali's family. Keshe nomads had raided the house of Naphtali's close friend, Mordechai the Mason. He had resisted and they had murdered both Mordechai and his wife. At the time of the attack, the couple's eight-year-old son Jacob had been playing in the basement. The miracle of the child surviving this tragedy was something everybody marveled at, but what—they all wondered—would happen to him? Nobody knew. Naphtali gave the boy food and shelter. Weeks passed, but no one was willing to take him—not even Solomon the Grocer whose wife was barren, for, as he said, he and his wife were too old to have children. "My wife's thirty and I am forty-years-old! Who has the energy to raise a child who's only eight?"

When Naphtali's efforts to place Jacob in a good home came to naught, he declared, in spite of his wife's shock, that he would take the boy himself.

"We can barely survive on the meager income you earn, *agha joon*—my dear man. How are you going to feed another hungry mouth?" Ruth complained to her husband.

"I can't put him out on the road, can I? God answered my prayers and blessed me with our son, Ruben," he reasoned to his wife. "Now it's my turn to thank Him for His favor."

After adopting Jacob, Naphtali worked long hard hours and struggled to make ends meet in the hope that he would earn enough to support the whole family, including the newly added Jacob. But soon it turned out that Jacob was a troubled child. In the middle of the night, he awoke screaming. At home, he constantly hit his sisters. Worst of all, he hated Ruben, and both Naphtali and Ruth had to keep a permanent eye on the child lest he hurt their baby boy. Making matters even more difficult, Jacob habitually disobeyed his new parents and frequently disappeared. Ruth and her other children would look for him everywhere, first in the house and then in the neighborhood, but had no luck finding him. And then, hours later, when everybody was exhausted, Jacob would come back, his clothes, hands and face covered in black dust. "Where were you?" they asked, but he wouldn't answer.

So one day Ruth followed him as he left home. Keeping her distance so that he wouldn't see her, she caught sight of him walking the turns of the Alley until he came to his parents' abandoned house and sneaked in, going through the courtyard down to the basement. She walked into the empty house. Three months after the gruesome carnage that had taken place here, the bed of red roses that Jacob's father had planted, attended and was so proud of, had died of thirst. The banisters on the sides of the stairs to the veranda were stained brown with dried blood and the house was filled with a nauseating stench. In the dead silence, Ruth could hear the screams of the victims. With trembling knees, she walked towards the basement. Then stealthily she went down the stairs and stood on the last step. At first it was too dark to see well. The air was stuffy and laced with the smells of wood, pickles, wine and vinegar. She rubbed her eyes and then, behind a curtain of sunlight, she saw Jacob with his back to her, sitting on the pile of charcoal bags that rose up to the ceiling window. With his knees up under his elbows and his face held in the palms of his hands, he was gazing down into the backyard. Ruth was breathless. She wanted to speak, but she didn't know what to say. And so, for those few long minutes, the two of them, she and the boy, remained silent, although it was as if waves of words were sailing over the brightly illuminated dust particles between them. Words of pain. Words of sympathy. He is too small for an eight-year-old child, too thin, Ruth thought.

Jacob was the first one to break the silence. "Five," he said, as he stretched out the open palm of his hand, showing his five tiny fingers to Ruth, then turned his head back again to the window. "I was there, where you're standing now. I was playing. I heard Baba screaming. I climbed up here to see what was happening. There were five of them. Five big, big, Keshe nomad men. They were carrying bags. 'In the name of Moses and Mohammed,' my Baba begged them, 'don't take everything we have.' Then they got angry and said very bad things to Baba. And then they jumped on him. Mani begged them to let go of him and they called my mother a *jendeh*. I was so scared. I opened my mouth to scream, but I covered it with my hands. Then two of them held Baba. Baba was screaming, so one of them took his own turban and stuffed it in Baba's mouth. The other four pulled off Mani's chador and then tore off her clothes one by one—her shirt, her skirt, all of it, all, until she had nothing on. Then one of them took his robe off and threw himself on her. She cried and cried as the Keshe man made strange sounds and laughed. Then he stood up, and the second man did the same thing, and after him the third man, and the fourth and the fifth. Then the biggest one of them said, 'Send them to hell.' And the other four pulled out their daggers. And like the chickens the rabbi slaughters, they cut Mani's and Baba's throats. And there was blood — so much blood. And I was crying with my mouth shut."

Ruth stood there, glued to the stair, biting her fingers. Now her eyes had become accustomed to the dark and she could see Jacob's face. There was fire in his thickly lashed eyes and a sad smile frozen on the corners of his young lips.

"I will kill them." Ruth heard the words come out of Jacob's mouth in a voice that was not his, not the voice of a child, but of the man he would become — hungry for revenge. She walked towards Jacob as he slid down the charcoal pile and held him in her arms. He accepted the warmth of her embrace, but she could feel something rigid, determined and unyielding in the hard muscles of his small body.

In the months and years to come, Naphtali's family learned how to tolerate and cope with Jacob's moods. As he grew, he learned how to control his anger, but his bitterness and hurt never left him. By the time the boy was thirteen, Mullah Shimon declared him capable of reciting his prayers and released him from his *Sheik*. That's what teach-houses were called. At his Bar Mitzvah, as they saw him standing on the mishkan, reciting the Torah portion of the week, Naphtali and Ruth could barely hold back their tears of joy and sympathy. Although they had taken good care of him, the poor young boy had not grown much since they had adopted him. He was small and fragile.

Then Naphtali took Jacob into his shop, where he taught the boy the tedious job of unraveling old suits. Over time, Jacob mastered this craft so skillfully that the Jewbarites bestowed on him the title of Unraveling Jacob. He worked hard and was of great help to Naphtali. He rose early in the morning and by the time Naphtali arrived, Jacob had cleaned the shop, brewed tea in the teapot sitting on the top of the samovar, and was hard at work. Over time, Naphtali married his four daughters to fine suitors. Rachel, who grew up to be one of the tallest girls in Jewbareh, became the wife of Moshe the Poplar. Ruben and Rachel were closer to one another than to their other siblings. "Because," Ruth used to say, "as the

oldest of my girls, she was always like a second mother to my son."
Debra, quiet and shy, married her first suitor, Shelomo, son of
Rabbi Shimon, and a relatively well off jeweler. Mohtaram's
husband, Mansur, was the son of David the Butcher. Mansur
worked for his father and, unlike Shelomo, struggled hard to earn
his bread. Kafi married Yehuda the Mason, the chubby son of
Tannaz the Barrel. All these blessings Naphtali attributed to his
pious act of adopting the orphan child, his son Jacob, whom he
married to the boy's murdered mother's cousin, Setareh the Star.

In 1831, when Ruben was twenty-two, his father Naphtali
died, and Ruben was immediately installed as kadkhoda of
Jewbareh by Rabbi Shimon and Mayor Haskell. What Naphtali left
for Ruben was his business of tailoring, the family's secret wine
recipe, Abram's Magic, and Jacob in the shop, for Naphtali had told
Ruben, and even written in his will, that he should never forsake
his stepbrother.

In the mornings, Ruben now walked along the path to work
that he had taken with his father for so many years. From their
house, where he lived with his mother, he would pass the familiar
shops, all lined up next to each other. On Fish market Alley, there
was Abe the Fishmonger, "Catch of the day, Kadkhoda Ruben!" he
cried, showing off a one foot long trout he had caught that morning.
"And hello to you too," Ruben teased the old man. "What a
beauty!" He paid for the fish and asked Abe to give it to his mother
when she came shopping later that morning. Next were Yohai the
Shoemaker, Nehemiah the Baker, and finally the shop of his old
friend Nissan the Fabricseller. Ruben stopped at each shop, greeted
the owners and asked them about their business. The Shoemaker
was upset with the Fishmonger. "Like a town crier declaring his
king's conquest of another land, he howls until he's sold his last
fish." Nehemiah the Baker was unhappy because he was no longer
the same young man he had once been. "I simply can't stand the
heat, or the cold for that matter," he complained to Ruben.

"But why don't you get your young strong son to help you?"

"No, Kadkhoda Ruben. No!" He raised his whitened palms.
"I've burned enough bread here. Not my child. If someone younger
would buy this place and let me go home and wait for my day to
come…"

"God forbid Agha Nehemiah. May you live to be one hundred

and twenty years old. I will spread the word and hope we'll find you a buyer."

Then he turned into Meat Market Alley, where his own tailoring shop was located. At the junction of these two market roads, he would sometimes pause at a shop that had been turned into the burial site of *Pir Pinehdooz* — Saint Cobbler — a Muslim who, in addition to his reputation as a wonderworker, had been a shoe repairman as well as a poet. Jews and Muslims alike lit candles at his gravestone, and listened — as Ruben sometimes did — to Dervish Mohsen, the turbaned blind beggar in a long robe who sat on its steps, singing or reciting the Saint's poems with his enchanting voice, his milky stone eyes staring up into the blue. Dervish Mohsen knew people by the sounds of their voices and by the scent of those who passed mutely by. People gave him a coin or two in exchange for his assurance that the Saint would grant their wishes.

Perhaps feeling the vibrations of Ruben strong steps, stretching his arm and opening his palm, the beggar called "Salam Kadkhoda Ruben. Make a silent wish and let the Pir make it come true."

"I say it out loud," said Ruben putting a few coins in his palm. "Let there be peace and health for all. Muslims and Jews alike."

In Meat Market Alley there were the shops of two Muslim businessmen. From Asghar the *Allaf* — fodder-seller — people bought forage for the sheep they kept in their backyards and slaughtered on happy occasions such as circumcisions and weddings. As always, Asghar was the first to say Salam.

"*Alik-al-Salam*, Asghar Agha. How's business?"

"*Alhamdollah*"--thanks to Allah — he said, smiling as always.

On the contrary, Samad the Attar--the grocer — never responded to anyone's greetings. He's angry at himself, people said about him as he sat behind his scale with a permanent knot between the thin, gray eyebrows that sat atop his dark brown eyes. "What sin have I committed to deserve such requital — to have to earn my bread from najes hands?" he had often said to his Jewish customers. Past the Allaf and the Attar, facing Ruben's store, on Meat Market Alley, was that of David the Butcher.

Finally, when Ruben arrived at his own shop, he went up a few steps and greeted Jacob, his always frowning stepbrother, who, as on every other working day, had opened the shop and made fresh tea, setting the teapot on the brass samovar, where it was ready to be served. Ruben greeted Jacob and instead of responding, Jacob pointed at the teapot and the brass samovar. Before sitting down behind his working table, Ruben poured two glasses of tea, put one in front of Jacob and another on his own table.

And so it happened that Ruben the Rhino, son of Naphtali the Tailor, with his good mind and kind heart, proved to be a young leader capable of resolving many difficulties in the life of the people of Jewbareh. Ruben had been born and raised during the reign of Agha Mohammad Khan, the founder of the Qajar Dynasty, who ruled Persia from 1742 to 1797. This king was a merciless eunuch and people attributed his cruel rage to the fact of his predecessor had castrated him. During his reign, throughout Persia, the oppression and persecution of Jews intensified, and once again since the conquest of Persia by Arabs, Persian Jews were put under immense pressure to convert. As an apprentice going to meetings of community leaders, Ruben had discovered that the problems of the ghetto were many. But when he took the place of his father as the governor of Jewbareh, Ruben discovered that doing something about attacks of murderous Keshe nomads and preventing tensions between Muslims and Jews would not be an easy task.

In his first meeting as kadkhoda with the mayor and the rabbi at his synagogue, Ruben shared his concerns with the other two men. "What bothers me," he said, "is the way we act in the face of the nomads' atrocities. They invade us the way foxes and jackals attack flocks of sheep, and we don't fight back. Since time immemorial, our community has taken these acts of violence as an inevitable part of its destiny. They steal from us in broad daylight and they rampage through our homes and all we do is to sit back and cry silently or cringe and cower under the malicious deeds of these monstrous predators. They put their daggers against the throats of our loved ones and we beg them for mercy. And when they have severed their heads, we plead for our own lives."

"What's happening to you?" Rabbi Shimon grunted in a surprised tone. "For all the years that you've been attending our meetings, I had hoped that our young, kadkhoda-to-be was learning enough to think with his head, and act with *chutzpah*--not with emotion. Not once during all these years have you ever spoken about this problem. Why? I guess because you already knew the answer," he said, caressing his long, gray beard. "As it has been written, as long as we Jews live in Diaspora, we will be attacked. You know very well that, unfortunately, we are the Keshe nomads' convenient prey. They live only a few streets away from here in their disgusting shacks and get such generous subsidies from the mosques in the area that unlike other nomads, even when the weather is freezing cold in Esfahan, they don't travel to the warm southern regions. And worst of all, with the money that they have saved from donations, they buy rooms in Haji Ghazi's caravansary. Their men don't work and their women march through our alleys as their brass bangles clink and clang like devils of the night, luring our ignorant women to open the doors of our houses to their blasphemy, sorcery and spying eyes."

"Your kind evocations are impressive, rabbi. But has it also been written that we should simply surrender to our sufferings?" Ruben looked steadily at the old man who had spent so many years studying the Torah, but knew nothing about self-defense. "We can't take their cruel attacks as acts of God and do nothing about it. With all due respect, Rabbi, I'm convinced that we are victims of our own wanton weakness."

The rabbi shook his head, his beard waving in the air. "You're too young, my son. Too young. I know that from time to time in our defense you have bravely confronted these vicious nomads, but if that's what you have in mind as a permanent strategy, I will not allow it."

Then it was Mayor Haskell's turn to admonish Ruben. "If it doesn't itch, don't scratch it," he said, waving his unusually long, thin forefinger sideways. In his late forties, Haskell owned the ghetto's public bath, which he had inherited from his father. As a younger man, he had worked as an "exfoliator," rubbing layers of soiled dead skin off the bodies of his customers. This strenuous job had tightened his muscles, which danced like that of horses under his dark skin as he moved his gloved hand back and forth over his clients' backs and arms and legs. Brown was his favorite color. His robe. His shirt. His kippah. Even his beard, which he colored with henna. This brown aura made the color of his skin look much darker than it really was. "This situation, my son," Haskell continued, pulling on his earlobe, as brown as the rest of him, "has been going on since the time of my father, and the father of his father and many generations before that and there's nothing to be done about it."

This matter was taken up in a number of subsequent meetings until Ruben became convinced that neither of these two men, nor any other Jewbarite, was willing or able to confront the problem of the Keshe nomads who lurked only streets away and served as a constant threat to every man, woman and child in Jewbareh with possibility of sudden, uninvited murderous violence.

One morning in the winter of 1832, Ruben entered his shop and he found Jacob sitting behind his table, his small figure all tightened up, his face pale. He was gazing into nowhere. Ruben looked around and noticed that the samovar wasn't on and that the ashes of the previous day's fire had remained undisturbed. "What's happened?" he asked and heard no response. He went up to Jacob and put his arm around his shoulder. "Talk to me, older brother. Are you having problems at home?" he asked, kissing Jacob on his cheek which Ruben realized it was wet with tears, and that frightened him. He asked if anything had happened to Jacob's wife or his two young boys. But Jacob shook his head and then broke down sobbing.

"I swear you on the soul of your mother," Ruben pleaded. "Talk to me, Jacob!"

"My mother!" he roared. "Just like my mother…"

"Like your mother *what*, Jacob?"

Early that morning, Jacob told Ruben between sobs and gasps, he had been passing the home of Nehemiah the Baker, when he noticed the door to the house broken wide open and heard Nehemiah and his wife, Misha the Clothwasher, begging for mercy. "It was like hearing the echoes of my mother's pleadings. I don't know why, but I barged into the house and froze seeing the scene in front of me. Out in the courtyard Keshe nomads were raping Misha in front of Nehemiah and their two young girls. And me…" Jacob broke down again. "I ran away. I couldn't take it, brother. I couldn't. It was just like seeing a recurring nightmare in the day-light."

With his heart full of pity and outrage, Ruben nevertheless felt torn. Should he rush to Nehemiah's house and try to stop the attack, knowing quite well that he would be outnumbered and possibly killed, or instruct Jacob not to keep quiet about this and cover up the whole incident? After all, it was the honor of Misha, Nehemiah and their daughters that was at stake. He tried to put himself in Nehemiah's place and wondered how he would feel if the same thing ever happened to him, although at this point in his life, a wife and children were the last things on Ruben's mind. It didn't take him long to decide. He rushed out of his shop and ran as fast as he could to Nehemiah's house. When he got there, he put his ear to the broken door, which had already been put back in place, but not fixed. Hearing nothing, he knocked gently.

"Who is it?" Nehemiah called, his voice weak.

"I was just passing by. I saw your door broken. Is everything all right?" Ruben said in a low voice. He stood there, waiting for a response, wondering whether he should just go in. Then Nehemiah opened the door. His face was bruised, his clothing torn. "What has happened to you?" Ruben asked.

"They raided my house, attacked us, stole everything we had and took off. That's all," he said, as if reporting a routine matter. Deep down the Rhino praised the man, who was obviously protecting his family's name, although Ruben was certain that plagued by this brutal assault, Nehemiah might never again touch his raped and "corrupted" wife. "My dear *kadkhoda*," he concluded beseechingly with an old Persian proverb, "*Did you see a camel? No, you didn't!*" – which essentially added up to: "Keep your mouth shut."

On his way back from the baker's house, Ruben came to the realization that he would have to fight back against these atrocities singlehandedly, for, when it came to even trying somehow to lessen the hardships imposed upon their people, Rabbi Shimon, Mayor Haskell, Nehemiah and the rest of the Jewbarites had surrendered to the abuse to which these outsiders chronically subjected them. *Outsiders*, he thought, as a revelation dawned on him. It was so obvious! The redemption of his people had to come from outside Jewbareh. Those inside had neither the will nor the vigor. But the question was: Who would be this redeemer?

Some weeks later, on an early Thursday morning of a cold winter day, Ruben arrived at his shop to find Hakim Akbar waiting for him, warming his bare hands in the steam of his breath.

"Salam," Ruben said in greeting. "What brings you here so early?"

"Alik-el-Salam," – Greetings to you. "Open the door and let's go in first. I have been here a long time and I'm freezing."

"Sorry Hakim. I thought you knew that Thursdays are Jacob's day off and that I don't open the shop as early as he does."

A Hakim was a holistic doctor whose knowledge had been amassed and handed down through generations. Hakims were medical practitioners whose advice and treatment were based solely on years of experience and a detailed understanding of herbs, potions, and all sorts of old wives' remedies. In his seventies, Hakim Akbar was a slender man who wore a permanent smile. Many Jewbarites were his patients, and they liked him. Although a Muslim, he cared about them regardless of their faith. He went around carrying a fat brown leather briefcase filled with medicines; indeed, the Hakim and his briefcase were inseparable. "You never know," he said. "Somebody may suddenly get sick."

Ruben's father Naphtali had dealt with Hakim Akbar on a barter basis — free treatment for free tailoring *and*, once in a while, a mysterious canvas bag, whose exact contents Ruben did not discover until sometime during his adolescence.

"Nobody, not even your mother, should ever find out about this, or it will have grave consequences for our people," Naphtali had warned his son one night on their way home from work, just before confiding to him that the contents of the bag were in fact bottles of his famous wine. As a strict Muslim, Hakim Akbar didn't drink wine, but he knew its medicinal properties and used it as an ingredient in some of the medications he prepared. The Hakim had come to know about Abram's Magic through a ranking prince in the Esfahan governor's mansion and had subsequently become a regular customer of Naphtali's, and now Ruben's.

Hakim Akbar climbed the steps into Ruben's shop, and sat down on the rough, charcoal gray cotton cushion facing Ruben's worktable. Ruben took the samovar and the brazier outside and filled them with charcoal. As he lit the rich black chunks, two columns of smoke swirled up. Then he came back in and sat down, facing the old Hakim, who was still blowing into his hands.

"Sorry Hakim. As soon as the charcoal glows red, I will bring it in. So, tell me, why have you come so early?"

"Well," said Akbar rubbing his eyes with the backs of his forefingers. "I have a special request, but I'm embarrassed to tell you what it is."

"Oh?" Ruben said with an encouraging smile, tilting his head to look into Hakim Akbar's eyes. "If it is anything I can help you with, you know I will."

"I don't know how…" the Hakim twirled his hands hesitantly as Ruben sat back and waited patiently. Presently, Akbar slapped his thigh and began. "All right. This is the situation. I have a patient who is very influential. This man has been suffering from a chronic stomachache. Last month I gave him a small bottle of your wine laced with valerian root extract, but unfortunately the impious man was able to detect the Abram's Magic in the syrup. I'm sure he has sampled your wine somewhere, perhaps with one of your customers, because he mentioned something about having heard about Abram's Magic. Since then, he has relentlessly been asking for more medication. 'Although it works miracles,' he says, 'the effect doesn't last too long.' He hates the valerian in the potion," Hakim added, shaking his head. "This means that he wants the wine only and what's even more unfortunate, he wants it in large quantities."

Ruben looked at him slyly. This 'very influential' person could be of help to Jewbarites, he thought as he went and brought in the brazier and put it in front of the Hakim. Next he brought in the samovar and placed it on a tray by his side. "If you don't mind my asking, who is this patient of yours?"

"I can't divulge his name!" said the Akbar firmly.

"Is he in the government?"

"No. He's not and please ask no further!"

"Is he a member of the clergy?"

Hakim Akbar didn't respond. It was time for Ruben to ease the pressure on the poor man by changing the subject. "This stupid samovar takes forever to boil the water."

"Are you going to help me?" Akbar pleaded.

"But of course, Hakim! Tell me how many bottles are we talking about?"

"I guess three to four bottles a week. But," he raised his voice, "I will be the one to pay for them."

"You know I will never accept money from you, Hakim Akbar. But why don't you tell this person, whoever he is, that you simply don't have access to such a large supply?"

Saying this, Ruben began blowing into the charcoal furnace of the samovar as he watched Akbar from the corner of his eye. The water began boiling and steam spewed out of a valve hinged on the lid of the samovar, making tapping noises as it popped up and down. Ruben put some tealeaves in the teapot, filled it with boiling water and placed it on furnace of the samovar. Shaking his head as though feeling sorry for himself, the old Hakim said, "I told him yesterday. I said, 'Your Holiness...' Shit!" Akbar realized the slip of his tongue.

"Mullah Ahmad?" Ruben stared at Akbar and let out a great laugh, even though he saw that the old man had turned pale.

"In the name of Allah and all His prophets and the soul of your father of blessed memory, I beg you, Ruben. The lives of my family and my own life are at stake here. If he finds out that I have revealed this, especially to a Jew... Oh, how stupid of me!" This time he slapped his forehead.

The Rhino knew full well that as the chief clergyman of Esfahan, Mullah Ahmad was a part of the top leadership of the Shiite Muslim clerics who were in turn the moving force behind the kings of the Qajar Dynasty. If he could get close to this man, he would have an excellent opportunity to mitigate the Keshe atrocities and at the very least, bring relative calm to Jewbareh. "Take it easy Hakim," he reassured the Hakim in a cheerful voice. "If I'm ever stupid enough to say a word about this, I'll be the one who's executed, without hesitation." He grinned at the Hakim, who was still nonplussed. "Now, back to your problem," Ruben continued. "He wants wine? He gets wine! It's as simple as that! So, relax and let's talk about the details."

"What details?" Akbar asked, throwing up his hands. "What are you up to? I thought you said you couldn't come up with so many bottles a week!"

Ruben reached for two cups, filled about one third of each with the dark brewed tea and the rest with the hot water of the samovar, putting one cup before the Hakim and keeping the other for himself. Then, ignoring Akbar's misgivings, he said, "If I get him, say, four bottles a week, I hope he doesn't expect *you*, our respected physician, to be his runner."

"What do you mean?"

"I mean all you have to do is to tell him that you have arranged for his medicine to be delivered to his house."

Hakim Akbar hollered, "Aye..." and began coughing as he gulped the hot tea. "Forget it," he said, standing up. "You!" he pointed at Ruben, his hand shaking, "You don't seem to understand the seriousness of the situation. Nobody knows that the Mullah drinks wine. He doesn't even admit to me that he wants it. He calls it medicine. I am the only person who can and should do this." He picked up his bag and was about to head toward the front door when Ruben stood in his way, with two fresh cups of tea in his hand and coaxed him to sit down. Then he wheedled and cajoled until Hakim Akbar calmed down and gave in.

"But only on the condition that you, yourself, Ruben, deliver the wine."

Only after Ruben swore on the soul of his father that he would make the deliveries himself, did the Hakim relent, and the two of them sipped their tea in friendship and peace.

One early evening about a week later, just before sunset, Ruben stepped out of his house into the serpentine ripples of the Alley of Eleven Twists, a heavy canvas bag slung over his shoulder. It had been snowing all day. From a distance, he could hear the muffled chime of caravan bells, and the eerie voice of Muezzin Ali chanting Allah Akbar from the top of the minaret of the Juma Mosque, inviting "the people of faith" to begin their evening prayer. The shopkeepers, who were busy closing their stores along the Alley of Eleven Twists, saw Ruben's tall and powerful figure passing by. They greeted the patriarch and the governor of their ghetto, but Ruben was too distracted to respond. Many thoughts were going through his mind.

He came out of the ghetto and went to Haji Ghazi's caravan-sary. Here he would wait for night to fall before setting out along the city's streets. Haji Ghazi, a Muslim friend of Naphtali, was known for his notoriously long moustache, which covered his lips and came down his chin on both sides. Theirs was a friendship of mutual interest. When Keshe nomads planned to raid Jewbareh, Haji Ghazi was on the alert. He hated these nomads for two reasons. "Firstly," he said, "Because they are like primitive and brutal animals whose acts contradict the Koran. Secondly, after they depart, not only do they leave a mess behind, but they barely pay me." So, after a while, whenever the nomads showed up, Haji Ghazi immediately sent word to Naphtali — and now to Ruben — that they had settled outside, behind the walls of his caravansary, to the interior of which he had refused to admit them. These warnings were invaluable to Jewbarites who would immediately lock and block their doorways, hide in their houses and take as many precautions as possible to reduce the virulence of the forthcoming raids. Naphtali and Ruben would reciprocate the favor by occasionally giving the caravansary owner free wine. Now, in the room where Haji Ghazi lived, Ruben and the caravansary owner sat, drinking tea and chatting.

"Tell me, my friend, what do you have in that bag?" Ghazi asked the Rhino.

Ruben reached into the bag, took a bottle out and handed it to his friend. "This!" he said. "Taste it and tell me what you think. I'm taking the rest to a customer in the city."

Ghazi took the bottle, put it next to him and said, "At this time of night, you, the Jew, want to walk the streets of Esfahan with a bag of wine bottles hanging from your shoulder? Are you out of your mind? I mean, who's this customer of yours and why doesn't he get someone to pick up his order? Allah Akbar! You Jews have become so goddamn arrogant!"

"Calm down my friend. I know it's dangerous, but this has to be delivered by me. In person."

"I'll tell you what," Haji sighed deeply. "I will have one of my people accompany you. Really, there are so many vagabonds on the streets at this time of night."

By the time Ruben had politely rejected Ghazi's insistent offers, it had become so dark that Ruben knew he had to be on his way. The streets were almost empty, except for groups of homeless beggars who stretched their arms out at Ruben with open palms and occasional drunk or drowsy city guards who would stop him to inquire about the contents of the bag, insisting that he was a thief carrying stolen merchandise. Ruben would appease them with a bribe and continue undisturbed toward Mullah Ahmad's house, which was about a mile away from Jewbareh, on a side street just off Shah Square in the center of the city of Esfahan.

With an area of over nine hundred thousand square feet and almost four hundred years of history, the Shah Square has one spectacular monument on each of its four sides. On the north parameter, where Ruben entered the Square, stood the Safavid Bazaar with a magnificent arch shaped gate, embellished with colorful floral designs made of miniature mosaic tiles, artfully put together. As Ruben headed to the southern end of the square, which led to Mullah Ahmad's house, on his left he saw the moonlight-struck beige and blue mosaic tiles of the dome of Sheik Lutf-Allah Mosque. And as he walked closer to where Mullah Ahmad's residence was located, on the southern side of the square, the tomb of the Shah Mosque was an enormous glowing gem of detailed mosaic tiles with elegant designs on a dark blue background. Finally, on his right he saw Ali Ghapoo Palace, a seven story structure. For the obvious reason that Jews were considered najes, they were not allowed to step inside any of the mosques, but Ali Ghapoo Palace was the exception. Ruben had been to Ali Ghapoo only once. His father had taken him there when he had been eighteen. Climbing the spiral staircase of this palace, Naphtali had explained to his son how Shah Abbas, the most powerful king of the Safavid Dynasty, would celebrate the Persian New Year by entertaining noble visitors and foreign ambassadors in this palace. Ruben had seen murals of floral, animal and bird motifs by the renowned master and court artist, Reza Abbassi on each floor. The music room on the sixth floor had especially fascinated Ruben. There were shelves carved into the plaster walls in the shape of different musical instruments for the musicians to fit their instruments after they had entertained the king, his guests or his harem. Naphtali had told his son many stories about the atrocities of the kings of the Safavid Dynasty — the patrons of the Shiite sect in Persia. With every detail that Naphtali had narrated for his adolescent son, the enigmatic ambiance of this seventeenth century palace had captivated young Ruben's imagination even more. He had felt the spirits of the cruel kings who had lived there hundreds of years ago and could see their women-slaves, concubines imprisoned within for the kings' pleasure, the eunuchs who guarded their harems, the African slaves, brought through the Persian Gulf by Portuguese merchants and handpicked for the royal court, the young men, who were dressed as women and kept in separate harems to entertain his majesty's change of taste and appetite for variety, should he tire of his women.

Naphtali had explained to his son that there were some men who were attracted to both men and women, or to men only. Later in his life Ruben would learn that although homosexual behavior was considered an abomination in Islam — and all other Semitic religions, for that matter — and was punishable by death, it was nevertheless widely practiced throughout Persia, mainly because women were kept away from men. Kings, however, were exempted by the court clergies from many religious protocols, for they were

considered "The Shadow of Allah on Earth." There was a fine line
between the Allah and his shadow, and therefore, in order to
distance the kings from the risk of becoming the Allah himself, they
were required to commit certain sins such as drinking and having
young boys for their sexual pleasure.

In the pitch-dark night, hesitating in front of the mullah's door,
Ruben shuddered as the freezing air entered his lungs and
intensified his anxiety. He put down the bag, making sure the
bottles didn't clink against each other. "In the name of God," he
whispered, raising his fist to knock on the door. Then his arm froze
and his heart sank. Time and again, he had rehearsed what to do at
this moment, but now that he was there, his courage deserted him.

Beyond the entrance to the house were the "private quarters" of
Mullah Ahmad, to which Hakim Akbar had instructed Ruben to
deliver the wine. But in the entire history of Jewbareh no "infidel"
had ever talked to the Chief Mullah of Esfahan face to face. He was
to knock on the door, tell the Mullah that he was delivering the
Hakim's medicine and leave at once. Within their larger houses,
men of Mullah Ahmad's standing had their own havens. Private
unto themselves with a separate backdoor, these important figures
received their personal guests where no wives, concubines and
children were allowed to enter. And that was exactly where Ruben
the Rhino stood quailing, within inches of the Mullah's very private
quarters and too scared to knock. Suddenly, the enormity of the
action he was about to take dawned on him. Too many thoughts
were going through his head. "Who are you?" the mullah would
ask upon seeing his face, "And what are you doing here? And what
is *this*? And how dare you bring wine to my house? And do you
know who I am? Come and arrest this najes Jew and break the
bottles on his head. And since when have you infidels become so
arrogant?" Then, Ruben thought, the mullah would declare *jihad*
against the Jewbarites, and issue a *fatwa*: "Plunder their belongings
and pour their filthy blood!" After such a catastrophe, how would
Ruben raise his head among his people? "Oh God! Help me," he
sighed.

"Excuse me?" answered a voice. Ruben raised his head to see
the mullah standing in the frame of the door. He was a small, neatly
dressed man of elegant appearance. He wore a black turban, a long,
white coat with a green shawl round his waist, the uniform of the
mullahs who were considered *seyed* — of the posterity of the

prophet Mohammed. His thick black eyebrows sat above his gentle eyes. Ruben's heart was stuck in his throat.

"*Hazrateh Agha*" – Your Holiness. I am… I have… Hakim Akbar has sent me…" He bent down and lifted the bag, handing it to the Mullah. The bottles in the bag rattled as his hands shook. "Your medicine, Hazrateh Agha."

"I thought you were Hakim Akbar. All right. Why don't you bring it in? It's too cold outside and you are shivering, young man."

Ruben was beside himself. Did the most important Muslim cleric in Esfahan know he had invited a najes Jew into his home? Ruben thought as he stepped inside Mullah Ahmad's private quarters and followed him into a small courtyard. They passed by a pomegranate tree, its bare branches covered with snow and then a tiny *hoze* – a pond Muslims use for ablution before prayer. On either side of the hoze were traces of two flowerbeds hiding under a blanket of snow. Facing the backyard was a red brick building. The two men climbed up the stairs to the veranda and entered what was obviously Mullah Ahmad's private quarters. He and Ruben took off their shoes and entered a foyer lit by some tall candles. Its marble walls rose to the ceiling and the floor was covered with a rough, inexpensive Persian carpet. Mullah Ahmad opened the door to his large living room, inviting the Rhino in. Ruben entered and baffled at what he saw, stopped – frozen in his tracks. The room was illuminated with candles placed in the large chandelier hanging from the ceiling and sconces on the walls. There were two full length windows with thick, beveled crystal panes on his right that opened onto a long veranda and a smaller one on the opposite wall that overlooked the back street. The walls were decorated with carved plasters and painted skillfully, matching the floral designs of a large Persian carpet that covered the floor. The air was filled with the aromas of brewed tea, wild rue and frankincense. Never in his life had the Rhino been in a house with such luxurious ornaments. Ali Ghapoo was one thing, for there lived the *kings*, he thought. If this were only one room in the private quarters of this mullah, he wondered, what would the rest of his house look like?

Ahmad, who was facing the windows onto the veranda, turned around and sat down at a spot where large pillows covered with fine tapestry had been arranged, some on the ground and some against the wall. "Now bring the bag, sit next to me and let's see what we have here," the Mullah called from where he had just sat down. Then, as Ruben placed the bag on the floor in front of him, the elegant cleric winced and his eyes widened. "What the hell is this?" he said, glaring at Ruben.

Drops of sweat streamed down Ruben's forehead. "I... I mean..."

"This insane Hakim has sent me a year's supply of medicine!" cried Ahmad, laughing.

Ruben tried to say something, but he felt as if his tongue had stuck to the roof of his mouth.

"And where on earth has my Hakim found himself a giant of a footboy like you?" he stared at Ruben. He then paused and asked, "Why are you so nervous, young man? Sit down and tell me who you are," he commanded, pointing to the pillow facing him. "Have I seen you somewhere?"

"I'm Rueben. Ruben the Tailor, Your Holiness," said the Rhino, sitting down.

"Jew?"

"Ye... Yes, Hazrateh Agha," Ruben stammered.

Mullah Ahmad poured a cup of tea and put it in front of the deliveryman. Then he looked inside the bag and shook his head. "*Five* bottles! I hope the old Hakim hasn't laced his fine wine..." he took his turban off and scratched his head. "What was its name? Abram's Wine... or was it Abram's Magic? Anyway, let's hope that these are not mixed with that nasty tasting valerian root extract. You see. I've tasted that wine, and no other comes close to it."

"Your Holiness. I make this wine myself and I can assure you that it is Abram's."

The Mullah's eyes widened. He took a bottle out of the bag, opened it, poured a little wine into a clean teacup and tasted it. Then he smacked his lips, and as if he had found a treasure, clapped his hands joyfully. "It *is* Abram's Magic. That little Hakim knows where to get pure fine Jewish wine." Saying this, the mullah stood up. Ruben immediately jumped up too. "What's the matter with you, young man? Sit down and drink your tea," he said, putting his hand on Ruben's shoulder and pressing him down gently. Then he took the bag and put the bottles in the closet near where he sat. When he returned, he gave Ruben the empty canvas bag and said, "If somebody were to ask you what was in this bag, what would you say?"

Ruben put the bag under his jacket and said, "What bag, Your Grace?"

The mullah screamed with laughter. "You're my kind of Jew. Now, how much do I owe you for this favor?"

"Nothing, Your Holiness."

"I guess you don't know me," Mullah Ahmad said with a smile as he sat back on his pillow. "I pay for whatever I get. Besides, I want to feel comfortable when I ask you for future refills."

It was the right and crucial moment for Ruben to muster his courage and negotiate his terms with this compellingly powerful authority. "This is only a mere token of appreciation from my community for your support," he said with his head down. For the long moment of silence that followed, he did not dare to raise his head to look at the mullah and see how far he had angered him. Then Ruben heard him roaring with laughter from deep in his belly. "In the name of Allah, since when have you Jews learned to speak like this? 'A mere token of appreciation?'" he imitated Ruben. "Anyway, how much?"

Ruben exhaled in relief. "Hazrateh Agha. Jews believe that wine is sacred and priceless."

"You know what?" Ahmad chuckled. "I sort of like you, big man. Surely you know how to make nonsense sound meaningful, but what you don't know is that I know your religion better than you. So don't tell me that Jews never sell wine. Now, if you don't want to charge me, that's a different matter."

"Surely it is, Your Holiness." Ruben stood up to leave.

When Ahmad had accompanied him to the door, Ruben asked, "When do you want me to come and take back the empty bottles?"

"Make it four weeks from now," replied Mullah Ahmad, caressing his thick beard at the same time.

But Ruben did not wait another four weeks. Two weeks later he brought five more bottles and this time the Mullah, who was delighted with Ruben's surprise visit, invited him in to have a drink of "the fine Jewish wine, Abram's Magic." And as the two were drinking to each other's health, Ahmad told Ruben that his wine had been so superb that he had already finished all the bottles Ruben had brought on his first visit. Another two weeks, another five bottles and Ruben hadn't yet dared tell the other two community leaders about what he was up to. Eventually, after an interval of several months, he felt obligated—in spite of the fury that was bound to follow—to share his unauthorized arrangement with the rabbi and the mayor. And once he told them, just as he had expected, they condemned his irresponsible, dangerous scheme and cursed the day they had voted him their kadkhoda for, they said, they now realized that he was void of his blessed father's merits. They called Asher the Ewe, Ruben's uncle and Ruth's brother, for help, for Asher had become the family patriarch after Naphtali's death. They asked the Ewe to convince his young nephew that taking wine to the Chief Mullah of Esfahan was most imprudent and deeply dangerous for the security of the Jewbarites. But despite his avuncular authority, Asher's demands on the Rhino to stop his 'foolish' plan were to no avail. So, despite their disapproval, the rabbi and the mayor had no choice but to follow their young leader in what seemed to them like madness.

Soon, to everybody's surprise, especially the Keshe nomads, Mullah Ahmad delivered sermons in Juma Mosque, quoting verses from the Koran favorable to the Jews.

"According to *Kalam-Allah*—the words of Allah—Zoroastrians, Christians and Jews are 'People of the Book' and are therefore not to be considered infidels. It has also been written that Imam Ali kneeled down in front of a Jewish girl to take a thorn out of her foot. So, it is upon us to follow his footsteps." But since Ahmad also knew that his people's abhorrence of non-Muslims was deep-rooted, and that it was necessary to quench their thirst for hatred, in his sermons he also prescribed a small dose of bigotry. "However, because of their ignorance and since they are not enlightened enough to convert to Islam, we will let them live their lives within the confines of their miserable ghettos."

Thus, although Keshe nomads didn't stop their habitual trespassing through Jewbareh, they did put a halt to their brutal raids during periods of scarcity such as harsh winters when caravans they would have otherwise ambushed and preyed upon were unable to pass through the frozen deserts that led to Esfahan. It was in such times that, like locusts, they came in waves, though now, to everyone's utter astonishment, they only begged for food. This meant a good deal to the Jewbarites, who naturally had no idea what was behind this unexpected blessing and were talking about the imminent coming of the Messiah. Ruben thanked Ahmad every time he brought him wine and the mullah cautioned him that this situation was not going to last forever and that it would only take something like a serious year of famine to unleash the latent evil in the ruthless nomads. "Then, even I will not be able to stop them."

Over time, as they became drinking companions, Ruben learned that although Mullah Ahmad was a high-ranking member of the ruling clergy, he deplored what many of his colleagues were doing to the masses of poverty-stricken Persians, especially the people of their own faith. He told Ruben that while he was a firm believer in those principles of Islam that taught love and brotherhood among mankind, he had his own approach towards his faith. He believed in the inevitable logic of cause and effect. Forbidden by his religion, and ironically contradicting his own teachings, he drank wine alone and unknown to the rest of his family, but shared the pleasure of having musicians play prohibited music for himself and his family in the privacy of his home.

When he spoke, Ruben listened intently, asked questions like an eager disciple and gained knowledge of many things he had thus far known nothing about. He hung on every word Ahmad said — words that had awakened in Ruben a thirst for broader knowledge and understanding of other faiths. What Mullah Ahmad had to offer was so unique to Ruben that he could not help being fascinated by it. The mullah respected all prophets and admired many philosophers, but he did not believe in a great God of mercy and forgiveness and a petty Satan of temptation and evil deeds, as all Semitic religions taught. Inspired by the philosophy of Zoroaster, the ancient Persian prophet, he believed in two primal spirits as the creators of the universe: Good and Evil, and that life and existence were a product of the eternal conflict between these two spirits. "We are all trapped in a no man's land, between good and bad, light and darkness, God and Evil," he told Ruben, who listened with intense pleasure and attention to the mullah's reflections. "I praise the beauty of seeking the light of love and avoiding the darkness of hatred among mankind. I believe that by giving, you take."

And so, Ruben the Rhino gained knowledge from the insight that Mullah Ahmad possessed and passed it on to his children and their children.

Chapter 4
The Year of Famine

As soon as it became clear that food supplies were dwindling throughout Esfahan, Ruben remembered Mullah Ahmad's repeated warnings that he would not be able to help Jewbarites in time of famine. The disastrous specter of what might happen in such dire circumstances—should Jewbareh fail to keep the goodwill of the Mullah—alarmed Ruben. So he called upon Rabbi Shimon and the Mayor Haskell, stressing the urgency of the matter, persuaded them that it was high time to prepare the people of Jewbareh for the coming ordeal. They held a meeting in Mullah Shimon Synagogue and invited the rabbis of two other smaller synagogues and all those who were in day-to-day contact with the Jewbarites, such as the owners of the bathhouse, the bakeries and the food stalls, and asked them to alert their families, customers and friends about the potential calamity. In their sermons, Mullah Shimon and his colleagues in other synagogues warned the community that drought was like fire and that it burned wet and dry alike. They cautioned the Jewbarites that before the coming of hunger, starvation and death, they would have to protect themselves from the equally hungry and ruthless Keshe nomads, who were certain to invade Jewbareh without mercy in search of food. They pleaded with the members of the community to at least buy wheat and flour which, although expensive, was still available on the market, or whatever else they could put their hands on that was needed to get them through the coming catastrophe, and to store these provisions in safe hiding places. It would be necessary as well for them to secure their houses.

"He who creates a hungry mouth, provides bread too," people complacently responded.

"Are they blind? And deaf? Don't they understand that famine brings looting, rape and murder in its wake?" Ruben complained to the rabbi.

"I thought you — as our kadkhoda — knew your own people," he shrugged.

And this struck Ruben like lightning. It dawned on him that if he were not the governor, but an ordinary inhabitant of this godforsaken ghetto, his responsibility would have been limited to his immediate relatives and himself. That was something that he was easily capable of handling. He would not have risked his life bribing Mullah Ahmad with wine — of all things — to protect these unruly people. No matter how he looked at it, the governorship of his ghetto had not been his choice. Neither had been his name, Ruben. Nor his epithet, the Rhino. He was no king, for a monarch's subjects follow his orders, whereas the Jewbarites, who came to him with their problems, at a crucial time like this, they listened neither to his nor the other community leaders' recommendations. He was a governor, he concluded, who actually could not and did not govern.

For weeks, Ruben contemplated all this and eventually came to the conclusion that he simply couldn't cope with such unbearable weight on his shoulders. So, during a Saturday morning service at Rabbi Shimon's Synagogue, he went up to the mishkan and announced that he intended to bestow the office and the title of kadkhoda upon anyone willing to take his place. It was as though they had announced Ruben's death. Women screamed from the balcony that surrounded the synagogue and men sitting around the mishkan groaned.

"Once a kadkhoda, always a kadkhoda!" said Yohai the Shoemaker.

"I said this when you were born and I say it again, Ruben!" Henna the Midwife exclaimed, shaking her bony finger. "People like you come to this world once in a hundred years."

"Our destiny is in your hands," screamed the tall Nehemiah the Baker, standing up. "What do you mean you are leaving the leadership?"

And when his mother shrieked, "My husband must be rolling in his grave," there was a commotion. Men and women in the congregation screeched simultaneously: "*He* was a real kadkhoda... May he rest in eternal peace... How come he never complained?... Don't we all miss him..."

"Hush!" Rabbi Shimon shouted and suddenly there was silence. "I have something to say, first to all of you and then to my friend, Ruben. To all of you, I say your ignorance is driving the three of us—the mayor, the kadkhoda and myself—out of our minds. Week after week after week, we have been going around and begging you to prepare yourselves, for famine is imminent. O people," he raised his voice. "Don't you hear? Famine is coming! And what have you done? Nothing! Absolutely nothing! You have all ignored us. Actually, knowing you, I'm sure you will wait until you are perishing of hunger and then you will blame us, not yourselves. How Moses put up with us, his tribe, is beyond my comprehension."

The stunned congregation remained silent. Then the rabbi turned to Ruben and said, "You can't leave. You do have a responsibility to your community that comes not only with your position, but with your heritage. As the old saying has it, 'This food's been cooked by your aunt. You can't refuse it.' In front of this crowd of your fellow Jewbarites, your friends and neighbors, and in front of the Torah, as your rabbi, I instruct you to take back what you said." It was at that moment that the Rhino realized that his commitment to his community ran in his blood; in fact, it *was* his blood. He bowed his head to Rabbi Shimon, women in the crowd ululated, men called, "Blessed be our kadkhoda," and that was how Ruben the Rhino was reinstated as the governor of Jewbareh. Still, once the three leaders realized that their pleas and warnings about the oncoming famine were in vain, they gathered a small group of Jewbarites to help them. A dozen other volunteers, mostly their immediate family members, joined them. They went around and obtained money from a number of well-to-do Jewbarites and from there Ruben took it upon himself to buy and hide provisions in the basement of the synagogue for the hard days ahead.

The year of the third famine hit in the spring of 1833, and when it did, the Jewbarites panicked. As predicted, these people suddenly became angry with their community leaders, especially with Ruben. They blamed anybody but themselves for their failure to store enough foodstuffs in advance. And when, in the summer, this year of famine reached its peak, Jewbareh was dreadfully stricken. Businesses were closed. The hidden reserves of wheat, flour, dried fruits, nuts and even barrels of stale bread that had been stored as the last resort in the synagogue had long been depleted. Starvation and death struck everywhere. Mostly Ruben, but also the rabbi and the mayor, ran through the alleys, trying to help people, no matter how little they could do under the circumstances. From behind thick brick walls, they heard men, women and children wailing in agony. Slouching figures stumbled and staggered through the alleys like ghosts.

In the summer of 1833, on *Tisha B'Av* – the ninth day of the Hebrew month of Av – the already starving Jewbarites fasted to commemorate two of the saddest events in Jewish history – the destruction of the First Temple, originally built by King Solomon, and the destruction of the Second Temple, which had been rebuilt with the help of the Persian Emperor, Darius the Great. Those two events had occurred about 656 years apart, both on the ninth day of Av. Although the recitations prescribed for this day to bewail the loss of the Temples and the subsequent persecutions of the Jewish people are more or less similar throughout the world, Jewbarites had come up with an additional ritual unique to them only, obviously derived from Shiite mourning traditions.

On *Ashora*, the anniversary of the martyrdom of Imam Hussein, the men mourners join different groups, each group representing three teams: *sineh-zanha* – the chest-beaters; *zanjir-zanha* – the chain beaters who beat their bare backs with bundled chains and *ghameh-zanha*, who slash their shaven heads with daggers. As these groups proceed from different parts of the city towards their nearby mosques, women mourners line up along the path while each group leader sings lyrics depicting the brutality with which Imam Hussein was mutilated and martyred. Women cry, screaming and bewailing the gory viciousness of their prophet's martyrdom. The group members that follow their assigned leader recite the verses in unison, their faces wet with their sweat and tears and, depending on which group they are part of, either beat their chests, slap their backs with heavy chains or slash open their bare skulls.

Since their liberation from captivity in Babylon by Cyrus the Great, Persian Jews have kept both their faith and loyalty to Persia. Unlike other minorities, they have not only treasured all aspects of Persian culture, but made remarkable contributions to it. With the emergence of the Shiite faith, however, many features of cultural life such as music and theater were subjected to prohibitions and, instead, mourning and self-torture were enforced as a religious obligation. Ever since Shiites had been ruling Persia, the Jewbarites, living among a majority whose sole pleasure was sorrow, had discovered their own outlet for the frustrations and grievances they suffered on account of the hostile intruders and had come up with their own version of Ashora, which took place on the night preceding Tisha B'Av. Fasting men and women gathered at the entrance to the ghetto and headed from there along the Alley of Eleven Twists to their synagogues. Mullah Shimon directed the ceremonial procession. The mourners would beat their chests, although not as hard as their Muslim compatriots. On this specific night of the year of the third famine, they had many reasons to cry and cry hard. They bemoaned the miseries that had befallen them, remembering the loss of their Temples, but again, very unique to their tradition, they beat their chests for the martyrdom of the prophet Zechariah, who had been stoned to death for his public rebuke of the worship of idols. On their way to the synagogues, Rabbi Shimon recited a song with lyrics that were rooted in the depths of the history of the Jews in Islamic Persia:

Dear Zechariah, oh our brother
Never been nursed from the breast of his mother
Young, he was martyred
Strong, he was martyred
When he was killed
All over the world his blood was spilled
Dear Zechariah, alas
Bloodied and martyred, alas

The book of Lamentations was chanted, mourning the loss of the Temple, the sufferings of the Jewish people and the desolation of Jerusalem. Also particular to the Persian Jews, was the reading of the book of Job. "Naked I came from my mother's womb, and naked shall I return there," recited Rabbi Shimon when the mourning crowd reached and settled in his synagogue, his voice trembling and his eyes tearful. Along with him, his congregation bemoaned the calamity that had befallen them.

To everyone's utter surprise, Ruben did not attend these rituals. "I would rather bemoan my own people's stupidity," he said to the rabbi who asked the reason for his absence. "Look at the Armenians. Can you tell me why the Keshe nomads don't raid Julfa—their little township? Let me tell you why. Because, first, they have a leadership that they listen to and second, Armenians are brave and fight back. Why would you lead such a stupid procession in which — with all due respect to you — we, like monkeys, imitate Shiites?"

"As the rabbi," Mullah Shimon said in his own defense, "I am the guardian of our traditions. And," he raised his voice, noticing that Ruben was about to object, "these poor souls needed to cry, to express their miseries."

Then, in this year of famine, even on Tisha B'Av, the murderous nomads, themselves suffering from famine, escalated their raids on Jewbareh. They came in waves, plundered everything you had, killed you if you resisted, and the question now was how you would survive the next attack. The Jewbarites, at the mercy of the violent Keshe, had no voice with which to cry and no tears to shed. Soon, the alleys' walls became stained with the blood of those with little or nothing for the nomads and their streets were littered with the corpses of their victims.

Ruben and his friend Nissan the Fabricseller had fortified the twin houses that they had built together with locks and fences. Nissan helped his relatives to do the same, but Ruben moved Jacob, his sisters and their many children to his own house. Once a group of hungry nomads followed Ruben and tried to break into his house, but the Rhino subdued them all singlehandedly. From then on, the Keshe nomads stayed away from him. They knew enough to fear his powerful body and his fearless courage. Haskell the Mayor bought two trained, vicious wolf dogs to protect himself and his family. The rabbi's protection came, as it turned out, in a rather ironic way: as it happened, the nomads superstitiously believed that harming a Jewish mullah would bring death of the worst kind to the perpetrator and his family.

Ruben's prime concern being the safety of his own people, time after time he appealed to Mullah Ahmad for help, and each time the mullah reminded him of what he had told him in the past: that he could not contain hungry nomads, for, he told Ruben, "My words can mollify them for a while, but as it's been said, a hungry belly has no faith." The benevolent mullah did give Ruben money to buy provisions and distribute them anonymously among the Jewbarites. Ruben, the rabbi and the mayor went from house to house, handing out these meager yet welcome supplies they had acquired with Ahmad's funds. They also organized a group that went around Jewbareh, gathering corpses which they piled in a carriage, and buried at the Jewish graveyard outside Esfahan.

Chapter 5
Wandering Frozen Deserts

In the dark of night during Purim in the winter of 1834, Mullah Ahmad heard someone tapping on the door to his private quarters. "It's me, Hazrateh Agha." Ahmad recognized Ruben's voice. "It's open, come in," the old cleric called out, wondering why Ruben had unexpectedly come to see him. As Ruben opened the door and stepped in, Ahmad was taken aback. The Rhino's clothes were soaking wet, his face clearly injured, and blood streamed from his left shoulder down to his fingers.

"Allah Akbar!" Ahmad exclaimed. "What has happened to you?"

Ruben fell down on his knees like a melting iceberg.

"So, what is it?" Mullah Ahmad kneeled down and peered into Ruben's eyes. "You are badly wounded. You must be in a lot of pain."

"Your Holiness," Ruben panted. "I..." He began sobbing like a child.

"Stop crying and talk to me. What are you trying to say?"

"I killed someone... A Muslim," Ruben said as though whispering to himself.

Mullah Ahmad jumped up. "You have killed a Muslim? You have killed a Muslim and dared to take refuge in *my* house?"

Ruben raised his head. "I'm sorry, Hazrateh Agha. I had nowhere else to go. This nomad was killing an old man. The fishmonger. I only tried to stop him. But, then he attacked me. I asked him to leave. I intended no malice, but..."

"But you killed him!" Ahmad exclaimed as he began to crack his fingers nervously.

"I slammed him against a wall to protect myself from him — and he was killed by the blow. I'm so sorry," said Ruben as he stood up and began to head for the door. "You are quite right. I should never have come here."

"And where in the name of Allah do you think you're going now?" Ahmad called after him. "If you are caught by the mob, they will hang you—and worse! Sit down, shut up and let me think."

Ruben obeyed the mullah as he stood over him, scratching his beard abrasively. "May Mohammed himself help me out of this mess. First of all, did anybody see you come here?"

"I don't think so. I'm a very fast runner and I ran faster than ever."

"Now, tell me exactly what happened?"

Ruben described the scene as Ahmad paced the room and when he was finished, the old cleric asked, "How can we be sure you haven't been followed?"

"I kept on looking back as I ran. I'm almost certain no one followed me," Ruben said as his facial muscles contracted in pain.

"Your shoulder. You're bleeding badly." Ahmad took a towel out of his wine closet.

"Hazrateh Agha."

"Quiet!" Ahmad dropped the towel and cupped his hands behind his earlobes. "Do you hear a noise out there?"

Ruben listened, then nodded in horror. The mullah hurried to the window and looked out. "May Allah Himself help us! What is this crowd at my house? Obviously you *were* followed." He rushed toward Ruben, grabbed his hand and pushed him into the closet. "Stay here, be quiet and pray for your life... and for mine!" But before closing the closet door, he tossed the towel at Ruben. "Here! Take this and press it hard against your shoulder. You're bleeding badly."

Opening the front door, Ahmad saw the crowd and the crowd saw him, their sullen murmurs escalating into an uproar, with all of them shouting Ruben's name over and over again and the name of someone else, whom he took to be that of Ruben's victim. He raised his hand, inviting them to silence.

"Brothers! I hope you realize that I cannot hear you if you are all speaking at once!" The crowd quieted down. "Repeat after me: *Praise unto Mohammed and his tribe!*"

"*Praise unto Mohammed and his tribe!*" the crowd shouted back. As required, he said this prayer two more times and they recited after him.

"Now I want one of you, and only *one* of you, to step forward and tell me why you are here."

Zain's master opened his way through the crowd. "May no Muslim hear and no infidel see what I saw, Hazrateh Agha! That Jew, the big, najes Jew, killed our Brother Zain."

Ahmad tasted a sharp bitterness in his mouth. "And..." he paused, dreading the answer. "Where is the murderer? Bring him here to me."

"He has escaped. We don't know where he is, Hazrateh Agha," Zain's master replied. "We can't find him because, as you know yourself, Agha, these Jews have a bonding with *jens*."

"And they hide in the shadow of these demons," one of his men added.

Ahmad was relieved to know that they had lost the Rhino.

"My two other brothers and I saw him kill Brother Zain and disappear," said the master. "He was there one second and gone the next, and his family has disappeared too." Then the chief turned to the crowd and shouted, "With the help of Allah, once Hazrateh Agha has issued his *fatwa* and declared *jihad* against the Jews, for the Muslim blood that has been shed, we will do away with all of those filthy Jews in Jewbareh!"

Mullah Ahmad stood silent as dozens of eyes gazed at him, awaiting his fatwa to massacre the Jewbarites. All he knew was that he had never issued a decree to kill and he was not about to do so now. As he was pondering his next move, the crowd became impatient and he heard words of protest. That was when the mullah raised his hand, indicating that he was about to speak. To the surprised crowd, who were expecting the fatwa, he said only, "Where is the body of our slain brother?"

The chief pointed his finger in the direction of Jewbareh and said, "It's over there."

"Over where?" Ahmad demanded firmly. "Are you telling me that you have left the sacred body of our slain Muslim brother in dirt and mud and have gathered here?" His voice gradually rose. "Are you aware of the sin you have committed?" Now he was shouting. "Do you know that the poor man's soul, as it sits next to his physical body, is waiting to ascend and can't do so before his body is buried?" The crowd became absolutely silent. "I want you all to go back," Ahmad said in an assertive voice, "clean up the body, put it in a coffin and take it to the Juma Mosque, so that the poor man's soul can rest in peace. After that, I want you all to go back home and do nothing but pray for our slain brother. Tonight I will hold a vigil. I will pray for a solution and I will get my answer from Allah. Then, in the morning, after we have escorted him to his eternal home, I will tell you what to do."

Ahmad turned around, stepped into his house, closed the door, leaned against it, inhaled deeply and exhaled with relief. He had performed well. Meanwhile, there was much to be done in the next few hours. He opened the closet and asked Ruben, "How's your wound? Let me see." He came closer and examined the injury. "It's deep," he shook his head. "Stay here until I will tell you to come out." He called his servant and ordered food, hot water and more towels. He cleaned Ruben's shoulder wound, applied some herbal balm over it and covered it with a clean cloth. He gave him food to eat. Then he began pacing back and forth in the room, thinking. Time and again he grabbed his turban tightly, then slapped his forehead. He kneeled down and prayed. He consulted his prayer beads. Finally he took the Koran and with his eyes closed, opened it to a page and read the first verse that swam into view, for that was meant to be the answer. "Allah said to Mohammed: I didn't make you a prophet unless you forgive." Ahmad smiled. He stood up and said, "It's good, Ruben!" But with his head down, Ruben was crying.

"What are *you* crying for?" Ahmad put his hand on Ruben's shoulder. "You can't possibly be as scared as I am. I have so much more to lose than you. Calm down, young man."

"I'm not scared for myself, Your Holiness. Of course the mere thought of having killed someone shatters me. But for what I have done, I have foolishly put you, my family and all my people at risk. 'By giving, you take,' is what you've taught me, Agha. I have given death. What shall I receive?"

"Trying to get close to God, one can land in the kingdom of Evil," Mullah Ahmad said with a dark laugh and continued, "This is no time to get philosophical, Jew boy. Somebody was about to be killed, you intervened and the would-be killer has been killed. There is no law or commandment that condemns that. The immediate problem is *you*. You need to disappear, and right away too—not into the shadow of demons as those idiots out there believe, but to a very faraway place, hundreds of leagues away from here."

"But where can I go, Your Holiness?"

"That decision is yours. Anywhere that is days and days and months and months away from here. Leave now. You must go out of the gates of Esfahan before dawn, and then keep walking. I suggest you travel on foot until you are so far away that nobody can recognize you. Only then take a carriage to get even farther away."

"I can't run away from myself, Hazrateh Agha. I have killed. Let me surrender myself."

"Yes!" Ahmad yelled impatiently. "Surrender yourself and get mutilated! You don't seem to understand the situation, my friend. You, a Jew, have killed a Muslim! They have every religious right to kill you, your mother and in fact all the Jewbarites. Luckily, I have subdued them for now."

With his hand on his wounded shoulder and his face grimacing in pain, Ruben shook his head. "The weight of this sin is too heavy for me to go away and never come back, Hazrateh Agha."

Ahmad sat down, facing Ruben and said calmly, "You are very nervous now and I do understand it. Please try to remain calm and accept what has happened. Don't worry, I will bring you back. As far as the safety of your family and your people are concerned, leave that to me. But this mess needs to be taken care of first and this means a lot of work and time. Not only do these people have to be calmed down, but they must also be encouraged to forgive you and your people. Believe me, you deserve to be forgiven, because you are a good man." Saying this, he stood up, walked over to the window and stared out into the dark night with his hands clasped behind his back. For a few minutes there was silence. Then Mullah Ahmad spoke. "Why," he said softly, as though talking to someone just outside his window. "Why can't people just live, for the sake of Allah? What's wrong with loving each other for a change?" Then he turned around and continued, "I think you should leave now."

"I apologize," Ruben whispered.

As he stood up to leave, Ahmad noticed how the upright, monumental Rhino had become somehow shortened and withered. He had always liked Ruben, for he was different from any other person he had ever known. This big man came from a community of people who were historically belittled, humiliated and continually pushed into a ghetto, where they were made invisible except for the times when they became convenient scapegoats. Yet, at this dismal moment in the mullah's life, beyond the pale of Ruben's fair-skinned face and dimmed greenish-brown eyes, there was a helpless good man who deserved respect. Alone, out of a community of frightened and cautious people, the Rhino had emerged to pass a formidable test of courage in defending the life of an innocent man. Unfortunately, he had killed the aggressor.

"I don't want your apology, Ruben. I need you to pull yourself together and be strong. As I said, go far, far away. Once you reach your destination, let your family know your whereabouts, and as soon as I have put out the flames of this crisis, I will have them signal you to come back."

"Please pray for my deliverance, Hazrateh Agha," Ruben said in a low voice as he reached for Ahmad's hand and kissed it. "You are a merciful man of God."

"Ah!" Ahmad held Ruben's hand, looked into his eyes and smiled. "Who the hell is going to get my 'medication' while you're away? I have to save your life and get you back here as soon as I can for my own sake, can't you see that? Now, quickly, write a note to your mother and I will have it delivered to her. Tell her you're safe and that you're leaving for a long time. Tell her also that an unknown person will take care of her financial needs while you're away."

Mullah Ahmad gave Ruben warm clothing, bread, money and a pair of comfortable shoes. "Go, and may Allah protect you!"

At dusk, the caravan passengers coming from the west saw the dark figure of a man, tall and sturdy, leaning against the wind in the haze of the snowstorm as white flakes danced wildly around his long, black overcoat. With his woolen cap pulled down over his ears, he had one hand jammed deeply into his pocket while with the other hand he held onto a bag hanging from his shoulder.

"Salam brother!" called the caravan leader coming from the opposite direction. "Where are you headed? There are no shelters ahead and the desert is unsafe."

But Ruben, without answering, pressed on and then disappeared into a thick wall of snow. The caravan leader watched him for a long time, shook his head, and whispering this old Persian adage to himself. "I said: Let me be your watchdog. You don't want me to be? So be it!"as he wondered at the ways of Allah.

The night lay between the infinite expanse of the white desert and the vastness of the dark skies. A freezing wind pierced through the warmth of Ruben's coat into his open wound. Yet, despite the pain, he kept walking with the fortitude of a rhinoceros as fast as he could, crushing the icy snow under his feet, as though fleeing the ghost of the nomad he had killed. He was hungry, but he did not stop to eat. He strode through the night. He cursed Jewbareh, the day he was born and his destiny as the leader of his people. Had he been fated, after all, to kill? Had that also been part of the plan? He thought as the pain caused by the intense cold penetrated his skin — especially his open wound — into his flesh and deep into his bones. And then, his knees began to shake under the weight of his body as he crumbled onto the icy snow.

He was on the verge of passing out when he realized that he could easily freeze to death out here in the cold desert. He drew himself up to his feet, shook off the heap of snow that had covered his body, and resumed walking deeper and deeper into the desert. Gradually the intensity of the snowstorm lessened and eventually stopped. A full shimmering moon lit the expanse of white frozen desert that lay before him. He had no idea where he was going, but he had to keep moving, hoping to find a caravansary where he could stop to rest and board a stagecoach that would take him as far away as possible to someplace, he hoped, where, Zain and his tribe wouldn't reach him. But as he kept moving into the night, the desert only stretched further and further ahead. His mind wandered back to the story of the Israelites and their escape from the slavery of Pharaoh. Was he experiencing what they had experienced, feeling what they had felt? In the Biblical desert, he reflected, there were many wanderers *and* a great leader. Moses. A man who spoke to God and to whom God spoke in return. *Moses said to God, "Who am I, that I should go to Pharaoh and bring the Israelites out of Egypt?" And God said, "I will be with you."* In this frozen no-man's land, though, Ruben felt that he, who had hoped to deliver his people from the nomads, who had wanted to save their lives and preserve their community, was no Moses. He was alone and yearning for a sign of help and mercy.

Stopping abruptly, he lifted his face and cried, "Oh, God, forgive me!" His voice pierced the air and was lost in the vastness of the desert that was empty but for the stars that flickered above him and, like him, were struggling to free themselves from the cobalt blue sky. Then, in the distance, he saw a star that had fallen on the snow and was blinking on and off. "I must be seeing things," he thought. He stared at the light as it appeared, disappeared and reappeared again. He had heard that those lost in desert snowstorms imagined seeing light in the distance. Was it a mirage or a sign that he hadn't been left completely alone in this vast, frozen desert? Heading toward the light, he soon made out a small cottage with a thin column of smoke rising lazily from the chimney. "Surely," he thought, "if they let me in, in that cottage there will be a fire to warm me, food to eat and a place to rest." He pushed himself forward and with his ebbing energy knocked with his big fist against the cottage door.

"It's open," said a phlegmy voice.

Upon entering, Ruben was flooded with a warm mixture of scents--opium, tea, charcoal smoke, frankincense and fried food. The cottage was in fact a teahouse.

"Salam," he said, greeting the man who had invited him in.

"Welcome, my brother. Go back outside, shake the snow off your coat and shoes, then come in and close the door behind you."

Ruben stumbled outdoors and returned seconds later, heading straight towards the old man, who obviously was the teahouse keeper. He sat cross-legged on a large wooden bench behind a samovar and a brazier holding a pile of red-hot burning charcoal, an opium pipe and a very large, glazed teapot. Over time, heat had baked tea stains and changed its color from white to a dark brown. Next to the brazier, there was an oil lamp that sputtered a dim light. Ruben shifted his gaze from the lamp to the innkeeper's face. His drowsy, opium-brown eyes were sunken into his flesh. There were a few strings of white hair in his thin beard, which ran from underneath his bowl-shaped gray felt hat down to his chin. He was wearing a long, worn-out brown cloak over a black shirt covered with a crust of shiny dirt. The teahouse keeper took a deep drag on his long tobacco pipe, and then spat into a copper spittoon next to the brazier as he talked and coughed at the same time. "You looked like a ghost when you came in," he said with a grin that showed his protruding, stained brown teeth. "Are you stay- ing for the night?"

Ruben nodded. He could not speak. His voice was frozen.

"What did you say?" the innkeeper shrieked, bobbing his head.

"I can't hear well. You're shaking, brother! Go put your bag on one of those beds." He pointed to three wooden beds near a fireplace at the back of the room. "Then warm up by the fireplace, and I will bring your tea there."

Taking his bag, Ruben shuffled toward the beds. On each there was a rolled up cotton mattress and quilt. He threw his bag down on one and stood close to the fireplace, leaning his body forwards and stretching his palms towards the fire, as though worshiping the flames. The innkeeper brought him a tall glass of hot tea and a cup of crystal sugar on a small tray. "*Besm-Allah*" – In Allah's name – he said, putting the tray on the small platform in front of the fireplace. Ruben sat on the platform and reached for the small saucer that held the cup, but he was shaking so hard that half the tea was emptied into the saucer. He took a piece of sugar, threw it into his mouth and gulped down whatever was left of the hot tea in the cup. "May your gracious hands never suffer any pain, Haji," he said, finding his voice.

"Jafar. My name is Jafar. And what's your name, brother?" asked the man who was now sitting by the fireplace next to Ruben. But before Ruben could answer, he brought his face close to Ruben's, inspecting it. His breath reeked of tobacco, opium and vinegar and his eyes were dancing, moving swiftly back and forth. "Look at those scratches and bruises on your face!" he said. "Have you been in a fight?"

"Mustafa. My name is Mustafa," Ruben repeated loudly, hoping to distract Jafar from examining his bruises.

But Jafar pointed to Ruben's face, "And these, brother Mustafa?"

"Bandits, brother. Bandits attacked me on the way here! There were six of them, all young and strong. But, with the help of Allah, I handled them all."

"Is that so?" Jafar squinted. "Six of them and you managed them all," he muttered, sewing his suddenly lifeless eyes to Ruben's. There was a hint of suspicion in the teahouse-keeper's demeanor and it bothered Ruben. He wondered if the news of the nomad's murder had already come this far. Then, with his shoulders hunched, Jafar turned around and scurried back to his bench, where he took his opium pipe from the brazier and stuck a piece of dark opium on its porcelain bowl. He picked up a burning piece of charcoal with a metal clip, put it next to the opium and inhaled deeply, first holding his breath and then exhaling as he talked. "Would you care for some, Brother Mustafa?"

"No, thank you, Haji Jafar. But I'm very hungry."

"Because of the harsh weather, no carriages have been passing through the desert in the past few days to bring me provisions. And even if they did, in this year of famine, there would be very little that I could offer you. Anyway," he yawned, coughed and beat his chest. "The best I can come up with is eggs and bread and I can either boil the eggs or fry them."

"I like them fried, please," said Ruben, relieved that he had not been offered something non-kosher.

"I will have to make at least ten eggs for a big man like you!" Jafar chuckled, his words interrupted by percussive coughs.

"Four will be enough, thank you." The words caught in Ruben's throat.

Jafar stood up, supporting his back with his palms. "Oh my back!" he complained and immediately continued, "Four fried eggs, with bread and tea, will cost five *dinars*. Do you have the money?"

Ruben brought a fistful of silver coins Mullah Ahmad had given him out of his pocket and showed them to Jafar, who nodded and then disappeared into a backroom.

Two weeks before, Ruben remembered as he put the money back in his pocket, it had been the first night of Rosh Hashanah, the Jewish New Year. Ruben had been celebrating this religious feast with his whole extended family, reciting prayers for escaping the slavery of Egypt, full of hope and prayer that famine would give way to fertility. "What hope?" he now muttered to himself under his breath as the door to the teahouse opened and a man entered, followed by a gust of snow.

"*Ya-Allah!*" — In the name of Allah — bellowed the newcomer. "Each snow flake is the size of a mother-whore quilt!" As he talked, he shook his body like a wet dog and stomped on the floor, letting the snow fly off his clothing. "It's as if God has eaten ice and is shitting snow on the earth," he added, moving toward the fireplace and unwinding the shawl wrapped around his cloak. "This freezing, bastard snowstorm calmed down awhile ago and then all of sudden it started up again." He stretched his arms out over the flames and asked Ruben, "You! Are you the *ghavechi?*"

Ruben shook his head. "No. He's in the back."

"Like a horny bitch that locks her mate inside her," said the man, talking to the flames, "the wheels of this carriage that was bringing me from Esfahan got stuck in the snow a few leagues from here and wouldn't move." He shifted his gaze from the flames and glared at Ruben. "Oh brother," he shrieked with laughter, "Doesn't your face look like a squeezed piece of shit. And who has re-arranged it for you?"

The man was short and bulky. He wore a full beard, a heavy moustache and his bald head was partially covered with a felt hat peculiar to hoodlums. Disproportionate to his body size, his shoulders were broad and looked strong.

"It's a long story," Ruben answered. "But tell me, did you manage to get the carriage out of the snow?" he asked immediately, trying to distract the stranger.

"We couldn't get that piece of mother..."

"Salam," said the teahouse-keeper, returning from the kitchen with a tray in his hand.

"*Aleik el-Salam,*" returned the man.

Jafar put down a tray with four fried eggs on a copper plate in front of Ruben and asked the new arrival, "What's your name, brother, and where are you coming from?"

"Bashi. From Esfahan."

"Your servant's name is Jafar," the innkeeper pointed at himself, and then to Ruben. "And he is Haji Mustafa."

The newcomer looked at Ruben's plate. The eggs were arranged meticulously like a four-leaf clover. Next to the paper-thin soft bread stood the salt and peppershaker, side by side like two parading soldiers. Ruben quickly held a piece of the bread between his fingers, twisted it into the fried eggs and took a big mouthful.

"*Ya Ali!*" – In the name of Ali – the innkeeper exclaimed. "You eat so fast! You *are* hungry, Haji Mustafa, aren't you? Let me get you some tea." Walking towards his tea-stand, Jafar turned around and asked the newcomer, "Did I hear you say you got stuck in the snow, brother?"

"Yes, Haji. Your testicles will freeze out there. And no matter how much I told this idiot of a carriage driver to walk with me, he refused to leave his mules. You know what I said to him? I said, 'You can stay here until the summer comes and the grass grows under your feet, but before then you'll be dead and gone, evaporated like a monkey's fart.'" He began laughing hard. "He and his mules must be icicles by now. Fancy that! Icicles of an ass and four mules!" He shook his head.

Jafar came back with three cups of tea on a tray. He set one in front of Ruben and the other two on the bed facing Ruben where the newcomer was now seated.

"So, when did you leave Esfahan, Brother Bashi?"

"We were supposed to leave Esfahan in the early afternoon, but this sister-whore of a snowstorm was coming down so heavily, the other passengers and I said to the carriage driver, 'Let's wait until tomorrow.' 'No,' said the bastard, 'I can sense the weather. I have driven many carriages. It will stop snowing soon. I know it.' And before we could do anything, he took off at dusk. So we went on our way, hoping to pass through the desert before it got dark, but we'd only been gone a few minutes — still in Esfahan, of course — and all of a sudden, guess what? There was a roadblock. 'What's happened now?' I asked the driver. 'Come and see for yourself,' the brainless idiot said. So I came down from the carriage and saw a large crowd gathered in front of Hazrateh Agha, Mullah Ahmad's residence. They were crying 'A Jew has killed a Muslim.'"

The mouthful of bread and egg stuck in Ruben's throat and he began coughing fiercely. Despite the warmth of the fire on his back, he felt a flow of icy water going down his spine. Bashi looked up and asked, "Are you all right, brother?"

"A Jew has killed one of our brothers?" Jafar roared as he clutched at his beard.

Ruben jumped up to his feet. Bashi raised his head and whistled, "Ya-Allah! What a shit-bloated giant *you* are! You seem to..."

"I seem to be *what?*" Ruben demanded.

"What the hell is with you, Haji Mustafa? You jumped up as if a termite had run up your bottom. I was saying, 'You seem to be enjoying your eggs.'" He turned to Jafar, "Can you make me, say, eight of those eggs? I'm so hungry I could eat a donkey with its pack-saddle."

"It's my leg, Brother Bashi," Rueben said as he sat back down. "I get cramps."

"Tell us about the najes Jew," the innkeeper urged Bashi.

"Get me my eggs first!" Bashi grunted, "I will tell you. I promise."

After Jafar made sure that the newcomer had enough money to pay for the dinner and lodging, he went back to the kitchen. Bashi sat facing Ruben, staring at him and licking his lips like a greedy dog. "Can I have a taste of your eggs?" he asked.

"Of course, brother. Come near and help yourself." Ruben pointed to his tray.

Bashi took a few pieces of bread, loaded it with whatever bits of egg were left on Ruben's plate, and shoved it into his mouth. "Sister-whore chicken!" he said with his mouth open, "It laid such a tasty egg!"

Just as Ruben was beginning to think that everyone had forgotten the conversation about Mullah Ahmad's house, Jafar came back with the fried eggs, put them in front of Bashi and asked, "So you were saying, Brother Bashi. Go on with your story."

"Which story?"

"The killer Jew and the crowd at Hazrateh Agha's home."

Bashi took a mouthful of bread and eggs from his own plate and began, "I went into the crowd and asked this nomad brother whose face was as red as a baboon's nose what had happened. 'A filthy Jew killed one of our brothers and escaped. I saw it happen.'" Bashi gobbled up another mouthful and said, "These eggs are so delicious."

"Go on, what happened next?" asked the innkeeper anxiously.

"What's the hurry?" Bashi took another big mouthful. "We have all night to talk. Anyway, the way this monkey-face brother screamed at me, you would think I was the najes Jew who had killed the bastard. So, because of this catastrophe, the crowd had gathered to ask His Holiness to issue a fatwa ordering the extermination of all the Jews and sending them back into the earth like the worms that they are. What do we need these damned creatures among us for?"

Ruben's heart started racing again. To change the subject, he asked the teahouse-keeper to get him another glass of tea. But Jafar, who was staring in disbelief at Bashi, simply pointed to the brazier. "Help yourself," he said to Ruben. Then he turned to Bashi, slapped his head and said, "It's the end of time. Jews are killing Muslims. So did Hazrateh Agha issue such a fatwa?"

Bashi shook his head. "Agha decreed, 'No. Go bury the slain brother first.'"

"You mean knowing that an infidel had killed a Muslim, His Holiness refused to issue a fatwa?" Jafar bellowed.

"Nobody knows why, but why are you shouting at me? Too

much opium? And who are you to question decisions made by His Holiness's?"

Ruben, whose attention had never left the conversation, returned to sit on his assigned bed with another cup of tea. Overwhelmed with the puzzle of Mullah Ahmad's decision, the teahouse proprietor was still in awe. "May I be stricken for questioning the decision made by our Ayatollah, but what has murdering our Muslim brother by a Jew got to do with burying him? I mean, didn't you find out?"

"No. All I did was to go back to the carriage, grab the mules' harness and help push our way out of the crowd. Let's hope, Brother Jafar, that by the time I return to Esfahan, Allah willing, Jewbareh will finally be erased from the face of the earth."

"But how? I mean, did that man you talked to, or anyone else, know who the killer Jew was?"

"Well, the baboon-faced brother, he sort of knew and he sort of didn't know. I mean, although he said he'd seen the Muslim-killer-Jew, he didn't seem to be completely certain who he was." Saying this, Bashi slammed his thigh. "If I had my way, I would kill all those seditious Jews once and for all to relieve Allah from a nasty job on the day of resurrection."

Ruben had to put an end to this conversation. He stood up, yawning loudly and made a show of stretching. "I'm so tired. If you brothers will excuse me, I'll go to bed now." Then, with all his clothing on, he slipped under the worn-out quilt and, pulling it over his head, said, "Sleep well my brothers and I will see you tomorrow morning." Soon feigning sleep, Ruben watched the two men and carefully listened to them as they resumed their conversation, both of them cursing Jews and their evil deeds. Was the man he had killed any different from these two whose ultimate desire was the eradication of all Jews from the face of the earth? Ruben wondered. And then he thought of the many of Persian Jews who over the past centuries had been massacred in the name of Islam and by the hands of cruel Shiite kings. "Oh God," Ruben sighed silently, "Did I not do everything in my power to help and protect my people?"

"Care for some opium?" Ruben heard Jafar asking Bashi.

"By all means. I could really do with some now. "

Through the hole in the quilt, Ruben saw the two men go over to the tea-stand. For a few minutes, the crackling of the wood in the fireplace and the chirp of the sizzling opium on the pipe-head were the only sounds in the teahouse. Ruben saw Jafar, slouched over the brazier as he inhaled deeply from the opium pipe and expelled the smoke into the air before asking Bashi, "I wonder how could a little Jew have killed one of us and gotten away?"

"Apparently this one is a big Jew with a strange name I can't remember." He slapped his forehead as though trying to pop the name out of his head. "Something like 'bull.' Was it...? No. I can't remember. Anyway, the man that I talked to said that our martyred brother fought the najes Jew to the last... Ah, I remember! They called him the Rhino something."

Ruben's stomach twitched in the sudden silence that followed. From underneath the quilt he saw the two men pointing at him, first nodding between themselves, then shaking their heads.

"I have a donkey's brain in my head. Of course it's him," Ruben heard Bashi whisper.

"Has to be him. Wounded, big as an ox," Jafar said softly as he reached under his counter and brought out two large knives. He took one himself and handed the other to Bashi. Then they slowly moved towards Ruben, their knives glittering with the reflection of the fireplace flames. Outside, the snowstorm howled and slammed against the only small window in the teahouse, wrapping itself around the cottage in the middle of the vast expanse of frozen desert where the Rhino was trapped like an antelope between two tigers. Determined not to kill again, Ruben jumped out of the bed and hollered, "What's going on?"

Jafar the innkeeper took a step forward. "Are you sure you are a Muslim?" he asked, his voice screeching like a rusty hinge.

"Of course!" Ruben struggled to sound confident. "And I would stake my life on that!"

"You are sure you are a Muslim?" Bashi parroted the innkeeper as he stepped closer, his knife pointed at Ruben. "And your name is Mustafa?"

"And you didn't lie to us about those scratches and bruises?" Jafar demanded.

"You *are* the killer Jew, aren't you? You najes worm," added Bashi spitefully.

"What the hell is the matter with you two?" Ruben roared as he stepped forward.

Startled by the big man's reaction, the men momentarily moved back.

"Of course I *am* a Muslim. My name *is* Mustafa and I *have not* killed anyone, let alone a Muslim brother."

"If you were a Muslim, you would have recited your evening prayer before you went to bed," said the innkeeper.

"I was too tired and…"

"All right," Bashi interrupted him, waving his knife in front of Ruben's face. "Here's a simple solution. Recite your evening prayer right now and recite it aloud."

"In the name of Allah and Mohammed," Ruben yelled at them in indignation. "I swear to you I am not a Jew. I have killed no one. But if you don't want me here, that's fine with me. I will leave."

Saying this, Ruben reached for his bag, but instantly, Bashi shouted, "You *are* the filthy Jew with our slain brother's blood on your hands!" He moved to pounce on Ruben, but before he could reach him, Ruben grabbed the man's fist and twisted it behind his back. Bashi howled in agony. Ruben took the knife from him and held it to his throat.

"Let go, you filthy Jew," Bashi cried. Then he shouted at the teahouse-keeper, "What the hell are you waiting for, you opium-head idiot? Kill the bastard!"

"If you take one step forward, Jafar!" warned Ruben, "I swear to Allah and the twelve Imams, I will slash his throat first and then yours. Now bring your knife here and put it on my bed!"

"Yes, of course," whispered the frightened proprietor as he immediately complied.

Ruben picked up the knife and propelled Bashi back against Jafar. The Rhino charged towards the two men with a knife in each of his hands. Jafar and Bashi ran and took shelter behind the tea-stand. Ruben stood over their heads, waving the knives under their noses as they begged for their lives. "You pathetic idiots," Ruben sighed. "If you are so certain that I am a Jew and a Muslim killer, then here!" He tossed the two knives at them and took two steps back. "Take these, kill me and you will have the blood of an innocent Muslim on your hands, not the blood of a Jew."

Neither of the two men moved. Then Bashi craned his neck to look at Ruben. "I confess to you, Brother Mustafa," he said in a brittle voice, "I feel like filthy dog shit to have suspected you. I'm a bastard, the son of a hundred filthy dogs. Please forgive me." He looked at Jafar and continued, "It was this opium-grilled brain-sister-whore who put this stupid thought into my empty head."

"I don't deny that," Jafar said with an obsequious tone. "It's this opium I smoke, may Allah burn the bones of my father in hell for encouraging me to indulge in this venom."

"Brothers," Ruben said calmly. "I have no time for this nonsense. I accept your apologies. I'm tired and if you will excuse me, I'm going back to sleep." Ruben began to move toward the bed, but after a few steps, he turned around and said, "You know, you have upset me so much, I want to say my evening prayers before I go to bed. Brother Jafar, where do you keep your prayer mats and seals?"

The innkeeper pointed meekly to a pile near the fireplace.

Bashi said, "Do you... may I... I mean do you mind if I join you?"

Jafar said, "And me?"

"Suit yourselves," Ruben spread a prayer mat on the floor, put a prayer seal at the side facing Mecca and stood on the mat.

In a gesture of respect, Bashi and Jafar insisted that Ruben lead the prayers.

"Allah's damnation on *Shaitan.*"

"Quiet!" Ruben snapped at Bashi and Jafar who stood on their prayer mats behind him. "Let us say our prayers and go to bed. I, for one, have a long journey ahead of me tomorrow. *Besm-Allah al-Rahman al-Rahim,"* — In the name of Allah, the Divine and the Merciful, — Ruben began the beginning part of the prayer that was allowed to be recited aloud.

Since childhood, Islamic prayer had fascinated Ruben. Whenever he passed the Juma Mosque near Jewbareh, he would pause to watch and listen to the praying men. He was intrigued by the splendor of their movements as they bent, kneeled, touched their foreheads to their prayer seals, stood, raised their heads, held the palms of their hands heavenwards, then repeated the ritual all over again as though in a mystical dance. Through the years, Ruben had watched them pray so often that he had come to learn every movement as well as many verses recited aloud during their otherwise silent devotions. This would be the first time ever that he had performed before two experts standing behind him who would probably be listening suspiciously and waiting for him to make mistakes. And so, as Ruben said the opening line of the prayer, he watched the innkeeper and the traveler from the corner of his eye, swaying sideways. Scared yet determined, he uttered the lines flawlessly. When he had finished, he turned and embraced the two men. Jafar rushed to his tea-stand and returned with a large tray of rice cookies, chickpeas, pistachios, raisins, walnuts, a teapot and three cups. "Let's have a snack before we go to bed, my Muslim brothers." And the three men sat around with their legs crossed, drinking tea and nibbling goodies from the tray.

Jafar said: "If you don't mind my asking you, Brother Mustafa, and I don't mean to be nosy, so please feel free not to answer if you don't want to..." He paused and shook his head. "It's none of my business. Forget it."

"Please. Ask what you like."

"Well," he said, refilling the cups with fresh hot tea. "You said tomorrow you have a long journey, and I'm just making conversation. Which way are you heading?"

Ruben gazed at the small frosted window on the opposite wall. "To Mecca!" he said. "I have been commanded to go to Mecca. You see, two years ago, my five-year-old only son got very sick--bedridden all the time. We took him to all the Hakims in town, but nobody could cure him. They all said that his disease was fatal. Only Allah knows what my wife and I have gone through." He shook his head. "Then, during one of my many sleepless nights, I had a vision. I was in Mecca, in the House of Allah. And I saw things that I am forbidden to talk about. I experienced emotions that I can't explain. But I can tell you, I saw a man with a glowing face. He put his hand on my head and said, 'Your wish has been granted.' When I awoke, the first thing I did was go to my son's room. And what did I see? This little boy who had been wasting away and couldn't even sit up in bed was walking around his room, looking the picture of health, as if he'd never been sick a day in his life." Ruben held his glass out for his host to refill with tea and took a bite out of a rice cookie, aware that his two listeners were waiting in suspense to hear the rest of his story.

"Allah Akbar!" Bashi exclaimed. "What happened next?" he asked earnestly.

"I don't know how to explain it to you, but my boy had had the same dream as I had."

"*La Allah el-Allah*," — there's no God but Allah — Jafar murmured under his breath. "This is an unbelievable story!"

"I myself was flabbergasted at my son's sudden recovery. So, the next day, I visited Hazrateh Agha Mullah Ahmad. I told him about the two identical dreams. His Holiness, may he live to The Day of Resurrection, interpreted the dreams. 'For this miracle that Allah has brought to your son, He has called upon you to visit His house in Mecca. This is an immediate call and you must begin your journey without delay.' 'Your Providence,' I told the holy man, 'Praise Allah, Mohammed and his posterity for blessing my family with a miracle, but can I not wait until the *hajj* season when all Muslims go to Mecca as pilgrims? I don't want to be ungrateful,' I said to Hazrateh Agha, 'but crossing the desert to Mecca in this freezing winter is a precarious journey. Can I sacrifice a sheep, or a cow, and give a sizeable donation instead until the hajj season in the summer?' 'No,' Agha answered. 'You have been called upon to Mecca *now*, not in the summer. This is the least you should do for this extraordinary blessing.'" Ruben sighed as he continued, "And His Holiness also said that I would suffer hardship on this journey." Ruben smiled, sipping his tea.

"Go on, go on," Jafar urged Ruben, as he put more wood on the fading fire. "Tell us more about what Hazrateh Agha told you. I'm all ears."

"Me too," said Bashi, beating his chest, "This is like a story in A Thousand and One Nights."

"Bite your tongue!" Jafar shouted at him from the fireside. "How dare you talk about Allah's miracles like that?"

Bashi punched his own head. "Because I have the brain of a donkey in here. Forgive me, Brother Mustafa, and please go on."

"That's it. As decreed by His Holiness, I left Esfahan *yesterday*," Ruben said, stressing the last word. "There were eight of us. We rode and rode in the heavy snowstorm into the desert and as it got dark, as I told Brother Jafar, six of my travel mates and our carriage driver turned out to be bandits. They took us off the main road and in the middle of nowhere attacked us. I was the only one amongst us who fought back and that's how I got these bruises on my face. All six of them were no match for me and I gave them a lesson they'll never forget."

"Well," Bashi laughed. "Hazrateh Agha told you that there will be hardship on your way to Mecca!"

"And was he ever right! First the bandits," Ruben nodded with a sad smile, "and then you two simpletons."

Bashi turned to Jafar and screamed with laughter, "Don't *we* know about that?"

Jafar looked at the frozen window and yawned, "This is the coldest winter I can remember."

"The wind shrieks like a coyote that's got a piece of shit caught in his throat," snarled Bashi.

"It's late," Ruben sighed, "Let's go to bed."

When at about midnight they finally turned in, Ruben was almost certain he had convinced the two men that he was not the Rhino, although he couldn't be absolutely sure that they had completely cleared him of suspicion. Moreover, despite his exhaustion, the guilt of having killed the nomad and his concern for the lives of other Jewbarites kept him awake. In the early hours of the morning, half-sleeping and half-awake, he had a vision of his dead father. Vividly present, Naphtali the Tailor stood in front of his son, Ruben the Rhino, and they spoke.

Ruben swore that he had not meant to kill the nomad.

Naphtali looked at him with reassuring conviction and told his son that this was the way he was destined to travel.

"To where?"

Naphtali pointed to the west. Ruben felt the strong hand of his father holding him by his arm, lifting him up into deep skies. They flew over a city shining with rays of silver and gold, the land around it flowing with milk and honey. He saw men and women singing and dancing as they rejoiced in the glory of their Promised Land.

From up above, Ruben saw Jerusalem, illuminated and divine, and knew that this was his destination.

Chapter 6
In the Circle of Dervishes

"Salam. Tea is ready, Brother Mustafa!" Ruben awoke in teahouse to the voice of the innkeeper. Anxious to put as much distance as possible between himself and the two men with whom he had spent the previous unnerving evening, Ruben nevertheless had a leisurely breakfast and then took off, continuing his journey toward Jerusalem. He walked half an hour to the nearest village Jafar had given him directions to, where he engaged a coach to take him to Kermanshah, the Persian city closest to Baghdad. From Baghdad he would proceed to Damascus and then Jerusalem.

Outside, the sky was clear and the sun glittered on the icy snow. The past two nights had taken a severe toll on Ruben. He had killed and had almost been killed. Despite the beautiful vision of the night before, weariness and worry accompanied him every step. Jerusalem beckoned—a place of atonement as well as refuge. At least, he thought, I will be among fellow Jews, and perhaps I can discover what, as a Jew, I can do to expiate my great sin. In the late afternoon hours, hungry, tired and bedeviled by these questions he arrived in Bisotoon, a small village a few miles away from Kermanshah. Here, the coach driver stopped for the night. Ruben knew about Bisotoon. Mullah Ahmad had mentioned this place when he had described to him how Persians had become Muslims. Bisotoon had been the last capital of the Sassanid Dynasty. To spread Islam, Omar, the second successor to the Prophet Mohammad, had conquered Persia. His mission was to eradicate Zoroastrianism and replace it with Islam. Thus, Omar's army ruined or set on fire all the Persian palaces, including the palace in Bisotoon and its library, with a magnificent collection of more than twenty thousand ancient books and manuscripts.

Alighting from the coach in Bisotoon, Ruben was enveloped in a thick fog. He put his bag down and rubbed his eyes, trying to see better, but he couldn't make out anything more than a few feet ahead. As the freezing fog entered his lungs, he smelled burning frankincense, a scent Ruben had known since childhood, when his mother would burn the black seeds of this aromatic substance inside a small brazier, reciting verses to ward off the evil eye. Ruben took this as a good omen and headed in the direction of the pleasant and familiar smell. Then he saw an arched doorway with a flickering lantern hanging from its top. Next to the lantern, there was an inscription in gold glazed into a tile with a turquoise background that read, *"Ya Hagh, Ya Hoo"* — He the righteous, He the only — and underneath it, *"Deyreh Darvishan"* — the Convent of Dervishes. As he stepped towards the light with his head up, he collided with a phantom-like man. "I apologize, Agha," Ruben said to the stranger who was wearing a tomb-shaped black hat down to his eyebrows and a long black cloak that covered the rest of his body.

"Follow me, pilgrim," he said turning and moving toward the light.

The stranger's odd voice resonated in Ruben's head. "Pilgrim?" he thought. "How does he know I am a pilgrim?" Haunted, Ruben followed the shadow of this tall man as it crawled along the snow-covered street, disappeared into the arched doorway and descended a flight of stairs to a basement on the floor of which the man stood waiting, his peaceful but compelling look inviting Ruben to join him. With the eerie feeling that he had no control over his movements, Ruben also went down the stairs, until he stood facing the stranger, their eyes locked. The man pointed his index finger to his right. Ruben turned his head and saw an illuminated room, crowded with many men, each with long hair and a thick moustache, wearing long cloaks and sitting cross-legged in the middle of the room. The man walked away as Ruben stood at the bottom of the stairs, transfixed. Then he heard a whisper, "Welcome Pilgrim. I am a *Morid* — a disciple — and your host tonight."

"Greetings to you Haji. My name is…"

"Hush! No mention of your name here. Follow me."

"Where am I?" Ruben whispered curiously as he followed him into the room.

"You are here for a reason. You will see that soon."

"Who was that man who brought me here and who are these

people?" Ruben asked as he sat down, near the stairs, next to this stranger who called himself Morid.

"The man who brought you here is our *Ghotb*—Axis—and the rest of us are his Morids. Those who are sitting in the center in black cloaks, facing the altar, are dervishes and the ones on the sides, like myself, are apprentices."

There was a raised platform facing the stairs where Ruben and his guide were sitting. In the middle of the platform—which the Morid told Ruben was their altar—they had spread a sheepskin carpet and behind it a group of musicians sat cross-legged with their instruments in their hands and their heads bowed. Two dozen younger men who were also apprentices and wearing brown cloaks and felt hats sat along the other three sides of the chamber, which was illuminated by candles and heated by large braziers of burning charcoal in each of its four corners.

The Axis now stepped up to the altar as the dervishes in the center stood up and for the next few minutes faced him with their heads still bowed in a meditative stance. Ruben could now see the Axis' face. He was cleanly shaven, except for a gray moustache that had grown down to his lower lip. His long snow-white hair ran from underneath his black felt hat and ended at his waist.

"*Ya Hagh*," said the Ghotb, announcing the end of the meditation. He then removed his cloak, permitting the dervishes in the center to do the same. Under their own black cloaks they wore white shirts, trousers, skirts and shoes, all of it made of coarse sheep wool—*pashmineh*. The Morid assigned to Ruben whispered, "They are preparing to begin the *soma* ritual, our spiritual dance." He went on to say that Rumi, their beloved philosopher and poet, who had lived over half a millennium ago, had inspired the soma ritual. "We believe that the whole universe revolves and as it does, it changes. We are made of cells that spin. We come from the earth and return to it. It is our human intelligence that allows us consciousness of this constant spinning."

The Ghotb descended from the platform and took his place in the center of the room. He stood in front of each dervish and bowed to him. Then he returned to his post on the platform and sat on the sheepskin. At a signal from *Morshed*—the dance leader—who stood at the head of their line, the dervishes knelt before their Axis. At that point, the flute players started to play. Remaining on their knees, the dervishes began to turn their heads in a circular motion to the music, whose rhythm was, at first, slow and languid, but gradually escalated in rhythm, so that the dervishes correspond-dingly moved their heads until the Axis raised his arm. At this point, the Morshed stood up, bowed his head to the Ghotb and began walking slowly around the chamber.

One by one, other dervishes stood up, bowed to their Axis and followed the dance leader. The men orbited the abbey three times, then formed a circle, clasping their arms—right hand over the left elbow in front of their chests. At this point the Ghotb stood up and examined each of the dervishes, nodding in apparent approval. Then, unfolding their arms and extending their right palm up, left palm down, the dervishes began to rotate around themselves as they also revolved around the room in slow motion, allowing—as the Morid explained to Ruben — the universal energy to enter from above, pass through the right palm into the body and exit to the earth below through the left arm. As Ruben watched them in astonishment, they whirled counterclockwise to the tune of the music, gradually going faster and faster as the musicians and the singers joined in. In what was a mystical voice to Ruben, the Ghotb sang Rumi's poetry. The Axis sang faster, the musicians played faster and the dervishes whirled faster. With their wide skirts billowing, they looked like fantastic birds. Soon the whirling of the dervishes to the speeding music was so fast that their faces were hardly visible. Then, as they continued to dance, the Ghotb walked into their center and slowly began to revolve.

"Now he is the sun and his disciples are planets spinning around him. This spiritual journey allows dervishes to concentrate on the unity of the three fundamental components of human nature: mind, heart and body."

Ruben was absorbed into this enigmatic ritual. The chants of the dervishes resonated in his head, becoming louder and louder, until they became as deafening as a thousand drums beating in unison. And as the dance continued, the dervishes fell to the ground, unconscious. "Anything wrong with them?" Ruben asked anxious-ly.

"No," whispered the Morid "This is the point when they feel the uniting of the mind, heart and body. They are outwardly unconscious, yet spiritually united with their creator. At this point their illusion has become their reality and reality, illusion."

Like a commander surrounded by the bodies of his fallen

warriors, the Axis stood in the midst of his disciples until the last one fell. The Ghotb's face was radiant. He returned to his position on the sheepskin, sat down and closed his eyes. Still in a state of ecstasy, slowly the fallen dervishes regained consciousness and again took their positions facing the altar. There was silence for as long as the Ghotb remained seated with his eyes closed. When he opened them, the dance master stepped forward and kissed his hand. "Will you share with us what you saw and the gift you have brought from beyond?" Before stepping back to his position, the dance master kissed the floor on which he stood.

The Ghotb stared at the front wall with eyes that were wide open and unblinking. "Moving eastward," he spoke slowly, "I passed many plains and villages till I arrived at a faraway place and descended into a small village of poor people living among twisted alleys. They were robbed, tortured and even killed by ruthless oppressors whose hearts, minds and bodies were not joined, yet they called themselves human beings. There, prudence and serenity had vanished and bigotry and ignorance had taken their place."

This is Jewbareh, Ruben thought in wonderment.

Still staring at the wall, the Axis continued, "Someone from this pool of misery has been sent our way. He is running away from the blood he has shed."

Ruben found himself standing, shaking, his eyes fixed on the Ghotb.

"This man amongst us is in search of peace. He is carrying his heavy heart to sacred grounds." As he spoke, he opened the buttons of his shirt and placed the palm of his right hand on his heart. "This pilgrim is in search of tranquility."

The Rhino felt a sense of relief that exalted him, but soon his feelings of awe turned to shock as he saw the man pressing the long sharp nail of his thumb into the skin on the left side of his chest, making a wide cut. Ruben saw no blood coming out of the incision, though he unmistakably saw flesh. As the Ghotb cut deeper, his throbbing heart was visible. "I opened my heart and put his troubled soul inside my body to share his agony and, with the help of Hagh, lessen his pain." Saying this, the Axis closed his eyes, moved his hand along the open wound and it was gone.

"Was that real?" Ruben turned to ask the Morid, but saw the Ghotb sitting next to him.

"What is illusion and what is reality?" answered the Ghotb.

"You come from ethereal places, Hazrateh Ghotb," said Ruben with a shaking voice. "And you know the unknown. You know the story of my life. Oblige me and tell me of my destiny."

The Axis spoke and said, "In two years you will go back to your village. Free. But for a long, long time, as the Almighty said to Cain after he killed his brother, Abel, the slain man's blood will cry out from the ground to the Heavens. Time, and only time, will silence it."

"You mean..."

Ruben opened his eyes to find himself at that very moment alighting from the coach in Bisotoon and enveloped in a thick fog. He rubbed his eyes, but he couldn't see more than a few feet ahead. He went towards the Deyr of Dervishes, where he had just been only a moment ago. Like a fleeting illusion, it had vanished.

Chapter 7
In The City of God

Next day, at a late afternoon hour, Ruben arrived in Kermanshah. He knew that there was a Jewish community in this city.
When he asked, people were surprised. "You don't look like a Jew,"
they said. "Why would you want to know?" Once again Ruben had
to lie. "One of them owes me money," he said and they gave him
directions to a synagogue.

It was only when he arrived at the synagogue that he realized
that it was the eve of the Feast of Purim, an occasion celebrated by
Jews throughout the world but with its roots in Persian history. As
recorded in The Book of Esther in the fourth century BC, Xerxes, the
Persian emperor, leaves his wife Vashti, because, despite his orders,
she refuses to appear "before the Emperor with the crown royal, to
show the people and the princes her beauty, for she was fair to look
on." Esther is thus selected from the candidates to be the Emperor's
new wife. In the meantime, the Emperor's Vizier, Haman, with the
assistance of his sons, hatches a scheme to persuade Xerxes to kill
all the Jews. To get things going, Haman builds fifty gallows to
hang Mordecai—Queen Esther's cousin and adviser—and his
family. Mordecai tells Esther and, at the risk of endangering her
own life, Esther warns Xerxes of Haman's plot. Thus the Emperor
decrees that Haman and his sons be hanged on the very gallows he
had built to kill the Jews.

It was early in the evening and the recital of the Book of Esther
had not begun yet. Seeing this monumental stranger at the entrance
of his synagogue, Rabbi Yoram, who was also the Jewish
community leader of Kermanshah, stepped forward and raised his
head to look at Ruben's face, for he was barely half the newcomer's
size. "Are you Jewish, Agha?" he asked. When Ruben introduced
himself, he noticed that the suspicious look in the man's eyes gave

way to panic. "Ruben the Rhino, the kadkhoda of Jewbareh!" exclaimed the rabbi. It turned out that the frightful news of Ruben killing a Muslim had reached the western region of Persia and now the Jews of Kermanshah feared for their own safety.

The nomad's vengeful soul was running ahead of him, Ruben thought. In killing a Muslim he had jeopardized the safety of the Jewbarites, but with this poisonous news spreading so fast, he had endangered the security of all Persian Jews. He knew he had no patience to hear another lecture consisting of "You did it in self-defense" or other extenuations. "I will leave immediately," he said. Yet, as he turned to go, the rabbi took hold of his arm. "Where do you think you're going?" he asked, astonished. "I mean, for your uniquely unusual figure and shape—your height, the color of your eyes, your size—you are so easily detectable, it's a wonder they haven't caught up with you so far."

If this man of God only knew what had happened to me in the teahouse, Ruben thought. "It is for this very reason that I have to go far, far away," he told the munificent rabbi, "To Jerusalem, to be exact."

That came as a shock to Rabbi Yoram. "Going to the moon is easier than crossing the Zagros mountain range in the winter. No. I insist we hide you here among ourselves—at least until the winter is over."

"Death is no threat, rabbi. I have such a heavy heart that I think it might even be a relief from what I am going through."

Rabbi Yoram played with his moustache as he stared helplessly at Ruben. "Why don't you come in and join us. We are about to start reciting the *Megila*. But before we go back to the synagogue, tell me, what's the name of your father?"

"Naphtali," Ruben looked at the rabbi, surprised.

"All right. If anybody asks you who you are, tell them your name is Naphtali and you are coming from Kashan, not Esfahan. That way, my people will have no reason to be suspicious or panic."

After reciting the whole Megila—the religious prayers of the night—Rabbi Yoram invited Ruben to join him and his congregation in the backyard of the synagogue to perform a further ritual called *Omar Koshan* or "the killing of Omar." Ruben knew that throughout Persia, Shiites celebrated the occasion of the assassination of Caliph Omar, whom they rejected as a successor to Muhammad. They would make effigies of Omar, take them into the streets and dance around them, singing songs in praise of Abu Lolo, Omar's murderer. At the end of the ceremonies, they would set fire to the effigies and stomp on them. To Ruben's utter astonishment, it was now Jews he saw performing the identical ritual, not on the same date as the Muslims, but on Purim. What amazed Ruben more was that there was a large community of Sunnis in Kerman-shah.

"Why would the Jews perform a Shiite ritual discourteous to Sunnis? Are you doing this to please Shiites?" he asked the rabbi.

"Not at all. Actually this ceremony doesn't go beyond the wall of this synagogue. People outside think this is part of our Purim celebrations. We cherish Omar's demise because when this ruthless caliph's army invaded Persia, it was not only our holy books in Bisotoon that they burned, but they also demolished all the Jewish synagogues. Most of our handwritten Torah scrolls and prayer books also perished. This first Muslim conqueror of Persia killed many Jews who refused to convert to Islam. The purpose of this occasion is to remind ourselves of our ancestors, who daringly withstood an oppressor and also to demonstrate our hatred of those who aim at the core of our faith."

That night, Rabbi Yoram took Ruben to his house and again tried to convince him to at least delay his journey to Jerusalem. The Rhino, however, was adamant. Besides his inner turmoil and his fear for his community, it was as if a mysterious energy was pushing him away from home and at the same time an enigmatic power was pulling him to where, in his dream, his father had told him to go. Jerusalem.

Finally, the rabbi surrendered to the Rhino's decision. "You have a precarious journey ahead of you," he said. "Now, let's see. How are we going to get you to Jerusalem? The rare Persian pilgrims who go to Jerusalem," he explained to Ruben, "invariably choose summer for their journey. They engage Ardalan the Eagle, a Kurdish, Jewish friendly caravan leader. He knows his way to Jerusalem as well as the palms of his hands." What Rabbi Yoram did not tell Ruben was that the journey was very costly and that this was one of the reasons why the summertime pilgrims traveled in groups of ten in each carriage. To get Ruben to Jerusalem, the hurdles ahead of the compassionate Yoram were many. So, next morning, he asked Ruben to stay in the guest-house of the synagogue while he made the necessary arrangements for his departure.

First he sent for the Kurdish caravan leader and asked him if he would be willing to go on this journey.

"How do your followers call you their mullah and the wise man of their community?" Ardalan chuckled. "No one has ever passed over the Zagros mountains alive in wintertime." Then he asked curiously, "What's your pilgrim's hurry, anyway?"

"Let's talk about the fare and leave these details for a later time," Yoram replied. "I know you're the best and that you will get my friend to his destination. Now tell me my friend, how much?"

When the Kurdish man left it to the rabbi to decide the fare, Yoram who had already collected enough money to help Ruben escape, doubled Ardalan's ordinary charge—something he could not resist.

Thus, along with Ardalan the Eagle, Ruben the Rhino began his dangerous journey to Jerusalem in the early days of March 1835. The two men climbed several frozen mountains and meandered through numerous snow-covered valleys. Despite Ardalan's astonishing knowledge of this perilous terrain, they had many serious mishaps. They slipped down the icy hills and were injured. At one point bandits blocked the road on them, though as soon as they recognized the Eagle—for he paid ransom to them regularly—they allowed them to pass. Despite his strength, Ruben's legs and especially his feet gave out on him more than once. Luckily, his expert guide had potions and balms with which he massaged his legs to help him carry on. What was astonishing about Ardalan was that he never failed to remember the nearest shelter, teahouse or small village where the owners who were all familiar with him, gave the two shelter on a stormy day or a dark night before they resumed their sluggish journey.

A week later, they spent the night at a caravansary in a small village not far from Baghdad. The following morning they set off for the great city, where they planned to travel through to Damascus and on to Jerusalem. About an hour after they had taken off, Ardalan stopped the carriage on a hill that overlooked Baghdad. From where Ruben stood, he could see minarets and domes surrounded by irregularly scattered small houses. The city looked much smaller than Kermanshah. If you took the domes and minarets away, Ruben thought, the place looked like an enlarged village. When Ardalan asked if Ruben wanted to tour the city, he declined the offer, for he remembered the words of Mullah Ahmad who had instructed him to go as far away as he could. The carriage rushed through the dusty streets of Baghdad and continued the two week journey to Damascus.

Along the way, the Eagle and the Rhino developed a peculiar bond. "Why are you in such a hurry to get to Jerusalem?" the carriage driver asked right away. Ruben, who had by now become a creative storyteller, took his teahouse version of why he was going to Mecca, changed the destination to Jerusalem and crafted a similar episode, trying his best to make it as believable as possible. Being both a Kurd and a Sunni, Ardalan had many complaints about the atrocities of Shiites who, as he put it, were everywhere—from Persia to Mesopotamia. "I know they treat you Jews who live among them no better than us. But we fight back. They kill us by the hundreds and if necessary, we retaliate with our claws and teeth."

Ruben expressed cautious compassion, but did not say very much. He noticed that the Kurdish man was excited about going to Jerusalem. He too was a pilgrim, he told Ruben. Once in Jerusalem, he would go to the Dome of the Rock—or, as he put it, the Mosque of Omar—and pray. "When we are there," Ruben said, "I too want to visit our holy places--first the Wailing Wall, and then all the other religious sites." But the Rhino knew that he could not be a casual pilgrim. Throughout the time that Jews had been expelled from their homeland, Ruben thought, they had lamented their exodus from the Promised Land. The wish to return to his homeland was in his, and every other Jew's daily prayers. But now that he was on his way to the land promised to his forefathers, he knew he would only be able to stay for a brief time before returning to Jewbareh, where his family and people were.

Initially, after Ruben left Baghdad, he kept track of time, but by the time he arrived in Damascus, he had no idea whether or not he had missed Passover—which is about a month away from Purim. Finally, after a long journey from Damascus over the mountainous terrain of Golan Heights to the heart of the Promised Land, in the early morning hours of a chilly day in the spring of 1835, the carriage stopped and the driver announced, "We are at the top of the Mount of Olives. Look out and see Jerusalem!"

He remembered The Mount of Olives from many mentions in Rabbi Shimon sermons. It had been the temporary replacement for the Temple Mount during times that Jews were not allowed to enter their Temple. From the top of the hill, Ruben gazed wonderingly at the tomb of the Dome of Rock, sitting atop the Wailing Wall. He was indeed in Jerusalem! He got down from the carriage, knelt, kissed the ground, stood up and recited the words of the Lord to Moses: "This is the land of which I swore to Abraham, to Isaac, and to Jacob: 'I will give it to your offspring.' I have let you see it with your eyes, but you shall not go over there." And now Ruben was going to enter the very land which God had denied Moses, but promised nevertheless to the offspring of Abraham, Isaac and Jacob. The Rhino was ecstatic, for, after thousands of years, he was one of the few Persian Jews who had been blessed enough to visit the Promised Land. No joy for Jews, he thought, was ever free of sorrow. Moses had been deprived of the happy fulfillment of his mission and although Ruben had arrived safely in Jerusalem, he carried with him a heavy heart, for he had blood on his hands.

"Get up," Ruben heard Ardalan standing over his head. "I'm tired of watching you sit here and whisper to yourself."

Ruben nodded and climbed back into the carriage as it took off. Once again worries that had followed him like a shadow through-out his journey overtook his mind. He came face to face with the necessity of having to stay away from home for an unknown period of time. It was one thing to merrily praise Jerusalem in your daily prayers, but the reality of living in this faraway land with no money and no family or friends was nothing to celebrate. Where exactly was he going to settle in Jerusalem? He had thought of Yadegar the Camel, a wool-seller and one of his father's second cousins who, as Naphtali had told him, had immigrated to Jerusalem before Ruben was born. However, the chances that Yadegar, who was older than his father, would still be alive were next to none.

"Where do you want me to drop you?" Ardalan's voice inter-ruptted his thoughts.

"Somewhere in the Jewish quarter." It was the only place Ruben could think of.

That was where the two men alighted from the carriage to bid farewell to each other. "Look over there," said Ardalan pointing to a cluster of holy monuments. Ruben saw the Wailing Wall, Ardalan the Dome of the Rock. "If our holy places can stand next to each other so gracefully, why can't our two peoples?" whispered Ardalan the Eagle.

"One day we will," Ruben said, reassuring him of something

that he himself was not so certain about. Then he embraced his Kurdish friend and they bid farewell to each other. With Ardalan gone, Ruben asked passersby in his broken Hebrew if they knew of a Jew from Persia? Yadegar the Camel? Or perhaps the children of a man known by this name? Any Persians in the wool business by any other name? He tried every conceivable combination he could come up with, using the little information he had about his father's cousin, but no one was able to help him. Although on this beautiful early spring day, Jerusalem had a lot to offer and a lot to be seen, with each and every shake of the head, Ruben's anxiety escalated. This was not an overnight stay. He had to stay here until Mullah Ahmad allowed him to return home. And worst of all, he had little left of the money that Mullah Ahmad and Rabbi Yoram had given him. He sat down, grabbed his bent legs and put his chin on his knees, feeling lost and confused. Why had he listened to Ahmad and come all this way? He could always have gone to a faraway location in Persia where nobody knew him. There were so many places to go—from the Caspian Sea to the Persian Gulf. But the news had reached the teahouse and later Kermanshah like lightning, he remembered. And then came the awakening realization that he was renouncing the blessing of being in the holiest of all places on earth.

"Shalom," a voice echoed above his head. He stood up to see a young man with blue eyes and a fair complexion. The man wore a caftan and a hat of fur, from which two long braids of blond hair hung down on either side of his face. "I heard you talking to yourself," said the man in a Hebrew dialect that Ruben found very different from what he had studied. "Are you a pilgrim? And where are you from?"

"Ruben is my name, I'm from Persia and I have just arrived," he answered, amazed at the way this man was dressed.

"*Mi Paras!*" – from Persia – the man said hesitantly and then introduced himself as Boaz. "Persian Jewish pilgrims who come to visit Jerusalem," he went on, "usually come in the summertime. You have come at an unusual time. And where are you going to stay?"

"I'm hoping to find a cousin of my father who immigrated to the Holy Land about forty years ago—a man by the name of Yadegar the Camel. I've been asking people if they know of him or his children, but…"

"Forty years ago?" the man shook his head, his braids waving in the air. "I don't want to sound pessimistic, but it's very unlikely that you would be able to find him, unless you know his Hebrew name, because Yadegar must be the man's Persian name."

Ruben nodded. He thanked the man, but he was not about to leave.

"So you have no place to stay."

"That's right."

"Well," the stranger grinned. "I don't think you can find anywhere to stay tonight!"

Was this annoying man having fun mocking him? Ruben thought. "So, I will sleep on the street, if it makes you happy. Why don't you leave?"

"Please don't be upset, my friend. Don't you know that tonight is the first night of Passover?"

Ruben was breathless. After his experience at the Deyr of Dervishes, was this yet another illusion? As if being in Jerusalem was not enough of a feat, to be in the City of God on the eve of Passover was like a dream turned nightmare. He was nothing but a poor and homeless vagrant who for the first time in his life had nowhere to go, and no way of celebrating the feast of Passover. Tonight, he thought, in every Jewish home they will sing and praise the Lord for the Israelites' liberation from slavery in Egypt. And now, thousands of years later, he had found a Promised Land with nowhere to go to and no shelter over his head. Could this be a mere coincidence or another otherworldly sign? Ruben wondered.

"So, might my family and I have the pleasure of having you at our Seder table tonight?" Boaz's voice brought Ruben back to the real world.

Ruben was flabbergasted. "I feel badly for being so rude to you and I'm speechless, sir. Why should I bother you on such a sacred night?"

"Listen young man. You're my God-sent guest for Passover and I salute you. You would be no burden but a blessing if you accept my invitation," said Boaz, taking Ruben firmly by his arm and helping him up. "Let's go. We will look for your old friend after Passover."

Walking towards home, Boaz asked his guest if he was there to stay.

"For a while if not forever. That's why I have to find a job to

74

earn my bread and a place to live."

This man's story was not the happy one of a Jew arriving at the Promised Land on Passover, Boaz thought. On the night that all others in Diaspora prayed for: *Next year in Jerusalem*, it was so obvious that this pilgrim—or a settler, perhaps—was not in a mood to celebrate. "Sorry, I forgot to ask you your name!" Boaz laughed.

"Ruben."

"*Adon* Ruben. In this city, on the eve of Passover, you can find neither a place to live nor a job. But since you're so concerned, rightfully so, there's this good friend of mine from Persia, Rabbi Daniel. He has helped many of his countrymen who have arrived here in the last twenty years or so. The day after tomorrow I will take you to his shop and together we will think of how to get you settled here."

It was late afternoon when the two men arrived at Boaz's house. Ruben remembered all the Passovers at home in Jewbareh—the rituals, the food and the festivities. A few days before the holiday, the Jewbarites would begin to clear their houses of *hames*—wheat, barley, bread and all other grains, which one is forbidden to eat during this feast. Then they would bring out all their copperware utensils such as pots, plates, bowls and cutlery and hire zinc-workers who would set up small furnaces in their backyards. On the furnaces, these professional polishers, melted zinc and applied it to the copperware with rough pieces of fabric, giving them a silvery shine and a gleaming new polish after a year of use. The next step was to give all these utensils a ritual bath in boiling water to make them spic and span for Passover meals.

Boaz and his wife Alisa, both in their early thirties, had seven children—three girls and four sons, all under ten. Alisa, who wore a long dress and a headscarf, welcomed Ruben. "You are twenty-five and not married?" Alisa was genuinely surprised. "It's written that girls and boys must find their destined spouses and marry them immediately after they come of age." Then she turned to her husband and continued, "We must find this young man the right match."

"Let him recuperate from his exhausting journey, then—if he decides not to go back home—at that time we will think of a wife for him," Boaz said to his wife. "For now, let's sit down and celebrate this holy night." As Alisa continued talking about finding him a wife, Ruben remembered his mother, who constantly nagged him to get married and for the first time, he actually missed her grumbling.

At dinner with Boaz and his family, Ruben found the Seder — the Passover dinner and its rituals — very close to that of the Jewbarites. Still, there were some interesting differences. Unlike in Persia, no cooked rice was served and when Ruben asked his host the reason, he was shocked by the answer. "I had heard and was very surprised that your people eat cooked rice on Passover," said Boaz. "As you know, no food that has been leavened is allowed in this period. That's why we eat matzo in place of bread." Boaz was further surprised to hear that in addition to rice, during Passover, Persian Jews also ate legumes. Then, towards the end of the Seder, when Boaz recited the song and prayer of thankfulness, it was Ruben's turn to be surprised. Similar to Persian Jews, the head of the household recounted each and every one of the many blessings that God has bestowed upon the Israelites during their exodus from Egypt, and the people around the table responded by singing in unison: *Dayenu* — It would be enough for us.

"If He had only split the sea for us." ... "Dayenu!"

"If He had only executed justice upon the Egyptians." ... "Dayenu!"

"If He had only led us through on dry land." ... "Dayenu!"

But here, his host and his family didn't do — and didn't know of — what the Persian Jews did when this part of the prayers was recited. Back home, at the time of "Dayenu," adults joined the children and enjoyed a rather silly but joyful game that was believed to be a re-enactment of the beating of the Jewish slaves in Egypt. When it was time to recite this song, everyone would grab a handful of spring onions, chase others around the room and with every recitation of "Dayenu," gave anyone within their reach gentle lashes. Upon hearing this detail, Boaz and his family burst into wide, astonished laughter, to which Ruben genially added his own.

At the Passover table in the house of Boaz, there was no rice, no legumes, no beatings with spring onions, but there was the love and compassion with which these total strangers had received the Rhino — himself a stranger to them — in what was, for all of them, the honoring of Jewish tradition, and one of the many ways by which the Jewish people had survived.

As promised, after Passover Boaz took Ruben to Rabbi Daniel's fabric shop, introduced him to the rabbi. On the other side of the counter, Ruben saw a small man in his seventies with a long beard and gray hair. While Boaz was talking, from time to time the rabbi turned his head toward Ruben as though measuring his huge size and smiled gently. Unlike Boaz, he wore a turban, smaller than what the mullahs wore in Persia, and a long, black robe.

"How do you two know each other?" Rabbi Daniel asked and Boaz explained how he had met Ruben on the eve of Passover. "So you've brought me Cyrus the Great himself?" the rabbi chuckled, looking at this tall and muscular man again. "*Khosh amadid,*" he said to Ruben, then instantly turning to Boaz, he added, "I'm sorry. I just welcomed him in Persian. It's nice to speak the old language once in a while. So, tell me about my countryman."

"This young man is a tailor," Boaz now explained, "and our main concern is to find him a place to live and a job so he can earn a living."

"Well, my friend, together we will find him a job. As far as a place to live, I have a spare room in my house for new arrivals where they are welcome to live until they begin to make money on their own. So, from this point on, the pleasure of having a guest who comes from the land of my forefathers will be mine."

"But I don't want to be a burden, rabbi."

"It is no burden young man, and I thank our friend Boaz for blessing my house with your presence."

Ruben embraced Boaz and thanked him, "You're a benevolent man," he said under his breath. "May the Master of the Universe reward you and your beloved ones with health and prosperity."

"Don't talk as if we were parting forever. We will be seeing each other soon."

Once Boaz left, the rabbi brought Ruben a cup of tea, sat next to him and asked what part of Persia he came from and whether he was a pilgrim or had come to stay — the question everyone on this trip had repeatedly asked him.

"Neither one," Ruben replied after a lengthy pause. "It is a long story. A sad story."

Seeing Ruben's sorrow, the rabbi tapped him on his shoulder and said, "All newcomers have different and interesting stories. The only thing that matters is that you are here. We are in the middle of the Passover week," he suddenly changed the subject, "and since, as you can see, I don't have many customers, I will try to close shop earlier and go home. So, after the first night of Seder with Boaz and his family, prepare yourself for a second Seder with mine."

"As I said before, I don't want to be a..."

"I will not tolerate any arguments," Rabbi Daniel said, caressing his beard. From now on, do me a favor and call me by my first name. You should also know, my brother Ruben, that this is a circle of righteousness that you've fallen into. When we first arrived here, we too were drawn into this loop of compassion. My father used to recite this Persian poem, 'Do good and let it flow on the Tigris River, for the Almighty will reward you in the desert.'"

"I am humbled, Daniel. I am humbled," said Ruben in a low voice, trying to hold back his tears. "Since I have arrived in Jerusalem, I've been nothing but a burden to kind and generous people like you and Boaz."

"Enough! Now let's eat," said Daniel as he spread a tablecloth in a small room in the back of his shop, put his lunch on it and invited Ruben to join him. As they ate in silence, the Rhino's mind wandered back and forth from Jewbareh to Jerusalem, from the circle of dervishes to the circle of righteousness—as the rabbi had just referred to it. Had he been destined to be here and was there some magic, if not logic, beyond the reality of the events that had brought him to this place? First there had been Boaz and now this compassionate clergyman. The rabbi sensed his guest's urge to open up, but he didn't want to sound as though he was prying. "So," he said, "Do you want to know how I ended up in Jerusalem?"

Ruben nodded, but before Daniel could answer, a voice sounded from the outer part of the shop, "I need fifteen rolls of that light blue silk you showed me the other day. Do you have that much in stock?"

"My friend Ariel!" Daniel called, jumping up and going to the counter. "Yes, I do."

"Sorry," said the man. "I see you have a guest and you're having lunch. Just have them delivered to my workshop as soon as you can, will you?"

"Of course. In the meantime, I would like you to meet my friend from Persia." He signaled Ruben to come to the counter. "He is a tailor and we are looking for a job for him."

"Who is '*we*'?" Ariel said to Daniel in a sarcastic tone, as he bowed his head to Ruben.

"As usual," the rabbi laughed. "*'We,'* my friend, is you, me and all the people around us."

"So, who am I to say no to a distinguished rabbi like you?" Ariel laughed. "Bring the fabrics and your friend from Persia tomorrow and *we* will see what *we* can do for him!"

To show Jerusalem to Ruben, Daniel closed his shop early. For the first time since he had arrived, Ruben was looking at the city, and the people around him. The hills surrounding Jerusalem were garlanded with evergreen olive trees and many sturdy plants with fresh, shiny spring leaves. The stony walls, cobblestone streets, the horse drawn droshkies, Arab shepherds in long head-covers and robes leading their flocks of sheep and goats, the peddlers who cried out their merchandise in a mix of Arabic, Armenian and Hebrew and the Turkish-speaking men in uniform who soldiered the streets, all struck him with the majesty of the city.

"Jerusalem is a mix and a divide," said Daniel, noticing Ruben's confusion. "In this city of about eight thousand people, we live under the rule of the Ottoman Turks, and by 'we,' I mean Jews, Arab Muslims, Christian and Armenians who separate themselves from other Christians. We all live within the confines of our quarters."

"Ghettos?" Ruben snapped.

"Not at all," Daniel shook his head. "Although we live in separate areas, in our daily life, we mingle and work together with minimal clash of faiths."

There were many Arabs in Persia and Ruben could easily recognize them because of the way they dressed. There had been Armenians in Esfahan from whom he bought grapes for Abram's Magic and he could recognize them when they spoke Armenian. Oddly, it was those whom Daniel called Jews that looked least familiar to Ruben. There were two very different groups. Although all the men were bearded, some—like Boaz— were dressed in long black caftans, shiny leather shoes and white shirts, while their heads were covered with either velvet kippas or hats of felt or fur, from which two long braids of hair hung down, one on either side of the face. And there was another group who, like Rabbi Daniel, were not so neatly dressed and wore turbans and worn-out cotton cloaks. The rabbi explained to Ruben that the nicely dressed men were called Ashkenazi Jews. "Centuries ago," he said, "after the Israelites were driven out of their homeland and scattered throughout the world, they gathered together in different regions and with the passage of time, they developed cultures unique to where they lived. Today," he went on telling Ruben, "Jews are essentially divided into two major ethnical and cultural groups: Sephardim and Ashkenazim. Sephardim are those who, after being expelled from Spain several hundred years ago, emigrated to the eastern Mediterranean and the Balkans, while the Ashkenazim came from Prussia in the Middle Ages to Russia and Eastern Europe."

Nothing was more striking to Ruben than the marked difference in appearance between the two. Sephardim had generally darker complexions, black hair and — to Ruben — regular features, whereas the Ashkenazim had pale skin tone, and sometimes light-brown or even blond hair. Except for their hands and faces, all the women were fully covered in long dresses, mostly in black or white — the Ashkenazi in more elegant outfits and the Sephardim in humbler attire. Daniel went on to tell Ruben that the Ashkenazim were more learned and prosperous than Sephardim.

Sectarianism in Judaism was something that Ruben could not digest, for his own roots went back to two and a half millennia ago, when Jews were nothing but *Jews*. He was feeling an overwhelming curiosity as he became aware of historical facts he had never dreamed of. Suddenly the world was more complex than he had ever realized. There were Jews who looked different from him and all the Jewbarites he had lived amongst. After all, was it not true that with the coming of the Messiah, Jews would gather here, where their Temple had once been, rebuild it, and praise the Almighty for bringing them back to their homeland? Those other Jews, who looked so different, were part of the same tradition. How could they have divided themselves over their geographical regions? How could they be different from each other but still be Jews? Overwhelmed, Ruben wondered if he seemed as strange to them as they did to him.

"Are you all right?" Daniel asked.

"I am... No, I'm not! To be honest, my head is throbbing. I have so many questions to ask, and yet I barely know where to begin."

"Well," Daniel smiled. "As it has been written, ask and you shall be answered."

"Fine. Let me try this. To which of the two groups do we, the

80

Persian Jews, belong?"

"You see, although our religious rituals are closer to those of the Sephardim than the Ashkenazim, we don't identify with either one of these two groups. We are undivided Jews who, throughout centuries of living in Persia, have remained loyal to the original religious heritage of our forefathers. What's ironic though is that Ashkenazim and Sephardim think exactly the same. Quite honestly, I identify with both groups and fortunately there are many others here who think the same way as I do. It is time we all went back to our origins."

The two men were around the corner from the Wailing Wall and it was to the Wailing Wall that Daniel now took Ruben, sensing in him something he couldn't quite name but that he was sure required the lamentations so often recited at the ancient remnant of the Temple. Once in front of the Wall, Daniel took out his small prayer book and as he was thumbing through its pages, he saw Ruben putting his forehead to one of the large stone blocks and whispering. Through the glaze of his tears, Ruben saw a tunnel that took him back more than twenty-five centuries ago. His presence at this strange but sacred place was overwhelming. Remembering what Rabbi Shimon had taught him from the books of Kings and Isaiah, he saw the soldiers of Emperor Nebuchadnezzar burning the temple that had once sat upon this wall after plundering its treasures which they took with them to Babylon. He had also taken Ruben's ancestors captive and taken them to Babylon as slaves. The Rhino had an eerie feeling that he was the reincarnation of one of those slaves, a nameless one who, perhaps as strong as him, had also murdered a captor, maybe on the day that Cyrus the Great had conquered Babylon and freed him.

Daniel closed his prayer book, put it on his forehead, kissed it and placed it back in his pocket. He turned around and was shocked to see this big man sobbing like a child, his fingers clawed into the niches of the wall. He held Ruben by the arm, shook him gently and said, "Look, it's none of my business, but you are the first person that I have ever seen come to the Promised Land so despondent. If I take home this huge grimfaced man," he chuckled, "it will scare my poor kids!"

His friendly expression was like that of Mullah Ahmad, Ruben thought. Moreover, he couldn't help but notice a certain sense of curiosity in Daniel's combined kindness and humor, as if he had suspected Ruben's secret and was yearning to hear the story of what the Rhino had gone through. The last person with whom he had shared the guilt of killing Zain was Mullah Ahmad. From then on, the thoughts of what he had done to the nomad and his people had ceaselessly pained his heart and flooded his head. He was sick and tired of being Mustafa, Naphtali and anybody but himself. Furthermore, he was destitute in this foreign land, except for Boaz and Daniel, two benevolent and generous men who had offered him refuge, accommodation and help in earning a living. He opened his mouth to tell Daniel all about himself, but the words stuck in his throat. "I've been through a lot," he barely managed to whisper. "Give me some time, Daniel, and I'm sure I will be fine."

"Let's talk about the things that worry you," said the rabbi, as he put some coins in the hand of an old beggar near the Wall. "You have a place to live until you stand on your own feet and your employment with Ariel is almost sealed. So, you don't have to worry about how you are going to support yourself."

That was the breaking point for Ruben. How could he withhold anything from Daniel or Boaz? They were such kind men. "I'm not here to stay," Ruben finally opened up. "I have a big family in Jewbareh—a mother, a stepbrother and four sisters with spouses and children. But I have run away because..." he hesitated. "Because a nomad was about to kill me."

"Wait a little," said the rabbi, sensing that a tragic story was on the tip of Ruben's tongue. "I want to hear everything you wish to tell me. But look now. You are here, in Jerusalem, where every Jew in Diaspora dreams of being. And you are here on Passover, of all the Almighty's days. So, let's take this as a good omen. You have a story to tell about why you are here and I have one of my own. Let's exchange our tales tonight, after dinner. Now raise your head and look around. Look at those two mosques on the top of the Wailing Wall—the holiest of places for us Jews and the only remaining wall of our sacred temple. The Muslims not only believe that this holy Wall is only a platform and foundation for those two mosques—Al Aqsa and the Dome of the Rock—they also believe that Mohammad ascended to heaven from here." Daniel shrugged his shoulders. "Next to these two monuments, there's the Church of the Holy Sepulcher where the Christians believe that their prophet was crucified and went up to heaven. But no Jew, Ashkenazim or Sephardim," the rabbi laughed loudly, "has ever ascended from any one of our synagogues. Now, let's go, because it's getting late."

And that comment triggered many questions that for Ruben had remained unanswered until now. "Do you mind if we resume our conversation where we left it before coming to the Wall?" Ruben asked as the two began to walk, "Because this separation between Jews baffles me."

"Of course I don't mind."

"If Ashkenazim and Sephardim are almost the same, then why do they label themselves differently?"

"We are all the same but our diversity adds to the richness of our culture. Curious to know about each other, we become closer and in that way, we care for one another. Here, as in Persia, we don't beat our chests to please the Muslims. And believe me, this is not unique to Persian Jews. Other communities who come from various countries bring with them--but soon abandon--their un-Jewish rituals. Give it some time and you will see it for yourself."

It was late afternoon. A day had gone by since Ruben had arrived here and he had been so preoccupied with the events of the last twenty-four hours that he hadn't noticed the freshness of the air or the way the many languages, dialects and accents with which people spoke mingled and resonated like a pleasant melody. Shops along the way to Daniel's house were more or less similar to those of Jewbareh; whether Sephardim or Ashkenazim, their proprietors greeted the rabbi. How similar it was, Ruben thought, to passing by the shops of Hassan the Allaf or Nehemiah the Baker. When they arrived at Rabbi Daniel's residence, Ruben found it to be a modest house with three small rooms and a shack that served as the kitchen.

"A guest from Persia, where our forefathers lived," said Daniel, introducing Ruben to his wife Miriam, who was busy preparing their dinner in the kitchen. Her jet-black hair, covered with a colorful scarf down to her shapely shoulders ran from underneath the scarf to her waist. Miriam turned around and welcomed the Rhino with a soothing smile. Then to her husband she said, "Why don't you take our guest in and I'll join you as soon as I'm done cooking."

"We have been blessed with two sons and their families who will be with us tonight," Daniel said as he ushered his guest in. Then, he showed Ruben to one of the three rooms, asked him to rest and told him that he would call him when dinner was ready. The room was small, with whitewashed gypsum plastered walls and its floor was covered with an old red and blue Moroccan rug. Ruben lay down on the bed. The mattress and the quilt were made of white cotton with bright orange stripes. He tried to rest and unwind the grip of thoughts that twirled around his mind like a mighty snake. At twenty-four, he had made his first journey to faraway lands. No one his own age in Jewbareh had gone as far away as Jerusalem. He had come a long way away from where he belonged, where his people were undoubtedly being persecuted for what he had done. And as he dozed off, he saw the nomads, savagely rampaging Jewbareh, stealing, beating, raping, torturing, killing...

"Are you having bad dreams?" Ruben opened his eyes to see Daniel standing over his head with a cup of wine in one hand and a decanter in the other. "You were talking very loudly to yourself, my friend. Here," Daniel said, handing him the cup. "Drink this. It will relax you."

Ruben gulped the wine, thanked Daniel and held out the cup for a refill. Daniel said, "Miriam has made us some chicken kabob and steamed rice." It was obvious that he was trying to distract Ruben from an apparent nightmare. "For all the years that we have been here, we find Persian food *the* most delicious of all. Now, get up, wash your face and refresh a bit. Dinner is ready."

So, on this second night of Passover, Ruben sat at the table set in the dining-room together with the rabbi, his wife and his two sons—Solomon and Yoel—and their families. Solomon, who looked very much like his father, was married to a Yemenite girl who had a dark complexion. They had three young sons who ran around the room as their mother tried to bring them to the table. Solomon was a jeweler with a business in the Armenian quarters of Jerusalem. Yoel bought hand-woven carpets from Arab villages and sold them in the main bazaar in the city. Yoel's wife of only a few months was a blond Ashkenazi with blue eyes. After the Seder prayers, both Daniel's sons were curious about their ancestors' motherland and Ruben answered them eagerly.

Later, when Daniel's sons and their families had gone, Ruben thanked Daniel and especially his wife Miriam for their kindness to him, who was a total stranger. Then Daniel addressed his wife and said, "After such a hard day's work, you need to rest. So, why don't you go to bed while our guest and I spend some time talking about our old country." With Miriam gone, the two men moved to the other side of the room and sat on the bigger and more comfortable chairs. Noticing that Ruben was much more relaxed than earlier that evening, Daniel said, "Before we came home, you said that you escaped Persia because a nomad was about to kill you. Why don't you tell me what happened next?"

Thus Ruben finally got a chance to tell the rabbi the whole story: of who he was, how he had killed Zain, what he had gone through before finally arriving in Jerusalem. He talked about the weight of the guilt he felt for having killed another human being, regardless of who he was. He talked about his anger at himself and at the universe and wondered why a Divine Power had not intervened to stop this unfortunate incident. When he had finished, he looked at Daniel for an answer. The man — it seemed to Ruben — had not been moved. He looked Ruben square in the face, nodded, reached for his Torah, thumbed through it, stopped at a page and said, "First, listen to what I read to you from the Book of Exodus, Chapter Two, Verses 11 and 12: *Now it came to pass in those days that Moses grew up and went out to his brothers and looked at their burdens, and he saw an Egyptian man striking a Hebrew man of his brothers. He turned this way and that way, and he saw that there was no man; so he struck the Egyptian and hid him in the sand."*

Ruben, who deep down was begging for someone to despise him for the sin he'd committed, moaned, "Who am I to be compared to Moses?"

"I'm not comparing you with Moses, but you have done exactly what our great deliverer has done. Can you be compared to him? Perhaps not. But nevertheless this parallel remains. Nowhere in the Torah does it say that Moses had a guilty conscience after he struck the evil Egyptian. Indeed, who are you to consider yourself more ethical than Moses?" Daniel took a sip of his hot tea and went on, "I think your presence in Jerusalem is far more than a simple flight. It was meant to happen."

"My killing of someone has been predestined? What sort of reasoning is that?"

The rabbi nodded as he paged through the Bible. "Well, I guess there's a lot to read, and I'm not sure if you have the patience to listen."

"Please go ahead," Ruben implored.

"All right. Here it is. Deuteronomy, Book 19," he said, looking from one page to another. "It's as if every verse in this book is about you," he chuckled. "Let me read Verse 4 word by word: *This is the rule concerning the man who kills his neighbor unintentionally, without malice aforethought. That man may flee and save his life.* And here you are, young man. Sinless in the City of God!"

"Isn't that something!" Ruben tugged at his beard nervously.

"So, the Torah, and not this rabbi," he said, putting his hand on his chest, "tells us that you are absolutely permitted to come here for the reasons you have. But personally, I think there's more to your presence here. You are here to learn a little more about becoming a Jew."

"I am a Jew, rabbi!"

"And a good Jew too, as this book testifies," he said, bringing the Torah to his lips and kissing it. "But especially because you are a community leader, there's a lot more for you to learn about Jewish laws."

"You are right," Ruben sighed. "I'm afraid my knowledge is very limited."

"Leave that to me. As soon as you have settled, I will try to walk you through the teachings of Judaism. The fact that this Muslim mullah has saved you from being killed is a miracle. Believe in miracles and soon this benevolent man will call you home. Now, let's talk about something else," said Daniel to distract Ruben.

"Of course," Ruben responded, much relieved. "You promised to tell me the story of how you came to Jerusalem. I'd very much like to hear it."

"Well, it's late and I know you are tired," said Daniel, "So I will try to be as brief as I can. It was about sixty years ago. My father of blessed memory was the chief rabbi of Shiraz. We were three brothers and one sister. Abdullah, the most influential and notorious mullah in Shiraz, had seen my sister Hannah, who was fourteen-years old at the time, in the bazaar near our ghetto and had ordered his disciples to kidnap her. When we got the devastating news, my father rushed to the Mullah's house, begging him to give Hannah back to us. '*Soghra*, you najes Jew!' Mullah Abdullah had said heatedly. 'That is her Muslim name. Soghra. And she's my *sigheh*' — temporary wife." It was obvious that Hannah had been forced to convert and become Abdullah's temporary wife.

"I'm sure you know that under the Qajar Dynasty, which still rules Persia, forced conversion of 'infidels' has become a common practice. My father appealed to anyone he could, but all he found out was that Hannah was not alone. Abdullah had also kidnapped nine other young girls—five Jewish, two Armenian and two Zoroastrian. 'As virgins they are converted to Islam and then, as my temporary wives, their conversion is sealed and thus the sword of Islam has spread its domination further and further,' Abdullah had said in his own defense. Headed by my father, the parents of the kidnapped girls got together to figure out how they could save their daughters from remaining in captivity. In the middle of their conversation, the mother of one of the Zoroastrian girls said that she was friendly with the hairdresser of Wife Number One in Abdullah's harem. According to this hairdresser, Wife Number One was furious with her husband's endless appetite for virgins. My father jumped at this tiny thread of information and came up with a plan whereby the group bribed the hairdresser to tempt Wife Number One to let the girls escape. In the absence of Abdullah, all the kidnapped girls fled their captor's house. At the same time, their families sold everything they had and hired smugglers to help them escape Shiraz. This occurred back in 1791. The five families and many others who also feared Abdullah's vengeance traveled by carriage to Bandar Bushehr on the Persian Gulf, and from there, by sea and land to the Promised Land."

That night, as Ruben lay on his bed and thought of his host's life story, it gave him a relative sense of relief to know that he was not the only one whose sufferings had taken him this far. He couldn't help thinking, however, that whereas Daniel's father had saved many lives, thanks to his intelligence and successful plan, Ruben himself, in executing his moral responsibility towards his people, had used his muscles, killed someone and put such a heavy weight of guilt on his conscience. He couldn't help thinking, however, that whereas Daniel's father had saved many lives, thanks to his intelligent plan, Ruben himself, by using his muscles in self-defense, had possibly jeopardized the safety of the very people he had dedicated his life to protecting. Then he thought of the joy of living in a land where, at least, he had some kind of historical root. If he were to settle in this land, he would encourage not only his immediate family but also all the Jewbarites to move out of that prejudice-infested village.

The next day, Ariel, who was a member of Rabbi Daniel's congregation, hired Ruben with a meager wage. He gave Ruben and the rabbi a tour of his factory's section which manufactured exclusively men's clothing and was only staffed by men. In the women's section, Ariel told Ruben, women's clothing was made only by seamstresses. "The place is blessed by His Holiness," he pointed at Daniel and laughed. "God forbid, if a man goes to the women's side, this agent of the Almighty will grill me alive!"

"I'm glad you are behaving," Daniel said, also laughing. "But seriously, I'm grateful for your kindness to our brother Ruben."

Soon after he had a job with Ariel, another member of the congregation gave Ruben a room to live in at his house for a nominal weekly payment. Other members each provided him with used pieces of furniture, kitchen utensils, a bed and many other secondhand items. But when it came to his clothes, nobody had anything in Ruben's size. That's when Ariel gave him some pieces of old fabric so that he could make himself new clothing.

And thus, Ruben the Rhino, the son of Naphtali the Tailor and the kadkhoda of Jewbareh, began his humble life in Jerusalem. During the daytime, he worked as an assistant to Menasha, one of Ariel's foremen—a little ginger haired man with a red face and two purplish-blue bags under his small eyes. Perhaps it was because of these bags that they called him "Menasha the Purple." He was short in height, but more so in temper. It didn't take long before the foreman realized that Ruben's mastery in tailoring, which surpassed his own, was a threat to his position. From then on, he did all he could to get rid of his rival. He overloaded him with work and treated him harshly. In the evenings Ruben came home exhausted, cooked himself a small dinner—part of which he put aside for his next day's lunch—and then spent most of his sleepless nights thinking of his family and the people he had left behind, contemplating the crime he had committed and fretting over Menasha's ruthless exploitation of him. Although he obeyed this insecure man's endless commands and put up with his contemptuous behavior, he could feel how his own integrity and self-confidence were gradually being sapped, and he was outraged at what was happening to him. Was he no longer the Rhino he had once been? Had he been transformed into a different creature? He thought again and again about Moses and the Egyptian. How was that possible? Did it not violate every rule he had been brought up with? Was *this* the "Promised Land" as he had always imagined? And worst of all, was he himself becoming so angry that he might lose his self-control and commit a crime again? The thought struck horror in his heart.

The only glimmer of hope for Ruben that prevented his fury from exploding was the thought that one day soon a messenger would arrive from Mullah Ahmad, giving his wine-bearer permission to return home. But who would this messenger be? He knew that some relatively well-off Jews from different ghettos in Persia had hired guarded carriages to bring them to Jerusalem and back. As a pious act, such pilgrims spread the word throughout the synagogues in Persia, seeking to carry letters of supplication to be placed in the niches of the Wailing Wall. They also accepted money from those who had made a vow to distribute alms to the needy in the Jerusalem. These were the most likely people that Ruben's family and friends might look for to communicate with him.

And then another chapter opened in the life of Ruben the Rhino in the city of Jerusalem. It was a few days before Shavuot, a feast of two major events in Jewish history—the day that Torah was given by God to the Jewish nation at Mount Sinai *and* the festival of grain harvest. It had been a week since Menasha the Purple, who always feared the Rhino as a threat to his job, had assigned Ruben to work ordinarily done by cheap laborers. Ruben had not objected, for not only he had been aware of the Purple's insecurities, but also due to the fact that his livelihood depended on his job. On this early afternoon, Menasha had instructed Ruben to load a carriage with a rush order for a customer. So, Ruben came out of the factory to the loading area located between the men and women's sections and began to work.

Ariel's factory was on a large lot that was like a platform that nature had dug into a mild slope on Mount Olive. From where he stood, Ruben had a clear view of the city and its surroundings. He could see colorful wildflowers that had began to bloom on the hills and the valleys, among cypresses, pines, almonds, figs, pomegranates and olive trees and the streets of Jerusalem full of people busy with preparations for celebrating the feasts of Shavuot. The air was filled with the generosity of nature and the celebrative mood of the people. In this contagious aura, Ruben found solace and deliverance from the web of anguish and frustration he had been trapped in, especially Menasha's harsh treatment. For the first time since he had arrived here, he felt that the dark black rock of despair that had constantly weighed on his heart was gone. Suddenly, and for no discernible reason, he felt liberated from all his misfortunes and miseries. As he lifted heavy bundles of clothing onto the carriage, he began murmuring an old Jewbarite folk song. It was at this moment that he saw a young woman, over at the women's section, supervising a group of female workers who, like Ruben, were loading piles of clothing onto another carriage. Ruben froze, enamored by one of the women's magnetic beauty. The Rhino had a feeling that she knew he was watching her. What he was not aware of was that many workers, men and women on both sides of the fence, were watching him. He was not aware of the length of time he had stood there, mesmerized by her. All he knew was that at one point she turned around and for a few short seconds their eyes met. She smiled, waved at Ruben and then, this tall, slender, young beauty disappeared into the women's warehouse. Ruben came back to himself when the carriage driver called out, "All right, she's gone!" This incited uncontrollable laughter from the other workers who were helping Ruben.

All that night, images of this unusually lovely woman over-shadowed all Ruben's nocturnal agonies. None of the Jewbarite girls, whom his mother had always claimed would die to marry him, had ever smiled at him with such delightful coquetry as this beautiful girl had today. It was in the early morning hours that the "prudent kadkhoda" in Ruben emerged—the man whose job it was to protect his people's reputation, the leader who had always guided his people from the realm of fantasy to the world of reality. And now, Ruben, this same kadkhoda, chastised himself with his ridiculously unattainable desire for a girl whom he did not even know. And once again, the Rhino's heart was filled with loneliness. He had to stop himself, but he couldn't stop Menasha who, the next morning, stormed into the workshop and shouted for Ruben to follow him. Time and again, the Purple had deliberately provoked Ruben in order to start a brawl, but had failed because the Rhino had tactfully dodged his insults. Now Ruben followed the foreman to the backyard of the workshop. Menasha looked around to make sure there was no one watching, then turned and pressed his forefinger on Ruben's chest.

"Tell me now and tell me the truth!" he growled as the veins on his forehead and neck began to bulge. "Do you have something going with Aviva?"

"Who? Who's Aviva?"

"Don't play games with me, young man. Yesterday, everyone saw you and Aviva signaling to each another. You and Aviva... The blond... Daughter of Ariel... Do you remember now?"

Ruben's arms went slack. So the girl who waved and smiled at him was the boss's daughter. "I didn't..."

"Stop acting innocent," Menasha grunted, again poking Ruben's chest with his finger. "I know that you have a secret understanding with Aviva," he said in a low voice. "I know that you're using her to take over my job. Don't lie to me and don't think I'm that stupid! Because of what you've done, these days Ariel wants to see you rather than me in his office. The reason he had so much to say about your *excellent* work is that, with Aviva on your side, you've been personally taking your work to him and comparing it with mine."

"He said my work was excellent?" Ruben asked, squinting with astonishment. "I haven't seen Ariel even once since I started working for him."

"Whom do you think you're fooling? I know the likes of you people who come from gentile lands."

"The likes of who?" The Rhino grabbed the little man by the lapels of his coat, lifted him up and held him against the wall. "What's the matter with you?" he said up close to Menasha's face. "Why do you treat me like this?"

Menasha began to cry for help, but Ruben blocked his mouth with the large palm of one hand as he continued to press him up against the wall. The red of Menasha's face turned purple-blue.

"I can kill you," Ruben roared. "And I will if you don't stop harassing me."

For a split-second Ruben saw the face of Zain in his last moments superimposed over that of Menasha. But at that instant, he pulled his arms back and the little man fell to the ground, howling in pain. The Rhino began walking back to the workshop when he heard the Purple called after him, panting. "Ariel is waiting for you in his office. Please go and see him."

But Ruben didn't turn around and didn't continue to the workshop. He began running. He ran as hard as he had run to Mullah Ahmad's house after killing Zain. He run back home, closed the door behind him, sat on the ground cross-legged and gazed at the opposite wall. He stayed in this position for the rest of the day and through the night, as though in a trance. *We are all trapped in no man's land, between good and bad, light and darkness,* he remembered Mullah Ahmad's words, telling him of the two primal spirits in the universe. As Ruben saw it, his problem was that he constantly swayed between these two poles, unable to hold firm to what he wanted to be--a good man. Today, the dark and negative force had almost taken control again. After all, he had patiently tolerated Menasha's mistreatment for as long as he had worked for him. Was it because he was not only attracted to, but truly in love with Aviva—someone whom he had only seen once? One smile. One wave of the hand. One beautiful woman. What else could the poor girl, who was under such strict surveillance by her father, have done to signal her love for him? The Rhino felt that—far from his ethics as a kadkhoda—he was falling into an abyss of lustful desire and exasperating heartache. The thought of being in love with Ariel's daughter shattered him. If Ariel heard of this, if it didn't anger him, if he didn't fire Ruben, if he gave Aviva's hand in marriage to him, and if they married, then he would have to stay here in Jerusalem, away from his mother, his sisters, Jacob and all of their children, whom he loved so dearly. But most importantly, weren't Jewbareh and his people all waiting for him? Didn't they need him? Wasn't it his responsibility to find a way to get back to them as soon as he humanly could? Yet to return too soon, without Mullah Ahmad's permission, would endanger his life. The more he struggled with these unsettling thoughts, the longer they kept him awake.

Next morning, Daniel knocked on Ruben's door and entered. "So, what makes you stay home instead of being at work? I saw Ariel earlier this morning at the synagogue. He told me that he had examined your work personally and found you an excellent tailor. Then he had sent for you, he said, and instead of going to see him, you abruptly had left the factory. Now, what's the story? What's going on with you?"

"Is that all he told you?" Ruben asked, curious to know what Menasha had said behind his back.

"Yes he did say something about your foreman..." He looked into the Rhino's panicked eyes. "And what sort of an expression is that?"

"Nothing, Daniel. I was just wondering."

It was obvious to Daniel that Ruben had a secret that was itching to escape. "Anyway," the rabbi went on, "Ariel said he wasn't happy with Menasha. Now, tell me why you left your work. I mean, I hope you realize that in this day and age, it's hard to earn your bread."

Ruben was too embarrassed to tell the rabbi about the incident with Ariel's daughter and his own excitement over this ridiculous fantasy. He was also ashamed of his vicious act against Menasha. But he had to answer the kind man. "You see rabbi," Ruben said, "Apart from how you interpret or excuse what I did from a religious or moral point of view, such as self-defense or protecting another person from harm..."

The rabbi, who had suspected that there was more to Ruben's story than his guilty conscience, interrupted him. "Let me see if I understand you correctly. All of a sudden, in the middle of your work, you remembered the evil nomad you had eliminated and decided to leave? I'm not going to pressure you, but this sounds too ridiculous to be true. Now, I want you to get up immediately, get ready and this is what we will do. Together, from here, we will go to my friend Ariel. But once we're there, if Ariel questions your sudden disappearance from work — which I believe he will — then we have to come up with a sensible answer."

Ruben remained silent as Daniel played with his thick moustache, took off his turban and yarmulke, scratched his head, raised his eyebrows and finally said, "Didn't you tell me that you make the best wine in Jewbareh? I remember you saying something about... was it Abram's Magic?"

Ruben nodded, surprised at this sudden question.

"All right," Daniel continued. "So you will tell him that I had asked you to make sure that I had all the necessary pots and jars for winemaking since its season is near and you had promised that you would help me with that."

"Rabbi Daniel!" Ruben's eyes widened. "You're lying and you..."

"For all I've done for you, don't you want to help me with making my wine this year?"

"Of course I do."

"So who's lying? You *are* helping me, aren't you?" He smiled.

And to such a pious clergyman, who would go beyond telling

the truth to help him, Ruben decided that he would teach the secret of Abram's Magic.

Once at Ariel's office, it became evident that—perhaps fearing the Rhino—Menasha had not reported Ruben's confrontation with him. Before the rabbi had a chance to give an excuse for Ruben's abrupt absence, Ariel jumped out of his chair, embraced Ruben and cried, "Welcome my friends, welcome!" Then he ordered Turkish coffee and cookies and sat facing them. "First and foremost, I have to thank you, my friend Rabbi Daniel, for introducing such a master tailor to me," Ariel began. "As it's been said, a businessman has to have oversight. I rely on my foremen to some extent, but examine each and every piece that's been sewn is my own task. 'Whose work is this and whose job is that?' I always ask them. Every piece that is the product of this man's blessed hands," he pointed to Ruben, "tops everyone else's work. So I salute you, my friend Ruben, and promote you to be my right-hand man and my eyes and ears in the factory."

"Mazel Tov," said the rabbi, nudging Ruben.

"God bless you and thanks," Ruben muttered, realizing that he had better show some gratitude.

"I have a suggestion, Rabbi," Ariel declared, rubbing his hands. "As this young man has been blessed with a wealth of wisdom and talent, with your permission, from now on, I would like him to become a member of the board of our synagogue. After all, he has been the governor of his ghetto and I'm sure he will be of great help to us."

The rabbi paused, stroked his beard with the back of his hand and said, "Of course. What a great idea! We can exchange experiences."

And from then on, Ruben the Rhino witnessed, learned and treasured the uniquely different and innovative approach these leaders took towards their community problems. As they discussed alternatives and possibilities, Ruben thought of Jewbareh and whether their methods could be put into practice in his ghetto. For instance, to finance their civic plans, they solicited money from the Ottoman authorities. To encourage immigration to the Land of Israel, they appealed to the European Jewish organizations. To preserve and promote Persian Jewry—which they believed to be the most ancient and authentic form of Judaism—they invited the Sephardic and Ashkenazi youth to lectures they held at the synagogue. And it came to pass that thanks to these sessions, the kadkhoda of Esfahan's ghetto learned more about being a leader than he had ever dreamed of before.

The day Ruben returned to work, after the meeting, Ariel took him to the factory and with his face beaming with pleasure announced the new position he had given his prized worker. As of the following day, Ruben the Rhino began his job as Ariel's Chief Supervisor. Although it was obvious that Menasha was far from happy with this change, to Ruben's astonishment he raised no objection, and neither did the other foremen. But soon, as the rumors about Aviva and Ruben's alleged clandestine relationship began to spread through the factory, it became obvious that Menasha wasn't just sitting silent. While this was a cause of concern for Ruben, he knew that Ariel was aware of every single thing that happened in his factory and this telltale was no exception. He has a headcount of the number of mosquitoes that fly in his workshops, people said about Ariel. But the thought that one day he would have to face Ariel and Rabbi Daniel and defend his innocence and that of Aviva, worried Ruben all the more. Would he be telling the truth to Ariel if he said that he was not attracted to his daughter? To make matters worse, every time Ruben met with Ariel, he was treated with such warmth and kindness that it made the Rhino more nervous than curious; Ariel had only words of friendship and affection for his master tailor. "Don't tire yourself, young man. Take a rest."

It was a few weeks after *Tisha B'Av*. Preparations for making wine had began in Jerusalem and, as he had promised, the time had come for Ruben to teach Rabbi Daniel how to make Abram's Magic by tutoring him every step of the way. Because Ruben was embarrassed to ask his boss for time off to help the rabbi choose the right grapes, he asked Daniel to do this on his behalf and when the rabbi did so, Ariel cried, "My master tailor makes good wine too? And what is Abram's Magic?"

"I have tasted this wine when still in Persia, and let me tell you my friend," said the rabbi, licking his lips, "You have never tasted anything like it in your whole life."

"What other magic does this big man have up his sleeve that he is hiding from us? All right. I will give him two days, more if need be, but you have to promise me at least twenty large bottles—and for that, I will make a big contribution to our synagogue."

With Ariel's permission granted, the rabbi rented a carriage with an Arab driver and the two men headed to the vineyards on the eastern hills of Jerusalem. Ruben spent the first day choosing the grapes, helping load them onto the carriage and taking them down when they arrived at Daniel's house. Throughout the process, he couldn't help but think about the long way he had come—from Julfa—the Armenian ghetto of Esfahan—to the Judean Hills. Back home, the Jewbarites would also be buying their grapes around this time. He remembered the caravan of carriages his people would hire to haul the grapes they bought, as well as the people like Noori the Scavenger, Daniel the Weedeater and many others who spied on him and bought the same grapes as he did in hopes of finding the secret to Abram's Magic. No wine had been made in the house of the Rhino since he had escaped the ghetto. This hiatus was perhaps the only one that had ever occurred since the birth of Abram's Magic. And in the middle of all this, his memory could not let go of the image of Aviva and the moment he had seen her.

That evening, Ruben supervised everybody in the rabbi's large family as they joined him in separating the grapes from their stems, squeezing the juice and pouring them into large earthenware jars to ferment. On the next day, he asked Daniel to accompany him to the bazaar to buy the ingredients that he used in his own wine. "You have to make a note of all the spices that I add to the wine while it's fermenting, so that you will learn the secret of Abram's Magic and pass it on to your descendants." But the rabbi refused the offer obstinately. "It is your family secret and your family secret it will remain, for your forefathers did not want it revealed," he said. "As Tehillim quotes, 'One of the merits with which the Jews left Egypt was that they didn't divulge secrets.' As it is, you are doing me the great favor of helping me make my wine this year, and that's more than I can ask for." Ruben insisted, but to no avail.

Thus, every night Ruben went directly to the basement at Daniel's house, and worked on his wine. The task of making the Abram's Magic in the Promised Land, where this treasure might have come from many centuries ago, thrilled the Rhino. But of more significance in Ruben's life was the knowledge he acquired from Rabbi Daniel who insisted every night that Ruben have dinner with him and his family after his work in the basement was done. Every night, after dinner, Daniel would read and interpret a portion from the Torah, the Talmud or any other holy book he could put his hand on. It was in these meetings that Ruben came to appreciate the rabbi's immense knowledge of Jewish ethics and learn from him the values inherent in his faith—something he would have otherwise never known. For the Jews in Jewbareh—although observant—were so busy trying to survive that few had time for the traditional study necessary to understand what it meant to be a Jew. Ruben's education in his faith had been meager, to say the least. And when he shared those thoughts with Daniel, the righteous rabbi told Ruben the Rhino, "One day, you will go back to Jewbareh—with a treasure of knowledge that you have learned here and a wealth of experience you have acquired—and you will govern your people wisely."

The next few weeks went by peacefully. Things were going well at work and Menasha appeared to be adjusting to the reality that he was junior in rank to the Rhino. Ariel's kindness to Ruben remained steady. Daniel's wine was coming along well. In the meantime, during his nocturnal tutoring, the rabbi came to learn a great deal about Ruben, and the more he got to know him, the more he realized the magnitude of the task he had undertaken in tutoring him. Although Ruben knew a number of Hebrew prayers, which he'd had to memorize for his Bar-Mitzvah, he really didn't understand what they meant. Having been influenced by his friend the Muslim mullah, Ruben knew Zoroastrian philosophy more than his own religion. And despite his selfless sacrifices for his people, he sorely lacked self-confidence—the first and foremost requisite for leadership. So, in the nights and days to come, the rabbi had a large task ahead of him—to reeducate his pupil, introduce him to the laws and traditions of his faith and invigorate him with the knowledge and courage of leadership.

As the record heat of the summer of 1835 in Jerusalem was yielding and a cool breeze began blowing into the city from the Mount of Olives, a new arrival from Shiraz brought a letter from Mayor Haskell—the first communication Ruben had had since his escape. The letter had travelled a forty day journey by the messenger and his group.

"Greetings of the people of Jewbareh to our benevolent and respectful kadkhoda, may he live one hundred and twenty years in health and prosperity," the letter read. Mayor Haskell then went on to describe in detail how the anti-Semitic atrocities had once again heightened in Persia and especially in Shiraz, so that many Shirazi Jews were escaping to Jerusalem. Since the people of the Shiraz ghetto had come to know about Ruben's situation, they had sent word to Jewbareh that they would happily bring him any messages the Rhino's family and friends had for him.

The mayor had written about how Mullah Ahmad had subdued and then restrained people from rampaging Jewbareh and inflicting carnage on its inhabitants. Haskell had said that immediately after Zain's funeral, "Mullah Ahmad, this God-sent savior of our people" had smuggled a message to Rabbi Shimon and himself. They had met discreetly in the mullah's private quarters. Ahmad had told them of his help in allowing Ruben to escape, and further that he had asked the Governor of Esfahan to increase security measures around Jewbareh. "We were astounded as Mullah Ahmad, may God protect him and all his beloved ones, brought out money and put it in the rabbi's hand with directions to give it to your mother, telling him to encourage her to ask for further financial assistance in the future if needed." Saying goodbye to them, Mullah Ahmad had instructed Mayor Haskell and Rabbi Shimon to get this information in whatever way possible to Ruben, who, he knew, was waiting for the Mullah's permission to return home. Before leaving, Rabbi Shimon had held the palm of his right hand over the mullah's turban and blessed him. "For the kind attention you have given our people, may the shadow of the God of the universe and the blessings of Moses and Mohammed be with you always." The Mayor had gone on to say, "Recently Mullah Ahmad summoned us again. This time he told us that he has plans to convince his followers that you are not the man who killed Zain and once he has done that, he will tell the rabbi and me to send you word to come back." The Mayor had guessed that Ahmad would finalize his plan in six months to a year.

Ruben was saddened for six months to a year was a long time to wait and, at the same time, pleased with the good news of what his friend, Mullah Ahmad, was doing to help both the Jewbarites and him. He had just begun to read the letter once again when he heard Menasha's voice over his head. "Ariel wants to see you in his office immediately." But before the Rhino was able to ask the reason, Menasha walked away, and that concerned Ruben. Why would his boss want to see him? Did Menasha have something to do with this, and if so, what could it be? Ruben went to Ariel's office. From behind the door, he could hear Ariel shouting and pounding his desk. "What does he think I am—a fool? This stupid idiot! I..." As Ariel went on ranting and raving, Ruben became convinced that the rumors about Aviva and him had reached his boss. Nevertheless, he decided, he had to go in and tell him the truth.

"Who's it? Come in!" Ariel yelled when Ruben knocked on the door. And after the Rhino entered, his angry boss pointed to the women's side of his factory and continued, "There! That girl. She has betrayed my trust."

"No, sir!" said Ruben. "If you allow me, I will explain the..."

"What the hell do *you* have to explain?" He yelled, holding a long dress in front of Ruben. "You be the judge, Master Ruben. Look at what this idiot of a seamstress Henna has sewn! An utter disaster. And she has made not only one, but three hundred of them. *Three hundred*, all of which have to end up in the garbage."

Ruben sighed—an obvious sigh of relief that Ariel took as a sign of sympathy. "Let me take a look at it, if I may." He held the dress up and examined it, looking at its back, then its front and finally the seams. Then he turned to Ariel and said, "I can't make any promises, but if they take a little bit from the sides and tighten the shoulders, I'm sure they can fix them."

Ariel, who was listening to Ruben intently, nodded, then suddenly jumped and embraced him. "Master Ruben, Master Ruben!" he cried. "What can I say?" He shook his head fiercely. "You are a life saver. You're right. I'll have them do exactly that. Thank you!" he exclaimed, drawing a bundle of notes out of his pocket and holding them out toward Ruben. "Here! And I should seek your advice more often, Master."

"No, thank you," Ruben whispered, taking a step back. "You're paying me generously already and this is a part of my job."

Ariel insisted, but the Rhino politely refused. "Of course," said Ariel putting the money back in his pocket. "If you insist."

"May I leave now?" Ruben asked.

"No," he laughed. "Wait a minute. This wasn't why I called you. Next week on Tuesday is the anniversary of my father's passing, may he rest in peace. After evening prayers at the synagogue, I would be honored if you would join my family and me for dinner."

That whole day Ruben was uneasy. He worried about his presence at the home of a man whose daughter's name was tarnished because of him, thanks to the gossipmongers. That evening at Daniel's house, he begged the rabbi to see him before dinner, and as soon as they were in his study, Ruben reported what had happened that day and sought his guidance on how to excuse himself from going to Ariel's house.

"Why?" the rabbi exclaimed. "This gracious man, your boss, has invited you to his house on such a blessed family occasion and you don't want to go? I would be very insulted if I were he."

"But..."

"But what? You prefer your loneliness? Listen. He has invited me also. So I'm going, you're going and that's the end of that. You know what Ruben? I don't want to sound rude, but there are times that I wonder how you acted as the kadkhoda of Jewbareh! Why are you making such a big fuss about a simple invitation?"

Ruben could not hold back his secret any longer. He took a sip of hot tea, sighed, and told Daniel about the day Aviva had waved at him and the rumors that had followed. Then he swore that they were not true.

"Of course they're not true. Is that all, Mr. Governor?"

Daniel's cynical tone left a bitter taste in Ruben's mouth, but more than that, it hit deep into his self-confidence. "I know I'm not the governor of Jerusalem," he said. "But if these innuendoes were to reach Ariel..."

"Ariel?" Daniel laughed hysterically. "Have you heard what they say about this man?"

"That he has a headcount of the number of mosquitoes in the air that surrounds him?"

"Exactly. But not only to him, the innuendoes have reached everybody. I know, Ariel knows, all of Jerusalem knows!"

Ruben's eyes widened. "If Ariel knows all this, why hasn't he thrown me out of his factory?"

"Because he is a wise man and as the Proverbs has it, '*Without wood, a fire goes out, without gossip a quarrel dies down.*' Ariel has become rich because of his wisdom. He knows how to take care of his business and he has the wisdom to deal with problems that surround him. Something you have to learn as a seasoned governor. And if you'll excuse me, Jerusalem is not Jewbareh."

Looking at Ruben's face, Daniel could see that what the young man was hearing was infuriating him. "Tell me what is on your mind, Ruben."

"You are a man of God," Ruben said, holding his head in his palms. "You, of all people, are telling me that it is all right if rumor-mongers go around and taint the integrity of a Jewish girl?"

"Calm down Ruben, calm down," Daniel replied, tapping the Rhino on his shoulder. "I too have lived in Persia. Gossip like this is truly dangerous within the confines of our ghettoes abroad because, if such rumors were to leak beyond the ghetto walls, non-Jewish men would target the... what do they call them?" he scratched his head, "the 'indecent girls'. But here, we do not live in ghettos. So, even if you like this girl and want to marry her, you've done nothing wrong."

"What?" Ruben cried. "I have no intention of getting married. I have enough on my mind, Rabbi. Down there, in your basement, squeezing those grapes in my palms, every drop of the red grape juice that slips through my fingers looks like the blood of the man I killed. It doesn't leave me, Rabbi. It doesn't. One minute I am here, the next minute I am in Jewbareh, wrangling with the nomad."

"Listen Ruben," Daniel refilled his glass of tea. "We are talking about two different subjects. About the nomad, time and again I have given you my opinion as a rabbi. As a friend, all I can add is that you have been given two blessings—physical and mental strength. On the matter of your confrontation with the nomad, you had no intention to kill, but only to restrain. And in doing so, you have become a victim of your strength. You seem too magnetized towards this Muslim mullah's interpretation of Good and Evil in Zoroastrian faith. Yes, there is 'Good' and yes there is 'Evil'. But in Judaism we believe in only one primal power that shows us His ways and leaves the choice to us. As it has been written, *'I have set before you life and death, blessing and cursing. Now choose life that both you and your seed may live,'*" the rabbi said, citing another portion of Deuteronomy. "What you seem to have missed here is that we live 'in between' and not 'at' these two poles. Unfortunately, through your mental strength, your conscience has mercilessly driven you from the reality that you are a humane person to the other end of the spectrum—to the point where you consider your act 'evil.' Are you enjoying tormenting yourself with this totally unwarranted guilt? I don't know what else to tell you. You are a kind, fine man who has become too sensitive, if you want my opinion."

Ruben held the rabbi's hand and kissed it. "Thanks," he said. "You are a man of immeasurable wisdom."

"So," Daniel laughed. "Back to Aviva. Is there anything else you want to tell me?"

"The truth is, Aviva smiled and waved at me. That's all. Now, what does that tell you?"

"That she likes you?"

"I'm not so sure. Maybe she was just being friendly, or flirting a little. But that's not the point. Even if she were interested in me, she is rich, I am poor. She's a Jerusalemite, I am a Jewbarite. She belongs here, I belong there. I admit she is a beautiful young woman and I have thought a lot about this. I don't want to cause her any harm. This is where I need your help, Rabbi. I beg you to tell Ariel..."

"Tell him what? That his daughter has smiled at you?" the rabbi threw his hands up. "If you are not interested in her, just let the story die away."

Ruben remained silent. The rabbi's wife — who seemed to have been waiting outside her husband's room for his conversation with Ruben to end — stepped in. "Do you men ever stop talking? And who do you make fun of all the time? Us? The women? *We* talk too much and you don't!" She laughed and then clapped her hands. "*Yallah, yallah!* Dinner is ready."

On the anniversary of Ariel's father's death, after the evening service, Daniel and Ruben followed Ariel to his house which was almost two blocks away from the Western Wall and was one of the largest Ruben had seen in Jerusalem. Two thick-mustached Ottoman soldiers in brown uniforms and Turkish Fez hats greeted Ariel at the entrance to his house. Ariel nodded, motioning them to step forward. He put some coins in their palms in exchange for a military salute. Later on, the Rhino would learn that Ariel paid generous bribes to the Ottoman governor of Jerusalem, who in turn assigned soldiers to protect Ariel's factory and his home.

In his boss's home, Ruben was surprised to see that in the room for receiving guests, the dining arrangements — unlike Daniel's — were traditional Persian. The guests sat on the ground, where tablecloths had been spread. Ariel's wife, Leah, who was strong and bulky, supervised two Arab women as they served the food. Just when Ariel asked Ruben and Daniel to sit on either side of him, Ruben saw Aviva come into the room and was stunned. She was gracefully dressed in a long blue silk costume and a short white headscarf that revealed most of her long, black hair. When she bent down and put a dish of lamb kabob in front of her father, Ruben saw sadness in her eyes, although she was smiling.

"Master Ruben. This is my daughter Aviva," said Ariel, interrupting this mute exchange between his daughter and Ruben. "She has the same job you have, but it's on the women's side in my factory."

Embarrassed, Aviva turned around and left. Ariel shrugged and smiled a strange smile. Looking at his boss, Ruben wondered what was on his mind. He was yearning to tell his host that the rumors about Aviva and him were all false. But Ariel didn't ask and Ruben didn't utter a word. Instead, Ariel called for all his guests to help themselves with the dinner that the women in the family and his servants had prepared for them.

After dinner, when all his other guests were gone, Ariel turned to the rabbi and said, "Because I think there's a lot that this fine artisan, Master Ruben, can teach my daughter," he pointed at Aviva who sat with her head down next to her mother, "I want to make sure that it is religiously permissible for Master Ruben to come here once a week and teach her all the things he knows about tailoring."

"But, of course," said the rabbi as Ruben began coughing severely. "Here at home, in the presence of your virtuous wife, Leah, of course it's permissible."

"Are you all right?" Ariel asked and the Rhino nodded, showing the glass of wine he was sipping.

"She is a fast learner, Master Ruben," Ariel continued as Ruben raised his head and looked at Aviva who smiled and he blushed. "I'm sure she will be a good student."

"So, because on Tuesdays our workload is low," Ariel went on, "I want both of you to take Tuesday afternoons off, and come here to the house so that you can teach my daughter your great tailoring techniques."

"Whatever you say," Ruben murmured, his throat dry.

It was late at night when Ruben and Daniel left Ariel's home.

There was a chill in the early autumn air. Jerusalem was silent, and so were the two men who, although each had a lot to say, both seemed to be waiting for the other to begin. So much had happened in the last few hours—enough to devastate Ruben and to awaken deep concern on Rabbi Daniel's part about the Rhino.

"Mazel Tov!" said the rabbi at last. Ruben remained silent. "Not that I want to dispute your mastery of your profession," Daniel continued, "but now I understand why my friend Ariel has taken such a sudden interest in you."

"I wonder what that could be!"

"I have to admit to you, I was wrong in my prediction that Ariel was indifferent to the rumors surrounding you and his daughter. But don't tell me that you don't find Aviva attractive."

"She is beautiful," the Rhino whispered under his breath.

"Of course she is. You see, almost every eligible man in the community is after Aviva, but, besides the fact that you could be a fine son-in-law for Ariel, perhaps he is hoping to subdue these rumors by marrying his daughter off to you."

"Please, Rabbi," Ruben stopped walking. "As I've told you before, marriage is the last thing on my mind. I don't want to be rude to you. I don't want to sound ungrateful for the blessing of being in the Promised Land. I also find Aviva strikingly pretty and Ariel's interest in me very heartwarming. But despite the hurt and injustice that I have suffered in Persia, I belong to the cage of Jewbareh, because the rest of me is there, in that cage. So, don't I have to tell Ariel what I just told you?"

Daniel put his hand on Ruben's shoulder and said, "But isn't there at least *some* possibility that you might stay here forever? If so, then you could do a lot worse than to marry someone whose father adores you and..." he paused. "Now that I think about it, with the wine that you make, you could start a winery here in Jerusalem. 'Abram's Magic.' That's not a bad idea, is it?"

"*You*, Rabbi," Rubin said. He rubbed his forehead. "Time and again, it's been you who has reminded me of my duties to my people. And now you are talking about me leaving my people behind and staying here?"

Daniel looked at Ruben and found him tense and gloomy. "I'm sorry. In the end, you may indeed return to your home and to your people, but for the time being, whatever you do, please don't reject Ariel's daughter so openly, because if you upset him, I don't know where else we can find you a job. Don't be in such a rush, my friend."

"I'm supposed to begin teaching her next Tuesday! I don't want to make any false promises to the girl or to her father. I don't want her to count on me. Please tell me what to do," Ruben begged helplessly.

"So begin teaching her, but be wise. If you're really not interested in marrying her, just behave accordingly. Don't flirt, don't lead her on. Trust me, as a woman she will respect you. In the meantime, just be patient and let me see what I can do for you."

The following Tuesday, Ruben left work at noon and went to Ariel's house. Standing behind the entrance to Ariel's house, he struggled with his dilemma. If it turned out that Aviva really did care for him, what would happen if he rejected her? What would happen if he didn't? He was caught between two completely undesirable moves and he knew that he would have to choose one of them. "Why don't you come in, Master?" Aviva said as Ruben stood there frozen—captivated by her soothing voice. "Who can resist this girl's dazzling beauty?" was the first reaction that crossed Ruben's mind as he forced himself to cross the threshold into the house. And as he followed her toward the parlor, silent reflections encircled his mind like a mantra. "I will withstand this attraction. I will do it because of my family and my people and my ghetto." This was the first time Ruben had stood so close to this young woman, the first time he was hearing her voice. Not only was she beautiful, but she seemed to have jumped out of the Song of Songs just as Rabbi Shimon had recited it, or the poems of Rumi as he had heard the dervishes singing them. Her skin was white as snow, her eyes the blue of the deep seas and her long, dark brown hair poured like a waterfall from beneath her white scarf down to her slim shoulders.

Once inside, the two sat at a table near the kitchen. On the table there was a set of brand new sewing machines and a complete set of tailoring tools. Ariel's wife, Leah, said hello from the kitchen and then, acting as chaperone, went back and forth, bringing Ruben tea, coffee, cookies, fruit and snacks—taking a good look at him as she did so. "Eat, eat," she said to Ruben. "Of course they're not as delicious as what we had back in Persia, but those days are gone. You'll learn soon."

Aviva sat next to Ruben and with her head down, began twirling in her chair.

"Aren't you going to teach her?" Leah called from the kitchen.

Ruben wanted to cry that he had never taught tailoring. Instead, he turned to Aviva and said, "All right. Why don't we... Why don't we start with, uh... fine stitching?" He took a piece of good quality cotton fabric, handed her a pair of scissors and said, "I want you to cut this very straight and then I want to watch you stitch the two pieces back together."

With her head bent, the mass of her silky hair poured down onto her face, veiling her deep blue eyes. The scissors were plainly shaking in her hand. She tried hard to keep them steady, but failed. What was it that was making her so nervous? Ruben wondered. Unlike the last two times that he had seen her, this time she was not smiling. Actually she was frowning. Frustrated, Ruben grabbed the scissors from her and cut the fabric in two in a straight line.

"I'm sorry," Aviva whispered.

"No. You don't have to be sorry. It's the stitching that matters," Ruben said, realizing that he had distressed Aviva, but with that, she raised her head and smiled. Sweet, reassuring, but not joyful.

For the second week's lesson, under Leah's constant surveillance, Ruben and Aviva did nothing but cutting, stitching and fitting. Then, on the third Tuesday, in the middle of the so-called training session, Leah came out of the kitchen clapping her hands and declared cheerfully, "If you two have an announcement to make, you'd better be quick. Rosh Hashanah is round the corner, in three weeks to be exact, and that's the most appropriate time to..."

"Mother, *please!*" Aviva cried, blushing as the Rhino reached for his handkerchief and wiped the sweat of his forehead.

Leah shook her head so robustly that her headscarf fell off, her hair flew in the air and her large breasts swayed. "I am your mother and I am telling you. Where the hell do you think you're going?" she shouted as Aviva covered her face in her hands and run off to her room. "She's a little bit shy, but she has her eyes on you," Leah said to Ruben as she put her headscarf back on. "I'm going to get her back and please, when she comes back, talk to her and let's do this on Rosh Hashanah—it's a good omen to have the engagement party on the first or the second day of the New Year." Saying this, she went off to talk to her daughter.

Leah spoke the two words—engagement party—with such an

irrefutable certainty that obviously, as far as she was concerned, the deal was sealed. And this awed Ruben as he sat mute behind the table, watching Leah go to Aviva's room. Not even sure about his own feelings for Aviva, now it was obvious that her heart was not with him. If it were, he thought, she would not react the way she had. In the middle of all this, what further alarmed him was the mere mention of the New Year. Almost a year had passed since he had killed Zain, and now, in a faraway land here, he was being forced to marry a woman who obviously had no intention of marrying him. He stood up thinking he would run away there and then, but where to? Enough of running away, he thought, as he sat down again. He heard the mother and daughter screaming at each other, and as Aviva's voice got louder, Leah became quieter. Then there was silence and some minutes later, Aviva walked out of her room—her eyes puffy, her face pale, followed by her mother.

"I'm sorry. I..." Leah said with a streak of tightened jaw muscles, as if she were chewing on a hard object. "Never mind. Go on with your work. I will have Ariel take care of this matter," she grumbled as she disappeared into the kitchen.

That evening, Ruben was busy bottling Abram's Magic in the basement of Daniel's house, mulling over what had happened that day.

"*My well-beloved had a vineyard in a very fertile hill.* Isaiah, Book Five!" Ruben heard Daniel announcing as he tromped down the stairs. "Shalom Master Ruben! Your dinner is ready to be served. Why don't you leave what you are doing and come up with me?"

"I've burdened you and your kind wife so much, Daniel."

"Who's troubling whom? Look at you. You are making me wine in this suffocating place and you think you're troubling me? All right!" He waved his hands. "Compliments accepted. Now, before we go upstairs, I have something to tell you."

Ruben put a half-filled bottle of wine on the shelf and sat down on an old bench near where he stood. "I'm listening," he said anxiously.

"It's about Aviva," said Daniel as he sat next to Ruben. "Since I promised to help you to take up this important matter with her,"—he smiled solemnly, though Ruben detected a twinkle in his eye—"twice I've sent word to her to come and visit me." The two men were alone, but the rabbi moved closer to Ruben on the bench they were sharing. He tilted his head in Ruben's direction, speaking in very low tones. "Finally, she showed up at the synagogue this afternoon. We spoke, she told me what she had to say and I urged her to talk to you directly."

"Today… Never mind. What did she have to say?"

"Ethically, my friend, I can't divulge what she shared with me to anyone. All I can say is that it's good news. She told me to ask you to meet her tomorrow during your lunch break in the alley behind the factory."

Ethically? What ethics? Ruben wanted to cry. But despite his anxiety, he knew Daniel well enough not to argue with him.

The next day, Ariel called Ruben into his office. Ruben was tired after another sleepless night, but Aviva's father was relaxed and surprisingly friendly, although Ruben sensed a concealed rage in the man's voice. "So, how's your student doing?" he asked as he examined a jacket on his desk.

"She's doing fine. Very well, I mean."

"So you like her… you know," Ariel waved his hands in the air.

No, I don't know, Ruben thought. "Yes sir, I know," he said.

"Good, good," Ariel stood up and shook Ruben's hand. "Let me know how she's progressing, I mean how the two of you are progressing, and let me have your answer as soon as possible."

"I will, sir," he said knowing exactly what his boss meant.

Out of Ariel's office, Ruben went to the back of the factory and sat down to work, but he felt as if he were drowning in a whirlpool of relentless thoughts. He tried to digest Ariel's cordial but threatening words as he worried about his upcoming clandestine visit with Aviva soon. At lunch break, he went to the alley behind the factory. Aviva was standing on the corner of a side alley, her face mostly concealed by a long scarf. She signaled to Ruben and he followed her, keeping his distance from her until she turned into a remote side alley and stopped there waiting for the Rhino to catch up with her. She wasn't one to waste time. "I love someone else and I don't want to hurt you," she announced, looking him firmly in the eye.

Ruben clapped his hand to his jaws, which had opened in surprise. "But why… I mean the first time you saw me?"

"To be honest, you are exquisitely handsome and I'm sure you know it yourself. It would take a lot of control not to react the way I did and I'm sorry if I have conveyed the wrong message to you. No woman should run away from you. I wouldn't if I were not in love. That's why I couldn't take my eyes off you the first time I saw you. And then, all of a sudden my father came up with the idea of you as his son-in-law."

For a few seconds, Ruben stared at Aviva. He was speechless. No woman had ever complimented him on his good looks so candidly. Then he thought, no woman was ever allowed to make a flattering remark about a man in Jewbareh, or in Persia for that matter. Was this woman from another planet? Ruben thought. Her tenacity surpassed every principle and tradition he had been raised with. Aviva's willingness to disobey her father and find love on her own was something that didn't fit within the confines of his comprehension. The Rhino came from a place where both men and women were put together through intermediaries. Mothers, aunts, relatives and matchmakers decided who your wife would be, whereas in this sacred city, this wild girl would smile at a man she didn't know at all. And it didn't stop there. She had even told Ruben, a *man* as well as a total stranger, that she found him attractive and that if it were not because of *another man* she loved, she would willingly accept him as her husband-to-be. Had he, Ruben the Rhino, come to the City of God to be a witness to such blasphemy?

"Please don't be upset with me," Aviva said in a pleading tone.

"Of course not," said Ruben, shaking his head violently, as if trying to force out the thoughts that had stuck to his brain like leeches. But his curiosity didn't abate. "Let me ask you a question," he said. "Why do you disobey your father?"

"Because I love Dan," Aviva answered with a forthright expression on her face.

Despite his revulsion at Aviva's indecent behavior — as Jewbarites called it — Ruben was nevertheless very attracted to something about this girl that he couldn't put his finger on. Well, actually he could put his finger on it, he decided: she was brave and she was honest. And she was determined to decide for herself whom she would marry. He had been the one to ask Rabbi Daniel to bring this situation to an end, and now? No, he insisted to himself, he was not in love with her. But he had to admit that there was something remarkable about her — and admirable too.

"You were not thinking of marrying me, were you?" Aviva

asked as though reading his mind.

"If you don't think that I'm parroting you, I have to confess, you're so gorgeous that under different circumstances, I would have loved to marry you. But this is my situation: I have a mother and a whole ghetto to take care of and soon I return to Persia. I can't think of marrying now, and I can't think of marrying here. I couldn't ask a girl from Jerusalem, even a girl with a Persian background, to give up her city and her family, and spend the rest of her life where we face constant dangers. Now, enough of exchanging kind words," Ruben said, again with a laugh. "Tell me. Why aren't you married to the man you love? Is there anything wrong with him?"

"Yes, according to my father. You see, like you, my beloved Dan used to work here. He's a hardworking man and my father liked him as much as he likes you. The problem started when my father found out that, without his blessing, we had fallen in love. That angered him and he discharged Dan from the factory. I'm forbidden to even mention his name," Aviva said chokingly. "And my father's excuse is that Dan is Polish, an Ashkenazi."

"And I am not!" Ruben's eyes widened.

"That's right. All Persian Jews have a special place in my father's heart and that's why he wants me to marry you. I should have told you this before, but as you well know my mother was always present at our crazy tutoring sessions, and it was just impossible for me to tell you my situation. Luckily, Rabbi Daniel, who has a lot of influence on my father, is now involved and has promised to intervene on my behalf." Aviva looked around nervously and continued, "We have to rush. I need your assistance. My dad may pressure you to marry me. Promise me, please, that you won't!"

"Is this how much you love me?" Ruben roared laughing. Then noticing Aviva's alarmed expression, he continued, "I promise. Really, I swear I will." And he raised his hand.

Aviva jumped up, hugged the Rhino and went back to the factory.

"You seem to be fine with the way things are going, right?" Rabbi Daniel, who could sense Ruben's   tension, asked him that evening after the Rhino reported his encounter with Aviva.

"It's a strange feeling, Rabbi," Ruben sighed. "Paradoxical, in a way. On the one hand I'm coming to realize that I really love this beautiful, courageous girl. On the other hand, I love her even more for not loving me, because quite frankly it's a huge relief."

Daniel raised his eyebrows in surprise. He clapped and said, "Blessed be His name! You have become so pragmatic, so eloquent, so wise. You have learned from the hardships you have suffered to outgrow and rise above your ego, your weaknesses. I'm so proud of you. Forget about the tea." He reached for a wine decanter, poured two cups, took one and handed the other to Ruben. "Let's say *L'Chaim* to this happy occasion," he said, and raised his glass. Ruben did the same. "Now, let me tell you what happened this afternoon," Daniel went on. "Dan came to see me. He begged me to get Ariel's consent so that he and Aviva can get married. Although Ariel is stubborn and very hard to convince, I told him I will do my best." Then Daniel turned to the Rhino and continued, "That's why they call me the Resolving Rabbi!"

"A well deserved title!"

"Well, let me tell you about the problems at hand," Daniel said, beginning to count on his fingers. "Dan's problem. Aviva's problem. And, of course, your problem, since it is you who is caught very unfairly in this silly crossfire. All of that it is my task to resolve."

When Rabbi Daniel told Ariel that the Rhino had no intension of staying in Jerusalem and if he ever thought he was going to marry his daughter, he was wrong, it enraged Ariel.

"My father said and I, like the idiot, never believed him! He said, may he rest eternally in peace in the Garden of Eden, that people from uh... Esfahan's ghetto... what was its damned name?"

"Jewbareh," Daniel responded calmly.

"Yes. My father said that the people of Jewbareh were too clever to be trusted. Ruben, this ungrateful Jewbarite, should kiss my hands, throw himself on the ground and beg me for my daughter. You think I didn't know that he was giving my innocent girl a bad name? Next time you ask me to help someone, please check to see who he is. You shouldn't have relied on his lies and I shouldn't have trusted him," he bellowed.

"Calm down my friend," Daniel said, raising his hands. "Trusted him with what? Ruben is a fine, honest young man. First of all, you know better than I do that these rumors that are going around about Aviva and him are nothing but idle gossip. Ruben is a decent man of God. Many times you've told me how pleased you are with him. This man has an aging mother, a brother and four sisters back at home and he is the governor of his ghetto. He was a refugee and he would soon have to go back. I'm sure you don't want to send your daughter to Persia, do you?"

"So why didn't you tell me before?"

"I did tell you, my friend, when I first brought him here. But disregarding my advice, you went ahead and brought up this scheme of making a match with him and your daughter."

Infuriated, Ariel sat back staring at the wall behind Daniel, who was pondering how and where to start the next stage of his mission. Noticing that the rabbi kept standing there looking at him, Ariel finally spoke. "Anything else?"

"Well... yes. I don't quite know how to put this to you. It's about Dan."

"That damned Ashkenazi bastard!" Ariel jumped, pounding his fist on his desk. "Don't even mention him, may his name be erased! I'm telling you, rabbi, these Ashkenazim..."

Two weeks and many meetings later, one day Rabbi Daniel walked out of the factory, tired but happy that he had secured Ariel's trust in Dan, his son-in-law-to-be, and renewed his confidence in his master tailor.

Time went by. The Rhino celebrated the Jewish New Year with Rabbi Daniel at Boaz's house with their two families. In early 1836, at the feast of Danot, Abram's Magic was tasted, praised, bottled and laid to age. Once again the anniversary of the passing of Ariel's father came and went. Sixteen months had gone by since Ruben the Rhino had arrived in Jerusalem. Sixteen months of anxiety, catastrophe, doubt, reflection, and deep uncertainty about his role as a leader, compounded with hard work and intense study, had culminated in making the Rhino a person more conscious, more comfortable in his own skin and more thoughtful.

And then came the wedding of Aviva a few months later, to which the rabbi and Ruben took many bottles of Abram's Magic. The guests lavishly praised the wine. One loved its bouquet, the other its clear red color, the next its potency; in the end, they all agreed that it was the best wine they had ever tasted. Everyone asked for the recipe but didn't get it. The celebration was most unusual, a mix of Ashkenazi and Persian-Jewish traditions. Ariel's mansion was decorated with numerous ornaments and illuminated with huge candles. The groom's family had insisted that men and women should be separated, a demand that Ariel had accepted only on the condition that no partition would be put between the two sexes. Two musical bands—Ashkenazi and Sephardic—were stationed between the male and the female guests.

Ruben sat next to Boaz—who turned out to be a cousin of the groom—and watched Rabbi Daniel perform the marriage itself with all its accompanying rituals. Aviva and Dan were allowed to stand next to each other only this once on the night of their wedding. When the ceremonies were finished, the two bands took turns. Hasidic men, with their hands on each other's shoulders and their long beards waving in the air, danced in circles. Mesmerized by Aviva's beauty, Ruben, who could not take his eyes away from the bride, sat back struggling to push away the temptation that he felt as he watched this tall and majestic girl dancing, this outstanding woman who could have been his bride. And then came the big shock. Aviva looked back at Ruben, waved her hand and smiled. The Rhino was breathless.

"Isn't she beautiful?" Boaz asked as he waved back at the bride, obviously thinking that his cousin's bride was waving at him.

But Ruben's mind was somewhere else. This could have been *his* wedding, the thought came back to him. He saw himself marrying this wonder-woman and taking her to his ghetto as the wife of the kadkhoda of Jewbareh, like a king who brings his stunningly beautiful queen from a faraway land to his motherland. She would glow like a jewel among the Jewbarite girls—their complexions dark, their hair black. He thought too of the charm and the sheer comfort of finally being settled, of having a wife and many children. No more wandering. No more worrying. Just being home with the ease and pleasure of everyday family life.

But his dreams and his wishes remained just dreams and wishes. Ruben the Rhino, entangled in the web of his attraction to Aviva, but freed from the burden of an unwanted marriage and the fear of displeasing his employer, continued to live in Jerusalem in anticipation of news from Mullah Ahmad.

Chapter 8
The Homecoming

On the morning after Zain's murder, a large crowed of mourners gathered at the Juma Mosque. Their cries of anguish drowned the voice of the *ghari* — the man with a good singing voice — who was standing in their midst, reciting the Koran. In the shrine, under the Juma Mosque's tomb — that had been a Zoroastrian temple before the invasion of Arabs over fourteen centuries ago — Mullah Ahmad sat crossed-legged facing the stairs that led to the top of the marble altar, sipping his tea, playing with his prayer beads, and pondering how to calm this bloodthirsty crowd. He was wearing his usual black turban, neatly wrapped around his head, while his brown cloak covered the rest of his body. Although in the past he had pacified angrier crowds than the one he faced now, he nevertheless knew that today he was facing a major challenge, for a najes, infidel Jew had killed "a member of the faith." Certainly, the simmering, vengeful crowd would not allow its thirst for blood to go unquenched. The night before, he had tranquilized them with the excuse that Zain's body had not been buried yet, but today, he had no doubt, everyone expected him to issue a fatwa, condemning the execution of Zain and declaring jihad against all Jews.

It was under these circumstances that he, Ahmad, the Chief Mullah of Esfahan, was plotting to save the lives of the innocent Jewbarites, and in time, that of Ruben's as well. A cold sensation crawled up his spine, down into his arms and into his sweaty palms as he contemplated what he would say once he ascended those marble stairs and sat up there in the seat of judgment. Moments later, Haji Ali, the mosque attendant, knelt in front of him and whispered in his ear, "Hazrateh Agha. The people have been waiting a very long time. Will you be starting your sermon soon?"

"No," Ahmad said imperiously. "Tell the ghari to keep on reciting."

The attendant nodded, stepped back and signaled to the ghari to continue.

After struggling all night to little avail, Ahmad was now contemplating his dilemma. He felt the presence of *Ahriman*—the Devil—as defined by Zoroaster, defiantly struggling to penetrate his consciousness. Why should he, the highest religious authority in Esfahan, take such a big personal risk? Why should he make such a major sacrifice for a Jew? He could easily step up to the altar and issue the fatwa that the crowd expected. *Go make them pay for it. Go find our slain brother's murderer and lynch him. Chop him into pieces alive and hang every piece of him from each gate to the city.* And then he could order a raid on Jewbareh, as many of his predecessors had done. That alone would make him one of the most reputable and popular mullahs in the nation. On the other hand, *Ahoramazda*—the God of Goodness—stood next to Ahriman, cautioning Ahmad to listen to his conscience, to stop any needless bloodshed. Mullah Ahmad was torn between these two vigorous forces pushing him in opposite directions.

As though trying to untangle himself from these stifling thoughts, he suddenly stood up and headed to the altar. The ghari stopped reciting. The crowd became silent. At the top of the altar, he turned around and sat on the velvet pillow with his legs crossed. He could hear cries of "Fatwa! Fatwa!" that were escalating into a wild tumult. Mullah Ahmad took a deep breath and began reciting. *"Besm Allah al-rahman, al-rahim,"*—In the name of Allah, the forgiving and the merciful—"Repeat after me three times: Praise Allah, Mohammed and his posterity!" The crowd loudly repeated the verse and instantly became silent. Then Ahmad gave a long sermon, quoting every verse of the Koran he could remember that related to kindness and forgiveness until he began talking about Zain. "On the matter of our slain brother," he said, pointing at the coffin below the altar stairs, "a tragedy has befallen us." Men and women in the gathering cried loudly, beating their chests. The mullah raised his right arm and the crowd's moans waned. "As I promised those of you who came to my residence last night, I kept a vigil and prayed the whole night. And now I am ready to issue my fatwa."

"Allah Akbar!" shouted the ghari, the crowed repeated the verse three times after him and again there was a sudden silence.

"In my vigil, I was told by Higher Authorities to ascertain the identity of the murderer before I issue my fatwa."

A convulsion went through the crowd. Heads turned towards the three nomads present at the scene of the murder who were standing in the front row. "Speak up!" someone in the crowd shouted at them, and Zain's chief raised his head as though to respond, but it was Ahmad who quickly spoke. "Remember, my brothers. One could easily mistake the identity of the murderer that they saw on a dark rainy night like last night. Bear in mind also that our Holy Koran commands Muslims to speak the truth even if it is against themselves or their own families and that for testimony based on uncertainty and assumption, there is the same punishment as bearing false witness."

Ahmad was relieved to see that the nomads' eyes remained sewn to the ground and that they remained silent. But suddenly, their chief muttered something and the crowd shouted, "Louder! Louder!"

"Ruben the big Jew," said the chief again, raising his voice. "It was he who murdered our slain brother, Zain."

There was no question now. The chief had identified Ruben. Instantly, the Mullah motioned the mosque attendant to perform the swearing ceremony. Haji Ali took the chief's right hand and put it on the Holy Book, saying, "Repeat after me: I swear in the name of Allah, Mohammed and his posterity…"

The nomad withdrew his hand, as if stung. "Well, if it wasn't the big Jew, it was another big Jew." And as he tried to back away and disappear into the crowd, they surrounded him, hollering: "Coward! Traitor! Liar!"

Ahmad shouted over their heads "I ask you once again, brother. Are you sure the Jew you are accusing of killing our slain brother Zain is the one who actually murdered him?"

"I… I don't know, Hazrateh Agha."

"Liar! Coward! Bastard!" again the crowd roared angrily.

Mullah Ahmad raised his arm, once again silencing the mass. "We are all suffering the loss of a Muslim brother," he said. "But our faith doesn't permit the shedding of innocent blood motivated by rage and anger." And without giving his audience a chance to react, he continued, "In the name of Allah, here is my fatwa."

Aware that he was about to put his high spiritual leadership in jeopardy, he announced, with a quivering voice, "My brothers, I forbid you to use abusive language, especially against a pious man before us who understands the importance of giving testimony untainted by uncertainty. You, my brother," he said, pointing to the chief, "You have prevented me from issuing a fatwa that would take the lives of innocent people. Life is the greatest of God's gifts. It is something precious that only Allah can give and only Allah can take, whether that life be that of a believer or that of a najes infidel. As far as infidel Jews are concerned," he said, getting to the heart of his fatwa, "we must keep our distance from them. As I have said before, their refusal to believe in Mohammed bin Abdullah— greetings of Allah to him and his posterity—will bring them their own misery. Let them keep looking for their Messiah like bats flying blindly in the darkness of the caves of ignorance. Their journey to Hell begins here on Earth. Let them live their accursed lives."

As he continued his sermon, again referring to portions of the Koran that discussed self-control, peace and tranquility, the cries and shouts of the crowd diminished as the Mullah's confidence surged. "And now we must escort the body of our slain brother Zain to his place of rest, leaving his revenge in the hands of Allah."

Looking out over the newly calmed sea of faces before him, Ahmad stepped down from the altar, having for a second time saved the life of his friend, Ruben the Rhino. As Mullah Ahmad looked to his left and his right, the Devil was gone but Goodness was there.

During Ruben's absence, Mullah Ahmad was frequently in touch with Rabbi Shimon and Mayor Haskell, to whom he sent money for Ruben's family. In the meantime, he always kept a finger on the pulse of his followers, who were enraged with the unimaginable sin of a Jew killing a Muslim. After almost two years when the passage of time had finally blunted the people's obsession with finding and taking revenge on the man who had killed Zain, Mullah Ahmad decided that it was finally safe to bring Ruben home. The mullah had a plan, and he calculated that the most appropriate time to set it in motion was in his weekly sermon in Juma Mosque, on the Friday before the second anniversary of Zain's death. He had dreamt of Zain, he announced, wearing a robe as white as snow. "He looked beatific," the mullah said. "'Something is bothering me,' Zain told me. I asked him what it was and he said, 'There's something my people should know, for what is known to Allah should not be kept from His people.' And what he said, my brothers and sisters, was astonishing."

The crowd was hanging by his every word as Mullah Ahmad stretched out the moments as long as he dared. "...and here is what Zain said. 'My Muslim brothers must know that I wasn't murdered by a Jew.'"

A huge sigh came from the crowd. "Then why has Rhino the Jew disappeared, Hazart Agha?" someone called out.

"I asked Zain the same question and he said, 'It is sad that this innocent Jew has been wrongly accused of my murder. Bring him back, please.' 'Bring him back from where, Brother Zain?' I asked. 'Fearing execution, he has escaped to Jerusalem, our second Mecca. He is a pilgrim and for the hardship that he has suffered, he deserves to be recompensed with respect, especially among the Muslims.'"

"So who killed Zain?" rumbled the crowd.

"Here's what Zain told me," said the mullah, putting his index finger on his nose, signaling an invitation to silence. "'My murderer has been brought to justice.' Without saying more, Zain then disappeared." In the same breath, Ahmad continued, "So, my people of faith, we should be grateful to Allah for two blessings. Most importantly, we know that the murderer of our brother Zain has faced justice. Secondly we haven't killed another innocent person, be it a believer or not. To respect Zain's soul, this morning I sent a message for the Jew's old mother that her son had been pardoned by the mercy of Islam and that he can come home. I also let her know that we are ready to give her son shelter under the flag of Islam because he is a believer under the faith of Moses." Having done what he set out to do, Mullah Ahmad adjusted his turban and closed the service. "Repeat three times, Allah Akbar!"

The crowd complied and Ahmad was pleased. He was going to have his wine bearer back and Zain's death would be nothing but an echo from the other world. Later on, Mullah Ahmad called for Rabbi Shimon and Mayor Haskell and assured them that it was safe for Ruben to return. They in turn sent word to Jewish communities throughout Persia. Soon a family who was escaping from Kermanshah arrived in Jerusalem, and delivered the news to

Ruben.

In Ruben's absence, the year of the third famine had come to an end. Gradually, food supplies were becoming more readily available and life was getting back to normal. The Keshe nomads had moved back to stealing and away from killing. *Zayandeh Rood* — the River of Fertility — that passed through Esfahan and had been dry throughout the years of famine, had now started to flow again with ample water and plenty of fish. Furthermore, the country was at this time under the rule of a new king, Mohammed Shah of the Qajar Dynasty. This new king was young and inexperienced, but fortunate to have an intelligent prime minister, Mirza Abolghasem Farahani. He provided financial subsidies to the nomads who had originally come to the cities in search of food and lodging and were now willing to return to their tribes. Many nomads who had lived in shacks or caravanserais near Jewbareh took advantage of this subsidy and left for their distant villages. The Jewbarites had fewer creditors and were also blessed with the protection of the good-hearted Mullah Ahmad.

The night before Ruben left Jerusalem, Aviva and Dan — now husband and wife — held a big goodbye party for him at Ariel's house. They were also celebrating Aviva's pregnancy. Daniel had brought many bottles of Ruben's wine, Abram's Magic, which the guests drank, enjoyed and praised. After dinner, Ariel gave a speech. "I'm so sad to see my Master Tailor go. But what makes me sadder is this," he said raising his glass. "The great, great wine that only he knows how to make. So let's drink to a master tailor, a king of winemakers and a..." Ariel began to choke up as the rabbi took over, "It has been written by Isaiah, *The Torah will go forth from Zion, and the word of the Lord from Jerusalem*. So, our friend Ruben will take with him the words of our Lord to faraway lands and tell them about the beauty of Jerusalem."

The guests danced to music followed by eating and drinking until the early morning hours, when they saw Ruben off to the carriage Ariel had personally paid for which would take him from the City of God, over the Zagros Mountains and away to his homeland. Rabbi Daniel put a bag of coins into Ruben's pocket. "Money put together by Dan and Aviva to for the road you have ahead of you," he whispered in Ruben's ear and then blessed him.

Ruben had come to Jerusalem in the season of cold with a knapsack of grief, guilt and destitution. And now, two years later, he was returning home—this time grateful for all he had experienced and learned, appreciative of what Mullah Ahmad of Persia had done to save his life and thankful to the friends he had made who had helped him in Jerusalem, especially Rabbi Daniel, Boaz and Ariel. A few weeks later, the Rhino stopped the carriage outside the gates of Esfahan and waited for the night to fall, and when it was dark enough, he rode into the city. Before anyone else, he wanted to see his savior Mullah Ahmad. Standing behind the door of Mullah Ahmad's private quarters, he could not believe that he had been away almost two years, and that four years ago he had knocked on this door for the first time. When Ahmad opened the door to find Ruben standing there, the two men embraced.

"Hazrateh Agha, I don't know how to..."

"Your rabbi brought me good wine," Ahmad interrupted him. "But I am so happy to have *you* back, because no wine comes close to Abram's Magic."

Ruben grabbed Mullah Ahmad's hands, held them tightly and kissed them. "Allow me to thank you, Your Holiness," the mullah heard the Rhino whisper as he felt the warmth of his tears on his skin. Releasing one of his hands, Ahmad caressed Ruben's face, "What is this *Jude baazi*—Jewish weeping? Two years ago, when you left my house, you were crying. Now you're back and again you are crying. Have you been crying in between also?"

"*Agha-ye bozorgavare man!*"—my compassionate master—"If it were not for you... I mean my people owe their safety to you. I owe..."

"You owe me your wine, you big Jew. That's all. What a nice man he is—this Mullah Shimon of yours! I like him. Now, go home and come back and see me after you have seen your people who have been waiting for you all this time."

It was late at night when Ruben headed towards Jewbareh. He passed by Haji Ghazi's Caravansary and into the ghetto. No one was walking the alleys. In long strides, the Rhino passed by the Meat Market Alley and his own shop, turned to the Fish Market Alley and here he froze. Zain came to his mind. Although over the past two years the guilt of killing this man had little by little waned, the reality of being present once again at this very location made him shudder. He felt an outburst of rage deep in his heart, and it resonated throughout his body. And then he ran. Ran from the renewed memory of the horrific event that had never stopped eating at his soul. He ran all the way to his house where his mother, his brother, his sisters and their husbands and children cheered his safe return. Before he could so much as sit down, they showered him with all the questions they had asked each other while he had been away. Ruth wanted to know how her son had survived in a distant place like Jerusalem. Rachel questioned, "Who cooked for you?" Shelomo, Debra's husband and the son of Rabbi Shimon, was curious about the Wailing Wall and Mohtaram wanted a detailed report about the things he had seen. Kafi was curious about the events her brother had experienced.

And then Jacob spoke. "My brother has had a long journey. Let's all go home and let him rest." He stood up and motioned to his wife, his sisters and their families to leave. On their way home, Setareh asked her husband Jacob heatedly, "What's with you? Not only did you not have anything to ask your brother after such a long time, but you also turned everybody else away."

"Because," Jacob responded, "there's nothing he has to say. Every wrinkle around his eyes and every strand of white in his hair is witness to the sufferings he has endured. This man has been through a lot. It was heartless of them to barrage him with such petty questions."

"Well, I hope your sisters are not angry with you," Setareh sighed. "But that aside, he's not the same person as he used to be."

"He is not the man I grew up with," Jacob nodded. "There have been deep changes in my brother. I feel I must get to know him all over again."

For a whole week the ghetto celebrated the Rhino's home-coming. Every day, they gathered in front of his house, welcoming their kadkhoda and cheering the end of his wanderings. Then they accompanied him from his house to his shop. When passing by the shop of the Jew hater, Samad the Attar, they lifted Ruben above their shoulders and recited Jewish prayers of gratitude—one of those small revenges that the Jewbarites considered themselves entitled to. They brought candies and dried fruits of all kinds and distributed them among the people who came to his shop to welcome him. They lit candles at their homes and even at Pir Pinehdooz and gave alms to its blind Muslim curator. On Saturday, they decorated his seat in the synagogue with flowers and ornaments and had Ruben recite *birchat hagomel* — a prayer only to be recited by a person who has safely crossed the desert. And this is how the Jewbarites received Ruben the Rhino as their hero and embraced him once again as their kadkhoda.

Back in the business of tailoring in his shop, a few steps above the alley, Ruben sat back again on his late father's pillow, which lay on the ground. In front of him stood a small, short-legged table with the tools of his craft. Now in his thirties, Jacob was like a thin woman with twins. His stomach was pregnantly swollen caused by starvation during the years of famine, whose effects had stayed with him and many other Jewbarites. Once again, facing Ruben, Jacob sat with his elbows resting on his belly, using a sharp knife and the sharpened nails of his forefingers to unravel old suits. He then patched the torn or worn-out parts, had his wife wash them at home, brought them back to the shop when he ironed them and then handed the pieces to Ruben to start sewing them together.

In the days that followed, Ruben took every chance to thank Jacob for having kept their business alive while he was away. And Jacob was the first to whom he opened up and told all about what he had experienced in the past two years. The more Jacob listened to his brother, the more he marveled. To have seen Jerusalem! To have prayed at the Wailing Wall! To have met so many different Jews from so many other lands! To have studied with someone like Rabbi Daniel and to have plunged into the bottomless depths of the Torah and Talmud! To have met a girl like Aviva, determined as she was to control her own fate! Although he saw as well that Ruben still bore the scar of his fatal encounter with Zain, and still grieved and felt stained by that terrible event, he understood that his brother's whole existence had been immeasurably enriched by his journeys and adventures, and that Ruben had come home not only ready to take up his responsibilities as kadkhoda but to do so with a wisdom and maturity he had not yet achieved when he had first fled the ghetto.

Soon Ruben held meetings with the mayor and the rabbi in the synagogue. He thanked them for assuming his responsibilities during the time he had been away and when he shared with them the plans that he had in mind to improve the lives of the Jewbarites and make Jewbareh a better place to live in, Haskell quipped with a slap to his forehead, "Not again! Not another 'Wine for the Mullah' idea, please!"

"You're wasting your breath, Agha Haskell," Mullah Shimon laughed. "Don't you know our kadkhoda? No matter how much we disagree with him, eventually he will do whatever he wants to do. So," he turned to Ruben and continued, "tell us, son of Naphtali, how in the name of sanity are you going to get funds from this anti-Jewish governor of Esfahan to rebuild our najes ghetto?"

"Don't tell me, my dear Mayor that we've not benefited from our friendship with Mullah Ahmad. As they say, *Throw the free clod, it might hit the free sparrow.* I mean, there's no harm in trying."

"So our honorable Kadkhoda Ruben of Jewbareh," said Haskell mockingly as he bobbed his head back and forth, "His Excellency will go to the Muslim Governor of Esfahan and say: 'You! You give me money for my Jews or else?' A fine plan! I'd like to see the expression on the governor's face when you present him with this excellent idea!"

"How about me encouraging my friend, Mullah Ahmad, to request money from the governor for the repair of the Juma Mosques *and its vicinity.*"

The year 1836 is recorded in the history of Jewbareh as the year that, thanks to the efforts of its kadkhoda, major funding was obtained from the government to repair the pathways of the Alley of Eleven Twists, the ghetto's synagogues and the communal bathhouse.

Chapter 9
The Bone of Contention

On the other side of the alley, facing Ruben's shop, stood David the Butcher's store, in front of which matrons would gather from around ten o'clock in the morning, each carrying her meat-bag — a handmade sack of rough white cotton stained with dark red dried blood — gossiping while they waited for the butcher to arrive from the slaughterhouse and open up for the day.

"I don't see Badri the Petunia around, do you?"

"No, I don't. Anything going on?"

"Well, I've heard that Shamsi the Radish has asked for Badri's daughter's hand for her son Elias who's so poor, he doesn't have a star in seven skies."

"You've got to be kidding. The guy can't even sniff his own snot!"

"Whereas Shamsi's riches are… Who said that her husband has found an ancient treasure?"

So, to avoid being the subject of gossipmongers, all of whom mastered this art, Badri and Shamsi and every other Jewbarite woman made it her business to be at the Meat Market Alley, in front of the Butcher's shop, as early as possible, or else she would become a victim of their innuendoes. They arrived with babies in their arms, with eligible daughters by their sides, and as they chit-chatted with each other, they kept a lookout for the most eligible bachelor in Jewbareh — Ruben.

"What a shame," Badri whispered to Misha the Clothwasher, who had just arrived. "He's not the same pleasant youth he used to be."

"Angry," Shamsi the Radish chimed in. "He's so angry and serious. It's as if the whole world is indebted to him."

"But nothing lessens his appeal" Wartfaced Monir whispered even more quietly. "He has an awesome... How do you say it?" she looked at the Rhino with a lecherous smile.

"What part of him do you find so *awesome?*" Tannaz the Barrel sniggered, nudging Monir. "You're married, shame on you."

"Really, Tannaz," Monir retorted, suddenly taking a serious tone. "I find our young and handsome tailor and kadkhoda a good match for my niece — Narges. She's so..."

"Yes, yes, yes. Narges of course! Whom do you think you're fooling?" the Barrel said, teasingly.

Back and forth, women speculated about why their community leader had changed so much, for he had turned into a serious, reticent man who concentrated on his work and acted as though he had just punished an unruly person. But at the end, they all agreed that this new attitude had given him a tantalizing aura as he worked in his shop, above the alley and from time to time glared down through the window at them. After all, they concurred, he was the first kadkhoda of their ghetto, who, defending his people, had killed a Muslim. And so, the eligible girls watched him stealthily as their mothers exchanged words of seemingly little consequence but of great implication, and Ruben couldn't help but overhear what they said.

Once they were finished gossiping, they talked about each other. Someone might say about the beauty of a baby girl: "God help the man who marries this ugly child!" and everyone knew that this was supposed to ward off the evil eye and really meant, "Lucky the man who marries this beautiful girl." Then while they went on grumbling about their husbands' mothers and sisters, the issue that was really foremost on every mother's agenda was finding a suitor for her eligible daughter or son.

"Nobody," said Nosrat the Lavender, shaking her head in absolute conviction, "I mean no man can even come close to being the right match for my sweetheart, Batia."

"Not that I want to exaggerate," rebutted Misha the Cloth-washer about her own daughter, "but I swear on her own life, thousands of talents drip from each and every one of her fingertips. She is not even fourteen, but look at her dress. She made it herself with no help, neither from me nor anybody else."

"Enough, enough!" the elderly Henna the Midwife shrieked. "Aren't you afraid of the evil eye?"

"May the evil eye be blind and sightless," Misha resumed. "But can you imagine? Not even *once* did she ask me to hand her a needle or help her cut a piece of the fabric."

"God bless her, but let me tell you about my grand-daughter," Henna the Midwife said in her screechy voice. "If you only knew what a great cook she is. May God take all her ailments and put them right in my eye sockets. My precious girl is such a fine housekeeper. She takes care of her two younger brothers as though they were her own children." And then in a lower voice, "I don't know how her mother will survive without her once she is married!"

"Shifra khanom," the Pockmarked Taji said to Shifra the Hen. "I know you're looking for a match for your son, Musa. Have you seen my niece, Shokat? Aren't they made for each other?"

"Made, not made, who knows?" said Shifra, and as she swaggered away, she added, "May they all be lucky and prosperous."

"But tell Musa to consider her," Taji persisted.

The crowd was matchmaking, marketing their eligible children in a friendly and civil manner, when all of a sudden there was a mass frenzy. Somebody had announced that she had just seen the butcher arriving. At this point tranquility disappeared and mutual respect vanished. The same people who kissed and hugged and wished each other well, the very people who claimed that they would give their lives for one another, they suddenly pushed each other, swarmed the closed door of the butcher's shop and took up positions as close as possible to the lock. The rule of "first come first served" was strictly adhered to, in that whomever forced her way to the spot nearest the lock on the door of the butcher's shop would get in first and thus have her pick of the choicest cuts of meat.

David the Butcher would eventually arrive with blood-stained saddlebags filled with viscera hanging down from the two sides of his donkey as well as two sheep corpses strapped on its back.

"Women! Give way, will you?" David cried, but the crowd remained still. "Do you want meat or don't you?"

Now a chorus of haphazard responses followed: "No, we're here to watch you and your donkey... Don't be so coy for God's sake... Come on, open the shop... Do we have to go through this every day?!"

"But ladies, please. First I have to get there to open the door," he said, pushing his donkey through the crowd, unlocking the entrance, and carrying the carcasses in. As soon as he put them on the table, his customers mounted a full-scale attack. They hooted at him and at each other all at once, while holding tightly onto the part each claimed: "Cut me this piece... It's not fair... Any part I ask for, you always want... I know I'll go home again without the liver that my Agha has been asking for, and I'll have to face his sour frown... Hurry up... We've been waiting for you all morning..." But David refused to be hurried. As he worked at his own methodical and deliberate pace, his cleaver went up and down, chopping bones, and with a large knife that he sharpened every now and then on a jasper-green stone, he cut the meat into artfully shaped pieces.

An hour later, the sheep were gone and so were the customers, and there was silence, blessed silence, in the shop and the Alley. At this point, David the Butcher sat down exhausted on the steps of his shop, wiping the sweat from his forehead and tossed the leftover bones to the stray dogs that, unlike his customers, always waited patiently for their turn. They wagged their tails to get his attention. But, perhaps out of consideration, they didn't bark. Obviously they knew he couldn't take another moment of infernal racket.

David was a musician also and performed on happy occasions in Jewbareh. He played the flute and had a beautiful singing voice. No teachers—he had learned it all by himself. And it didn't stop there. He was a bonesetter too. This he had learned from his father. "If he wasn't born Jewish," Ruben remembered his father, Naphtali, saying, "David would have been a court musician instead of a butcher earning his bread from the hands of such needy people." Naphtali had liked David. In a way he had felt sorry for him and Ruben now shared his father's sympathy. No Jewbarite was so loved and hated at the same time as David. As a butcher they hated him, because they always expected to get more meat and fat than their money's worth. As a bonesetter, however, they couldn't help but acknowledge his healing powers, although many believed that through the force of his evil eye, he broke peoples' bones just so he could fix them. "It is shameful the way he makes money out of his vicious supernatural powers," they said of David. Yet as a musician, they couldn't help but praise his mastery. With the flute positioned on his lower lip and his eyes closed, he took off to another space, another world. Then he would open his eyes, pause, and start to sing. No matter how marginally happy the "happy occasion," when he played his flute and sang along with his own music, he created delight.

This was the part of the day Ruben hated most because it was now that women with eligible daughters lingered, and on the pretext of complaining about the quality of the meat David had sold them, went up to Ruben's shop. Nosrat the Lavender was the most persistent amongst them. Ever since Ruben had returned from Jerusalem, she had been bringing her daughter Batia to the market in hopes of arousing Ruben's interest.

"Look here!" Nosrat said, climbing up the three flights to Ruben's shop, leaving Batia waiting at the bottom of the stairs, and showing the contents of the bloodstained meat-bag to him. "I swear on the lives of all your loved ones, just take a look at the liver David has sold me. It's as black as a spleen. And it's all meat with no fat at all. As my husband says, whatever you cook without fat will taste like steamed wood! Tonight *her* uncle," she added, nodding towards her daughter outside the shop, "and his wife, are coming for dinner. Can you imagine what my husband's brother and his wife—that snake who hates my family and me—will think of my cooking with no fat at all? Now, as our respected kadkhoda, I'm sure you will do something about this, Haji Ruben. David shouldn't be selling us garbage meat." And before Ruben had a chance to react, Nosrat called for her daughter, "Come up my love, come up. Now, don't be so shy, Batia jaan!"

Blushing and embarrassed, the young woman climbed up to the store and stood next to her mother. She was short and barely fifteen. On the left side of her face there was major damage from scar tissue, *salak,* a disease common among the Jewbarites, caused by mosquitoes that carried its virus. The bite of the insect caused a boil that ate into the victim's skin and flesh, leaving behind a permanent and unsightly scar. Batia's left palm rested all the time on the scar, covering the telltale disfigurement—as if she had a chronic toothache.

"Nosrat khanom," Ruben shrugged impatiently. "Isaiah writes: *Those who are wayward in spirit will gain understanding; those who complain will accept instructions.* Now, here is my advice to you. If you are not happy with what you get, there are other butchers in Jewbareh."

"What do you mean?" Nosrat said as she looked in confusion from the Rhino to Jacob and back to Ruben. Jacob kept his head down and stared straight at the jacket he was unraveling "What are these words you are speaking, and what does *wayward* mean? It sounds rude. "

"No..."

"Yes it is. You don't have to be so impolite, Kadkhoda Ruben, and show off your learning like that," she grumbled as she knotted the top of her meat-bag. "You know what? You're not the same kind person you used to be before you..." she pointed to Abe the Fishmonger's store. Then she grabbed her daughter's hand and marched out of the store.

Behind his working table, the Unraveling Jacob was running his knife and sharp nails into the stitches of an old jacket while muttering something under his breath. This was his way of voicing his disapproval of Ruben's response to Nosrat the Lavender. Knowing what was going to follow, Ruben ignored him. And as was his wont when Ruben paid no attention to him, Jacob frowned, squinted, squeezed his lips tightly, sighed and finally grunted, "None of my business."

"What is it Jacob?" Ruben sighed impatiently.

"Nothing," he murmured. Ruben knew that this was a prelude to a bitter lecture. "The way you treated this woman was not right. This is not how your father of blessed memory ran this business and this is not the way you used to be before that incident. Before..."

"Before what? Go ahead. Finish what Nosrat didn't say. Before I killed the nomad?" Ruben yelled.

"No!" Jacob answered. "Before you went away. Before you became such a high-toned sophisticated person in Jerusalem and came back to your poor provincial charges in Jewbareh!"

"I killed him in defense of one of these selfish, ungrateful people who don't care about anyone but themselves and their meat and fat and how their sisters-in-law judge their food and above all, marrying off their ugly daughters to some poor, unsuspecting someone!"

"Keep it down, Ruben. People in the alley can hear you."

"Let them hear. My father and I have served these shameless people for years now. What do they want from me? To call poor David names because the Lavender isn't happy with the liver she bought? I'm up to here with them." He pointed at his throat.

"I don't want to argue with you, Rueben," Jacob put his

unraveling knife down and looked at his brother as he spoke. "This utter frustration and annoyance is not becoming of you. Look now my brother. You have every right to be furious at what happened to you with Zain, but be fair Ruben. Every Jewbarite knows that you killed him in self-defense. For all the time you were gone, Jewbarites remained loyal to you, supported our business, praised you for your sacrifice and didn't try even once to replace you. Jewbareh went on without a governor for two years. Why? Because in their hearts *you* were their kadkhoda and when you returned, they embraced you as if you had never left. The least they deserve is your respect. For God's sake don't let their petty complaints destroy all the wisdom you've gained from your time away."

Ruben took a handkerchief out of his pocket and dabbed his eyes. His brother was right, he thought. He had to overcome his rage. "I'm sorry," said the Rhino. "You have been nothing but a caring brother to me and I appreciate that. You have taken care of our shop, our mother, sisters and the whole extended family in my absence, and I'm grateful."

"You are your people's hero, their savior," Jacob said with his hand on the Rhino's shoulder. "They all think of you as a bigger and wiser man, especially since you've become so fluent in Jewish quotes which they mostly don't understand — and, by the way," he chuckled, "neither do I!"

"Oh, shut up," Ruben giggled.

"All I'm trying to say is that I know poor Nosrat is trying to put you together with her unattractive daughter," Jacob went on. "Any other mother would do the same. All you — the kadkhoda that you are — have to do is to act calmly and be compassionate. This way, as they say, 'You've killed two birds with one stone.' You have listened to the problem she's pretending to have and yet, you have not driven her away from your business."

"What has her trying to match her daughter got to do with our business?"

"Simple. In the same way as she is trying to sell her daughter to you, you should be selling your service to her. *You want a peacock? You go to India!* That's all."

"You and your maxims, Jacob," Ruben shook his head. "I neither want a peacock nor do I want to go to India. But seriously, how am I supposed to make a customer out of a woman who's complaining about bad meat and not enough fat?"

"Use your charm brother. Be nice to her. Can't you loosen up a little?"

"Fine," Ruben said, raising his hands in submission. "*You* know how, then *you* do it."

"Enough my dear Rhino," Jacob called as he untied the knots on his lunch cloth and laid it on a small *sofreh* – table cloth – on the ground. "Setareh's dinner last night was so delicious, I've brought the leftovers. Your sister-in-law has insisted that you should have some, so let's eat and forget about all this."

Ruben shared the meal with his brother. Yet, as he ate, the words he had exchanged with him kept wandering through his mind. "Like the old days... Loosen up..." Had he changed so much? Ruben thought. Had rage penetrated his soul so deeply that it had become second nature? Had he been purged of kindness and care?

"Come on Ruben, eat!" Jacob's voice interrupted the Rhino's thoughts.

"I don't know who I really am," Ruben said, his tone submissive. "You are right. Despite all my efforts to free myself from this nightmare, it keeps sucking me in like a whirlpool." He took a sip of his tea as his hand shook noticeably. "Please do whatever you think appropriate to bring us business, but don't get me involved. Give me some time."

"All right, I will." said Jacob, smiling. "But do me a favor. For the time being, when these women whine and complain, show a little interest, a little compassion."

The word "compassion" resonated in Ruben's head like thunder. Hearing it poignantly reminded him of those many people who, in spirit and deed, had accompanied him on his long journey. People like Mullah Ahmad, the dervishes of Bisotoon – whether real or imagined – Rabbi Yoram, Ardalan the Kurd. And then in Jerusalem, Boaz and his caring wife, Alisa, Rabbi Daniel and his kind spouse, Miriam, Ariel who had given him a job and his wife Lea, the beautiful Aviva and her beloved Dan. He wondered if the hooligans in the teahouse in the middle of the desert and Menasha in Jerusalem had been put on his path to elevate him to a higher plane and make him a kinder person, a better leader. And now, his brother who was telling him how to be compassionate. He wondered what was standing between him and all the knowledge and experience he had gained. And the answer was obvious. Zain! *So you will purge from yourselves the guilt of shedding innocent blood, since you have done what is right in the eyes of the Lord,* he recited to himself, recalling Rabbi Daniel quoting this verse of Deuteronomy. Zain's blood hadn't even been "innocent."

Now Jacob was in charge of public relations in Ruben's business. Next day at the Meat Market, Nosrat the Lavender was noticeably upset and much quieter. After buying meat from David, she immediately took her daughter's hand and turned to go home when Jacob, looking out the shop window, called after her. "Nosrat Khanom. Why don't you come up and show me what David has sold you today. This morning Kadkhoda spoke to him about your complaint."

Nosrat turned around and Ruben noticed her expression, which swung between surprise and disbelief. "He did?" Then she looked at her daughter and said, "What did I tell you, Batia? Didn't I tell you that Haji Ruben must have taken care of this?"

Ruben, who had pretended not to be listening, was taken aback by this exchange. Jacob's report sounded so real that now Ruben wondered whether his brother had actually gone to poor David with Nosrat's ridiculous complaints. "You haven't, have you?" Ruben mouthed. "Of course not, Jacob whispered back. Nosrat bounded up the stairs of Ruben's shop like a young child, dragging her daughter behind her. Now inside the shop, Nosrat stood in front of Ruben and called out, "God bless you Haji! See what David has given me today and compare it with the meat of yesterday." But just as Nosrat was about to untie the top of her meat-bag and show its contents to Ruben, Jacob said to her, "Today Kadkhoda Ruben is very busy. Will you show it to me, please?"

"Of course," said Nosrat, opening the meat-bag on Jacob's table. Jacob narrowed his eyes as he inspected the cuts David had given her. "A lamb shank," he turned the meat from one side to the other and nodded. "Good meat with a lot of fat. Um, two big kidneys. A big piece of light and shiny liver. Surely, this is an excellent deal," he murmured in approval.

"Come Batia jaan," said Nosrat to her daughter again. "Come and listen to this."
But the young woman didn't budge.
"As I was saying," Jacob remarked, ignoring the woman's

struggle to get her daughter into the shop and in front of Ruben, "My brother and I care for you and your family. But now that you are here, it is an appropriate time for me to tell you something that happened a couple of days ago. It's about your son, Joseph."

What about Joseph? Ruben wondered.

"What about Joseph?" Nosrat asked curiously.

Jacob sighed as he poured a cup of tea from the samovar next to him and set it down before Nosrat. "Have some tea."

"Thanks. But what about Joseph?"

Yes, what about him? Now Ruben was equally curious.

"Ah, people, people! My sister, Nosrat khanom," said Jacob, tapping the table with his sharp nails. "As they say, 'You can close the gates to a big city, but not the mouths of gossipmongers.' The other day as young Joseph was passing by here, I heard somebody far below your family status and dignity make a rude comment about the young man's outfit."

"Who?" Nosrat demanded.

Jacob leaned back, rested his forearms on his big belly, looked at Ruben, and then at Nosrat and after a long pause, he finally spoke. "I won't mention her name because I don't want to cause trouble." Then he took his snuffbox, pressed some snuff between his thumb and forefinger, sniffed it up his nose, sneezed loudly and blew his nose into his handkerchief.

"Bless you," said Nosrat, "but, please tell me. Who is this person badmouthing my poor boy?"

"You said it! Poor is what she said. In fact what she was saying quite loudly to another woman was," now Jacob whispered, "'Is his father so poor that he can't get this kid a pair of pants?'"

Pretending to be busy but listening intently, Ruben wondered how it was that, unexpectedly, in the time that he had been away from Jewbareh, his brother had become such a deceitfully persuasive salesman.

Nosrat sighed. A sigh of relief, but Jacob continued with the same enthusiasm, "I swear on the life of all of those whom you love, Kadkhoda Ruben got so upset that had I not intervened, he would have beaten her," averred Jacob.

"What a strong blow would *that* have been!" Nosrat said, giving Ruben a coquettish smile.

"But my Joseph never complains about his clothing," Nosrat went on. "He is such an understanding sweetheart." Then she turned to Batia again and called sharply, "Come closer, I'm telling you!" Immediately changing her tone, she continued tenderly, "Come my precious. Come and let's tell them about your brother." Batia complied as her left palm covered her facial scar. "Now let us tell you about my Joseph."

"So you agree that the young man needs at least one pair of pants, don't you?" Jacob cut in.

"Certainly. I will look to see what extra old pants his father has and, of course I will trouble you with a new pair of trousers for him..."

Nosrat went on praising her son, but as far as the Unraveling Jacob was concerned, he had just won himself a new customer. The rest of what Nosrat had to say went in one ear and out the other. While she blabbed away, Jacob tied the top of her meat-bag and handed it back to her. But Nosrat wasn't finished yet. Holding Batia's hand, she went up to Ruben.

"My Joseph is only twelve, but I swear he has the head of a forty year old man on his small body. Now, as I said, I will trouble you to make him a new pair of pants, but this kid understands his family priorities. Let me share the truth of the matter with you Haji Ruben, for after all you are like a member of our own family. My husband and I are frankly putting much more money aside for Batia's dowry than our boy's outfit. Everything we save we either set aside as cash or use to buy carpets and jewelry for this sweetheart." She looked at Batia, who clutched at the scarred left side of her face nervously, pulling her eyelid down. "We believe, Haji, that when Batia goes to the house of her destined man—and let me tell you, the man who will marry this jewel will be the luckiest man ever—and people in this community examine her dowry, we shall be able to hold up our heads with pride."

"I understand," said Ruben, keeping his eyes focused on the work between his hands. "May God bless you and your provident husband."

Jacob smiled.

Chapter 10
The King's Bride

Shortly after Naphtali died, Ruth and her daughters started looking for a wife for Ruben, but their efforts were interrupted by his escape to Jerusalem. On the Rhino's return, once again they resumed the task of trying to find him a match. Ruth spread the word that he was available, which encouraged many mothers like Nosrat to bring their eligible daughters to the Meat Market Alley in the hope that they would catch Ruben's eye. But Ruben would not pay any attention to these hopeful young women and their mothers. And as a few months went by without any results, one day Ruth confronted her son. "You are twenty-seven and you have to have a family of your own, so the sooner the better. Look at your next-door neighbor Nissan. Now there's a fellow who knows how to manage his life. He is your age, he's been married to this angel for only two years and now their sweet little baby girl is running around their house like a beautiful little butterfly. At this rate, they'll have a houseful of children before you get married."

Ruben and his best friend, Nissan the Fabricseller, had bought two adjacent lots on the second twist of the Alley of Seven Twists a year before the famine and had built two identical houses next to each other that had come to be known as the twin houses.

"So, in a little while I'm going to be an old spinster?" Ruben teased his mother. "Marriage can wait," he added, giving her a hug.

"No it can't" said Ruth, freeing herself from her son's arms. "Because I am the one who does your laundry, if you see what I mean!"

"Mother, please!"

"Don't *mother please* me. You can't sit up there in your shop, look down at all those women, come home, go to bed, and dream of them! You can and you will marry the prettiest girl in Jewbareh."

Ruth was right. Under the Islamic regime, all women, Muslim or non-Muslim, were obliged to cover themselves with *chadors*. But, intentionally or not, that did not stop the Meat Market Alley women from exposing whatever they could from under these dark, enveloping garments. On broiling summer days, when their thinner and more transparent dresses stuck to their sweaty skin, mothers and daughters alike used the "unbearable heat" as an excuse. "God forbid! It feels as if the sky is raining fire!" they said, as they flapped their chadors, more open than closed, some showing off their dresses and others with only apparent unconsciousness unveiling their voluptuous figures to Ruben, who sat in his shop, higher than the Alley's level, like a king in his harem viewing his wives parade before him. It was on days like this that the Rhino's hungry eyes traveled over these women's bodies at every rustle of their chadors; and no matter how hard he tried to conceal his glances, the women were on to him, and knew that he was looking at them. "Such a God-given beauty," they whispered to each other about Ruben. They adored the color of his eyes, his wide shoulders and thick neck, his white skin, graceful hands and brown hair – each trying to outdo the others in her assessment of the young man's charms. And the eligible young women, who heard their mothers' exchanges, imitated them.

"I wonder if his hair *down there* is also brown! Can you imagine that?" Malka, the teenage daughter of the Pockmarked Taji giggled, whispering to her friend Dolat, the daughter of Shamsi the Radish.

"God forbid. The man is devouring us with his eyes!" Nina the Singer murmured to her friend Khatoon Donbaki. "Why doesn't his mother get him a wife?"

"Don't blame the poor man!" snapped Henna the old Midwife, who had overheard the two. "Why don't *you* cover up properly?"

"Well, excuse me! Why don't we blindfold him?" objected Nina. "Is it my fault that the weather is so hot, old lady?"

"Just whom are you calling 'old'? Why, you've already got more wrinkles in your neck than folds in your chador!"

And the two women became so combative over the word "old" that they went for each other as the matrons tried to separate them, without luck. They called the Rhino for help, but he remained exactly where he was, high on his perch above the alley, with a premium view of chadors falling off the women's shoulders and revealing their sweaty flesh as they shrieked at each other.

Then, one morning, in the hot summer of 1836, as the big crowd of the butcher's customers were waiting for him to arrive and Ruben was busy working, he heard a woman yelling, "We have a bride!" followed by, "It is Sara the Fox with her daughter Tuba." "Oh my God! When did she grow to become such a lovely young lady?" "May she be protected from the evil eye."

Then the group cheered and began singing the ancient song for this occasion.

I have a girl that the King doesn't
She has a face that the moon doesn't.

In Jewbareh, once a girl began to menstruate, her mother would bring her to the Meat Market Alley to declare her eligible for marriage. This trip would inaugurate her life as an adult. The day before, the mother would ceremoniously bring the daughter to the public bath, where her skin would be scrubbed with a coarse rubbing glove and her hair colored with henna. The next day the girl's hair would be dressed and she would be beautifully clothed and accompanied to the market, where her mother would show her off to the mothers of eligible sons and the shrewdly appraising matchmakers. In Ruben's case though, there was no need for matchmakers, because there was hardly a mother with an eligible daughter who didn't want him as her daughter's husband and there were almost no eligible girls who didn't struggle to find favor in the Rhino's eyes.

As custom had it, a mother would bring candies in a clean, shiny silver tray—the tray that would become the first item in her daughter's dowry. The larger trays were indicative of more substantial dowries. A girl's future husband would take the girl with her dowry and domestic skills into his parents' home to start a family within that larger family, and thus increase the clan. The man that she would marry would pledge his loyalty first to his own parents and then to his spouse and children while he would expect his wife also to give her loyalty to his parents first and then him and their children.

I won't give her to just any hooters
For she has many, many suitors

Young Tuba was excited and noticeably embarrassed. "Come on dear!" said her mother, pulling her forward by the arm. Women hugged her and whispered chants of good luck in her ears. They surrounded Sara and took candies off her silver tray, putting some in their mouths and some in their pockets. Sitting up there in his shop, Ruben impatiently heard the women's squeals and songs:

I'll give her to someone who's "somebody"
Velvet his clothing, handsome his body

"Another one of those days," Ruben complained to Jacob. "Another girl put on the market! Tomorrow her mother will probably be on my doorstep trying to get my attention and again I won't be able to get any work done. Of course she has many suitors?" Ruben said in a cynical tone. "Then marry her to one of them instead of bringing her here to give us a headache."

But Jacob wasn't listening. With his eyes narrowed, he was looking into the crowd. "Instead of fretting over nothing," he said, "stop nagging and look at this girl. Raven-haired down to her waist, olive skin like the Queen of Sheba, eloquent and so beautiful. And listen to this: you're not going to believe it, but she's someone's little girl whose life you saved — Abe the Fishmonger. When did she grow to be so tall and gorgeous?"

Hearing the Abe's name, Ruben felt a tremor gripping his arms and legs. When he had returned from Jerusalem, Abe the Fishmonger and his wife, Sara, had been the first to come to visit and, they had brought Ruben a basket of fruit and candy as a token of their appreciation. "I owe my life to you," Abe had said again and again.

"He really does owe his life to you," Sara had chimed in, echoing her husband. Ruben had listened, impatiently waiting for them to go away, hoping that by some mysterious magic they would take with them the horrific image of the nomad. Ever since then, he had tried to avoid Abe.

"Jet black eyes, joined eyebrows, two thick braids of soft, shiny black lush hair, slender and tall. Look at that serene face! She's made for you," Jacob chuckled, brandishing his charcoal-heated iron on a piece of wrinkled cloth.

"Jacob," Ruben groaned. "Do me a favor and don't play my mother's game! I have no intention of getting married and that's the end of that. So, go on with your work and leave me alone."

"As they say, 'Hearing is nothing compared to seeing.' It doesn't hurt. Just take a look for yourself."

Ruben turned around, saw Tuba and—with a threaded needle between his thumb and forefinger, a thimble on his middle finger and a piece of fabric in his other hand—he froze.

"*Now* what do you think?" said Jacob, bobbing his head and neck like a turkey. But Ruben wasn't listening. This girl's face glowed like sunshine under the thin cloud of a sheer navy blue chador she wore over a light lavender satin dress. She had an unearthly beauty. Tuba raised her head and looked at Ruben and their eyes locked—long enough for women in the crowd to notice how intently the two were looking at each other.

The King arrives with his warriors and his army
"I'll make you my Queen, he begs, if you honor me"

"Agha kadkhoda!" whispered Jacob. "All the women down there are watching you."

"What? I was just looking… I mean, yes, I was looking at the crowd," he stammered.

"You were not looking at the crowd, my brother." Jacob snapped as he scratched his neck. "You were devouring that poor girl with your eyes!"

Ruben winced and threw the needle that had missed the thimble and pricked his finger against the wall. The mere idea of marrying the daughter of someone who had been the cause of his killing a man was like hiring someone to remind him of this heinous incident for the rest of his life.

"Listen Jacob," Ruben said in a low voice. "I have to start sewing the unraveled pieces you are working on. I have promised Yohai the Shoemaker that his son's suit will be ready before his Bar Mitzvah next Saturday."

"Do you want me to talk to your mother?"

"About what?"

Jacob shrugged his shoulders, looking first at Ruben, then shifting his gaze to Sara's daughter, and back again to Ruben, nodding and smiling as he put his palms together as though he were shaking hands with himself.

"No. Please don't tell her anything," Ruben laughed nervously at Jacob's gesticulations. "As it is, she doesn't leave me alone."

"You're the boss," Jacob said. "But I assure you, within the next few hours, the news will be all over Jewbareh and your mother will know it too, because," he whispered, "everybody here saw how you two looked at each other." Then Jacob joined the crowd in singing

in a whisper:
And here's my response
Maybe I will maybe I won't.

Down the steps of Ruben's shop, Sara the Fox was milling through the crowd carrying the silver tray, offering candies to the women and speaking loudly. "May Satan be deaf, may the evil eye be blind... *help yourself, take some more,*" she interrupted herself, "with the help of the Almighty... *more, more...* and with happiness and a joyful heart, once I give her hand to be a bride... *why only one? Come on, take some home...* then I will have the extra hair between her eyebrows plucked." Suddenly she climbed up the steps of Ruben's shop, stood next to him and from there she continued her monologue. "Only then will you all see what a God-given beauty she is."

Ruben jumped. He was speechless. "Thank you," said Sara, as if he had stood up to show respect for her. "I don't see your mother here today. Do me a favor and take some candy for Ruth khanom." And before Ruben was able to react, Sara took a handful of sweets from the silver tray, put them on his table and walked down the steps. Like a man in a trance, Ruben picked up one of the candies and put it in his mouth. Then he turned around to take another look at Tuba, but Sara and her daughter were gone.

"What happened to them?" he asked Jacob. "Where'd they go?"

"Sara did her shopping; now it's your turn."

The butcher-shop crowd dispersed and the dust of the Alley settled. Jacob finished unraveling the pieces of fabric Ruben was waiting for and put them on his table. The heat of the day plummeted as the afternoon went by. David the Butcher closed his shop, said goodnight to Ruben and Jacob and went home. The bell on the neck of Samad the Attar's small donkey tolled, followed by the braying of Asghar the Allaf's mule, breaking the silence of the Alley and signaling the end of another day's business. Jacob tidied up his table and went home. Evening fell. Like a statue, Ruben sat behind his worktable with a threaded needle in one hand, pricking it in slow motion into the old fabric he held in the other hand, and staring into the dusk as if in a dream. Ever since Zain's death, he had been at the mercy of a permanent vision that incessantly haunted him, an indelible tableau splashed with the blood of the victim as all the people at the scene of the killing shrieked and moaned: the nomad, his boss, the boss's protégé, and even Abe the Fishmonger. Yet, from the moment he had caught sight of the Fishmonger's daughter, an ocean-blue curtain of tranquility had fallen over this calamitous image. When he thought of Tuba's face, he felt, for the first time since the killing, at peace.

Just as he was closing his shop for the night, he heard a woman calling him. "Agha Ruben!" He turned around and in the weak light of dusk, saw Sara the Fox. "I need your help," she whispered "It's about my daughter, Tuba, whom you saw this morning. You see, Kadkhoda Ruben, Tuba has two suitors. They are both fine, hardworking young men, but she neither approves nor rejects either one of them. She seems to have a problem making a decision."

Sara paused as if waiting for an answer, and when Ruben didn't say anything, she continued, "The poor girl is so confused. I think she likes them both. But she simply doesn't know which one to choose. Still, I'm not sure. How can I know what's in the girl's head?"

"You..." the Rhino swallowed – his throat dry. "You *think* she likes them? Are you sure?"

"No, no. I'm just guessing, really. Actually the other day, I asked her 'Which one of the two suitors do you want to marry, Tuba?' and she said she didn't know. Then her father talked to her and threatened to decide for her, but to be honest with you, both fellows are such nice boys, we ourselves couldn't decide on one or the other."

"Shalom, kadkhoda," a passerby greeted Ruben. Sara covered her face with her chador as Ruben returned the man's greetings and waited for the stranger to disappear into the next turn of the Alley. Then Sara went on, "So, we sat down with Tuba and talked and talked and at the end of it, my daughter said, 'Why don't you consult Kadkhoda Ruben? He advises all the families in the ghetto when they have problems.' You know, Agha Ruben, since her childhood, she has always had a lot of... how can I put it? A lot of affection and respect for you. And since you saved her father's life so bravely, she has a very special place in her heart for you."

At this compliment, Ruben began to relax. "Before you go any further, Sara Khanom," he said in a serious tone, "let me ask you one question. Having talked to Tuba, what do you think? I mean is there a chance that she's hesitating because she's not interested in either one of them?"

"Yes," Sara answered at once. "I haven't told her father, but I fear she might have her eye on somebody else." She looked knowingly at Ruben. And right away she continued, "Why don't you think about this and let me know tomorrow?" Then Sara the Fox abruptly turned around and walked away as Ruben the Rhino stood there, behind the door of his shop, watching her stroll to the end of Meat Market Alley and disappear into Fish Alley.

Fixing the lock on the latch, Ruben knew Tuba had filled the emptiness in his heart.

As Jacob had predicted, the talebearers immediately went to Ruth with the news of what had transpired that morning on Meat Market Alley between her son and Tuba. Before Ruben had so much as crossed the threshold of his house, his mother accosted him. "So, I'm hearing some good news about the daughter of Sara the Fox! Is there anything you want to share with your mother?"

"There's nothing to share, mother."

"You like her, don't you?" Ruth said, smiling. "And what's more, her father owes his life to you. I'm sure if you decide…"

"*If* I decide," he cut in. "For your information, I haven't decided yet."

But of course Ruben had decided. He spent the whole night thinking of what to say to Sara the next morning when she came back to the Meat Market. "You should wait," he would tell her. "You shouldn't push her." "But why kadkhoda?" Sara would ask. "Because what? Would it be appropriate for him to say, "Because I love your daughter and I want to marry her?" Of course not. Or, maybe, "Because she is too young?" "But she's already fourteen!" Sara the Fox would say, stressing her daughter's age. "Fourteen isn't young! She's definitely not too young to get married."

The summer of 1836 was hottest the Jewbarites could remember. Scorching easterly winds whirled around Esfahan and blanketed the city with desert sands. On that mid-August night the heat pierced the Rhino's skin deep into his flesh and bones. Pacing his room, he talked to himself, waving his long sweaty arms in the air, alternatively shaking and nodding his head, rehearsing what to say to Sara. It was in the early morning hours that the answer dawned on him. "Why don't you wait until my mother has spoken to you?" That would be formal and conventional.

But the next morning Sara didn't come to the Meat Market and as time went by, Ruben began showing signs of nervousness.

"Anything the matter?" Jacob said, squinting at him

"Nothing. It's too hot," Ruben replied unconvincingly.

"I get it. Might as well say: None of your business!"

Ruben had neither the time nor the patience to be affable. His anxiety only heightened as the hours passed slowly by and Sara the Fox didn't show up. It seemed that the sizzling hot day had no intention of ending. In the early afternoon Ruben was so frustrated that he could no longer just sit at his worktable and sew. "Today you close, Jacob," he said as he put down the pair of trousers he had been cutting and left the store.

The Rhino had no idea where he was heading. He kept walking aimlessly, worried that Tuba might have already made her choice, or been forced to accept, one of her suitors. Maybe she had gotten sick, perhaps with a life-threatening illness, because it was impossible that her mother wouldn't have come to Meat Market Alley that morning. "Why don't you think about this and let me know tomorrow?" Sara had told him the night before. So, where was she?

Hours later, as it was getting dark, Ruben passed by the bathhouse. That was when he realized that since he had left work that afternoon he had walked to the farm north of Jewbareh and from there had rambled aimlessly until he had arrived south of the ghetto, at the bottom end of the Alley of Eleven Twists near Tuba's house. There he slowed his pace, hoping to see Sara or Tuba. He waited a long time, but neither one showed up.

A week went by and Sara did not come to the Meat Market. With the passage of each day, Ruben became increasingly tense and couldn't sleep a wink. It seemed that both Sara and her daughter had disappeared off the face of the earth. Not to be seen by Jewbarites, every day after work, he walked to the farm and from there to the end of the Alley of Eleven Twists in hopes of seeing either the mother or her daughter. But they were nowhere to be found. He had to come home and face his mother's interrogations: Why was he so pale? Why wasn't he eating? Why... why... why...?

Now, every night, in the static air of the sweltering nights, Ruben waited in the dark near Sara's house, in hopes of seeing her and finding out where she was and what had gone wrong. But not

once did he catch so much of a single glimpse of her. After two
weeks, one night – when, after a long wait Ruben turned around to
go home, a woman passed by, wrapped in her chador. For a brief
second he thought he had seen Tuba. But no fourteen-year-old girl
would dare to walk alone the empty alleys of Jewbareh at this time
of night. Yet he noticed that her walk was exactly like Tuba's the
day he had seen her. It was the fourteenth night of the lunar month
and there was a full moon. He followed this veiled woman as
though he were her shadow. "Excuse me," Ruben called. The
woman turned her head and unveiled her face in the moonlight.
Ruben recognized the passionate glint of her black eyes. She was
Tuba. She turned around and accelerated her pace. So did Ruben.
When he got very close to her, she suddenly stopped, turned
around and gazed at him.

"Do you wish to speak to me, kadkhoda?" Tuba said
innocently. "You frightened me to death."

They stood motionless, like two statues. Then, the Rhino took
her head between his hands, looked into her eyes and kissed her
passionately all over her face. He wrapped his arms around her,
holding her tightly. Tuba struggled a little, but the warmth of
Rhino's breath on her face and the vigor of his grip around her
body disarmed her. "What are you doing?" she gasped,
nevertheless melting into his embrace. "What if someone sees us?
Let go of me, Ruben!"

For the first time Ruben heard his name in the mouth of his
beloved as no one had ever uttered it. She sang every vowel and
devoured every consonant.

"I will if…" He couldn't finish. He wanted to beg her to marry
him. He wanted to tell her that he loved her. Instead he opened his
arms to let her go, but she didn't. Tuba stood there firmly, face to
face with him.

"Is there something you want to tell me?" she asked, her voice
quivering.

Ruben saw his wife and his children in this young woman. Her
voice, which was like a thousand nightingales, gladdened his heart.
"You're so beautiful," he whispered as he reached for her small
hands and held them. Tuba bent her head down. A lock of black
hair fell over her eyes. Ruben clawed the hair away from her face
and caressed the back of his hand along her cheek.

"I want to marry you." There was fire in his voice.

Tuba was trembling. "You know this is not up to me. It's for my parents to decide."

Saying this, she ran away. Ruben stood there while the shadow of another woman passed by him, following Tuba into the dark of night.

Was it Sara the Fox?

The night was breathless. Blistering heat crawled along the alleys of Jewbareh. On such nights, women watered the miniature herb gardens in their tiny courtyards and sprayed water on the surrounding brick walls to cool their small houses before the men came home. Then they spread their worn out carpets on the ground next to their herb gardens and put old sackcloth pillows around a sofreh in the middle of the carpet where they served food to their husbands and children, going back and forth to their kitchens. It was on the night that Ruben kissed Tuba that Badri the Petunia saw them together from her kitchen window, which opened onto the Alley.

"Hey, are you there?" whispered Badri to Shamsi the Radish, her next-door neighbor. "Look out your window. There's a scene."

"What is it?" Shamsi whispered back.

"Hurry, hurry and see for yourself!"

"Oh, my God! Who are they?"

"The big man can be none other than the Rhino. But the girl? I don't know."

"What do you mean you don't know? Of course she is Sara the Fox's daughter."

"You're right! She is the Sara and the Fishmonger's daughter. Tell Monir to watch."

"Hey Monir. Look out your window. The Fishmonger's daughter and…"

"Are you there?" the Wartfaced Monir called her next-door neighbor.

And so, the message spread from one house to the next like a brushfire. Soon the women of the bottom end of the Alley of Eleven Twists crowded the windows of their hot and airless rooms, watching the two young lovers in each other's arms in the moonlight. They beat their chests, slapped their foreheads, pulled their hair, ran their nails across their cheeks and murmured lamentations.

147

"Woe to us, woe to us. What a sin!"

"May the Almighty spare him!"

"That's what happens when the master of a house lets his wife take charge!"

"First he was our patriarch, then he became a killer and again we were so stupid, we allowed him to remain our kadkhoda."

"What an impertinent bastard."

"For God's sake, why doesn't someone inform the poor girl's parents?"

"If they cared, they wouldn't let their daughter walk these dangerous alleys at all hours of the night."

"No, my dear. You don't seem to understand. He saved her father's life at the cost of risking all our lives and now she is… who knows, perhaps, how can I put it… thanking him?"

"Demons have possessed them both."

"But the poor girl is a virgin. Her eyebrows haven't even been groomed yet! How dare he touch her?"

"A virgin seduced by Kadkhoda Ruben."

"Well. She is 'not' a virgin any longer."

"It's the end of time. The Messiah is coming!"

"Oh, may the God of Abraham, Isaac, Jacob, Moses, Aaron, David and Shelomo protect us all from the fury of the Almighty!"

This conversation went on into the late hours of the night. The next morning, the women of the infamous Alley, escaping from the stifling indoor heat of another summer day, came out to their front porches to spread the news of what they had seen the night before.

"May ten scrolls of the Torah distance my beloved daughter from this disgraceful girl!" said The Wartfaced Monir. "I swear on my children's life, I saw the two of them, you know… they were… you know!"

"You saw them what?" asked Rana the Coyote, who hadn't been home the night before. "They were what? Either finish whatever you're saying or don't say it at all. Now, you saw them doing what?"

"They were right in front of my house. I went to open the window. You know how hot it is in the evenings these days? Look at the weather now…"

"Come on!" Rana cried, irritated. "Tell us what you saw. Who cares about the weather? Did he… you know… do it to her in the alley?"

"Of course!" Monir whispered. "I saw it with my own eyes. May I become blind if I lie. After all, there was a full moon. Not only did he kiss her a thousand kisses, first he opened her chador, then he pulled her long skirt up and put his hand under it. Those two idiots couldn't wait for a dark night or at least hide in a dark spot."

"She's right," said Badri the Petunia. "I saw them too from my window. They were right in front of me."

"Now, wait a minute," said Rana impatiently. "You two are at least five houses apart. How could you both see them, uh... mating—may they bear the torment of their sins?"

"Maybe they did it once near my house and once near her house. Who knows? Young men, unlike our husbands, can do it more than once."

They all sighed loudly, shook their heads, swayed back and forth, sympathized with the poor, ignorant parents of the innocent girl and cursed Ruben, their killer patriarch, with the worst of curses, for he had committed such a sin, and then eventually concluded that it was in fact all Tuba's fault, for a girl should be able to control herself. They begged one another not to tell anybody else because, after all, they said, both Ruben and Tuba were unfortunate young souls. Especially, they stressed, the girl, Tuba, who might yet be able to salvage some sort of future to look forward to, even possibly getting someone to marry her, an elderly man perhaps, in need of a caretaker in his old age.

And their venomous words traveled into the air like swarms of stinging black bees and eclipsed the sun over Jewbareh.

Chapter 11
At the Feast of Scavengers

On the night after Ruben kissed Tuba, Noori the Scavenger and his men gathered at Noori's house. The guests brought bottles of homemade wine and vodka. Tonight, instead of boasting about the taste and potency of what they had brewed, Noori and his pals had a novel topic to brag about. They were there to celebrate what they called "the most illegitimate and shameful intercourse in the history of Jewbareh."

"That's why it's been said by our blessed forefathers that the first suitor who knocks on your door for your girl is the best," Noori lectured his peers. "Just give them away and let them live with their destiny." Then he lifted his glass of vodka and made a toast, "*salamati!*" as the others echoed him and drank their own vodka down. "But think of that bastard of a Ruben, what a ladies' man! Don't all women go to him for words of wisdom? Now I'll tell you what wisdom he's shown the daughter of the Fishmonger. This!" he grabbed his crotch and pulled it up. The vagabonds laughed frantically and shouted, "More! More!"

"Let me tell you," Noori, upbeat now, continued. "Women are all the same. All they need is your *wisdom*," he said, again pointing between his legs, while the intoxicated crowd imitated his gesture, shouting, "Wisdom! Wisdom!"

They danced a gruesome dance, they laughed the laughter of demons, they sang evil songs, and their shrieks and shouts flew like arrows over the walls of the Scavenger's house, cutting into the silent, hot night when...

"Stop!" they heard Rabbi Shimon roar, as he yanked the door open and entered the gathering. "Shame on you, Noori! I could hear you from two alleys away. Are you insane? As they say, nobody sees his own faults, but God sees all. Do you think God will forgive you for what you're doing?" There was silence as the rabbi went on. "What if these two young people were your children? Tell me, how can you enjoy celebrating other people's miseries? *Thou shalt not give false testimony.* Remember? Can anyone of you answer me?"

Noori the Scavenger stepped unsteadily forward and muttered, *"Thou shalt not commit adultery.* Is this not one of the Commandments also, Rabbi?"

"What adultery?" the veins on the Rabbi's neck bulged as he cried. "Noori, I saw you going home late last night. It was about midnight and you were drunk as usual. So, there's no way you could have witnessed any of the nonsense you're hollering about. But having known you for as long as you have lived, I realize that nothing can stop you from swearing that you've been wherever you want your alcohol-laced thoughts to take you."

The rabbi grabbed Noori's hand, put it on a small Torah he took out of his pocket and said, "Can you swear to the truth of this baseless and sinful gossip you are spreading?"

"I guess... to be precise... I mean...I heard it from him," stammered the Scavenger, pointing at Daniel the Weedeater. The rabbi stared at Daniel, who shrugged his shoulders.

"Oh God," Mullah Shimon hollered. "'The man to whom you gave wisdom, what did you deny him; and to the man on whom you did not bestow wisdom, what then did you give?' I have nothing else to say except that you have to answer to Him." He pointed upward and turned to leave. Behind him, he heard a tumult. Some of the men were sniggering and some mocking him. Then, suddenly, in front of him, from the darkness of the night, emerged the formidable silhouette of a man.

"You imbeciles!" The voice roared like thunder. Noori and his crowd were sure that, as predicted by the rabbi—behind whom they all ran to take refuge—an angel had descended to make them pay for their sins. As the looming figure advanced into the room and they realized it was Ruben, they were no less frightened. With his bloodshot eyes, Ruben looked past the rabbi and found Noori.

"Now Ruben! You listen to me," said the rabbi steadily as he stepped forward and stood in his way. "You are not..."

"Yes I am." Ruben pushed him aside gently and walked up to Noori, who had been trying to hide behind his gang members. Splitting the shield of his men apart, Ruben grabbed Noori by the two sides of his collar, lifted the smaller man up until he was face to face with him, then slammed his forehead forcefully into Noori's nose. Everyone in the room heard the sound of the Scavenger's nose breaking. He screamed in agony, shaking his arms and legs in the air as he tried to release himself from Ruben's grip, blood shooting out of his nose and mouth.

"You pathetic, pitiful, filthy animal!" Ruben shouted, still holding him in the air. "Let this be a lesson for all of you and whoever else dares to speak vile and ugly nonsense about me or Tuba." Saying this, he lifted Noori even higher and threw him at his pals so hard they all fell back against the wall. Then he turned and walked out.

One by one, Noori's guys stood up, staggering and whining. "Do you still take *his* side, rabbi?" moaned Daniel the Weed-eater.

"Hah!" said Mullah Shimon, smiling broadly as he left the room.

For the next two days, Ruben's nocturnal activities consumed Jewbareh, as people gossiped about his Monday night's misconduct with Tuba and his Tuesday night's ruckus at the Scavenger's house. The ghetto was rocked with shock and confusion because of these two outrageous events, which were so clear to everyone that no embellishment was necessary. What was up with their kadkhoda, everyone wondered. First killing a Muslim, then doing whatever he'd done with a virgin girl and now pounding his own people?

On Wednesday morning, people who had come out into the Alley to do the day's business, looked through the window and saw Ruben provoked and wrathful as he sat at his table. He looked intent like an angry rhino. "You don't step on a wild animal's tail," women whispered to each other. "And especially when he's lying in wait to attack." For the first time anybody could remember, the customary hustle and bustle all along Meat Market Alley below the stairs to Ruben's shop was so quiet you could hear a bee fly across the way to the butcher shop. Women were neither arguing about the piece of meat they wanted, nor complaining about the insufficient fat. They whispered what they wanted to the butcher. David's cleaver went up and down somehow noiselessly and his knife cut the meat gently. Nobody uttered a sound and everyone tiptoed around the fuming rhino. Even Jacob didn't sigh. It was only after they had finished their shopping and they were one or two twists away in the Alley that the women resumed gossiping in whispers.

"Eat!" Ruth cried at her son at dinner on Wednesday night. "And don't tell me you're not hungry. You haven't eaten for days now."

Ruben didn't budge as he sat on the ground in front of a copper tray his mother had prepared for him full of steamed rice, eggplant stew, bread and pickles. Ruth moved close to him and ran her fingers through his shiny brown hair.

"Why didn't you just tell me you wanted to marry Sara the Fox's daughter?"

Ruben sat straight and stared at his mother.

"No wonder you refused other girls I suggested to you. If you had just told me, we wouldn't have to deal with all this." She gestured vaguely toward the window—and the world outside.

"I'm sorry, Mani, but there's nothing you have to deal with." Then Ruth shook her head and smiled. "All right. What do *you* have to deal with?" She moved the tray closer to him. "Eat and I'll tell you. You cornered Abe the Fishmonger's daughter in the dark of night and I'm not sure if you … you know?"

"If I what?" Ruben pushed the tray back. "You want to know if I took her virginity?"

Ruben started to get up, but Ruth took his hand and motioned for him to sit down. He complied, ill at ease. Then she put her arms around his wide shoulders and kissed his head. "I only asked you a question as a mother. If you don't want to answer, you don't have to."

"I only held her in my arms as you're holding me now. Does that make me evil?"

"Do you want to marry this girl?" she asked abruptly, ignoring his question.

Ruben was taken aback. "I don't know. I suppose so."

Ruth smiled and said, "Then let's get it done. Perhaps when you have a wife in your bed, you'll have less violence in your heart."

"I don't think it's going to be all that simple, mother. I'm surprised they haven't already come after me."

"They did. Sara the Fox was here this morning. She's a strange woman and I don't particularly care for her." Ruth scratched the back of her hand and continued. "This woman, Sara, wept so hard, you would think she'd peeled a hundred onions. But as soon as I promised that I would take care of the matter, her tears dried up. Anyway, after she left, the Scavenger's mother came, complaining about her son's broken nose and front teeth. And then came the wives and mothers of the other men whose bones you broke. You've been very busy my son."

"I'm sorry to put you through this," said Ruben, his head down. "And not only this, but also the troubles you had to endure because I killed the nomad. Mani, I don't know what's come over me these past few years. Maybe the Devil himself."

"Stop this nonsense, my dear. As my father of blessed memory used to say, 'Neither that salty, nor this sweet.' The world we live in is neither black, nor white. Gray is our world and that's what makes us human beings — sometimes dark gray, sometime light gray and sometimes elegant and handsome like you," she added, tickling Ruben under the chin like when he was a child. He pushed Ruth's hand and looked at her, annoyed. "Stop that, mother," he said.

"You're the most heedless person I know," she said. "And your recklessness is just going to cost us a few more invitations." She sat back, looked at her son, visibly jubilant and said, "I had to invite all the complainers and their families to the wedding."

"Whose wedding?" Ruben demanded in alarm.

"The wedding of my only son."

Chapter 12
The Wedding

Ruben the Rhino married Tuba the Woman in the late fall of 1836. To put an end to what was considered a disgraceful situation, the families of both Tuba and Ruben decided to forgo the usual engagement ceremonies and because Abe the Fishmonger was so poor, Ruben pleaded with his mother — and she accepted reluctantly — not to pressure Tuba's parents for a sizeable dowry. After consulting with Mullah Shimon, they set a date for marriage that was associated with good omens. Sara the Fox asked the rabbi to do whatever he considered necessary to officiate the engagement of her daughter to Ruben. "So that people won't talk behind my daughter's back if they see her together with the kadkhoda," she told the rabbi. Thus, after a brief engagement ceremony, the families of the bride and the groom began inviting their guests and making preparations for what was known as the seven-days-and-seven-nights-ceremonial-wedding, which, in fact, over time, had dwindled down to three days and three nights.

For the first time since he had killed Zain, Ruben was at peace with himself. The vigor of his love for Tuba — this beautiful, young woman he would spend the rest of his life with — overshadowed his continuing sense of guilt. In a way, this unexpected love had brought him closer to the reasoning of his family and friends — Mullah Ahmad in Esfahan, Rabbi Daniel in Jerusalem, his half-brother Jacob and his mother in Jewbareh — all of whom believed and had told him again and again that killing another man in self-defense was permissible in every religion and that he had no reason to be tormented by his conscience. Furthermore, no matter how selfish it was, deep down Ruben had the gratifying feeling that the woman he was marrying would always appreciate his bravery in saving her father's life.

Nevertheless, as the families of the bride and the groom were getting ready to go door-to-door to invite their guests to the wedding, the rumormongers, never ones to pass up the chance to gossip, got together and cackled like hens about how brazen the bride and the groom were.

"They have no shame!"

"My husband and I won't go! Will you?"

"Of course not! We refuse to be a part of a union so cursed that it will bring calamity upon the whole community."

"We all know the bride is not a virgin, not a girl any more. She is a *woman!*"

And that was how Tuba had come to be known as "Tuba the Woman."

Still, with the arrival of the hosts on the thresholds of their guests' houses, the relentless condemnation of both the bride and the groom began to wane, because, after all, the Jewbarites' sufferings and misfortunes were so plentiful that they couldn't afford to refuse whatever small dose of joy came into their dreary lives, even if it was vicarious. And though this was an invitation to the wedding of a "woman" and an "adulterer," still a happy occasion was so rare an event that it simply couldn't be passed up. So it was that many of those who had sworn to each other not to go to the wedding, actually accepted the invitation.

"Ruth called on me every day for two weeks and made me swear on the lives of my children to go," said Shamsi the Radish to her other gossiping friends. "I gave up. What else could I do?"

"The same here," said Shifra the Hen. "I'd told Ruth that the midwife had assessed my daughter's delivery date for the day of the wedding and I don't want to risk being away from her—an excuse, of course, you know—but she wouldn't take no for an answer. So eventually I too surrendered."

So, while in the alleys of Jewbareh a swarm of buzzing lies flew out of the mouths of Shamsi, Shifra and the like, happiness and excitement peaked in the house of Ruben the Rhino. Gaiety, as has been said, is contagious. For the time being, all the Jewbarites were happy. In the meantime Ruben wanted the wedding ceremonies— which as custom had it, were the groom's responsibility—to be outstanding, something that everyone in Jewbareh would remember for always. "Money is no object," he told his mother.

"Please make sure we have plenty of the best food and drink. Poor Tuba has gone through so much because of me, I want to make sure that this wedding is the most memorable event of her life."

This demand, however, irritated Ruth. "Sure," she yelled at Ruben. "First you forbid me to negotiate a dowry. Then you want me to spend my entire late husband's savings on your *poor* Tuba's wedding! You might have lost *your* mind, but I certainly haven't lost *mine*," she shouted, slapping her chest.

Ruben had sensed the real cause of his mother's frustration. After all, Ruth was losing her only son to another woman and although, time and again, Ruben had reassured her that no one would take her place in his heart, he knew that Ruth was unhappy at having to yield to another woman what she believed to be her right to her son. On the issue of the dowry, which Ruben had insisted on as a way of honoring his bride and her family, Ruth simply wouldn't relent. And as the wedding date neared, Ruben's concern heightened, for he feared that his mother might cause a commotion. He needed help—neither from the rabbi nor the mayor, but someone in the family. On his domestic problems, his uncle, Asher the Ewe, had always been there to help. Furthermore, Ruben knew that his mother was receptive to Asher's advice, for he was her older brother. So, he invited his uncle to his shop and, over a cup of tea, shared his problem with him.

Asher's long speech began with an ultimatum. "If you want my help, you have to swear on the grave of your father that from now on, no matter how provoking the circumstances, you will never, ever again lose your temper."

"If these people leave me alone," Ruben exhaled noisily as his hand shook and the cup of tea he was going to put in front of Asher spilled on his working table.

"You see? I talk to you and you lose your balance. What has happened to you, my dear? Calm down and listen to me. As the kadkhoda of Jewbareh, what you have done for your people has made you a hero in the eyes of your people. Then you turn around and, inexplicably so, beat not only a vagabond like Noori the Scavenger but also his gang. Now, what does all of this do? It makes people suspect your bravery and wonder whether both acts were equally out of rage. That's when they conclude that no longer they can trust their governor to stay his hand. What you don't seem to understand is that the gossip that Noori and other Jewbarite hens were spreading about you and Tuba was like a small pimple on its way to drying up and disappearing and with what you did, you made the venom of these gossiping bitches spread and poison your mother's head too—so much so that she now believes Tuba is not a virgin."

Ruben jumped up and hurled his cup against the wall. "How many times do I..."

"I'm leaving," said Jacob as he put his jacket on.

"Did I say anything wrong?" asked Asher the Ewe.

"No, Uncle Asher," Jacob said smiling. "But I have to leave. There's a lot to be done for Mr. Rhino's wedding. Your lovely sister has given me so much to do that if it were not for my big belly, my back would have broken by now."

The three men laughed. Jacob was happy, for he had capped his brother's rage and Asher appreciated the nice man's thoughtfulness.

"Look," Asher said to Ruben after Jacob left. "You are getting married. It's the happiest occasion of your life. So, why in hell, instead of going around and breaking worthless people's bones, don't you celebrate?"

"Because my mother nags me night and day about the dowry and about Tuba's virginity."

"Calm down and I promise I'll take care of the problem."

Later that day, when Ruben and his uncle met with Ruth, first Asher assured his sister that Ruben had not deflowered Tuba. Then he encouraged her not to be intransigent with Abe and Sara about the dowry. "Let them give her whatever they can afford," he said.

"These..." Ruth opened her mouth to object, but her brother cut her short.

"On the grave of our father and mother, swear that you'll do as I say."

Ruth raised her arms in surrender, but soon it turned out that she was infuriated by what she had come to know about Sara the Fox. "Turan the Turtle—Sara's sister—was here yesterday..." Ruth began, but became silent. Asher and Ruben were looking at her intently to continue, but she shook her head.

"So? Turan was here and...?" Asher bobbed his head forward.

"This family makes me sick. Can you believe that this cheap woman was here to betray her sister?"

Ruben and Asher sat back and waited for Ruth's prologue to end and the betrayal part to begin, and when it did, Ruben especially began chewing his nails, because what his mother had to say was something that he had suspected from the night he had kissed Tuba near her house. Based on Turan's story, Sara the Fox had plotted the whole scenario of getting Ruben to marry her daughter. She had brought Tuba to the Meat Market Alley, faked the story about the two suitors, asked Ruben for his opinion, disappeared on him and watched him waiting for Tuba night after night. Finally, she had let Tuba loose to pass by Ruben that night. The Fox had stood in the shadows, Turan had said, and watched Ruben embrace her daughter. It was this part of the story that, for Ruben, rang true, because that night he had seen a woman who looked and walked precisely like Sara pass him by after Tuba had run away.

Ruben felt betrayed. "I swore on my father's grave not to act unwisely, Uncle Asher, and I will keep that vow. But I'm going to straighten this matter out and if what Turan has said is true, I will cancel the wedding."

"You two!" Asher said, pointing at his sister and Ruben. "You are both totally irrational. You believe the Turtle? Someone who doesn't have any sympathy for her own niece and especially you who ignored her attempts to draw your attention to *her* daughter? The more important question is whether you and Tuba love each other, and I know you do. So, none of these stories is worth a copper coin." Then he turned to Ruth and continued, "Name me one wedding without such problems. All that matters is the future of the newlyweds — may they find happiness with each other. And most important, my dear sister, you know your own son and how much he cares for you in particular. About whether or not Sara has plotted to put these two young people together, I have my doubts. But even if she has done so, number one," he raised his thumb, "it's not Tuba's fault — the poor girl has just turned fourteen. Number two," he opened his index finger, "since Ruben loves her and she loves him, then so be it."

Asher talked and talked to Ruth and Ruben until they seemed to calm down. Reassured by her brother's advice, Ruth got to work. Since the official engagement, Ruben had been dining almost every evening with Tuba's family. Sara the Fox was smart. She always invited Ruben with his mother, but Ruth invariably rejected the invitations, giving different excuses. For a day or two, while still under the influence of his uncle's reasoning, Ruben let his love for Tuba overtake his urge to find out the truth behind what the Turtle had said. But at last, one night after dinner, he decided to put the question to Tuba. He asked Abe and Sara if he and Tuba could go out into the courtyard.

"But of course," cried Sara the Fox just as her husband opened his mouth to say no. "After all, that's why Abe and I had Rabbi Shimon officiate at your formal engagement. Go, go," she shooed them out the door.

It was late October and the relentless summer heat had not yet abated. Ruben and Tuba walked to the far end of Abe's small courtyard and sat on a wooden bench under an old pomegranate tree whose leaves had creased in the burning temperature of the day. Ruben was squirming restlessly. He didn't know where to begin. Tuba, who was alone with a man for the first time in her short life except for that night in the Alley, was nervously waving a straw fan in front of her face, waiting for her husband-to-be to say something.

"I have a question to ask you," Ruben finally whispered, for he could see Sara's shadow on the curtain of her room, obviously spying on them.

"Yes?" Tuba murmured in a shaky voice.

"All I want to know is if your mother was present the night I embraced you in front of your house," he asked, his eyes still fixed on the figure behind the curtain.

Shivering uncontrollably, Tuba began to cry. The Rhino turned his massive body around, facing her. *If what Turan has said is true, I will cancel the wedding,* he remembered having promised Ruth and Asher.

"I know it will upset you," Tuba finally spoke. "But... I mean, that night my mother told me you were waiting near our house. You wanted to see me because you loved me, she said. I told her I was scared and asked, 'If he loves me, why doesn't he come for *khastegari* and ask my parents for my hand to marry to you?' She said it was because you were shy, because you wanted to see me in the moonlight, because... I don't remember what else she said. Oh yes. After I told her that I was afraid to go alone to the dangerous Eleventh Twist, she said she would stand in the dark and watch me. But really, I came out because I... I... you know, I wanted to see you."

"You shouldn't be crying, Tuba," Ruben said, wiping her tears. Now he knew that there *had been* a plot, but this young woman had been an unwitting accomplice in her mother's plan and only because she truly loved him as he loved her.

That night, when Ruben came home, he shared all that had happed with his mother and begged her to rein in, if not forgo, her disdain for Sara and Turan and let the wedding preparations go on without further complications.

"I'll never like this woman," Ruth said of Sara. "But because you love her daughter, I will somehow put up with her."

With the road to the wedding ceremonies now paved, the only two seamstresses in Jewbareh—Talat the Seamstress and Badri the Petunia—were working day and night, Talat sewing exclusively the wedding dress for Tuba as well as the outfits for the families of the bride and the groom, and Badri plying her needle for the guests. For fittings, Sara brought Tuba and her friends to Talat's house on the tenth twist of the Alley of Eleven Twists. Talat was Sara's cousin and conducted her business from her house. Sara and her entourage went there with yards and yards of white silk fabric—one of many presents from Nissan the Fabricseller for the wedding of his best friend, Ruben. The fittings were festive occasions. Sara brought sweets and candies, the girls whispered naughty words in each other's ears and giggled, and everyone sang songs.

Talat had her own way of announcing the end of a work day. "My back is exploding with pain," she moaned. "We'll do the rest of this tomorrow." At this point, after all her customers went home, Talat poured two cups of tea and she and Sara sat down together for some serious gossiping. Meanwhile, Tuba and Gohar the Bud—Talat's daughter and Tuba's best friend—shut themselves in the Bud's room. Gohar, who was quite chubby, had a round face, large light-brown prying eyes and a small mouth like a bud, which was active relentlessly, either eating or talking.

The next fitting for Tuba's wedding dress was on the day after Ruben had questioned her about her mother's plot. Gohar noticed that her friend looked miserable. "Everything all right?" she whispered, but Tuba didn't answer. She only shook her head. Gohar had to restrain her curiosity until after the fitting, when the two of them once again went to her room. Talat was busy putting stitches in the dress and chatting with Sara the Fox.

"Look at this statue of beauty, look! And you're telling me Ruben's mother had the gall to ask for a dowry? Shame on them!"

"Of course I won't send my daughter away with *no* dowry, but we're not as rich as they are. I mean..."

While Talat and Sara were exchanging vicious remarks about Ruth, Tuba was contemplating the way her mother had brought her together with Ruben. It *was* shameful. Awkward. No wonder people called her mother 'the Fox'—the deceitful creature in all those bedtime stories of her grandmother. Still, understandably, she was happy with the outcome of the trick the Fox had played on both her and the Rhino. She loved this man. Or did she? She was confused. Who was this huge, imposing person? Although Tuba was one of the taller girls in Jewbareh, when she stood next to Ruben, the crown of her head was slightly above his elbow. At twenty-seven, he was thirteen years older than she—almost twice her age. He had killed someone. How could she be sure that he wouldn't kill her? Again she wondered if she really loved him. But worst of all, the man hadn't asked for her hand voluntarily. It was her mother who had conspired to put him in this thwarting situation where he had no choice but to marry her.

"Now tell me. What's the matter with you?" Gohar asked Tuba once they were alone. "Is there anything you want to share with me?"

Tuba felt humiliated even to mention how her mother had schemed to bring Ruben and her together. But she had a worrisome question to ask her friend. "My mother says..." she hesitated. "I don't know how to put it, but she has told me *things*."

"What things, Tuba dear?" Gohar cupped her chubby hands under her chin and looked straight into Tuba's eyes.

"Well," Tuba blushed. "My mother says that on the wedding night, I will bleed."

"Wait a minute! But you can't marry during the time you're *jahanami*—worthy of hell. You must *not* be bleeding on your wedding night. You have to be clean, go to the *mikveh*—the Jewish ritual bath—and then marry."

"No you silly. You think the rabbi would've approved the wedding day without checking on my menstrual period? It's not that. My Mani says that Ruben's thing," she pointed at Gohar's crotch, "will go in... Oh my God, I'm so embarrassed."

"Tell me, tell me. It goes where?"

This time Tuba pointed at her own crotch and with her head down, she continued, "Mani says, once he does that, it's painful and I should be a good girl and not scream. Most importantly, she says, as he does what I told you, I will begin bleeding. At that moment, I should immediately wipe myself with these white cotton napkins which she will place ahead of time under the pillow of my wedding bed."

"Oh... my... God!" Gohar covered her face with her hands. "How come *my* mother hasn't told me about this?" She reached for the plate of cookies and shoved one in her mouth. "Have some," she said. "And go on, go on!"

Tuba pushed the plate away. "You know nothing about this?" she asked. "All right. The morning after, I should give my bloodied virginity napkins to my mother. Then, Mani said, she will show them to the whole world to prove that no man has ever touched me. I'm so scared."

Gohar imagined her thin friend lying under this giant of a rhino and him doing this to the woman who was going to be his wife for life. "Can't this be done, for example, a year after you are married? I mean, don't we bleed enough when we are *jahanami*? What I want to know is why they have to do such a dirty, hurting, bloody act on a wedding night?"

"'Once you've done it, you will know,' Mani said to me."

Although she had expressed part of her worry to her friend and consequentially felt lighter, she was still afraid.

As for the men, the only tailors in Jewbareh, were ironically, Ruben the Rhino himself and his brother Jacob. It was they who made new suits for many of his guests and, of course, his own wedding suit. Ruben designed and sewed himself a *nimtaneh* – a long jacket – made of shiny blue velvet, a *tonban* – a baggy pair of trousers – made of soft wool, and a *pirahan,* a long white shirt made of cotton. Standing on top of a stool with two steps, Jacob, with pins held between his thin lips, turned a patient Ruben slowly around as he fitted the shoulders of the Rhino's jacket. Once he had finished the seams, and the pins lay expertly inserted in the deep blue fabric, he burst into song. "*A lover suffered a great deal of hardship to get to his beloved...*" Then he stopped. "You will be, my brother, the most elegant and the most distinguished looking kadkhoda and groom that Jewbareh has ever seen."

"And his brother gave him a heart attack, fitting his wedding suit, before he'd even taken his bride's virginity," Ruben groaned.

"Aren't we in a big hurry to get to that wedding bed?" Jacob chuckled.

"You're driving me..."

"Hush. Don't move." He held Ruben by his shoulders, examining the jacket carefully. Then he stepped back, squinted and continued, "I think the right shoulder is half a knuckle longer than the left shoulder.

"Two weeks ago we agreed that the wedding date should be in four weeks. Fourteen days have already gone by. In this fourteen days, I have had to make arrangements for the wedding and deal with," Ruben began counting on his fingers, "the baseless gossip surrounding Tuba and myself, our mother who doesn't stop bickering about my not asking Tuba's family for dowry, and, of course, *you* who are acting as though you're sewing for a sultan."

"You talk too much, my brother," Jacob said, again turning Ruben around.

"Ouch!" Ruben shouted, pulling out of his jacket a pin that had apparently pricked his skin.

"I'm so..." Jacob bit his forefinger, but his big belly bouncing up and down betrayed his stifled laughter.

"Laugh! Laugh at me. The world has laughed at me, why not you?" said Ruben in a playful tone. "Just make sure that when you're fitting my trousers, your needle does *not* prick me down there," he said smiling as he looked down at his crotch. "I guess you know that it has to remain undamaged for the wedding night!"

"If I cause any hurt in that area..." Jacob began laughing hysterically.

"What?" Ruben giggled, knowing that something funny was on his brother's mind.

Jacob took a deep breath and continued, "If I hurt you there, the day after the wedding, Tuba will pin *me* to the wall!"

This made the two brothers laugh so heartily that tears came to both of them.

"Listen," Jacob said, his words interrupted by hiccups. "If you want me to say how sorry I am for what you've gone through, you're wasting your breath. Sorrow is gone. It's time to laugh. Laugh at the pin that pricked your skin, laugh at what the gossipmongers have to say and treat our mother nicely over your bride's dowry, or rather the lack of it." Then, as though talking to the jacket, he said, "Don't worry. I'll get this done on time. All right?" And went on singing, *"A lover suffered a great deal of..."*

Ruben waited four more days for Jacob to finish his work before he took his wedding suit and shirt to Mohammad Khan—an embroidery master in Esfahan bazaar and a business associate of both Naphtali and Ruben. In less than three days and with no charge, Mohammad sewed detailed paisley-design silk embroideries on the groom's jacket, trousers and the shirt. "Tell your brother," he said to Jacob, "this is Mohammad's wedding gift for the big Jew."

As the bride and the groom were busy fitting their wedding outfits and making arrangements for the wedding, they saw each other frequently—of course chaperoned by Sara. Uncle Asher reassured the Rhino that he had Ruth under control. And on Tuba's side, Gohar had been assiduously gathering information about what happens to girls on their wedding night.

"What matters most is the amount of blood that comes out of you," Gohar said pointing her plump forefinger at Tuba, suddenly as if an instructor. "Now that she know that you have told me, my cousin Mehri who got married last year told me to tell you that you have to bleed a lot and make sure that it all goes on your virginity napkins. It's the proof of your purity and the flag of pride for your parents. So, no matter how much you hurt, you shouldn't resist until—I'm quoting my cousin—he's fully 'deflowered' you."

"Deflowered?" said Tuba, her eyes widening in horror. The image went through her mind of a vicious hand pulling a rose off of its stems and tearing off its petals.

"But Mehri says, the next time it doesn't hurt at all. In fact it's supposed to be..." Now, even Gohar blushed, and the two girls dissolved in laughter and curiosity and wonder that they had finally reached the age when they could talk like experts about such things.

A week before the wedding, friends and relatives of the bride and the groom volunteered to help with preparations. Make no mistake about it, Ruth was in charge and she had every task planned ahead of time. Men volunteers, she declared, were to work under Nissan's supervision and women volunteers under that of Zilfa, Nissan's wife. Perishables had to be delivered a day or two before the first day of the wedding on the following Tuesday and non-perishables, sooner. Carefully budgeting expenses, Ruth gave each one of the volunteers his or her assignment and with their allotted funds, they went out to fulfill her commands.

Ruth brought out of hiding a bottle of wine — Abram's Magic — that had been specially brewed with care by Naphtali for his son's circumcision ceremony and to be blessed once again and tasted at his wedding. From the large vats in the basement of Ruben's house, dozens of other wine flasks of Abram's Magic, many dating back to the days of Naphtali, were filled and brought up. Additionally, Joshua the Aragh-Kesh — the distiller — delivered twenty large bottles of raisin vodka, "As potent as rabid dogs," he boasted. Ammeh Manzal, Ruben's warm and caring aunt, was assigned the task of making sure there were enough pickles, relish and other preserves. And then deliveries began to arrive according to schedule.

On a Monday in mid-November of 1836 — one day before the first day of the wedding — Jacob brought two sheep and many chickens that he had arranged for David the Butcher to slaughter, and Asher, four donkey-loads of rice, vegetables, herbs, fruits, groceries, sweets, nuts and other provisions.

"So much work, so much work," Jacob complained as he put his hands on his back and bent backwards.

"And there's no other man here to give us a hand," Asher joined in. "Once everything is ready to be gobbled up, then all the fellows will ask if they can help," he laughed.

"Your poor wives," Ammeh Manzal shook her head sideways. "Do these men grumble as much at home?"

"No, don't worry!" Ruth answered. "It's only for their own family that they act like babies."

The volunteers got busy arranging the deliveries in separate groups and carried them to the basement of Ruben's house, where it was much cooler. Abe the Fishmonger, accompanied by his wife Sara, delivered a basket of fish and when Sara declared that it was a part of her daughter's dowry, Ruth lost control.

"What? Fish? A part of..."

But before she could continue, Asher, who knew his sister was looking for an excuse to start a brawl, heard this exchange and rushed upstairs from the basement. "Yes," he interrupted Ruth. "Even at *your* wedding, Ruth, I remember fish was served on the day your dowry was negotiated." He angrily gazed into Sara's eyes, signaling her to shut her mouth. Then Asher politely instructed Jacob to escort the woman and her husband out. They left, but a few minutes later, Abe the Fishmonger returned. He was apologetic. "I owe my life to your son and I ask your pardon, Ruth khanom," he said. "Of course fish can be no one's dowry. You have to pardon my wife. She is... you know. I've had to put up with her all these years. Please understand. I'm poor and I'm embarrassed. But this is my daughter's wedding too and I beg you to let me help and also to be kind and forgiving and let my wife be of help as well."

"Of course, Abe, of course," said Asher to Ruth's utter astonishment. "We need as much help as we can get here." He nodded toward the two sheep carcasses near the kitchen that Nissan and Jacob were busy preparing. "But before joining these two great men, why don't you go and bring in Sara khanom. We need her help too."

Abe nodded joyously, ran outside and came back with Sara. "Apologize to Ruth khanom!" he instructed his wife. "I'm sorry," said Sara and all the women helpers ululated and sang together a tribal Persian song particular to the occasion.

It's me, me the mother of the groom
I'm the celebrated one, my place up in every room...

Having restrained an imminent clash, Asher clapped his hands and called out joyfully, "Come on! We have a lot of work ahead of us." Everybody resumed his or her assigned task, except Ruth, who took a while longer before she stopped grumbling.

With the kitchen being too small to cater to such a large number of guests, Nissan offered his kitchen, adjacent to that of Ruben's. A short wall that stood between their houses had eroded so much that finally it had collapsed near its tail end—where the neighboring kitchens were built—and had created an open space between the two houses. But still this was not enough space. So outside the conjoined kitchens, huge pots and pans were placed on metal tripods with burning wood underneath.

A group of women helped Ammeh Manzal scrape the scales off the fish, washed and dried them with towels made of rough cotton and seasoned them before they placed them in the frying pans of sizzling oil and turmeric.

"The smell of this fried fish is all over Jewbareh," Ruben yelled as he walked in. "And the moment it reached my shop, I knew it had to be Ammeh Manzal's cooking. She's the best."

"What are you doing here?" Ruth cried. "I swear he's gone *majnoon* — crazy with love," she added addressing the others. "Who's minding the shop?" she asked Ruben.

"The shop is there, I'm here, life is beautiful, it's my wedding and I'm going to stay here and help. I've told my neighbors that we will be closed for the next few days. And... *and*... Guess what?" His huge body swayed cheerfully. Then he went back, opened the door and to everyone's surprise, came in a shy Tuba.

Women ululated, clapped and sang, "*Yar mobarak bada, ensha-Allah mobarak bada* — Blessed be your wedding, God willing it will be blessed." Tuba's parents froze. Ruth screamed, "What...?" But before she could finish, Asher interrupted his sister, raising his voice and singing in unison with others. He then grabbed Ruth's hand and pulled her to dance to the tune of yar mobarak. Ruth danced towards her son and the bride, held their hands and before long, everybody else left their assigned tasks and joined in the dancing and singing.

Their jubilance resonated beyond the walls of the Rhino's house into the nearby alley and soon many neighbors and by-passers entered and joined this ecstatic crowd. Ruben was euphoric. A head and neck taller than anyone else, the Rhino stood and watched so many uninvited Jewbarites streaming into his house, singing and dancing in celebration of his happiness. The sincerity he detected in their eyes and the joyous way they looked at him, gave Ruben the feeling of being purged of his grief, which had also accumulated over time. His people loved him, he reasoned, or else they wouldn't be showing such joy and affection toward him and his beloved. They were dancing, twirling like the dervishes he had seen — or dreamed of on his way to Jerusalem — and in the waves of their movements, he saw Zain evaporate, Menasha disappear, Noori the Scavenger dwindle and he, Ruben the Rhino, rising with an exhilarating feeling, like a phoenix from the ashes of his incessant, chronic grief.

"Enough!" Uncle Asher announced. "We have three days to dance and sing *and* drink."

On their way out, people wished the betrothed couple well. "May the bride and the groom live one hundred and twenty years," said one. "With twelve mighty sons like our kadkhoda," said the other.

"You Ruben!" Asher called once everyone had left except for the family and friends who had returned to their assigned jobs. "Why don't you give Nissan, Jacob and your father-in-law a hand? And what about this beautiful bride?" he asked Ruth.

"Well..." Ruth laughed loudly. "Let's see. Since it was *only* the great smell of Ammeh Manzal's fried fish that brought her and my son here, I think Tuba should roll up her sleeves and help Ammeh."

Holding Tuba's hand, Ruben went up to where his aunt was sitting on a stool in front of the frying pan, kissed her head and said, "Here's your gorgeous helper. Take good care of her, but before I go to the work that His Majesty Uncle Asher has assigned to me, can I please have one piece of your delicious fish?"

"You? Of course not, you spoiled kid!" Manzal retorted, pretending to frown. "Don't you dare touch my fish! This is *only* for the wedding of my beloved nephew. Who are you?" she chuckled as she took a piece of fish and handed it to Tuba, saying, "But your beautiful bride, that's a different matter." Ruben roared with laughter as he grabbed his small aunt from under her armpits and lifted her off the stool. Ammeh Manzal looked at Ruben and shook her head. "It's as if it were yesterday that you were born." She put her arms around Ruben's neck and kissed him.

Ruben got to work and together, the three men skinned the sheep, set aside the heads and legs for *kaleh paacheh* – a rich, gelatin-thick soup to be eaten for breakfast the next morning.

"Pew, this stinks," yelled Jacob who stood over the kaleh paacheh pot.

"Add some saffron," called Ammeh Manzal. "And a bit of turmeric," said Sara. "That will take care of the bad smell."

"I hate kaleh paacheh," Jacob said and shook his head.

"What the hell are you talking about," said Asher light-heartedly. "I've seen you devouring this delicious meal at breakfast so many times."

Done with frying the fish, Ammeh Manzal and her crew cleaned the viscera and handed them to Zilfa's group of women, now joined by Sara, to have them filled with dumpling, sew them up and make *gippa* – a traditional meal Jewbarites ate mostly on

Saturdays when they came back from the synagogues and also on special occasions like weddings. In doing this, Zilfa's hands, up to her elbow, went in and out of the pot, mixing the ingredients of dumpling: rice, cumin seeds, saffron, raisins, parsley, leeks, minced meat and — strangely — Zilfa's tears, which dropped into the pot.

"Anything the matter?" asked her sister, Henna who was helping also.

"Nothing!"

"What do you mean 'nothing'? What are you crying for?"

Zilfa brought her shoulder forward and wiped her tears with her shirt. "Remember my wedding? Our Mani — may she rest in peace — made fifty of these, each gippa more delicious than the other. And she did it all on her own. She was one strong woman!"

"What are you sisters up to?" said Ruth, who had also noticed Zilfa's tears. "Come on, it's getting late. And why aren't we singing more on this happy occasion? "Yar mobarak bada, ensha-Allah mobarak bada," she began and others joined in.

The men working on the sheep put different parts of the meat in separate piles, each to be blended with various spices. With bulky wooden pestles, they mashed the rest in large stone mortars to make ground kabobs. Another group prepared the chickens, stuffing the larger ones with the same ingredients used for gippa and chopping the smaller ones to make chicken kabobs. Before dawn, the first lot of kaleh paacheh and the gippa was put on the tripods to cook on a low fire to be served next morning for breakfast.

These series of festivities continued for three days and three nights. Every morning would begin with friends and the family of the bride and the groom gathering at Ruben's house to enjoy the kaleh paacheh and gippa, followed by the preparation of lavish dishes, herbs and fruits for each day. They also ate and drunk and when darkness fell, this noisy working day gave way to calm and tranquility. Except for the burning wood crackling under the tripods and the barking of stray dogs, there was silence over the house of Ruben the Rhino — serene and peaceful in anticipation of the joyous event ahead.

Towards the end of October, the smoldering heat subsided and the sand storms ended. Jewbarites swept away the heavy dust that the blizzard had left behind in their houses and washed the dirt from the alleys in front of their houses. On a Tuesday morning of a beautiful day in the fall of 1836, when the air was fresh and the bright sun shone on the yellow leaves of fruit trees, the marriage ceremonies of Ruben the Rhino and Tuba the Woman began. Before sunrise, Jacob turned the lock to Ruben's house with the key he had kept from all the years he had lived there, and let himself in. He went directly to the pots on the tripods, tasted the kaleh paacheh and gippa, which would be served for breakfast, and *ghormeh sabzi* – Herbs and Vegetable Stew – for dinner, making sure that each one was well-cooked and spiced. Ruben, who had always been an early-riser, was the first one to wake up. Together, they spread a sofreh on the veranda and arranged the plates and the silverware. As Ruben rushed to Nachamia the Baker's shop to get the freshly baked bread, Jacob put red-hot charcoals in the large samovar's burner to make tea and placed baskets of fresh herbs and bowls of relishes on the sofreh. When the breakfast was ready to be served, Ruben began to sing the song his father used to sing to wake him: "Laziness bring sleep to your eye..." And he sang loudly as Naphtali had.

"Save some of that energy," yawned Uncle Asher who had slept over that night. "You'll need it later!"

Jacob laughed loudly and that woke up Ruth, who complained, "What's the hurry?"

In late morning hours, the guests, among them the Rabbi and the Mayor, began to arrive. Tuba and her mother would not attend the breakfast, since they were preparing for the afternoon event. They all sat around the sofreh – men on one side, women on the other. Jacob and Nissan brought the two large pots of gippa and ah pacheh up to the veranda and put them in a corner near the stair-case next to copper bowls in which they would be served. David the Butcher was the first to praise the food.

"I'm sure gippa has to be Manna God sent the Israelites to relish for forty years in the desert and never get tired of. Please, everybody!" David called. "Inhale the aroma of this heavenly food before you put it in your mouth." He brought up his bowl to his nose and closed his eyes as if sampling the fragrance of a perfume. "The appetizing smell of cumin seed, hand in hand with saffron and parsley and leek and," he raised his voice, "*my* fantastic meat!"

"Before you start writing another book about the kaleh paacheh," Rabbi Shimon remarked with the wave of his hands, "I wonder why we haven't said the blessing for the wine."

"And since today we have a lot to be thankful for," Mayor Haskell added, "Why don't we break a bottle or two of Joshua's homemade vodka?"

An hour later, Ruben and his uncle Asher were the only sober ones in the midst of this jubilant, intoxicated crowd. The rest of them chased Jacob, grabbed him and made him eat the kaleh pacheh he claimed he hated. They challenged Ruben to raise Asher's heavy teenage twins and swirl them around. "Of course he can't," the twins said in chorus and Ruben proved them wrong. Some bragged about their businesses, some about their children and then, one by one, they lay down next to the sofreh and passed out. When they woke up, the sofreh was gone and the veranda had been cleaned by Ruben and Asher, who served the intoxicated guests tea *and* a shot of vodka, as prescribed by David the Butcher. Now refreshed, they joined Ruben, to whom Ruth had relegated the preparation of kabobs for lunch.

And so, as the men were busy getting the lamb and chicken ready to make kabob for lunch, women in the kitchen struggled with the heavier task of putting together the ingredients for various stews, to have them ready to be cooked one or two a day for the next few days. They cooked different types of *khoresh* — stew. There was khoresh *fesenjan*. Turan the Turtle, Sara's sister, was famous for her expertise in cooking fesenjan and did she make a show of it!

"No, no!" she shouted at her daughter, Mahin the Frog. "Don't put the meat in yet. How many times do I have to tell you? We have to wait for the pomegranate juice and the ground walnut to boil and blend first. Then a touch of saffron, a little bit of…"

"Enough, enough!" Sharona, Uncle Asher's wife, roared, laughing. "As they say, '*They count the chickens after the eggs are hatched.*' Once you've tasted my khoresh *gheymeh*, you'll see for yourself how the lamb meat, fried potatoes and yellow split peas dance in front of your eyes to the music of the secret spices I have put in."

The Turtle took a deep breath to counter, but Zilfa pointed at her sister, Henna the Nightingale, who was busy cooking also and said, "No matter what you do, neither the fesenjan nor the gheymeh you are cooking can come anywhere near the *khoresh* ghormeh sabzi my sister is cooking. I mean, anybody can put lamb shank, kidney beans, chopped chives, coriander leaves and scallions in a pot and boil them together. What matters…"

"All right women!" Jacob said, waving his arms in the air. "You are all master cooks. At one time or another, each and every one of you has been the *ashpazbashi* of His Majesty's kitchen. Now, get on with your work."

"How can we, Jacob?" said Ruth, waving her arms in the air as though dancing. "How can we *not* mention my beloved cousin's *khoresh bademjan* and the taste of her eggplant stew?"

At dinner, all these stews, which were cooked with one or more spices such as saffron, turmeric and dried Persian lime, would be eaten with a variety of *polo*—steamed rice—some white, some blended with various vegetables, dried fruits or herbs. They washed different fresh herbs—red radishes, tarragon, sweet basil, spring onion, mint and sweet fennel—and placed them on large plates in tasteful arrangements. They prepared melons, cantaloupes, honeydews and all sorts of other fruits in season to be served as dessert.

As the family and friends of the bride and the groom did all this cumbersome work, they joked, laughed, sang folk songs that praised the beauty of the bride and listed the attributes of the groom. By the time kabobs were ready to be served with steamed rice for lunch, the men had gone back to drinking wine and vodka. On her way back from the veranda, Ruth went to the basement, brought up a bag to the kitchen and took out two bottles of 'Abram's Magic.' "We need to relax too!" she proclaimed. The women in the kitchen cheered and began drinking too, out of the sight of the men, for it was considered unbecoming for a woman to drink like men.

In addition to cooking and other preparations that had to be taken care of, each day was marked with a festivity. The first day, a "women only" event began in the early afternoon when the women of the Rhino's household handed the responsibilities of the kitchen to the men and left home. "Please be careful," they begged their drunken husbands. "Everything is cooked, ready and put on a low fire to keep warm. Just keep an eye out so that…"

"So that the cat won't get to it," said one man in a wine-laced voice.

"And the fire won't burn it," added another.

"And the daytime robbers won't attack it," said a third

Escorted by Nina the Singer, who accompanied herself on a

stringed instrument called *taar,* and Khatoon Donbaki, a bulky woman who played the Persian drum, *donbak,* the women of the groom's family paraded to the bride's house, singing and ululating all along the way. This day was set aside for ceremonies involving the grooming of the bride's eyebrows, for only on her wedding day was a girl allowed to have her eyebrows groomed and her excess facial hair plucked. This was definitely a "females only" party. The only man who was allowed to be present was the groom and he was confined to a separate room until he was no longer needed, at which time he was excused. On their arrival, the guests were taken to *panj-dari,* the guest room and the largest room in Tuba's small house. In the middle of panj-dari, Tuba sat cross-legged on a red silk cushion. The women surrounded her and began to clap their hands, singing along with Nina the Singer and Khatoon Donbaki. Facing Tuba, sat Mehri the Tweezers—whose job was grooming eyebrows and plucking excess facial hair—also cross-legged and ready to get to work. But before she started, Tuba's mother, Sara the Fox, moistened a gold coin, placed it on the middle of Tuba's forehead and pressed it hard. For as long as the coin stayed on her forehead, the women counted seconds: one, two, three… To make the coin stay longer, Mehri the Tweezers cheated. She put her hand under Tuba's chin, pushing her face up. When the counting passed the sacred number of twenty-six, representing God's name in Hebrew numerology, the excitement of the guests peaked, Nina relaxed her hand, the coin dropped. Sara picked up the coin and put it in Tuba's palm. This would be the lucky coin that she would keep and use for the same purpose for her first daughter's wedding.

Mehri ululated loudly and got to work. First she took a thread and tied both ends together. Then she double-folded the thread, making a triangle out of it by wrapping it around her thumbs on two corners of the triangle and holding the third corner between her protruded front teeth. Then she bent forward, placed one layer of the thread in between the bride's eyebrows and, moving the second layer, plucked the first hair. "Ouch!" shrieked Tuba and all of a sudden the women broke out and sang.

Eyebrows curved like a bow
Lashes long, each like an arrow
Take an arrow and put it in the bow
Aim at the groom's heart and let it go

Then came the comments. "You call this pain? … Wait till you give birth! … And not only to one, but God willing to twelve sons…

"And when the Rhino breaks her virginity," Zoli the Midwife whispered in Badri the Seamstress's ear.

Mehri then took the first plucked hair, put it on a sugar cube and gave it to the bride's mother, who then carefully wrapped the sugar cube and the hair in a silk handkerchief and brought it to the room where Ruben was waiting in solitude.

"You've caged me here for such a long time, just to give me a hair, mother-in-law?" Ruben laughed. "What sort of a silly tradition is this?"

"But this is only one of many signs that your bride's virginity is still intact." She handed him the handkerchief and continued, "You should take this with pride and dignity, and as you know…"

Ruben regretted having had this conversation with Sara, for she went on lecturing him about the virtues of virginity as though this "virtue" was her own.

"I wonder," Ruben interrupted her, "if you have ever heard of this old saying: You can't fly with borrowed wings."

"Meaning?"

Ruben waved the handkerchief in front of her eyes and said, "Meaning… You are right. Now, if you excuse me, I'm leaving. After all, this is the only reason why I was kept here. So, I'm going home to help and you, Sara khanom, now go back in there and enjoy yourself."

Sara returned just when Mehri was attacking the bride's face, bobbing her head back and forth like a chicken, plucking her eyebrows and facial hair. And when she was finished with her work, like an explorer announcing something newly discovered, she exclaimed in her shrill voice, "Look at this face!" holding Tuba's chin up and tracing her eyebrows with her finger. "It's as if the clouds have melted and the shining sun has come out."

The guests carefully examined Tuba's features, complimenting Mehri on her work and the bride on her beauty. Except for what remained of her eyebrows, there was not one extra hair left anywhere on her hot and inflamed face. Relieved that the plucking ceremony was finally over, Tuba was looking forward to being able to sit back and enjoy the presentation of her meager dowry and the gifts from the guests.

"From the hard earned monies of selling fish," Sara sang to the accompaniment of musicians, "We have brought this beautiful bride a valuable present!"

"And what have you brought her?" the crowd countered.

"We have brought her this *toureh naghdeh* that my mother of blessed memory gave me at my wedding." Sara held up an old white silk scarf handcrafted with gold threads, and then she placed it over Tuba's head.

"May she wear it on many, many happy occasions!" responded the guests.

There was a musical interlude followed by singing and dancing before the next article was presented.

"We have more and we are bringing more," said Ruth, taking a turn.

"What have you brought this beautiful rose, your son's bride?" sang the crowd.

"From the hard earned monies of tailoring," Ruth recited, "I have brought her this beautiful tablecloth, embroidered by not one, but many masters of the craft and sanctified by my father and mother, may they rest in peace. She will keep it clean and fresh and God willing she will give it in happiness to the bride of her own son!"

"Amen," the crowd answered, singing and dancing.

"From the hard earned monies of selling fish," Sara chanted, presenting the rest of Tuba's dowry item by item, followed by the cheers of the guests, "We have brought this bride this silver necklace... This wine decanter... This embroidered bag for prayer books... This quilt..."

Then the guests presented their gifts.

"We have more and we are bringing more," sang Zilfa, Nissan the Fabricseller's wife. "From the hard earned money of selling fabrics, I have brought this beautiful bride of Ruben, my husband's best friend, two pieces of hand-woven silk cloth, red and blue, with elegant paisley designs." Zilfa walked around and showed off her presents.

"We have more and we are bringing more," sang Talat the Seamstress, the wife of Shokri Adasi, dancing and imitating the way Shokri stirred a pot of *adasi* – lentil soup. "I have brought this couple, groom the king and bride the queen, one bag of rice and a vessel of cooking oil."

"We have more and we are bringing more," cried Wartfaced Monir, the wife of Saleh the Carpenter. "From the hard earned monies of carpentry," she chanted, dancing as if she were working with a saw, pushing and pulling her body back and forth, "I have brought our gorgeous bride this especially handmade stool. A stool for the kitchen, so that when she's cooking for her beloved husband, she won't have to stand up and tire her beautiful legs."

"We have more and we are bringing more. From the hard earned monies of selling meat," sang Morvarid, David the Butcher's wife, imitating the way her husband would slam a cleaver on his butcher board, cut the meat and put it on the scale. "We have brought our soft-skinned bride this set of knives, specially ordered and masterfully sharpened by my husband."

This ceremony went on until late in the afternoon and as the guests took their leave, they were reminded that they were invited back with their families to Ruben's house later that evening for more festivities. "Who has the strength for more celebrations in one day?" a woman asked. "It's a happy occasion and the Almighty *will* provide each of us with sufficient energy to celebrate His blessings until dawn if need be," responded Tavous, Mayor Haskell's wife.

And when night fell, after the guests had gathered and feasted on the food and wine served at Ruben's home, and had sung along with David the Butcher and his band, Rabbi Shimon performed solemn and festive officiating ceremonies, after which Ruben and Tuba were officially engaged to be married — but not yet married — for, at the end of this gathering, as the guests left, Tuba also went back home with her parents.

On the second day, which was a Wednesday, the ceremony was centered on the bathing of the bride and the groom. Since the Jews were considered najes and not permitted to use Muslim bathhouses, they were confined to the only bathhouse in Jewbareh. It was a large, enclosed, heated room with two reservoirs of hot and cold water. On weekdays, men had the bath to themselves from four till nine o'clock in the morning, at which time the women took it over until late afternoon. Ruben's bathing ceremonies started before daybreak. The men of the two immediate families and the wedding party guests gathered at Ruben's house and accompanied him to the bathhouse as David the Butcher and his band sang and danced alongside the groom and the escorting guests. Every few steps, the musicians stopped and sang a folksong specific to the occasion.

I'll build you a bathhouse, one of those
With forty pillars and forty windows
For dignified men, tilted their hats, young or old
Covered from head to toe with jewelry and gold

Jacob, who was walking side by side with Ruben, noticed the Jewbarites lined up along the route and cheering. He saw mothers who after glancing at the groom raised their heads to the skies and wished the same ceremonies for their own sons. He noticed younger women he knew who, having had had their eyes on Ruben for themselves, sighed and passed by. There were children who had come to gather the pieces of candy that the groom's entourage had showered on him for good luck. And finally, Jacob saw the uninvited, very poor men who followed Ruben, hoping for a free wash.

On arriving at the bathhouse, the musicians put aside their instruments and joined the rest of the men in undressing and covering themselves waist-down with loincloths. Isaiah the Exfoliator, the most senior worker in the bathhouse, scrubbed and pounded Ruben's skin with *kiseh* — a rough woolen glove — washed him head to toe and except for his face and head, he applied depilatory paste to every hairy part of his body. After Isaiah was done, Ruben looked down at himself.

"In the name of Moses, what did you do to me?"

"You look like a soft marble statue," Jacob roared with laughter.

"I'm not done yet, kadkhoda," said the Exfoliator. "Just sit back and let me complete my work."

As a finishing touch, Isaiah applied henna to the groom's hair and beard, the palms of his hands and the soles of his feet. Waiting for the color to take effect, everyone relaxed as they were served a mix of sherbet while the musicians sang.

Our groom is applying henna
To his hand and to his sole
The henna as colorful as his love
As the fire of love in his heart, in his soul

When the bathing ceremonies were over, the men dressed and returned to the alleys, again singing and dancing as they delivered the groom back to his home. Now Sara, Ruth and her friends and family left for the Fishmonger's house, to take Tuba for her bathing turn. From here, women of both families accompanied by Nina the

Singer and Khatoon Donbaki, headed for the public bath. Here, Tuti the Exfoliator applied depilatory paste to Tuba's pubic area, legs and armpits. She then applied henna to her hair, the palms of her hands and the soles of her feet while Nina the Singer and other women present sang the famous song of "Forty Pillars, Forty Windows." Finally, they soaked Tuba in the chilled water of the mikveh.

As they accompanied the bride back to her house, women who would otherwise have been embarrassed to sing in the presence of strangers joined in with the musicians.

Our alleys are narrow? They are, oh yes!
Our bride is gorgeous? She is, oh yes!
Don't touch her lovely hair
Ornamented with pearl straps – a pair.

When the bride and her entourage were passing by Ruben's house, the men guests came out to the alley and clapped their hands to the music and songs of the women. Here Ruth told Tuba's mother that she was going home to help make preparations for the next day.

"No," said Sara assertively. "You can't because it's a bad omen. We're only a few alleys away from our house. You have to see your son's bride home, or…"

"Or what?" Ruth shouted so loudly that everyone froze. "You've played enough tricks on us. Where, in the name of all the sacred messengers of God, is it written that it would be a bad omen if I didn't follow you to your miserable house?"

Tuba rushed to her mother's side, tugging her sleeve and pleading, "Mani. Please."

But her outraged mother was not about to stop. She pushed her daughter aside and yelled, "We tricked *you* or was it *your* son who… Don't make me open my mouth, Ruth!"

Ruben jumped and stood in front of his mother. "What happened? Please keep calm, Mani!"

"No," Ruth pushed the Rhino aside. "If I don't respond to this woman, I will explode. I've had it with her up to here," she said, pointing to her throat. Then to Sara, "My son who *what*? Whom you and your daughter deceived? Is that what you want to say or do you want to admit that he killed, and he killed a Muslim, to save your husband's life at the cost of two years of wandering the world. And if Ruben did what you claim he did to your daughter, you grabbed him and stuck your daughter up his…"

There was a sudden tumult. "Oh my God! Tuba just fainted." Gohar, the bride's best friend, shrieked.

Ruben cut into the crowd and went to Tuba's side. "Please get me a glass of water," he asked Tavous, the mayor's wife.

Asher grabbed his sister by the arm and whispered in her ear, "We must save face. Do you know what you're doing?"

"I don't care. I want everybody to know that in this rush to the wedding, they have gotten away with avoiding all the expenses of the engagement ceremonies, which should be *their* responsibility. What is their contribution to their daughter's wedding? A tiny basket of worm-like fish and a piece of old fabric!"

"Mother!" Ruben protested as he helped Tuba drink from the glass of water Tavous had brought. But Tuba was crying so hard, she couldn't drink.

"Take care of your bride," said Asher to Ruben, and then whispered to his sister, "Look now. You're giving Ruben a heart attack. I said, stop it."

Although Ruth fell silent, it was Sara's turn to holler. "Your son has disgraced my innocent daughter, and now you're trying to take the upper hand?"

At this, Abe the Fishmonger jumped in and yelled at Ruth as he waved his hands in the air: "The least I should have done to buy my integrity back was to kill your son! But this woman of mine," he pointed at Sara, "stopped me."

Ruth laughed frantically. "You? You little thing? My son can twist you into a thin string." Then she suddenly stopped laughing and hollered, "You ungrateful fish. You wanted to kill the one who killed another to save your miserable life?"

Tuba began screaming hysterically. Asher grasped the Fishmonger by the back of his coat and his wife by her arm, and persuaded them to move on.

"Don't worry," the Rhino whispered in his bride's ear. "I will take care of everything." His hazel eyes and his tender look calmed Tuba. She nodded, tears streaming down her face. "I trust you," she whispered as she walked toward her house. Now Ruben grabbed his stunned mother and carried her out of the crowd into their house. "What has happened to you?" he asked once he closed the door behind them. "If you didn't approve of her from the beginning, why did you wait so long? Now you have made a spectacle of yourself!"

Ruth threw herself into Ruben's arms and cried. It took every bit of patience and forbearance as well as the diplomacy of a real kadkhoda to quiet his mother's distraught nerves.

The next day, a Thursday, was the appointed wedding day. After the previous day's quarrel, Asher and Ruben had spent a long time talking to Ruth, again calming her down and cheering her up until she relented and became absorbed again in helping with the remaining part of her son's wedding ceremonies. Ruben, who had been worrying the whole time about Tuba, was finally able to slip away to Abe and Sara's house. Half-warningly and half-jokingly, he persuaded them to keep calm. Finally, before heading back home, he spoke to his bride and reassured her that the wedding ceremonies were going to be carried out as planned.

Throughout the day, family and friends arrived in groups, went to the kitchen to lend a hand and then joined other guests to eat, drink and sing folksongs to the accompaniment of the musicians. Toward the end of the day, all the groom's friends and relatives together with the musicians gathered at Ruben's house and, as tradition required, they left together to fetch the bride at her house and escort her *to her destined home.*

Meanwhile, since the previous day's clash between the two mothers, the mood in the bride's house had been tense. Tuba was frightened that, despite his promises yesterday, Ruben might change his mind, and so were her parents, though they made an effort to appear calm. With the help of family and friends, Sara the Fox had been working the whole day preparing the bride. They painted Tuba's cheeks red with *sorkhab,* rouge made of rosebuds, and to her lashes applied *sormeh,* a black mix of ground silver-sulfate and almond oil, but the flow of her tears smeared their work.

"Wasn't Ruben here today and didn't he tell you that everything is all right?" Sara shouted at her daughter. "What is the problem with you?"

"I'm running out of patience with you, Sara!" complained her cousin, Talat the Seamstress, who had been sitting down, facing Tuba, and working on her makeup for a long time without luck. "If Ruth didn't want to come here yesterday, why did you have to make such a fuss about it and put this poor soul through such an ordeal?"

As Sara remained silent, Talat put her hand under Tuba's chin, raised her head, kissed her on the cheek and said, "Trust me, my dear. You'll get married without further commotion. So, don't cry and let me finish my work. We don't have too much time left before your groom and his crowd show up."

With Tuba now calm, Talat the Seamstress dressed her in a long white gown she had sewn her, ornamented with a strand of small pearls stitched around the collar and silver coins around the waistline. The seamstress then gave the last touches to the dress to make it look flawless. The women covered the bride's head with the gold woven scarf Sara had given her as a wedding gift. They put *golab*, fragrant rose water, on her neck, arms and hands.

Now Sara took Tuba to her room and kissed her. "You're so beautiful, my daughter." Then her tone became remorseful. "I'm so sorry for what I did yesterday." And as Tuba was beginning to feel relaxed, once again the Fox brought up the subject of the virginity napkins. "They're already under your pillow on the wedding bed at Ruben's house," she said.

"I know, Mani. I know. You've told me about this a hundred times. I swear I know. Please don't talk about it again, I beg you."

Sara ignored Tuba's pleas. "You have to make sure to place them under your buttocks before the groom enters you so that the napkins will be stained with blood upon the loss of your virginity, especially with all the rumors..."

Realizing that her mother was not about to shut up, Tuba stormed out of the room where, luckily, her friend, Gohar, was waiting for her.

Meanwhile, the guests on the bride's side started coming into Abe the Fishmonger's house. "What a moonlike face," they said, praising Tuba's beauty. "May her fortune be white and may she have many healthy sons." Still, no compliment of any kind diminished Tuba's concern about yesterday's quarrel between her mother and Ruth. What if Ruben's mother had enough influence on her son to call the marriage off? After all, considering the way she had attacked her mother, Tuba thought, she was capable of doing anything. And would Ruben give in if she directed him to do so? As it began to get darker, Tuba's anxiety escalated. Now, along with her parents and their guests, she quietly stared at the entrance at the other end of the courtyard, in anticipation of Ruben's arrival. The time stretched out and Tuba watched the guests looking apprehensively at each other. She turned to her parents. Their mouths were silent but their eyes betrayed their worry.

"So, where are they?" finally said her father, as he ran his hand across his face. "They were supposed to be here before dark?"

"But it is not dark yet," said Sara, glaring at her husband and raising her eyebrows.

Tuba saw her father's distress and forced her nails into her skin. It seemed to her that the worst of her fears was coming true.

"Yes. It's not dark yet," said Turan the Turtle, putting her arm on Tuba's shoulder and smiling a fake smile.

"You shouldn't have raised a fuss about Ruth's wanting to go home yesterday," Abe whispered to his wife.

"All I said was that..."

"You don't have to tell me. I was there, I heard you and I repeat. You shouldn't have done what you did."

"Leave me alone!" Sara said loudly and all the heads turned towards them, but nobody said anything. The curious silence continued until, just when Tuba thought that she would collapse, someone shouted: "They're here!" There was a short pause, and then a joyous uproar: "Open the door! Open the door!" And as they did so, David the Butcher and his band, followed by the groom and his guests, entered singing:

Here we are, here all right
To pick this flower who's cotton white

After Sara hurriedly refreshed Tuba's makeup, which had again been smeared by her hidden tears, her sister, Turan the Turtle took the bride's hand and walked her to the door, at the same time motioning the bride's family and guests to accompany her in singing the traditional response:

I won't go, I won't go. I'll stay where up I grew
My dad's home is better, better than anywhere new
In my father's home I live in comfort and peace
A comfort and pampering that will never cease

Tuba, who was gradually recovering from the almost continuous shock that she had been experiencing since the day before, now began to relax. Noting this response, the bride's crowd enjoyed the traditional "mock" negotiation. Turan demanded a "worthwhile" present to be given by the groom to the bride before she gave her consent to leave her father's home. On behalf of the groom, Nissan offered a gold coin.

"A gold coin?" Turan exclaimed. "How dare you think that my sister would exchange this precious diamond of a girl for a gold coin?"

The musicians sang and the crowd, both on the bride's and the groom's side, sang along.

"I won't go, I won't go. I will stay where up I grew. My dad's home is better..."

Ruben was pleased to hear Ruth's singing voice loud and cheerful. Obviously, his and his uncle's pleas to ease her tense mood had worked.

Nissan pointed at Ruben and asked Tuba, "You see this *oversized* gold bullion?" The crowd laughed loudly.

Ruben blushed and looked down. "Shut up and let's have this over with, Nissan!" he whispered under his breath as people were laughing and singing.

"Tonight is the night!" Nissan whispered back as he laughed loudly.

Ruben shook his head in frustration, but before he was able to say anything, Nissan cried, "Hush! Fine. We will raise our offer to two gold coins. How's that?"

Again the musicians and the whole crowd sang, *"I won't go, I won't go..."*

Ruben had no choice but to wait until the end of this fake traditional transaction where in reality no gold coin or even two were exchanged. At the end, Ruth took Ruben's hand and had him stand next to his bride. The families and guests of the bride and the groom crowded behind the couple and the procession in which Tuba was to be taken to her new home finally began. From Abe and Sara's house at the bottom end of the Alley of Eleven Twists, the couple walked to the late Naphtali and Ruth's house on the turn of the third alley, with the musicians leading the way.

Walking side by side, Tuba and Ruben saw their reflection in a large mirror—symbolic of a future life bright with happiness—held by two strong men, one on each side, who walked backwards, turning their heads every now and then to make sure the path was clear. In the mirror, Tuba saw Ruben in his beautifully sewn wedding suit. She noticed that her husband-to-be was taller than she by exactly two heads and necks, and she liked it. For the first time she spotted his dark brown freckles, which matched the color of his hair, and she found that attractive too. She saw his wide, masculine shoulders and his gentle and reassuring looks and she felt her heart caressed by soft peacock feathers. Tuba was confident that she loved this man in the mirror. And when she realized that he was staring back, examining her from her toes to her hair, she lowered her head to conceal her excitement.

When they arrived at Ruben's house, the whole crowd was singing and dancing so enthusiastically that Ruth had to wait a long time before she asked them to sit down, enjoy the dinner as they listened to Jewbarite musicians David the Butcher, Nina the Singer and Khatoon Donbaki perform as a woman from outside Jewbareh, Robabeh the Raghas, danced to their music. Pillows for the guests were set alongside the walls of the panj-dari and the veranda. In front of these pillows, many long, colorful sofrehs had been laid, and on each sofreh the best of the wine, food, fresh herbs, and fruits were arranged.

The guests started eating and drinking, the musicians played jovial songs and Robabeh performed vigorously. She whirled and her skirt opened like an umbrella, revealing long slender legs with strong muscles running up to her underpants. This excited the men who shouted as they drank wine and vodka, toasting each other's health, wealth and the marble of the dancer's legs as their embarrassed wives turned their faces away, pretending they hadn't noticed their husbands' bawdy carousing. But eventually a brawl broke out between Joshua the Aragh-Kesh who became emboldened and called to his wife, Pari the Clothwasher, asking her opinion about the dancer's legs.

"Despite your cooing, Joshua, you'll come back to your pigeonhole at the day's end," Pari sniggered as she walked away.

"Don't turn your face Pari khanom! I asked you a question and as my wife you are going to answer," Joshua insisted in an intoxicated voice.

Pari turned around, pointed at the middle part of her husband and said, "Plough your own land — of course if you can!"

Now Pari had emboldened other women, who joined her by mocking their husbands. Then Wartfaced Monir pointed her finger at her husband Saleh the Carpenter and said, "For your wives you have no appetite, but for other women you're starving!"

Talat the Seamstress added, "Feast your greedy eyes till they pop out!"

Rana the Coyote said, "As the saying goes, 'How can it rain when there are no clouds?'"

The bride, the groom and their guests all laughed, the dancer danced, the musicians played and the few intoxicated men, who would have ordinarily punished their wives for their sassiness, just shrugged it off and kept on drinking. The feast went on until late at night when Rabbi Shimon ordered the *chuppah* to be set up where the bride and the groom would stand and the rabbi would perform the wedding itself. The chuppah was simply the *talit* — prayer shawl — that Naphtali had inherited from his father and was now Ruben's. It was held from its four corners by four eligible bachelors who stood on stools to accommodate the Rhino's height. Then the rabbi called the bride and the groom to stand under the chuppah and began to perform the traditional rites — universal in the Jewish world except that, here in this small ghetto, as the rabbi was trying to perform the ceremonies, men and women kept on interrupting him. Each time he finished reciting a line of the prescribed prayers, and before he had a chance to start the next, the men sang folk songs they had sang for as long as any Jewbarite could remember as the women ululated along with them.

You've become the groom
Let His blessings be with you
So that you'll be the head and the patron
Of the tribes of Israel

Standing next to the Rhino, Tuba was nervous. Thinking of this enormous man throwing himself on her when the rabbi had finished and they would finally go to their *hejleh*, their wedding room, scared her. Noticing Tuba's obvious anxiety, Ruben whispered in his bride's ear, "You're so beautiful." Tuba smiled and to hide her blush she bent her head. What Tuba didn't know was that the Rhino, also a virgin, was equally nervous, for almost all the men of Jewbareh remained virgin until they got married. Uncle Asher knew this from experience for he too had never been with a woman until he was married. Bizarre and embarrassing was the only thing he said to a friend about his own wedding night and he soon regretted the slip of the tongue. Although he spoke no more about this, many ingeniously funny stories — a craft mastered by Jewbarites — had begun to sprout up around the subject of Uncle Asher's wedding night. That was why, only two weeks before the

Rhino's wedding, Uncle Asher took Ruben for a walk and lectured him on how *not to mess up* this most important night of his life. "Sharona was only fourteen," he said, beginning to tell Ruben the story of his wedding night. "I was eighteen. We both had a vague idea about what we were supposed to be doing, but to tell the truth we really were ignorant about these things. To make a long story short, your aunt wept like a baby and I shivered like I had a life-threatening ailment... What the hell are you laughing at? Anyway..." Asher went on telling his nephew as clearly as he could how to take his bride's virginity. Ruben wasn't surprised at the details, but the thought of actually following his uncle's instructions filled him with trepidation about his potency as well as worry that he would actually have to inflict pain on his bride. After the bride and the groom said their vows, the guests left and the rabbi gave Tuba's hand to the Ruben and sent them into their hejleh.

The following morning, Sara carried her daughter's blood-stained "virginity napkins" into the Meat Market Alley. Tucking them discreetly under her chador, she showed them to the women there who examined them carefully. After all, the rumors surrounding this marriage merited such close examination. They looked at the evidence and shook their heads sideways, meaning approval and appreciation. They congratulated Sara for being such a protective and caring mother. "Your daughter made you proud," they told her. "She saved your family's face. May she have twelve healthy and handsome sons."

But these women were not about to let go of a topic as hot for gossip as fake virginity. So, as soon as Sara left, whispers began.

"There's plenty of blood in a fresh liver or in a chicken. Who knows...?"

Gohar, who was at the Meat Market Ally with her mother, Talat the Seamstress, heard about the infamous napkins and was curious to know what had happened to her best friend the night before. After she got her mother's permission to visit Tuba, she rushed to Ruben's house.

"Tell me, tell me! What happened last night? But before that, why were you so shy at the wedding? I mean you blushed so much that at one point I thought they shouldn't have applied sorkhab to your cheeks. And the man you were standing next to—he looked so handsome in his wedding outfit. I mean, sitting behind his work table in his shop is one thing and standing there next to my beautiful friend, saying his vows and..."

As long as Gohar didn't shut up, Tuba was happy because she knew why her curious friend had come there. However, half an hour later, out it came. "Did it hurt? Did you bleed a lot? I saw those napkins your mother brought with her. My goodness, they were bloody. Tell me!"

"He was very gentle," was all Tuba had to say.

"Gentle? That rhino of a man? How did you handle his weight? Don't you want to tell me?"

"My dear," Tuba held her friend's hand, "I'm not keeping anything from you. Honestly, I don't remember much of what happened. All I can tell you is that first I felt pain and then I felt pleasure. I don't know how else to put it."

"I don't believe you," Gohar said laughingly. "You've already forgotten?"

"No I haven't. I think it was something that happened, and it's over and... Please don't look at me that way. All right. I give you my word. When I remember, I will share all the details with you."

Gohar was not upset. In fact she was happy for her friend. But when she left Tuba, she too suspected what the women at the Meat Market Alley had speculated upon. That on that moonlit night, near Abe's house, when Ruben had embraced Tuba, perhaps, there and then... Who knows? But upon reflection, she said to herself, who cares? What difference does it make?

Although Ruben the Rhino married Tuba the Woman in the late fall of 1836, the indelible skepticism regarding Tuba's true virginity lasted for many years to come, for the superstitious Jewbarites believed in and dreaded the phantom of this frightful thought that sooner or later, doom would follow and that the newlyweds would be punished for this unforgivable and disgraceful sin.

Chapter 13
Her Master's Wife

Ruben and Tuba were too happy together to be troubled by the gossip that continued to circulate about them. Ruth who lived with them, was especially happy for her son. She noticed a big change in Ruben's behavior. For the first time in a long while, the young man was in high spirits, looking forward to having a family of his own.

No longer a bachelor, Ruben had stopped being the target of mothers with eligible daughters. As a result, the number of complaints about David the Butcher dwindled and so did Jacob's "catches," as he called their new customers. But even as the number of tailoring jobs slowed down, Ruben's winemaking business soared. Over time, the reputation of "Abram's Magic" had spread so far that demand was continually on the rise. The bulk of the orders came from the governor of Esfahan's mansion and rumor had it that most of these orders were shipped to the capital and ended up in the palace of His Majesty Mohammad Shah Qajar. Although Ruben considered the prosperity of his wine business a blessing resulting from his marriage to Tuba, in reality it was her hard work and also her marketing insight that helped the business grow. Majid, a friend of Tuba's father, was a famous glassblower whose workshop was in a village near Jewbareh. "It's as if he blows his own belly when he puffs into the melting glass," Abe told Tuba of Majid on their way there, where Tuba ordered bottles that she herself designed. She sat down with Majid—a short and plump man who laughed at whatever he said or heard—and watched Tuba carefully as she drew the designs of the bottles and explained them to the young man. "Your daughter is so talented," Majid said to Abe. The bottles she wanted were large and made of clear glass with colorful floral designs. They were at least six times the size of a regular bottle and vaguely in the shape of a woman's body. Her idea, she had told her husband only, was that gradually, as a bottle of the wine was emptied, it was as if a woman were taking her clothes off—a trick to lure her customers to drink more and more. Not only the unusually excellent quality of Abram's Magic, but these uniquely designed bottles appealed to the wealthy. "Let's get rid of the cheap customers and go to the rich," she suggested and Ruben approved. And that's how, thanks to Tuba's ingenuity, their wine business boomed and Ruben's love for his wife escalated as time went by and he discovered her hidden talents.

But besides all of these, Tuba had a much more serious task ahead of her. She had to make children—many sons for Ruben. Ruth and Sara were the first to prod them to start a family and then their friends and relatives joined in. Tuba and Ruben reported to their respective mothers that they were trying to have a baby, and the couple's parents all waited for the newlyweds to present them with grandchildren. But as time went by they became impatient and began to show their concern. Ruth told her sisters-in-law, Manzal and Sharona, that she suspected that Tuba was barren and Sara wondered out loud to her husband whether Ruben was able to make children. Those small and private conversations eventually started spreading throughout Jewbareh and soon people began giving unsolicited advice and suggestions. The strain of trying to conceive, as well as the constant nagging from their mothers and the community, began to wear on Ruben and Tuba. In fact it was harder on Tuba, for each time she went to the Meat Market Alley, she was faced with other women's perhaps sincere but taunting advice.

"Leave the wine business to your man and concentrate on making a baby," Talat the Seamstress, Sara's friend, said sympathetically. "I know you are trying, but don't give up. Anyway, be quick, because raising children is not easy at all and the older you get the harder it becomes."

Rana the Coyote, who had always envied the superiority of Ruben's wine to her husband's, Joshua the Aragh-Kesh's brew, would inevitably chime in, "Children are the lights and blessings of one's home. Like me, you must have many children. Graceful sons, God willing, in different sizes and shapes, and let your chicks chirrup around you."

"And when finally they grow up and become real people," Shifra the Hen would say, "They will be crutches for you in your old age. Who else would support you when you get old?"

"You know Isaac the Goat and his wife Pouran the Rose?" the Widefoot Marjon remarked. "They couldn't have children, and look at them now. They are both old and bedridden with no one to do so much as hand them a glass of water. Only Pouran's niece visits them now and then, and for this, may God give her good health and a good match…"

Mehri the Tweezers interrupted Marjon, "And why do you think Pouran's niece goes through the trouble?"

"I know, I know!" This was the Wartfaced Monir. "So people see her more and talk about her. Everybody knows that she's looking for a husband."

"That's right," said Marjon. "Poor girl. She is already over twenty."

And Badri the Petunia would conclude, "Tuba jaan. May God bless you with what He has blessed my son. Five sons and one *other* – a girl, you know – may she also be blessed with a good match and a breadwinner."

Then there was the infamous Nosrat the Lavender who for years had unsuccessfully tried to marry her daughter Batia to Ruben. Like a snake, Nosrat sat in ambush, waiting to launch her long-contemplated, deadly sting. "Not all women are fertile," she said, raising her brows and shaking her head. "It's how long now? Nine months you've been trying? *And* with no luck? I don't know!" She bit her finger in a sign of hopelessness.

Whether out of sympathy, like their best family friend the Seamstress, or out of animosity, like the Lavender, they were heedless of Tuba's apparent distress and their words wounded Tuba's heart. Only after they saw her tears did they keep their mouths shut. Tuba raised her head to look up at Ruben, up in his shop, sewing and pretending that he wasn't listening to this conversation.

A year passed and, as Tuba wasn't yet pregnant, her mother took her to every midwife in Esfahan. One examined her belly and guaranteed that she would become a mother in less than a year; the other checked her genitals and declared her perfectly fertile. But another year went by and Tuba remained childless. She became desolate, while Ruben said nothing. But Ruth wouldn't stop complaining, often to her sister Manzal, loud enough for Tuba to hear no matter where she was in the house.

"Zilfa, our neighbor," she said pointing at Nissan's house, "Has been popping out children, one after the next, since nine months after she got married—may God bless them all." Then she would beat her chest and cry, "And for my doomed child Ruben, not even one after three years."

Tuba knew that Ruben's silence was worse than a thousand cries and curses. He had married her in order to have a child. Many children. Male. For his seed to bear fruit. For his posterity to flourish. But now, three years into his marriage, he had none. Not even a female child. Her own motherly desire aside, Tuba's worst nightmare seemed to be coming true—that she had failed at what she had been raised to consider her natural duty. It didn't help when, seeing her misery, her husband said, "We will keep trying and God willing, we will have many children."

In the meantime, Ruben consulted his old friend, Hakim Akbar, who, although he was of course forbidden to touch women, prescribed a lotion made of linseed oil, balsam and catkin flowers to rub on her belly as well as a bitter potion that had a light aftertaste of ginger to it and was to be taken before sex. After Hakim Akbar's treatment failed, Sara took her daughter to Hakim Salem, another reputable holistic practitioner who traveled around Persia and visited Esfahan twice a year. Salem gave Tuba a green liquid of herbs. It made her sick, but not pregnant.

In the fourth year of her childlessness, Tuba and her mother visited the most famous witchdoctor in Sedeh, a village near Esfahan. Mortaz Naji's diagnosis was that she had been locked. So, he asked Tuba and Sara to sit in front of him—a large bowl of water between them. He held a big open lock in front of the two women's eyes, locked it, held it in his palms and, for a long while, whispered unintelligible incantations to the lock. Then, all of a sudden, he threw the lock into the bowl, crying, "Open and let her womb be unlocked!" Then he closed his eyes and recited more incantations. "Wait," he said in a low, otherworldly voice. "Wait and my powers will open it." He went on chanting and shaking his body back and forth for a while until all of sudden he dipped his hand into the bowl, took the lock out and showed it to Tuba and her mother. To their utter surprise, it was open.

So the lock had opened, but Tuba's womb didn't. The fifth year was the year of soothsayers. The notorious gypsy, Afsaneh the Miracle, read her palm, put her hands over Tuba's head and said strange things. "Oh you the evil spirit of Jamura, the daughter of Rakshavash the son of dogs of faraway jungles! Get out of her and burn in the deserts of Uravishi!"

Despite his unhappiness throughout the first three years of their marriage at Tuba's infertility, Ruben remained affectionate and supportive of his wife. He kissed away her tears, embraced her and reassured her that soon they would have a baby. "Guess who came to see me today?" he began, relating a story in the hope of relaxing Tuba's evident distress. "The Bearded Mordechai!" he said, answering his own question. "And what was his problem? His wife, Tuti the Exfoliator. 'I have waited *four* years,' he says, raising his palm showing four fingers. 'Four years and no child, Agha Kad-khoda!'"

Tuba reached for her husband's hand, gave him a smile of gratitude and said, "You don't have to..."

But Ruben cut her short. "I tried to pass him on to the rabbi, but Mordechai wouldn't relent. 'After all, you're our patriarch. You are our wise leader who has been to Jerusalem and has returned with a wealth of knowledge. Please tell me what to do?' Now I had to wear my rabbi's hat," Ruben said as he put his hand on Tuba's knee and caressed it gently. "'Be patient Mordechai,' I preached to the Exfoliator. 'God said to Abraham, whose wife Sarah was barren, *Your wife will have a son,* and when both of them were very old, Sarah gave birth to Isaac. So, have faith,' I said to him, 'but never, ever suspect His might. Sarah did and that angered God. Now, go my friend,' I said to Mordechai. 'Go, don't question your destiny and, God willing, your wishes will be granted.'"

Despite such rhetoric, Ruben admitted to himself that, even without children, he still loved Tuba. "What do I want a child for? Thank God, I have you, better than a rose. I have been blessed with a good job and a full table. If this is our destiny and it is God's will for us not to have children, so be it. Who am I to disobey Him?"

But Tuba wouldn't relent. She spent another three years recycling each and every practitioner, but all to no avail. Finally, Tuba and her mother sought a self-proclaimed healer who lived next to the palace of the governor of Esfahan and was known to be the spiritual advisor to the governor's many wives. The healer's sessions took place in Sara's presence. Like many others, he chanted and recited incantations, but they had to revisit him many times — each time for a fee, of course — until Sara raised objections to the man's procrastination. "It's your mother," the healer told Tuba. "It's her negative energy that comes between you and your unborn child," he declared. Half way through the first session alone with the healer, Tuba stormed out, cursing him. According to rumors, which began flying around at once, he had tried to impregnate her himself — and forcibly, too.

Eight years passed and Tuba remained childless. Now, the same women who defined children as "the lights and blessings of your home" and "the crutches for you in your old age," switched their tune. Invariably, this happened right in front of the Rhino's shop and was said loud enough for him to hear too.

"What do you need a child for? Children are nothing but headaches, believe me. As the old saying goes, 'A childless woman is a carefree queen.' God bless them and may they live one-hundred-and-twenty years, but look at me. I have so many sons and daughters, and what have they done for me? Nothing! I mean *not a thing*. And how about Abba the Quiltmaker? He has four sons. I wouldn't wish the wolves of the desert that man's fate! After his wife, the Pockmarked Taji, passed away, he became crippled. And now, old and spent like a candle, among many sons, daughters, grandchildren, daughters-in-law and great-grandchildren, there isn't even one, and I mean *not a single one*, who would give this poor disabled soul a hand. None of them cares. You feed them, you raise them, make sacrifices for them and when they grow up, you go through hell to marry them off, and as soon as they're gone, the sons go and hide between their wives' legs and the daughters disappear under their mothers-in-laws' skirts."

Throughout all these years that she had been barren, Tuba's hurt in not having a child was compounded by her feeling of guilt, for, in Jewbareh, it was an unstated rule that infertility was the woman's fault. And then, there were gradual changes that she noticed in Ruben's behavior. A few times when she had gone to the Meat Market, she had seen Ruben measure a child for a new dress and observed his transparent sadness. By now, not only Tuba but all their relatives, and indeed every Jewbarite, was noticing the gradual surfacing of the Rhino's latent agony about his fruitless marriage. He came to work grimfaced and unresponsive, even to those who sought his advice as their kadkhoda. "What's the matter, Ruben?" Jacob would ask his brother frequently. "Anything you want to share with me?"

Initially, a headshake was the Rhino's only response, but as his frustration escalated, he opened up to his brother. He talked about the pain he felt deep in his heart—that to him, Tuba was the one and only woman he loved and that he didn't want to hurt her, but that there were times when his desire for a child was so ardent that it went beyond the boundaries of his patience.

Eventually, one night as they were having dinner, compassion gave way to resentment; the sleeping volcano within Ruben began to erupt, his impatience overtook his self-restraint, empathy yielded to fury. "Is this Zain's revenge from the grave?" he shouted at Tuba. "Is it because I kissed you before we married? Wasn't God there?" And as she sat there, remaining silent, the Rhino roared, "I asked you a question. Wasn't God there?"

"Wasn't God where, Agha?" Tuba whispered.

"On that last turn of the Alley of Eleven Twists, the night I did no more than kiss you?"

"I don't know, Agha."

"It wasn't my sin and it wasn't your sin," Ruben blasted. "My mother is right. It was that bitch your mother, the monster who trained you to seduce me. That's right. You don't know how she toyed with my emotions. You think I didn't see her that night when I kissed you? You think I don't know the game she played with me to get me to marry her daughter? As it is written in Psalms, 'No one who practices deceit will dwell in my house; no one who speaks falsely will stand in my presence.' And now, I am the one who is being rejected because of *her* sin. I saved your father's life and this is how your mother rewarded me," he roared, pushing his plate away, getting up and slamming the door behind him.

Once again, Zain was back and once again Tuba cried into the silence.

From this point on, Ruben's behavior deteriorated even more toward Tuba and the rest of the world. It was as if the tormented Ruben that had disappeared after he had fallen in love with Tuba had come to life again—like a sleeping monster roused to fury. And no one around him knew how to help him or hinder him. Certainly

Ruth did not help, for she made her son's problem and her own frustration public knowledge throughout Jewbareh. She would arrive at the Meat Market looking gloomy, bemoaning her fate and cursing the stars. This was her way of enticing her audience to ask what was wrong with her.

"What's wrong with me?" she grunted. "After all, a man is a *man*. He is not born with a bag inside of him to bear babies. There's no such a thing as a barren man, is there? Of course not! Was there any reason for me to agree to my beloved son's marriage to this woman—who acted so disgracefully before she married and sullied our family name—other than to make Ruben and me children? No!" Having answered all her own questions, now she shrieked, "Am I right or not?" Her audience mumbled, Of course... Obviously... That's right... "Therefore," she asserted, "something has to be done to save my son's seed."

"Like what?" asked Zoli the Midwife naively.

"I don't know," Ruth hollered. "Ruben is my only son. He must have a son and he must name his son Naphtali after my late husband," she said, tears rolling down her face. "This barren, indecent woman has kept us waiting for eight years now. Eight!" she screeched, beating her chest.

"Keep it down, Ruth!" said Zoli as she pointed at Ruben's shop. "He can hear you."

That got Ruth going. "I don't care anymore," she screamed louder. "Let him hear me. I should have died in place of my husband. It's true what they say, 'The wise man died, what a loss, and his foolish wife survived him, what a shame.' Let me cry my sorrow!"

"Why are you shouting at us, Ruth?" Nosrat the Lavender retorted. "Instead, go talk to your daughter-in-law. Talk to her firmly and tell her that she must do whatever you have in mind when you say 'she has to do something about her inadequacy.'"

Hearing this, Ruben went to the back of his shop and stepped down into the basement. When he came back, David the Butcher's customers had gone and the alley was quiet. Jacob was the first to notice how shattered his brother looked. He poured two cups of tea and put them both on Ruben's table. "Have your tea. I want to talk to you about what Ruth did today, down there. Does she really want you to divorce Tuba?"

"I'm not in her head and I don't care. Leave me alone, Jacob."

Ruben's voice was flat.

"Do you love Tuba?" Jacob said bluntly.

"Do I love Tuba?" Ruben echoed his brother's question. "What the hell have I been doing for the last eight years spending all my life savings on her to get pregnant? Who else would do what I did?"

"Nobody denies that you are a caring and compassionate husband, but you didn't answer my question. Do you still love her?"

Ruben was not sure of the answer. There was so much frustration and disappointment between him and Tuba that the love he had always felt for her seemed to have taken refuge in a place he couldn't find. "The things that I have learned," Ruben said, sighing after a long pause, waving his head sideways. "All those things that I have learned, brother! *'Guard yourself in your spirit and do not break faith with the wife of your youth,'* says Malachi, the messenger of God. How can I disregard my marriage vows, which I have spoken in the presence of the Lord?"

Do you still love her, Jacob wanted to scream, but realizing Ruben's frustration, he held his hands together as if shaking hands with himself, bent his head and said, "I am talking to you as a brother. I recognize the pain you feel being childless. I realize Ruth's desire to witness Naphtali's rebirth from Tuba's womb but I'm sorry to say that I don't understand what is happening to you. What I also don't understand is Ruth's cruelty. She is the same woman who adopted me, mothered me and raised me as her own son, for which I am grateful both to her and your father of blessed memory. I want you to know that I love her as my mother. But I think she has too much influence on you and that she hates Tuba."

"So, all of a sudden, my wife's infertility is our mother's fault?" Ruben groaned.

"Don't be silly, Ruben. I didn't say anything of the kind. All I'm trying to tell you is that because Ruth is a nice person, it doesn't make her right in every respect. Take this morning. Watching her disparage poor Tuba in public for a natural flaw that's not her fault, bothers me and it obviously bothered you, because as she was screaming, you disappeared into the basement. Ruth has more than a dozen grand-children, boys and girls, whom, as I have seen, you love very much and they are all from Naphtali's seed. Not taking into account my two boys who are not of Naphtali's seed, Rachel's four children are all boys. Debra has two boys and two

199

girls and Mohtaram, the same. Kafi is pregnant with her third after three girls. If, God willing, her child is a boy, why not call him Naphtali. And once you have your own son, you can name him Naphtali-Abram, for example. Why don't you talk to your mother about this and ask her to calm down?"

"I'm leaving," the Rhino roared as he stood up to leave. "I can't take this anymore."

Jacob stood up, face to face with him, and, blocking his way, he put a finger on the big man's chest. "If need be, take Ruth to the rabbi and ask him to rid her of the evil that has poisoned her heart and mind," he said in a voice charged with a mix of rage, passion and love. "You are the *man* of this household and you should calm your mother."

Ruben charged out of the shop and Jacob returned to his own working table.

The next morning, after Ruben left home, as Tuba was washing the breakfast cups in the kitchen, Ruth stormed in, her face pale, her brows twitching and her lips jerking with strain. "My son wants a child!" she hollered.

Tuba turned her back to Ruth and began to choke. Suddenly nauseated, she ran out of the kitchen towards the bathroom with Ruth following her like a hawk chasing its prey. But Tuba's stomach was ahead of her. She kneeled down in front of the small flowerbed of petunias and vomited on her mother-in-law's favorite flowers. Ruth stood over her head, hands on hips and legs set apart. "Hah! If only this were morning sickness!"

This was the first time Ruth had openly confronted her daughter-in-law on the matter of her childlessness. Tuba wiped her mouth with the back of her hand and stood up, facing the mother of her husband. There was only one thing she wanted to do — to spit in her face and run away from this house. But instead, she went to her bedroom, slammed the door behind her, sat down on the ground and embraced her legs. Soon Ruth yanked the door open and walked in.

"You have been running away from the reality of your infertility for more than nine years now and where has it gotten us? Talk to me, damn it! You act as if it is my son and I who are at fault. As they say, 'Leave the one who owes you alone and soon he will act as if you owe him.' It is *you* who is barren. It is *you* who seduced my virtuous son. Yes, *you* attacked my innocent son in the dark of the night, something that no decent virgin girl would do. It was because of your father that Ruben's hands were covered with blood and he had to leave his home for so long."

Ruth's words cut into Tuba's heart like a serrated knife, but as if numb to the pain, she looked at her indifferently, and this frustrated Ruth even more. "Dark is my world," the older woman muttered. "What has my poor son done to deserve this?" Tuba kept looking past Ruth and beyond the misery in the room at the beautiful bright day. Passover was around the corner and spring on its way. The swallows that had again come back from faraway lands were busy setting up their nest under the ceiling of the veranda. Soon they would settle, lay eggs and before long their babies would chirp. The fragrance of Persian jasmines in the courtyard would fill the air. The pomegranate tree next to the kitchen had given birth to its young leaves and blossoms and the sturdy white-berry tree near the pond in the center of the courtyard would be covered with large green leaves. By the summer, white berries would ripen, birds and bees would feast upon the sweet juicy fruit, and then they would fly beyond the tops of the trees — freely, without husbands, without mothers-in-law for whom they were obliged to make children. Then she heard a change in Ruth's tone.

"By now my dear, we're all convinced that you cannot have children. This is what every one of the hakims, midwives, sooth-sayers, healers and God knows who else has told us. Waiting any longer for you to bear a child would be like trying to extract sugar from a bamboo stalk or water from a stone. My son," Ruth went on as Tuba remained silent, "could have raised many children with the money that he has already spent treating your barrenness. He doesn't say anything to you because he is a kind gentleman and a very good person, but let me share something with you," she said, lowering her voice as though there were eavesdroppers behind the walls. "There are times when he gets upset and, out of his frustration of course, he tells me he wants to get rid of you, but I know how to control him. After all, who is better able to know her son than the mother who has delivered and raised him? But what can I say? You have no children to know better."

Keep on stabbing me in the heart, Tuba thought. *You're blind and can't see that more than you, your son or anyone else, I, myself, want to mother a child.*

"Now be sensible," Ruth concluded, "and *do something* about this situation and do it fast."

"Do what?" Tuba finally spoke as she looked at her in despair.

Ruth sat next to Tuba and whispered something in her ear.

It happened on an evening following a hot afternoon in the summer of 1846, almost ten years after Ruben the Rhino married Tuba the Woman. Ruth was not home. She was staying with her daughter Kafi. She had just given birth to her fourth child, a boy who, for fear of Ruth's rage, was *not* named Naphtali. Ruben arrived home from visiting his sister after work and found Tuba wearing his favorite red dress. He climbed the steps to the veranda where he noticed that on the carpet there was a colorful sofreh with floral designs and many of his favorite delicacies and side dishes on it. There were pebbled pomegranates put in a silver bowl and green herbs—fresh basil, radish, spearmint, tarragon, leek, sweet fennel and spring onions. Also, on the sofreh, there were various soured and salted pickles. The arrangement was highlighted by the best of his brew of "Abram's Magic," which Ruben loved when it was served in a Russian crystal decanter that was the nicest piece of Tuba's meager dowry. As he stood over the tablecloth, his eyes fixed on its contents, Tuba stepped up the stairs from the other side of the veranda, carrying a bowl. Ruben saw his favorite dish, white fish stewed with sliced onion, coriander seeds and turmeric.

"Are we expecting His Majesty for dinner?" Ruben said, kicking off his shoes and sitting down. "I mean, what's going on here?"

"I'm not done yet," said Tuba coquettishly, yet with a dry throat as she laid the bowl down and returned to the kitchen. She came back with a dish of saffron flavored rice, placed it on the tablecloth and sat down next to Ruben.

"Tell me. What's all this about?" He put a handful of green herbs on a piece of thin *lavash* bread and tossed it into his mouth.

"Nothing special, Agha," Tuba said, managing a smile.

"Do you by any chance… I mean could it be…" He looked into her eyes, but Tuba quickly turned her head away.

"What's the matter, woman?"

Tuba knew that when Ruben was annoyed, he called her *woman* and not Tuba jaan as he usually did. "Nothing, I swear. Just the onion I put in this fish stew. It's still burning my eyes." She wiped her tears with a napkin she always carried in her sleeve. "Please, let's start."

After the dinner, Tuba moved closer to Ruben and took his hand. Then, as she opened her mouth to speak, she felt a sudden, breathtaking pain in her chest. "Ah!" she exhaled.

"What was that?" Ruben said, worried.

"Nothing. There's something I want to talk to you about and I don't know how to begin."

"It's easy. Just begin." Ruben's tone was indifferent.

"Until when do you want to wait for me to get pregnant? I mean…" She couldn't recognize her own voice. The tears that had been threatening to fall now began to pour down her face. How much Tuba would have loved to hear Ruben say what he used to say in the early years of their marriage, that with or without children, he was happy because he had Tuba. Tuba who was better than a rose. But he spoke differently. "We are back to *that* matter again? Leave it!"

"Agha Ruben," she said, and wiped the tears from the corners of her eyes. "What would you do if I told you that I have a solution?"

"A solution?"

Tuba's body began to shake as she said, "We know I can't have a child of my own womb. So, I have found you a wife."

"What?" Ruben exclaimed.

Tuba looked deep into her husband's eyes. Greenish brown? Brownish green? Hazel? What was the true color of his eyes, the mirrors of a man's heart? For all the years that she'd been childless, in the same way that she had never been able to determine the color of his eyes, Tuba had not been able to determine Ruben's emotions. Then she heard him whisper a Psalm recited at her wedding by Rabbi Shimon and repeated by the Rhino many times thereafter. "Blessed are all who fear the Lord, who walk in his ways. You will eat the fruit of your labor; blessings and prosperity will be yours. Your wife will be like a fruitful vine within your house; your sons will be like olive shoots around your table. Thus is the man blessed who fears the Lord. May the Lord bless you and may you live to see your children's children." And then, there was silence.

"Agha jaan," Tuba finally spoke in a muffled voice. "Please listen to me."

"Listen to what? To this utter nonsense?" the Rhino roared. "What do you mean you have found me a wife? *You* are my wife.

Are you out of your mind? As if dealing with one wife is not burdensome enough, now you… What the hell are you talking about? Who allowed you to even *think* of this idea?"

"Hush, my husband, hush my master!" she put her index finger on the tip of her nose. "You will marry her and make everybody happy. I have talked to her parents already," Tuba continued in the same breath, "and they are willing to give their daughter's hand to you in marriage."

Ruben leaned forward, bobbed his head and brought his face close to Tuba's. "You mean you have found yourself a *havoo* and decided on *my* behalf to marry me to this second wife whose name I don't even know?"

And Tuba the Woman saw the real color of Ruben's soul, for now he was talking about the logistics of his wife's idea, not its unacceptability. Now she knew that all her husband's objections were nothing but empty rhetoric. Tuba nodded. She had no more tears to shed.

"And you are suggesting that we bring this woman into this house and have her live with you and me?"

Tuba nodded again, a bitter smile lining the two sides of her mouth.

"You expect me, Ruben the Rhino, the kadkhoda of Jewbareh, to go around and tell people that my beloved wife has found herself a havoo whom she wants me to marry? Who else has a second wife in this godforsaken inferno of a ghetto? Won't the Jewbarites scorn me for setting a terrible example and laugh at you for getting yourself a havoo, if I do what you say?"

If I do what you say. That said it all. "No, Agha," Tuba sighed. "You will not be setting a forbidden example. As your mother Ruth khanom has said time and again, many Biblical men — Abraham, David, Jacob, Solomon and even Moses himself — married more than one wife."

"But I am no prophet, no king."

Stop pretending distress! Tuba thought. "Yes, Agha jaan," she said. "You're the kadkhoda — the ruler of the ghetto. And if the Jewbarites have elected you as their governor, then you are their king."

"And you are their damned queen," he bellowed. "And my second wife will be a concubine and a member of your harem… my harem… whatever!"

Now you're declaring your conviction, man! "And she will bear you children and that's all right with me," Tuba whispered.

Ruben got up and began to pace waving his arms in the air like an inept actor. "How can you speak such garbage?" He bawled and from then on, his voice turned into vague sound bites in Tuba's ears. "If ten sturdy men were to subdue me," he declared, "hold me down, point a sharp knife to my neck, and threaten to decapitate me unless I say yes to your stupid idea, I would still not do it. And let me tell you something else, Tuba," he added, pointing both his stiffened forefingers at her. "If any other woman dares to step into our life, I will break her legs, and I mean *both* of them!"

Ruben's second wife was named Jewel. Tuba made the match, asking Yohai the Shoemaker, Jewel's father, for his daughter's hand in marriage for her husband. The marriage passed with no need whatsoever for ten sturdy men to cut Ruben's throat and Jewel's legs remained unbroken. Concerning Jewel, if you asked any Jewbarite why no khastegar had ever knocked on Yohai's door to ask for his daughter's hand, he would give you plenty of reasons. First and foremost, Jewel came from an impoverished family. "They're so poor," they said, "that the earth is their mattress and the skies their quilt." Furthermore, Yohai the shoemaker was a Cohen — a direct descendant of Aaron, brother of Moses. The common belief was that marrying a girl from a Cohen family could have dire consequences. Besides, the girl's skin was so white, the type Jewbarites call *bi-namak* — unsalted — and her hair so red, again not a popular color with the people of the ghetto. They likened her to a snowman with a bleeding head. And of course she was thin and had no flesh on her bones. "You want to grab some meat when you touch a woman," men said. But worst of all, she was tall — taller than any other girl of the ghetto. And then, there was her age. Jewel was twenty-two years old and at twenty-two, she was considered way past the age of eligibility. In short, Jewel was one fully pickled girl, and with her chances of being saved from spinsterhood being virtually none, like a bunch of grapes gone sour, she had earned herself the name of Jewel the Vinegar.

Knowing that her mother-in-law would reject the idea of marrying her son to a spinster — for Ruth believed that she could provide Ruben with the youngest and the prettiest girl in the ghetto — Tuba had kept her choice of Jewel as her havoo-to-be from

Ruth until she had closed the deal with Jewel's parents. Then, the morning after she told Ruben that he was to have a second wife, Tuba went to her mother-in-law's room to give her the news she had desired for so many years. Ruth, who was sitting on her cushion, fanning herself, jumped up, crying, "Congratulations!" She embraced and kissed Tuba. "I knew it," she said. "I was sure you would come to your senses and agree to let me get my son another wife."

Tuba untied Ruth's arms, pushed her back gently and said, "I've already done that."

It was as if someone had pulled back the skin on Ruth's face. "What?" she screamed. "No! As a mother, I am the one who gets my son a wife, not you." And when Tuba told her that she had already asked for the hand of the daughter of the Shoemaker, Ruth simply went berserk.

"That soured, ugly ostrich? Of course you looked for a monkey like her. I'm ordering you, daughter-in-law! In the same way as you took this donkey to the roof, you'll bring it down yourself. Who the hell do you think *you* are to get my son a wife? I'm not dead. Trust me, I will find him a fourteen year old girl who, unlike you, can bear him..."

As Ruth continued speaking, her words, Barren for so many years... She's too old to have babies... Do you know how many girls would die to..., buzzed through Tuba's head and their vibrations crawled down to her chest, squeezing her heart as she watched Ruth's facial expressions change from unattractive to ugly to unbearably repulsive. Her incessant jabbering echoed with all the contemptuous words and acts she had hurled at Tuba ever since she had married Ruben. With every word Ruth said, all of Tuba's muscles tightened. And then Tuba raised her clenched fist and threw a vigorous punch at her mother-in-law. The blow landed on Ruth's temple and her neck twisted to the side and she screeched, staying in that pose a few long seconds. Then very slowly, she turned her face and, to Tuba's utter astonishment, smiled a creepy smile as her knees bent and she sat down on the ground. She opened her mouth in an obvious effort to talk, but only unintelligible sounds came out. Tuba sat facing her and peered into her eyes. They were not moving. She took Ruth by both shoulders and shook her. "Talk!" No reaction. "Don't play this stupid game on me!" Silence. "Ruth khanom, speak!" Her mother-in-law's mouth remained open and still. "Talk, you old donkey." Ruth was staring into nowhere. Tuba slapped her face—right, left, right. Ruth's head swung sideways at each blow.

Tuba stood up, looked down at her and left.

It was the last Tuesday of the month, the designated day for Ruben to take wine to Mullah Ahmad and spend some time with him at his private quarters. On the way there, in the twilight, Ruben was contemplating Tuba's plan to marry him to a second wife. He was puzzled by the whole idea. Obsessed as he was with having a child, he was well aware of the consequences of such a drastic decision, yet he couldn't help hoping that someone—someone with magical reasoning—would give him the courage to go ahead and marry Jewel. That was why he had consulted Rabbi Shimon just that day.

"Here is the problem, my son," the old rabbi had told him. "Truth be told, there's no religious prohibition against marrying a second wife, especially if the first wife cannot conceive. Sara, the wife of Abraham, for instance, was barren, and because of that, the father of our people was permitted by..." he said, turning his head skyward, "You know... to marry his second wife, Hagar. But he was Abraham of Canaan, not Kadkhoda Ruben of Jewbareh. Having said all I've said, I am warning you. If having no children is only one problem, having two wives living together under the same roof is a thousand and one problems."

When Ruben arrived at Mullah Ahmad's home, the first thing he heard from the Mullah was, "What's the matter, Rhino Jew? You look so bleak. You haven't killed another Muslim by any chance?"

"No, Hazrateh Agha, I haven't. But I do have a lot on my mind."

"So, sit down, let's have a drink of your magical wine and it will drive all your worries away."

Ruben complied. Ahmad took two cups, poured the wine and gave one to Ruben. "*Besalamati*—to your health," he said, raising his cup. Then he gulped it down, refilled his own and signaled Ruben to finish his—which he did—and poured some more for the Rhino.

"Now, talk to me," said the old cleric, as he put his cup down, threw a few pistachios in his mouth and offered some to Ruben. "Tell me. What is it that's bothering you? I hope you have not had another nightmare with what was his name? Zaal? No.

Zain!" Ahmad made that particular remark because there had hardly been a night when he and Ruben had drunk wine together and his wine-bearer hadn't voiced his exasperation at the recurring images of Zain.

"No, Hazrateh Agha. It's a family problem," Ruben said as he went on to tell him about what had been going on in his life and asked for guidance.

"You're asking a Muslim mullah who has four wives whether marrying a second wife is all right?" He laughed a hysterical laugh, then suddenly stopped and asked Ruben, "By the way, did I tell you? Last month these two villagers and their families came to see me. They were neighbors and had a dispute over the portion of the village's water each was entitled to. I resolved their dispute, but before they left I asked one of them, who had fathered this beautiful fourteen-year-old, if he would give his daughter's hand in sigheh to me. As they say: 'What does the blind man pray for? Two clear-sighted eyes, of course.' One less bread-eater at the poor peasant's table made him happy. Now, what was I saying? Ah! Yes. I have four wives and with this most recent addition, one concubine. About your problem, if you were a Muslim, considering that you're twice my size," he began laughing again, "I would recommend twice as many wives and concubines. And there is nothing like a fourteen-year-old to give you the vigor of youth again."

Noticing that his words had not comforted Ruben, Ahmad took a more serious tone and said, "You see, big Jew. In Islam a man is allowed up to four wives plus few sighehs, but only if he can support them and treat them equally. I know of many polygamist Jewish prophets. Quite honestly, you are a Jew and I'm not the right person to be asked such a question. What does your own mullah have to say about this?"

"That's the problem. You see, Your Holiness, you're right in that there are people with more than one wife in our Torah, but in our little ghetto, this is almost unprecedented. Our Mayor talks about someone who many decades ago married two wives in some other ghetto, but what he says is more like a fable than a real story. I did speak to my rabbi too and the way he talks leaves me wondering whether he agrees with or disapproves of the whole idea."

"So," Ahmad chuckled. "He is a mullah like all of us mullahs. What we do," he said, as he took his half-empty cup of wine, drank it up, and continued, "Never mind. You want my opinion? Here you are. Why not? It's a shame you Jews can't have sigheh, because once you marry her, she will become your permanent wife. But, so what? Take this woman your wife has chosen as your new wife and have children."

That evening, when the Rhino came home, after Tuba laid the dinner and they sat down to eat, Ruben asked where his mother was.

"I haven't seen her since this afternoon. We were cooking together in the kitchen. Then she said she was not feeling well and was going to rest. She should be here." Tuba turned her head towards Ruth's room and shouted loudly, "Ruth khanom!" but there was no answer. "Let me go and take a look," she said as she stood up and went toward Ruth's room. She opened the door and saw that her mother-in-law was in the exact same position in which Tuba had left her that morning. "Ruth khanom. Dinner is ready, *befarmaeed shaam* – come and have dinner, please… Ruth khanom… Ruth khanom…" She called louder and louder and then screamed, "Oh my God, Agha Ruben, hurry!" Tuba had no idea that she was capable of acting so well, that she could be so evil. "Something has happened to…" she said, her voice shivering, as she began beating her chest.

Ruben rushed to his mother's side, sat down next to her and asked, "What's wrong, Mani?" Ruth was mute. "Are you all right?" he yelled. She didn't respond. "What's happened to you? Speak Mani, speak!"

Ruben took his mother's head in his hands. "Oh my God! What's happened to her temple? It's bruised!"

Tuba rushed to her husband's side, slapped the back of her hand and nodded, "You're right," and then shrugged, "I don't know!"

"My mother must have fainted and then fallen, her temple hitting the edge of this shelf," Ruben said, in anguish.

Aha, what a fine idea! Tuba thought.

"Please, get help!" he implored Tuba. "Hurry!"

They sent for Hakim Akbar, who, after thoroughly examining Ruth, turned to Tuba, narrowed his eyes and shook his head. "That bruise," he pointed at Ruth's temple.

"What about the bruise?" Tuba asked, her voice shaking, as she kneeled and then sat with her legs crossed.

"I see you are very nervous, Tuba khanom. Why don't you lean against that cushion?"

"Yes, what about it?" Ruben echoed his wife.

"Let me ask your wife another question. When..."

Like the buzz of a thousand mosquitoes, Akbar's voice began to resonate in Tuba's head. As it got louder, she could barely hear the hakim. Her whole body was shaking. The corners of her chador that she was squeezing tightly were wet with the sweat of her palms. She heard the Rhino's voice, "Answer Hakim Akbar," but it was as though her jaws were glued together. "All I want to know..." came the voice of the hakim and then faded away. "What's the matter with you, woman?" That was her husband shouting at her. Tuba began to cry. She had been betrayed and she could no more withhold the truth. "When I entered her room..." she sobbed. "I'm so sorry."

"Are you at all hearing what Hakim Akbar is asking you?" Ruben hollered. "You know Rachel has been very sick, don't you! All the hakim wants to know is when my Mani came back from Rachel's house today?"

"Leave her alone, Ruben," the hakim intervened. "The poor woman is in shock." Then he sat facing Tuba and spoke calmly, "You see Tuba khanom, I visited Rachel khanom last night. Your husband's sister has very rare *and* contagious form of sporadic cholera. Its major symptom is serious dizziness. Since, as Ruben tells me, your husband's mother has spent the whole morning there, it could be that..."

Tuba released her grip on her chador, licked her dried lips and sighed, relieved. "That's exactly what I told Kadkhoda Ruben before you came. She must have fainted and fallen. These days, the poor woman has been very busy with Kafi's childbirth and Rachel's sickness."

"Of course she fell. Her pulse is rapid and she has a tem-perature—a high temperature. I'm quite sure she's gotten the ailment from your sister," he said as he opened his infamous bag, filled two small bottles with different potions and handed them to Ruben. "Three times a day, five drops of each in lukewarm water. This will help her and shield you and your wife from catching the disease from your mother."

"And I hope it will cure her?"

"I'm sorry to say no, kadkhoda. I'm almost certain that she has damaged her brain. After all, my friend, she's over sixty! That's *very* old. These things happen to people who are even much younger."

"What things?"

"Most probably a stroke caused her fall. My friend Ruben," the hakim sighed. "If my guess is right, your mother, the wife of Naphtali the Tailor—what a man of virtue he was, may he rest in peace—will remain the same for the rest of her life, unless a miracle happens."

And Hakim Akbar was right for Ruth never recovered from Tuba's blow, much to Tuba's satisfaction, to aim her cruel insults at her daughter-in-law.

When Yohai the Shoemaker entered into marriage negotiations with Tuba, he was so anxious for a successful conclusion that he hurriedly accepted the unconditional terms that Tuba set. After telling, and shocking, his wife Widefoot Marjon about what he had done, the shoemaker called a family gathering to break "the good news" of Jewel's impending marriage. Her sisters and brothers— Shifra the Hen, Shahin the Rainbow, Rouhi the Quiltmaker and Solomon the Dwarf—came over.

"You don't know how lucky you are, my girl," the shoe-maker began. "I have something exciting to tell you, something so wonderful for you, for me, for all of us, that I don't know how to begin." Yohai gulped his hot tea, put the glass down and slapped his hands as his family members listened intently. "Our darling Jewel has been blessed with the unique opportunity to marry Haji Ruben, the man who suffered so much for our people, the kadkhoda of Jewbareh, and I have agreed to give her hand to him in marriage."

"Poor Tuba khanom. When did she die?" was Jewel's first reaction.

"I saw her in front of Samad's shop this morning. Poor soul looked fine and healthy," Shifra the Hen slapped the back of her hand.

"God forbid, no!" Yohai hollered. "The lovely lady is fine and healthy. But unfortunately, she is barren."

"So, Ruben wants to divorce his wife and marry my sister?" asked Shahin the Rainbow.

"No. He will keep her, but he will marry our beloved Jewel because Tuba is barren and our kadkhoda needs a fertile wife."

Beginning to realize what her father was saying, Jewel started to cry. Yohai nodded approvingly and said, "I know you're excited and these are tears of joy."

Jewel knew her father well. He was a kind man who meant no harm, especially to his own daughter. But as Jewel had grown up and no suitors had asked for her hand, Yohai's hope of having her married had given way to grief and eventually to the conviction that spinsterhood was his daughter's destiny. Now, Jewel knew, with the appearance of a khastegar, whatever his condition, it was as if his girl had come back from the dead. His judgment was overshadowed by his excitement.

"I've passed the age of eligibility," Jewel said as she sobbed. "I know I'm ugly."

"You are telling us that our kadkhoda is after a havoo for his wife?" Rouhi the Quiltmaker asked curiously.

"No, no, no! You don't seem to understand. He's not the one who's looking for a new wife; it's his lovely first wife instead. There's a world of difference here. It's not just consent on her part, in fact the whole thing is her idea!"

"And that makes it better?" Jewel bobbed in surprise. "The fact that the wife has asked for my hand in marriage to her husband?"

"Let me make one thing very clear, my dear," Yohai embraced his daughter and wiped her tears. "I'm not forcing you to marry this man. I told your mother and I'm telling you and your sisters and brothers too. If you don't want to do it, just say so and I will cancel the whole thing."

"But you want me to marry him?"

"That's right, Jewel jaan," said the Widefoot Marjon. "Those who don't see how gorgeous you are…"

"Stop it, Mani! I have known you all my life. Your expression belies your words."

"No! I mean it," Marjon put her hand on her heart. "You *are* beautiful. Blind are those who don't see your beauty. The problem that your father and I are facing is that we're getting old. All your siblings have gone to their destined nests and what worries us most is what will happen to you once we are gone. That's why women marry — to have the shadow of a husband over their heads."

"Tell me why does no one else in Jewbareh have two wives?"

Yohai told her about Pinchas and his brother Joseph, the twin jewelers, who, about forty years ago, after making a fortune, each married a second wife and moved out of Jewbareh to Kashan.

"But that was *forty* years ago!"

Younes the Dwarf, Jewel's older brother came to his father's help. "If you remain a spinster until our parents — may they live to be a hundred and twenty years old — have passed away," he threw his small arms into the air as though trying to ward off the Angel of Death, "you're most welcome to live with my family. But to have your own family," he said in the same breath, "*That's* something different."

"I deserve better."

"Ruben is your only chance, my dear," Shifra the Hen said, caressing her sister's soft hair.

Yohai the Shoemaker nodded approvingly. The Wide-foot Marjon hid her tears.

And so, feeling herself helplessly drawn into the downward spiral of her destiny, in the winter of 1846, Jewel agreed to become part of the household of Ruben the Rhino and Tuba the Woman, once again giving way to the talebearers who ran around and spread gossip about the house of Ruben the Rhino.

"As a kadkhoda, what sort of an example is he to our husbands?" Nosrat the Lavender had said.

"Bad, bad example. Very bad," Shamsi the Radish had responded. "As they say," she added. "'If the king picks one apple in the orchard of his citizens, his soldiers will uproot all the trees.' When our governor — may he himself bear the requital of his sins — treats himself to two wives, don't be surprised if half the married Jewbarite men don't follow his example."

"Our kadkhoda is becoming such an important man he acts like a pasha and takes two wives," Mehri the Tweezers said.

"And before you know it, he'll have a harem with fifty wives and five hundred children, like King Solomon!" chimed in Tuti the Exfoliator.

It was a cold day, a week before his second wedding, and Ruben was miserable. Tuba had decided to marry him to a second wife and despite his misgivings, he had at last surrendered. At least this was how he put it when he went and opened his heart to his best friend, Nissan. "Tuba is my one-and-only, but you have been a witness to the pain we have both felt for ten years now in our efforts to have a child." Ruben was angry at fate and the mysteries of conception which gave many children to one couple and none to another, though mostly he directed his anger toward the Jewbarites and their infernal gossiping. After all he had done for the good of his people, he told Nissan, he had hoped that his share in life would not be a barren wife. He was so sad for Tuba, he said, for he saw how she had subjected herself to the agony of finding him a second wife. And he realized, he told Nissan, that even though the idea had been Tuba's, he had clearly hurt her by acquiescing in it, even though he had resisted for a long time. He felt sorry for Jewel too — this poor, tall, white, redheaded spinster. But he had waited for a child for so many years. And he still could not imagine going through life childless. "What am I to do?"

"What do you expect me to say my friend," said Nissan. "Now that you've made up your mind just go ahead with it."

As for Tuba, the magnitude of her decision to marry her husband to Jewel was just beginning to dawn on her. Like Ruben, she too was furious at the gossip surrounding this impending event. First, she made sure that her havoo would not celebrate the traditional three-days-and-nights wedding ceremonies. Thus she limited the wedding to only one night and the number of guests to the immediate families. She even tried to skip a reception of any kind. "Let's have an early afternoon gathering," she suggested to Ruben. "We will serve tea and cookies and get it over with."

But Ruben disagreed. "You have already relegated this wedding to only one night instead of three and you have forbidden musicians. Now you are trying to reduce it to nothing. We must at least serve dinner to Jewel's family. We can't send them home hungry after the wedding and we cannot humiliate her in front of the whole world."

And this was just the first of many arguments they would have over Jewel.

"Look how excited you are about your new bride," Tuba said, choking on her words.

"Marrying me to a second wife was *your* idea, my dear wife, not mine," said an indignant Ruben. "And I am going along with it to give you your heart's desire: a child. But be reasonable, will you?"

That was like shaking the beehive of Tuba's frustration. She unleashed her fury on her husband. "Yes, it was *my* idea, but not rejecting it was *your* decision," she cried. "Believe me, you're not dealing with a fool! You could have said no. You could have said, as you used to, 'I love you with or without a child.' You could have said, 'You are the rose of my life.' But you have *not* said that for a long time. You are excited that you will get to take a new woman's virginity. I hope you're not counting me among your wedding guests, because I'm not going to be there!"

"I don't know what I have done to deserve all this," Ruben said quietly. "I do love you with or without a child. You are the rose of my life and you always will be. Now, make up your mind: do you want this wedding, and the child that may come of it, or not? Do not change your mind every two seconds for we will be living with the consequences one way or another for the rest of our lives."

"Listen and hear me well my husband!" Tuba said, ending the argument. "I arranged this marriage for reasons you're well aware of, and that's all there is to it. I'm offering you a new wife on a silver platter. You will marry her with or without me, and I wish you good luck."

They stood there, staring at each other. Ruben did not know whether to take her in his arms and comfort her or leave her alone to fume and sulk. He felt how hard it was for her. But wasn't his own position just as difficult as hers, and didn't he too deserve just as much sympathy and understanding? He reached out to touch her cheek, but she turned away. He went up to her and put his hands on her shoulders, which were as tight and solid as fortified walls. Ruben tried to turn her around to face him, but Tuba would not move. He understood now that they could never go back again to the loving and hopeful way things had been between them in the first years of their marriage.

Why had God made it so difficult for them to have a child? Was it, he wondered...could it be...? He dismissed the thought of Zain as quickly as it flashed through his mind. He had gotten rid of that horror for a long time now and he wasn't going to let it, like a thief in the night, rob him of his peace of mind. Though, at the moment, peace was in fact the last thing he was feeling.

He released his hand from Tuba's shoulder and left her alone in her room.

The wedding of Jewel the Vinegar to Ruben the Rhino took place on a Tuesday evening in the winter of 1846. Before the guests arrived, Tuba went to her room and closed the door behind her. She sat down on her bedding, which was spread over a Persian carpet on the floor, and gazed at her image in the mirror on the wall. She had shared this bed with Ruben for over ten years. She realized now just exactly what she had done to herself and her marriage in putting her husband together with another woman, and the thought of it struck at her like a hungry vulture. In the solitude of her room she remembered the beauty of the early days of her life with Ruben, auspicious days filled with the hope of having a family of her own. Then came the struggle to have a child and now this desperate act which she had dreamed up. Yet strangely, in the midst of her grief and self-despising thoughts, she felt sympathy for Jewel. She felt sorry too for Widefoot Marjon, who had pleaded with Tuba at the end of the negotiations, to treat her daughter as a younger sister. *A younger sister whom I allow to sleep with my husband?* Tuba had thought at the time. Not to hear the wedding guests clapping and singing, Tuba grabbed her pillows and pressed them against her ears. But the harder she pressed the louder she heard their singing voices and the uproar of the men raising their cups and wishing the groom and his new bride health, wealth and twelve strong boys. The room was cold, but she was feverish. She felt the burning sensation of a hot fluid that flushed through her body like molten red-hot iron and settled in her lower belly, right in her womb.

Once voices outside dwindled, Tuba knew that dinner was being served and finally she heard Mullah Shimon leading the exchange of matrimonial vows between her husband and his new bride. She heard Jewel say "yes" and the shrilling cheers of the women guests that followed. She turned around and buried her face in Ruben's pillow, inhaling his scent deeper and deeper, as if she wanted to absorb her husband into her skin and lock him there forever. She then heard the cheerful songs of the guests accompanying the bride and the groom as they made their way to the room she had assigned them at the other end of the house, next to the kitchen, where previously they had stored supplies of wood and charcoal. This was a small chamber with one door and no windows. The floor was covered with a worn-out rug and on the rug there was an old cotton mattress with a faded quilt. This was now Jewel's room, Ruben's wedding room where he and his new wife would consummate their marriage and it was to be hoped, make children. Knowing that they were at this very moment entering that room, Tuba felt that she was nothing more than a piece of merchandise that had been sold as flawless but had turned out to be hopelessly defective. The picture of Ruben and his new bride locked in each other's arms, making babies, was torturing her. She was delirious. She could see them in intimate sexual acts with Ruben's face in rapture as she had noticed when he made love to her on their wedding night.

She stood up and looked out of her window. It was snowing outside and the guests were gradually leaving. She turned around and caught sight of herself in the mirror. Methodically and slowly she began to undress, examining each part of her body and judging it bit by bit. She meticulously folded each garment that came off and put it on the bed, and then stared at her reflection. Finally when she was naked, she took hold of her breasts and squeezed them so hard that, when her hands came away, the tracks of her fingernails were visible in their soft skin. "You will never have milk flow within you," she moaned, "and no child will suck on you to be nurtured and grow. You will forever remain like two pieces of rock that never contain a fountain." Then she dug her fists into her guts and cried, "What a wasted belly, never to hold a new life, never to grow a child for my husband."

Suddenly, she raised both her arms high up in the air and with clenched fists she repeatedly slammed herself on her belly and between her legs. "Useless... barren...," she sobbed with her mouth shut as she again picked up Ruben's pillow, this time driving her sharp nails into the soft muslin cover until it tore open, and then slamming it against the wall until feathers fell like snowflakes all over the room. She threw herself back on the bed and laid quietly, the feathers settling over her naked body. She wanted to scream, but she didn't raise her voice. She cried in silence instead.

Lying naked on her bed, her body covered with feathers, in the cold of that late winter night, the night of the wedding of her master to a woman whom she had chosen for him to marry, to sleep with, to have sex with and to bear him children, Tuba the Woman was benumbed into a light, trance-like sleep. She felt as if she had been thrown into the eye of a whirlpool that was twisting her down beneath the water's surface. From those depths, she heard havoo scream and felt a sudden pang of pain in her heart.

Jewel had lost her virginity.

Chapter 14
The Graceful Rebecca

It was the fall of 1847 and Jewbarites were celebrating Sukkot. This traditional Jewish feast has dual significance — agricultural in that it is the harvest festival, and historical because it commemorates the forty-year period the children of Israel wandered through the desert and lived in temporary shelters after the Exodus from Egypt. For this holiday, Jews assemble such dwellings, called Sukkah, in the open air in the courtyard of their houses and live in them for a whole week. This year Ruben had reason to be in a festive mood, for Jewel was pregnant, and he had made a Sukkah, much larger than usual, where he and his two wives would live for seven days and nights. This year, though, they only spent the first night in the Sukkah because the next day, in the late afternoon hours, Jewel went into labor. They sent for Jewel's mother, the Widefoot Marjon, who brought with her all her immediate relatives and Zoli the Midwife. Jewel lay on her mattress, on the ground, in her allotted room by her havoo, next to the kitchen, shrieking with pain.

"Do me a favor, will you?" Marjon asked her oldest daughter, Shahin the Rainbow, as she ran back and forth. "Why don't you go to Ruth khanom's room and bring her here?"

"Are you out of your mind? The woman is totally mute."

"I know, I know. But the poor soul has been waiting all these years for a grandson. Who knows? Just go and help bring her here."

So, Ruth was there as well. *Or was she,* one had to wonder? She sat in a corner facing Jewel's wide-open legs. Whether she actually realized the birth of her grandchild was imminent, it was something that puzzled everyone. She sat in silence, tugging at the corners of her headscarf as frequently as her heart beat, with no expression on her face. None.

"Congratulations, Ruth khanom!" Shahin the Rainbow screamed in her ear, as if she were deaf. Ruth pulled back, gave her a
mystified look and then turned her head back in slow motion and
stared at Jewel who was screaming at the top of her lungs.

"You are about to become a grandma," said Zoli the Midwife,
who was taking her turn with Ruth. "Don't be scared. First labors
are often very long and exhausting, but she will be fine. She's in the
right hands," Zoli raised her palms in front of Ruth and saw no
reaction. Tuba was of course there witnessing her handiwork — the
noisy havoo, the crowd surrounding her husband's wife, the
amount of love and caring Jewel was getting and nobody, not a
single one of them, even looking at her. As she took in the scene
around her, perhaps in the hope of getting someone's attention, she
saw Ruth staring at her. Their eyes locked. Tuba tried to avoid her
victim's gaze, but it was as if Ruth had gripped her with her eyes
and paralyzed her. The silent woman's mouth opened and closed.
Not your child! Not your child!" Tuba read her lips and sensed how
much her mother-in-law hated her.

Frustrated, she cruelly screamed at Jewel in a voice foreign to all
who knew her "What is it? It's as if you were the only woman in the
world giving birth to a child! Keep quiet! You're crying as if you've
been beaten by a snake. We've sent for my husband Agha Ruben.
Now if he arrives and hears this tumult, God forbid, he will have a
heart attack."

The women who were attending to Jewel turned around and
looked at Tuba in astonishment. For all the months that Jewel had
been pregnant, Tuba had taken utmost care of her havoo, and now
this! "What's with her?" they whispered to each other as they ran
back and forth taking care of Jewel. They pleaded to Tuba to calm
down, but she was not about to give up. "Look at her," Tuba said to
Zoli the Midwife. "Swear in the name of all the sacred messengers
of God, tell me, have you ever heard any woman in labor making so
much noise? It's so obvious. She is playing up her pain to get my
husband's attention."

Tuba became more and more invisible as she groaned and
grunted. No one paid any attention to her cruel and nasty remarks
any more. Zoli shouted over Jewel's screams, "Marjon khanom! Get
me some more hot water and plenty of clean sheets."

"Hot water… Clean sheets…" said the Widefoot Marjon, as she

and her daughters, echoing her, ran back and forth from Jewel's room.

Ignored by the enthusiastic crowd surrounding her havoo, Tuba walked outside the little storage space near the kitchen that on Jewel's wedding night had become her room. She sat on a plank bench outside. Next to her, the flame of a tallow-burner flickered and came alive in the chilly breeze. The night was saturated with the mixed smells of the meal that was cooking slowly in the kitchen and the smoke rising up the chimney from the burning wood in the fireplace. Moonlight struggled its way through the autumn clouds, but barely reached the ground. Wherever she looked, she saw Ruth's face with that bizarre smile, staring at her, whispering, *"Not your child! Not your child!"* Turning away from this unrelenting image, at the opposite end of the house she saw the Sukkah, which was deserted, as were the veranda and the many rooms that Tuba had assigned to herself—empty, barren—while at this end of the courtyard, in the small room next to the kitchen, a long expected new life was making its way into the world.

Tuba had married her husband to Jewel nine months ago—nine months and nine days ago, to be exact. Her feeling that she had been flawed had not stopped there. Soon after Jewel's wedding, the Widefoot Marjon had gone to the Meat Market Alley and, with the grating loudness of a town crier, had bellowed the news of her daughter's virginity, and then, eight weeks later, she had repeated the same scene with the news of Jewel's pregnancy—both times with Tuba in the crowd and Ruben up in his shop, smiling the self-satisfied smile that Tuba hated.

Although during her negotiations with Jewel's parents and her husband she had insisted that Ruben would spend only one night a week in his second wife's room, after a while he had gradually changed the routine to two, three and at times four nights a week, and every time Tuba objected, he had made different strange excuses. "The poor woman had such a stomachache and I couldn't have left her alone... Her great-grandmother has died, for God's sake... I just fell asleep there, that's all..." What added salt to Tuba's wound was that, whenever Ruben did spent the night with her, *he* was the one who had always had a headache that prevented him from making love to her. Sometimes he held her, and she would wake up with his arm around her. But it seemed that he was incapable of the passion they had once known in the early days of their marriage. Often, as he slept beside her, she would cry silently. In the mornings, before he left her bed, he would tell her he loved her. But what did it mean if he could not take her as he once had? Had she become his sister? His aunt? His grandmother? It all made her feel old and unattractive and, worst of all, useless.

Sara the Fox, Tuba's mother, nagged her constantly for having given up on her husband. "In the first place, you should *not* have arranged for him to marry a second wife. But now that you have naively earned yourself a havoo, and she has practically taken your place in Ruben's household, you have to become competitive and outdo her by showering your man with love. You should push her aside and take charge. How? Be very nice to him. Dress provocatively. Be as coquettish as you can. And once you are alone with him, draw him to yourself. Thereafter, it's only a matter of safeguarding what you have achieved."

And it so happened that in the first three months of her pregnancy, Jewel had constant nausea worsened by lack of appetite and, what she never told Ruben, a sudden revulsion against his natural body odor. In the meantime, because Jewbarites believed that intercourse with a pregnant woman was the wasting of seed and husbands were therefore forbidden to make love to their expecting wives, it had been weeks since Ruben had slept with Jewel. She had to be looked after constantly. That was when Jewel's parents asked for Ruben's permission to take her to their house whenever she was very sick, so that the Widefoot Marjon could attend her daughter. So, the first time Jewel went to stay at her parents' house, Tuba made what she was best at—her famous fish stew. With 'Abram's Magic' in the Russian decanter, she sat close to the Rhino and held his hand—a near reincarnation of the night she had first told him about Jewel. The memory of that night saddened Tuba, but it did not stop her from seducing Ruben. Suddenly they were in bed, making passionate love. Later, as the two lay on their backs, staring at the ceiling, each had a separate perception. To Ruben, his first wife now seemed unexpectedly changed, warm and passionate when for so long now she had been grim and hardened against him. Tuba just as suddenly felt herself charged with confidence and power. She could indeed compete with Jewel. And compete with her havoo, she did! Whenever the pregnant Jewel was away at her parents' house, Tuba became a seductress, wining and dining her husband and making herself irresistibly desirable to him, so that the two of them spent wondrous nights together in her bed.

Nevertheless, once Jewel felt well enough to stay home, things changed. Tuba observed—as did everyone else—how her younger havoo had changed. Pregnant, she had earned herself some extra flesh. She had colored her hair black and she didn't look like a snowman with a red wig any longer. And standing next to Ruben —for she was the tallest girl in Jewbareh—she was only a head shorter than her husband. Now Ruben was one happy man, and he couldn't hide his joy from anybody, especially Tuba. He had impregnated his second wife on her wedding night, a living proof of *his* fertility and Tuba's barrenness. Inevitably, he stopped sleeping in Tuba's room. And again he lost his desire for her. As the pregnancy advanced, he became more and more solicitous of Jewel, and he even stopped coming to Tuba's part of the house to let her make dinner for him.

On the night of Jewel's delivery, Tuba was sitting outside, listening to her screams of pain. She folded her arms, embracing herself and piercing her skin with her nails. When she married Jewel to her husband, deep in her heart she had hoped that her havoo would also be barren. After all, she thought, she had shared her husband with her, why shouldn't Jewel be a partner in her miseries? But when Jewel became pregnant and a living proof of Tuba's infertility, she had felt an odd sense of belonging to this unborn child. She had looked after Jewel like a mother, a sister. And now that the moment had come, she felt a painful chill floating in her belly. She couldn't stand Jewel's screams. That clamor was *hers*. Those cries, those moans and groans and weeping and wailings, which she was certain Jewel was playing for all she could get, belonged to her—Tuba. And so did the baby.

As Ruben stepped breathlessly into his house and strode quickly towards Jewel's room, just then, from inside Jewel's room, he heard the baby's first cry of life, the taking of its first breath, followed by Zoli the Midwife's shouting, "Congratulations! It's a… well, it's a… girl!"

"A girl?" Ruben froze as in a split second a barrage of thoughts went through his mind. He had of course been hoping for a boy. He had to have a son, a son to be named Naphtali, his father's name, a son who would carry on the legacy of his ancestors, a son who would become the kadkhoda of Jewbareh, a son of his own who, when Ruben was gone, would take over the responsibility of his business and his wives. And then he heard a familiar voice in his head. It had to be his father talking to him. It was comforting. "Now you are sure that you can have many more children with your new, fertile wife," said the voice. "She will give birth to your first and then many more sons." At that moment, Ruben was relieved. He stood in the courtyard, behind Jewel's room, waiting for someone to bring his child to him, for no man was allowed to enter a delivery room before the mother of the baby had been covered. Ruben had to wait. It was at this moment that Tuba jumped up from the bench she was sitting on near Jewel's room and ran to Ruben, crying, "Congratulations, Agha! We have a daughter!" Then she went into Jewel's room and immediately came out, holding the infant in her arms. The Widefoot Marjon signaled her two daughters to follow Tuba to the courtyard. "Where are you taking my baby?" Jewel screamed. But heedless to the mother of the baby's objection, Tuba handed the infant to Ruben, who held his firstborn in his arms and looked at her as though he had found a long lost treasure. Then he put his nose on the soft crown of the baby's head and took a deep breath, savoring the fresh smell of her fine hair. He whispered in his daughter's ear a blessing: *He who blessed our fathers, may He bless my firstborn* – though he couldn't help grumbling, *Did you have to keep me waiting for such a long time?* He gave his child a lengthy report of the bitterness of his long, long ordeal. The baby, exceptionally quiet, was looking at Ruben as though she heard and understood every word he said.

In the meantime, Tuba wouldn't stop talking. "She looks so much like you, Agha. Like an apple cut in half. I mean, look at her hair, just like yours. Her fingers…"

"What the hell is she talking about?" Shifra whispered to her sister, Shahin the Rainbow. "The baby's hair is red like Jewel's, her face, her skin, all are like Jewel's."

"She's just babbling," Shahin whispered back. "Leave her alone, poor woman. She's distraught and doesn't know what she's saying."

Ruben was in his own world. He held the baby in his arms and raised her up above his head.

"For God's sake," pleaded Tuba. "Be careful, Agha!"

"I will not die forgotten. I will name you after my grandmother, Rebecca." He sounded as if he were making a declaration to the unknown future generations. "Rebecca, the daughter of Ruben, the son of Naphtali, the son of Rebecca, the daughter of..." he whispered unintelligibly, as if saying a prayer. "And God-willing," he said, raising his voice again, "After you, my many other sons will carry the legacy of my name, and that of my father, and my forefathers and pass it on to their children and the children of their children. Thank God my roots haven't dried up."

He examined the baby's features. Like her mother and not him, the infant had plenty of red hair, her brown eyebrows and lashes were full and her skin was fair and freckly. And, for a newborn, her small body was well defined. "My daughter is graceful," declared Ruben the Rhino, and that is how the newborn child came to be known as The Graceful Rebecca. "By the grace of God," he said under his breath, "all my sins are absolved because here is the living proof of His forgiveness." Then he turned to Tuba, "I owe this all to you. To your sacrifice and understanding. Please forgive all the pain and suffering I have inflicted on you because of Jewel. From now on, we will live—you, Jewel and me—in peace and happiness, I promise you."

"I'm glad I have made you happy," said Tuba, in a flat tone. "Please let me hold her also." Ruben gave her the baby. "She's beautiful," said Tuba, who began moving toward the veranda with the baby in her arms.

"Where are you going?" Ruben asked as he and Jewel's sisters followed her.

"To my room." She brought her head down and kissed the baby on her forehead. "You and I will raise Rebecca," she said to Ruben. "This is *our* child. Yours and mine."

"And Jewel's, of course," said Ruben as he tried to catch up with her.

"Didn't you just say that you owed this baby to me?" Tuba said, turning around and facing Ruben. "Jewel will bear more children and she is welcome to them. But this one is mine. Mine and yours." Saying this, she climbed the stairs to the veranda and disappeared into her bedroom. Jewel's sister ran to Jewel to report what had happened.

"What did you say?" exclaimed Ruben in disbelief as he yanked the door open and stormed into Tuba's room, suddenly realizing his first wife's vicious plan. "This is impossible. Now, please go give the child to her mother, come back and we will talk about it."

"*I* am this child's mother. I have waited such a long time and gone through so much for this one to come," Tuba said as she sat down on the bed with the baby in her arms.

"In the name of all of God's prophets, what are you saying?" Ruben pleaded as he went up to her and tried to take the baby back, but Tuba grabbed her tightly and screamed, "Don't come near my child or I swear to God, I will kill her and myself! This is *my* child!"

Enraged but restraining himself, Ruben flushed so severely that his freckles looked red. "Of course she will be our baby," he said as calmly as he could. "But you can't take her away from her…"

"Her what? If you were about to say 'her mother,' let me say it again. *I* am her mother. Understand?"

Ruben sat next to Tuba, put his arm on her shoulders and pleaded, "Please don't do this to me at this happiest moment of my life."

Tuba stared into his eyes and said, "Step into the world of reality, my dear selfish Agha kadkhoda! You are not the only one who matters. This graceful girl is *our* baby and that's the end of the matter."

Never, in all the years that he had been married to this woman had Ruben known that Tuba could be so stubborn, so fierce. "What has come over you, Tuba?" he said, his voice calm but laced with fury. "Why are you doing this to me? When did you come up with the ridiculous idea of having the child to yourself? Do you think I would have let you marry me to this other woman if I'd known you had such a crazy scheme up your sleeve?"

"That *other woman,* whose name for your information is Jewel, is your wife, not me," said Tuba, looking intently at Ruben. "I shouldn't have listened to your mother—may she remain dumb until she burns in hell. I shouldn't have married you to this *other woman* because, as they say, 'When new comes to bazaar, the old becomes bizarre.' I'm the old wife. I'm the one who sleeps in this empty bed night after night, while you have been up in the paradise of carnal pleasures with *her.* Wasn't she *only* supposed to make children for you and me? Instead, you took her and ran away from me, and you can't get enough of her. *This… child… is… mine…* And that's how it's going to be."

"Even if she were your baby… I mean all right, all right, let her be your baby, but Jewel has given birth to this child and taking care of her as an infant is her job, not yours. The baby will be here, in the same house with you and me. She will be taken care of and breastfed by Jewel and pampered by you. It is not right to take her away from her birth-mother at this crucial moment, is it?"

Tuba looked at the baby who, strangely, was still calm despite the raised voices surrounding her, then lifted her head and looked at Ruben. "I let your other wife have my husband," she said. "I allowed her to take you away from me into the privacy of her bedroom, to open her womb to you and let you make a child in her. From the first day she knew that she was marrying you to make you and me a baby. Don't you think I deserve to raise the child of my husband?"

"But she needs her mother's milk. She has to be fed. Don't you see? The poor thing is starving!"

"Leave that to me. There are many mothers in Jewbareh who would die to nurse my child. I will hire one of them."

Ruben threw his hands up. "You can be sure of one thing," he snarled. "I'm not going to tell Jewel about this ridiculous idea of yours."

"She already knows. I told Zilfa to tell her."

Ruben froze. The most precious thing he had ever wished for — a child of his own — was in the hands of a woman who seemed to have lost her mind. He tried to say something but managed a mere delirious mumble. He couldn't think. He heard noises in his head so loud that he felt dizzy. And then the noises became real. They were coming from Jewel's room. Ruben, followed by Tuba with the baby in her arms, rushed to the veranda. With a stained sheet wrapped around her body, Jewel had charged out of the bed in which she had just given birth and was running wildly towards Tuba's room as the Widefoot Marjon, her daughter Shahin, Zoli the Midwife, Zilfa and the other women who had attended her, ran after her, trying and failing to catch her. "My baby! My child!" she screamed as she climbed the stairs to the veranda.

Holding the baby in one arm, Tuba grabbed Ruben's hand, pulled him into her room and locked the door behind them before Jewel was able to reach her.

"Give me my baby! She is my child, not yours, you kidnapper!"

Ruben looked through the crack of the door and saw Jewel. All of a sudden, this submissive and belittled woman, although weak and breathless, had become a lioness reclaiming her stolen cub, kicking and pounding her fists on the door.

"Give me my baby, the fruit of my womb," she sobbed. Then she roared, "Tuba! I swear I will kill you, you filthy snake!" Saying this, her knees weakened, and she crumpled to the floor of the veranda.

The women who had pursued Jewel now surrounded her. "You shouldn't have been running after delivering a child. My God, the veins in your womb have broken. You're sitting in a pool of blood," Zoli the Midwife said as she sat down and put her arms around her. Then the midwife shouted at the locked door. "Be a man, Agha Ruben, I beg you. Swear on the soul of your father, Naphtali, may he rest in paradise, have mercy. The mother of your child is bleeding to death!"

"Get away from my room Zoli and shut your filthy mouth, you who earn your bread from between women's legs!" Tuba roared from within.

"Be a man, Kadkhoda Ruben," repeated Zoli, ignoring Tuba. "You are the man and your women have to obey you."

But she heard no response.

"Help me up," said Jewel breathlessly raising her arms.

"Put your arm on my shoulder and let me take you to your room," Zoli offered.

"Yes sweetheart," her mother nodded. "Here! Put your other arm on my shoulder."

Weak and exhausted, Jewel pushed herself up from the ground. With her arms around the neck of her mother and the midwife, she gave a mighty kick. The door broke open as she collapsed. There stood Ruben in the frame of the broken door, his eyes wide with horror as he looked from Jewel to Tuba, who was holding the baby tightly in her arms, then again at Jewel, who had passed out.

"Help! My child is dying!' screamed the Widefoot Marjon.

Other women joined in moaning and screaming. "Help, help! Somebody get us some water… Let's take her in… No… Leave her alone… Maybe she'll come back… Oh no, she's gone…"

Ruben rushed to Jewel's side. Her face had turned yellow and her lips were dark. He lifted her with his strong, muscular arms and as he carried her down the veranda stairs into the courtyard, her blood dripped on the yellow-red autumn leaves on the ground. He laid her gently on her bed. The women brought hot tea mixed with crystal sugar, as prescribed by the midwife, who opened Jewel's clenched jaws with a spoon and poured the drink into her mouth. Then the midwife ordered more towels and hot water to clean the bloody mess on the mother's body and applied a holistic balm inside her womb which stopped the bleeding. Ruben sat beside Jewel, held her hand and caressed her hair as slowly.

"You know something, Kadkhoda Ruben?" Zoli said, pointing her wrinkled finger at him. "I have been in this business for over fifty years. I have brought most of the Jewbarite children into this world. Never, ever, in all these years have I seen such cruelty that they steal somebody's newborn baby and give the child to another woman. You are our patriarch. You are good at solving people's problems. But it seems that, as they say, the potter drinks out of a broken cup."

"I… I mean, how was I supposed to know what Tuba had in mind," he muttered. "How?"

The midwife waved her torso sideways, signaling her disappointment in Ruben, and continued working on Jewel, who was breathing weakly until, a few minutes later, she opened her eyes. "She's back, thank God," said Zoli.

Jewel looked at people surrounding her as if they didn't exist, though she recognized Ruben. "My baby," she whispered as she held his hand. "I want her here in my arms. Please get her back, Agha. She must be very hungry. I have to feed her. My breasts are aching for her to suck. I beg you my master, don't let her take my child away from me." Her voice weakened, her eyelids fell and she turned pale again. Hurriedly, Zoli poured another spoonful of sweetened tea into her mouth and massaged her shoulders. When Jewel opened her eyes again, she saw Ruben's eyes burning with wrath.

"I will bring you the baby," the Rhino roared as he charged out of the room, went to the kitchen and came out with the largest knife there was. The Widefoot Marjon ran after him, "Please Agha Ruben!" she pleaded. "Have mercy!"

"He's going to kill Tuba!" called Shifra the Hen.

"Yes he is. He's going to kill again!" Shahin the Rainbow echoed her aunt.

Zilfa followed them, crying, "Please kadkhoda. Don't!"

Heedless of all the pleas of the women chasing him, Ruben went into Tuba's room with the knife held firmly in his hand. Tuba was pacing up and down trying to calm the baby, who was now screaming. "Give me my child!" Ruben hollered at Tuba, "Don't you see? She is starving." Ruben raised the knife and put the tip of the blade on his neck and cried, "If you don't give me the baby, I will cut my throat and free myself from this mess—and I swear on my father's grave, I will," he roared as he pushed the tip of the knife into his skin and a narrow line of blood began streaming down his neck.

"Don't Agha! Please don't!" Tuba screamed while the baby howled.

Hearing Tuba's cries for mercy, Zilfa run up the veranda, crying, "Help! He's killing her!" Shifra and Shahin followed her and the three women barged into Tuba's room to see Ruben holding the knife at his own neck. With the baby on the bed in front of her, Tuba had kneeled and was begging Ruben not to harm himself. "Here! Take her," she said sobbing.

Ruben threw the knife aside, picked up the screaming infant and rushed to Jewel's room. There, he put his daughter on her mother's chest. Jewel opened the top of her dress and pressed the infant's face to her breast. The baby rooted blindly, searching for the nipple until she clamped down on it with her tiny and hungry mouth. Suddenly Jewel's face became void of pain and peaceful. She raised her head to thank Ruben. "My God! Blood," she pointed at his neck.

"It's nothing. Only a scratch," he smiled.

Jewel took Ruben's hand and put it on the baby's face. "It's like the silk of Kashan, soft and soothing," she said with a smile of gratitude.

It was a few hours later, near midnight, when Jewel and the baby were sound sleep and the house was silent, that Ruben stepped out of her room. He took the tallow burner on the bench, went to the basement of his house and sat on a pile of wooden planks with his head on his knees. As a child, whenever he was sad, he took refuge in the basement of his father's house. Now, he was not sad, he was helplessly and hopelessly miserable. Once again he had tried to do good and once again he had become harsh and violent. Once again there had been a knife. So many knives. Zain's knife that had pierced his shoulder. The knife that he had held to his predators faces in the teahouse in the middle of the desert. The knife with which he had threatened Tuba today. Why was the universe playing so many crazy games on him? Zain had wanted to kill him, so had the men in the teahouse. But in this triangle in which he was caught, it was he, Ruben the Rhino, who had caused hurt to both his wives, simply because of his selfishness in wanting a child. Tuba was blameless, for being barren was not her choice and Jewel was innocent because of the humiliating circumstances that had forced her to marry him. No wonder this most blissful event of his life had ended up in violence and disaster. It was as if the Good and Evil that, according to Mullah Ahmad, were in eternal conflict with one another, had declared a truce and that, together were conspiring against him, lying in wait to make him happy and sad at the same time. Good had given him Rebecca. Evil had changed this festive occasion to a nightmare. "Damn it!" Ruben moaned, punching his leg. He had come close to killing Tuba. And Jewel could have died as she had run back and forth to get to her first child. His first child. Tuba's first child.

Caught in these unsettling thoughts, Ruben's mind swayed and swayed until there, in the basement of his house where he had taken refuge, on the night God had given him a child, he fell asleep.

So, this was the story of how The Graceful Rebecca, the daughter of Ruben the Rhino, Tuba the Woman and Jewel the Vinegar, stepped into this world and began her life — a life full of arguments over which one was her mother — Tuba or Jewel. A world in which, her father, the wise community leader and problem solver, had turned into an indecisive and helpless man, unable to bring about reconciliation between his two wives and he sought the advice of whomever he could think of. The Rabbi studied the relevant passages in the Torah and Talmud. He looked to see how Abraham had resolved quarrels between his two wives and how Jacob had dealt with the same situation. Then he went through his findings with Mayor Haskell and finally together they came up with what they thought was the best solution. They recommended that Rebecca's cradle be placed in Tuba's room while Jewel's role would be confined to feeding her child. Thus, if Rebecca were to wake up in the middle of the night, wanting milk, Jewel would be called upon to come to Tuba's room and breastfeed the baby. For agreeing to give up any other claim to the child, Jewel would be assured that if she were to have other children, Tuba would regard them as Jewel's and only Jewel's.

But Jewel rejected this wayward proposal. She refused to be the wet nurse of her own child. This rejection of the recommendations of the community leaders had its own consequences. Jewel's father was the first to shout at his daughter that *she* should obey the instructions of her husband and that of the community leaders. Yohai the Shoemaker had also emphasized that by marrying Jewel and saving her from the degradation of spinsterhood, and for that reason alone, he was eternally indebted to Ruben and Tuba. Jewel wouldn't budge and when the Shoemaker noticed that his pleadings were in vain, he went home and sent his wife and daughter to talk Jewel out of her stubbornness.

"No matter what the arrangements, my dear," her mother the Widefoot Marjon reasoned to her daughter, "the whole world knows that Rebecca is your daughter."

"Look at Tuba as a nanny for your child. Let her do the dirty work," her sister Shahin the Rainbow offered, agreeing with her mother.

"And when Rebecca grows up, whom will she think of as her mother?" her mother chimed in. "You, of course! Tuba can't show her belly to her and say, 'Here! This is where you were conceived and where you grew!' She can't say, 'You came to life from between these loins.' This poor woman has waited all these years for a child. Let her play with the baby as a desperate child plays with a doll.'"

And so they went on and on until Jewel exploded. "A nanny doesn't claim one's child. A nanny goes away after some time. A nanny gets lost!" she screamed at her mother and sister. "Go away and don't interfere with my life. You and my father married me to this married man," she pointed at Marjon, "Now leave me alone and let me deal with my own problems." And when her mother and sister left, they were convinced that motherhood had not only purged Jewel of timidity but filled her with courage. Then came Rabbi Shimon and Mayor Haskell with the same arguments, but these conversations also went nowhere. As a result, no steady arrangement was ever made about mothering Rebecca, so that there were frequent confrontations between the two wives. Every morning before Ruben left home, and every night when he came back, Tuba and Jewel fought like two wild cats over Rebecca. One day, Tuba stole into Jewel's room and took the baby while Jewel was napping and when she brought Rebecca back to be breastfed, Jewel refused. She told Tuba, "She's *your* baby? Then give her your own milk." Another time Rebecca was crying ceaselessly the whole day. "You shouldn't have given her sweetened water," Tuba grumbled, and then Jewel accused her havoo of causing *her* baby pain because she had given her chicken-rice soup. Tuba didn't want Jewel's mother around the baby for she had evil eyes. Jewel was convinced that Tuba stop short of nothing to get rid of her and have Rebecca to herself. To be away from the hassle at home, Ruben thought of sleeping nights at his shop, but the magnet of Rebecca always brought him back. He often asked himself, if he could ever love the sons that he was expecting to have after Rebecca as much as this outstandingly beautiful child who changed so rapidly, day by day, and became more and more adorable? Then, on one of his Tuesday appointments with Mullah Ahmad, once again, Ruben opened up to his friend about the hostility between his two wives.

"You want my advice? Impregnate your second wife again, and then impregnate her again after that, in fact, as frequently as possible. That way, trust me, the two women will be throwing your children at each other instead of fighting over them."

"But Hazrateh Agha. If one child has brought me so much misery, God knows how dismal my life would be with so many more. Besides, my first wife is so unpredictable that she might claim all my second wife's children."

"You know what?" Mullah Ahmad said with a laugh. "I think you've become the chicken who lays only one egg." He bobbed his head forward and looked at Ruben curiously. "Am I right? If so, see our friend Hakim Akbar. I'm telling you, Jew, he has given me this potion that I can take and have two of my wives in the same bed, making one of them pregnant and the other very happy."

Mullah Ahmad was right. The truth of the matter was that, after the chaos that had followed Rebecca's birth, Ruben no longer desired either one of his wives. He felt like a eunuch. Whatever it was, since the war between the wives over Rebecca, he hadn't gone near either of them even once. He came home, played with his daughter as he ate dinner, and listened to each of his wives telling him about the fights they had had that day. Then, depending on the assigned day of the week, he went to bed either with Tuba or Jewel and lay down in his bed lamenting his impotence, because no matter how much he was fed up with his wives, he wanted more children—boys.

"Try Hakim Akbar's potion," Mullah Ahmad's voice brought

Ruben back. And try it, he did, but to no avail. Tuba—with whom Ruben had not made love ever since Jewel had come home from her parents' in the middle of her pregnancy—was tormented by the thought that Ruben spent many nights in Jewel's arms, entwined with her in sexual rapture. One day when the two havoos were cooking lunch in the kitchen, Tuba stood over Jewel's head and suddenly yelled, "It's you who has again turned my husband against me. Why would the man who made love to me every night when you were vomiting your guts out, suddenly stop?"

Jewel burst out laughing. "Really?" she said, getting off the stool on which she was sitting and raising herself to her full height, from which she looked down at Tuba. Her expression was not, as Tuba had expected it to be, that of someone offended or insulted, but amused.

"What's so funny?" said Tuba, looking up at her rival.

But Jewel was not able to restrain her laughter.

"No!" Tuba cried. "It can't be! I mean, with you also?"

Jewel nodded, wiping her eyes with the corners of her scarf. "You can have him to yourself, my dear. For all time and forever," she said as she sat back on the stool and resumed her work, slicing vegetables.

"Nonsense. You are not telling the truth."

"Listen to me, havoo khanom!" Jewel jumped up again, put her forefinger on Tuba's chest and said, "I never wanted to marry your husband. *You* are the one who brought about this catastrophe. To be honest with you, not only I am not concerned about Agha's disability, but also even happy, because knowing you, if I were to bear any more children, you would claim each and every one of them. Maybe this is the Almighty's revenge on both of you."

"Disability?"

"He can't do it. His instrument fails him. Shrinks up like turtle retreating in its shell."

To Tuba, the thought of an impotent Ruben was unimaginable.

"At first I thought that he was just waiting for me to have my first period after the birth," Jewel went on. "But... let me put it this way. Our great fertile husband cannot do it anymore."

"What have you done to him?" Tuba exclaimed.

"*Done* to him? Why nothing, you fool, except give him the child that you and he always wanted and have now taken away from me.

I have served my purpose! And you see what use I am to him now! He sleeps with his back to me."

Jewel, who could not help noticing the look of joyous triumph on Tuba's face, went back to her cooking, convinced that it was lucky for her that with an impotent husband, she would never again have children. After all, Ruben had not prevented Tuba from either trying to take her baby, or for making incessant claims on her now. He never intervened to stand up for Jewel, the real mother, in her quarrels with that hateful woman. Deep down, in fact, she was pleased not to have to share her bed with a man she had never wanted to marry and had never loved.

And so, as he remained unable to make himself male children and Rebecca, whom he adored, remained the only child of his seed, Ruben the Rhino slowly began to turn into someone that even he himself didn't recognize. Little by little, a gigantic, vicious spider spun its thick web over his soul and choked his feelings.

It was in the midst of this battlefield — where she had to keep everyone happy — that Rebecca grew up. Tuba said, "You are my child because I have raised you," and Jewel said, "You're my child because you came out of me." And then there was the tormenting question both mothers asked her repeatedly: "Which of us do you love more?" Caught between the two women, little Rebecca was a sad child. *How come no other child in Jewbareh has two mothers?* She wondered. She witnessed Jewel's tears and felt it was she who caused them. She sensed Tuba's excessive love and considered herself unworthy of it. In truth, she could not stand either one of them for making her life, and their own lives, so miserable. The only person that she loved unreservedly was her father, with whom she shared her grievances about her mothers' incessant competition.

"Tell each one you like her more than the other!" Ruben suggested. "After all, this is what I have been doing since I married Jewel."

But Rebecca couldn't lie. She knew both her mothers loved her, but it was with a love so tormenting and so exhausting in its excessive and constant demands that she could not help craving the simple, selfless mother-love her friends got from their mothers. Its absence created a void she felt she could never fill.

Chapter 15
Like Ashes

The friendship between Nissan and Ruben went back to their early youth. Unlike the Rhino, Nissan—who was two years older than Ruben —was very skinny and remained so even beyond his late teens. He came in for his share of teasing, but it was Tannaz the Barrel who ridiculed the young man more than anyone else. "When your time comes to get married," she used to say, "I want you to make sure you'll marry a girl even thinner than yourself." Saying this—and she did so quite often—she would let out a bark-like laugh, slap her big belly and continue, "Because if a bulky woman sat on your lap, she would break your bones."

Nissan had to put up with the Barrel's mockery, because he worked in the shop of her husband, Samuel the Fabricseller. When he turned twelve, Nissan had come into the business as an assistant. He had just lost his father, Levi the Bricklayer, to cholera. The bricklayer's legacy to his only son was his wife Molook, four younger sisters and brothers and nothing to live on. After she placed Nissan with Samuel, Molook went to work for three years as a kitchen maid in the mansion of the governor of Esfahan. She came home exhausted every night to take care of her children, Nissan remembered. One of the governor's many Abyssinian slaves, a tall, strong man, had been assigned to accompany Molook home every night. When Nissan was fifteen, he found his mother dead. She had hanged herself with a rope tied to a ceiling beam in her kitchen. No one knew why she had committed suicide, leaving five children with no guardian. It had been the burden of life's hardships, the rabbi had declared at her funeral. But rumor had it that the Abyssinian slave had impregnated her and that she couldn't bear the shame. And so, what Molook left behind for her son and the rest of her family was disgrace, and for Nissan in particular, the entire responsibilities of taking care of four younger siblings. He worked all day with Samuel, keeping his shop in order and selling fabrics. In the evenings, he worked in the public bathhouse of Jewbareh. Here he scrubbed the floors, cleaned the place and after midnight, made a fire out of the wood he had carried from the bathhouse storage room to the furnace under the hot water tank. In this way he made sure that there would be enough hot water for the next day's customers before he went home in the early morning hours.

When Nissan was twenty, Samuel the Fabricseller died. Without a son to inherit Samuel's business, Ruben encouraged Nissan to buy it. Tannaz the Barrel wanted a lot for her husband's business, but Nissan's finances were as lean as he was. To assist his friend, Ruben pleaded with his father, Naphtali, who entered into negotiations with Samuel's widow. "You know me, Tannaz Khanom," Naphtali said to the Barrel. "As the kadkhoda of Jewbareh, I'm here to close this deal in such a way that, as they say, neither the skewer nor the kabob burns."

Poor Tannaz, who in fact had lost a great deal of weight while mourning her husband's death, told Naphtali tearfully, "I'm sure Samuel, from up there," she pointed to the skies, "is looking after me." And Naphtali of course understood her to mean that Samuel was watching the kadkhoda's every move during the negotiations so that he had better not try to cheat her. Naphtali assured and reassured her that although Nissan and his son were best friends, God was his witness that he was impartial. They went back and forth, finally settling on an amount that, to Naphtali's utter surprise and embarrassment, Nissan didn't have. It turned out that Ruben had deliberately kept Nissan's poverty from his father. His intention had been to ask Naphtali, once the deal was closed, to lend Nissan enough money to buy the business. Nissan knew about Ruben's plan and was nervous. He didn't want to be part of a naughty game Ruben was playing on his father, but as Naphtali's only son, Ruben knew that he had a special place in his father's heart—and he was right. At the end, Naphtali gave Nissan a loan and that's how Nissan became the owner of the only textile store in Jewbareh.

Thanks to the invaluable advice Ruben gave to Nissan, over time, his profits soared. He made enough money to repay

Naphtali's loan, marry Zilfa, have children, support his family and even save enough to buy a house. The two best friends bought a rundown house on a large piece of land on the third turn of the Alley of Eleven Twists, demolished it and built the two adjacent dwellings that came to be known as "the twin houses of Jewbareh."

In 1832—two years before Ruben fled to Jerusalem—to ask for Zilfa's hand in marriage to Nissan, Ruben attended the khastegari ceremonies and at the wedding, he helped "as no brother does for his own brother," in the words of Shokat, Nissan's sister. During Ruben's absence in Jerusalem, Nissan had been of extreme help to Ruth—both emotionally and financially. And eventually, on his return and especially when Ruben married Tuba, Nissan did his utmost to reciprocate his best friend's favors.

Unlike Tuba, Zilfa was fertile. Nine months after marrying Nissan, she gave birth to her first daughter. Their second child, again a girl, was born two years later. When Tuba married Ruben, Zilfa's two girls were three and one year old. A year into Tuba's marriage, Zilfa gave birth to her first son, whom they named Aaron after Nissan's father. Tuba, who hardly took an interest in any of Nissan's daughters, suddenly found a special place in her heart for this beautiful, calm and loving boy. She helped Zilfa change his diapers, bathe and pamper him. As Aaron grew, he became very attached to Auntie Tuba and spent a lot of time with her. Not only out of sympathy for her childless neighbor, but also because she was very busy taking care of her big family, Zilfa welcomed Tuba's involvement with her son.

Catastrophe hit the house of Nissan the Fabricseller when Aaron was seven on a cold and gloomy day in the winter of 1844. Aaron simply disappeared. One minute he was out playing in the street and the next, he was nowhere to be found.

"No, no! He hasn't died," said Ruth, who had brought the sad news home as Tuba sobbed, scratched her face and tore her scarf. "But the poor kid has simply vanished," she added ruefully. "He was there at the Meat Market Alley, right in front of my son's shop, and then, in the blink of an eye, he was gone. All of us called the boy's name, Aaron! Aaron! Poor Zilfa ran around, slapping her head and screaming her son's name until she passed out. When, after a few minutes, she regained consciousness, she froze. All of us were in a panic. Everyone was running back and forth, looking for him. 'Aaron! Aaron!' we kept calling. Zilfa looked like a statue made of white chalk, that's how pale she turned. It was as if her tongue had fallen into the back of her throat and she was choking on it as she tried to cry her child's name. Soon the news reached further and Nissan came running to the Meat Market Alley, followed by all the businessmen from the Fish Market Ally — your father, Nachamia the Baker, and I don't remember who else. Oh yes, Asghar the Allaf came and the good man recited incantations to shoo away jens who, he was certain, had stolen the boy. Then he muttered verses from the Koran to ward off evil spirits."

Hearing this, Tuba was weeping so hard she couldn't talk. "So?" she finally managed. Ruth wiped her own eyes with the back of her hand, sighed deeply and said, "It's not the first time that these Keshe nomads have kidnapped our children — unfortunately never to be found again. I heard Agha Ruben telling your father that he had seen a suspicious nomad woman in the crowd."

"I loved him just like my own child," Tuba said to Ruben's mother. "And how do they feel, poor Zilfa and Nissan? Just think of it. Their only son, after two daughters, is gone. Now what?"

"I don't know," Ruth whispered.

Time did not heal the wounded hearts of Aaron's parents nor did it erase his name from the memory of Jewbareh. "If he'd died, at least there would've been his grave to go to and mourn his death," Zilfa would sob. Nissan became silent. He sat in his shop, leaving its door and windows open — summer and winter — and stared into nowhere. It is as if he is looking for his son, people said. And if anyone, be it a customer or a friend, interrupted his thoughts, he got so incensed that he would, at times, throw them out.

Both Nissan's and Zilfa's relatives and friends used everything in their power to encourage the couple to have another child — a replacement for Aaron. But the two of them simply couldn't accept that Aaron was gone for good.

Nevertheless, three years later, Zilfa became pregnant. The son who was born was named Eli.

Chapter 16
Eli the Stallion

A year older than Rebecca, Eli was the fourth child born to Nissan and Zilfa. Contrary to his tag-name, the Stallion, that his father had given him at birth — perhaps imitating the Rhino — there was nothing of the stallion about Eli the child, physical or otherwise. He was a thin boy, timid and spoiled. Perhaps that was the reason why he and the courageous, ingenious Rebecca got along so well, since she was a leader by nature and he a follower. The members of the two families were so intimate that they roamed easily between the twin houses through the eroded bottom end of the wall that separated the two structures. In a way, they were happy to see the wall fall apart, especially Rebecca and Eli, who were inseparable. Each called the other's father "uncle" and the mother "aunt". For protection against nomad attacks, Ruben and Nissan had built hideouts in their basements. When she was only six, it was little Rebecca who discovered the den in her own basement and showed it to Eli. Then they found the den in Nissan's house. These basements became the places where the two young-sters played their favorite games through the years that followed.

"She's only six and I swear she has the head of a fifty-year old on her small body," Ruben said of his daughter, his only child, whom he worshiped and to whom he had become immensely attached. "Of course," people responded politely. "Poor Ruben had to wait so long to become a father. He is obsessed with his child and he has every right to be so."

Through the words of this six-year-old, no matter how childish, Ruben came to realize the great pain that he had inflicted upon both his wives — on Tuba when he had accepted Jewel as his second wife and on Jewel, whom he had married to be his child-maker. You couldn't ask Ruben how, but he swore that Rebecca had an enigmatic power that enabled him to regain his sense of responsibility towards his community, to make up for his selfish behavior towards his wives and to rejoice in his friendship with Nissan. Over time, Rebecca also became very attached to her father. After all, he was the only one of her three parents who did not fight over her. "Eli is my best friend," Rebecca shared her thoughts with her father, "and we love playing together."

And that made the Rhino happy. "You're a child with all traits of her father," he said. "Uncle Nissan and I were playmates also."

But by the time Rebecca was eleven, she had grown so fast that she looked much older than her real age and her closeness to Eli began to bother Ruben. "Soon she will hit puberty," he told his wives, "So, I'm not happy anymore with the two of them playing alone."

"But they are children, Agha," said Tuba and Jewel added, "They just play together."

"That's the point. You see, I used to get erections when I was younger than Eli, which means... You know what I mean. I want the two of you to talk to Rebecca," he went on to say. "Please encourage her to play with other girls."

The Rhino was too nice, too peaceful, and his wives did not want to argue with him. Actually, in a way they both tended to agree with their husband. There was nothing wrong with Rebecca playing with other girls. After all, this is what all the girls did.

The problem started on a Friday morning in the late winter of 1856. Although it was a bright day heralding early spring, Ruben's mood was dark. After his wives had repeatedly failed to persuade Rebecca to spend less time with Eli and find some girl friends, he had taken over and spent the best part of the night before arguing with his beloved daughter about the drawbacks of having Eli as her playmate. Frustrating as it was, he did tell her that boys and girls were like cotton and fire, that next to each other, they would catch fire. And what made him not only curious but furious was that Rebecca seemed to know exactly what her father was talking about. Actually, she made it clear to her father that she would not budge from her position. She had to be stopped, the Rhino decided, but he didn't want to raise his voice on the girl who was so precious to him. As time went by, Ruben's frustration gave place to anger, and anger to rage. Soon his heart was swollen with hatred for the kid next door, Eli.

On that Friday morning, Ruben couldn't wait to finish breakfast and leave home. When he was on his way out, he heard a robust pounding on the other side of the wall joining his house with Nissan's. He went to the side of the veranda closest to Nissan's house. Craning his neck, he saw Nissan standing on a ladder propped against the wall. He was making a hole there with a small hammer.

"Good morning. What are you doing, Nissan?"

"Good morning," Nissan replied, bringing his hammer down and pointing at the ground. "I planted this grapevine last year. The thing has grown so wildly that it has spread all over the ground. I thought I would make it into a trellis."

"But why are you hammering the wall?"

"I have to hook the top of the wooden pole somewhere. Don't worry. I'll make only two small holes — the size of two knuckles each."

"You can't do that, Nissan. This is an old wall. It can hardly support itself! You see how badly it has been ruined at the other end. I don't think you can use this for, of all things, a trellis." Filled with rage, Ruben spoke to Nissan with the coldness of a stranger.

"Ruben. Did you wake up on the wrong side of the bed this morning?" Nissan laughed in disbelief. "Is everything all right?"

"It was fine before this." He pointed to the wall. "Why don't you set up the poles on the ground next to the wall and put the top of the horizontal poles on them?"

"My friend, the trellis and the vine aren't heavy enough to affect the wall. So, let me finish this because I have some customers waiting at my shop and I'm running late."

"Not now. I mean it won't affect the wall now, but at the rate you're telling me the wild vine has been growing, it will soon get very heavy." Ruben could hear the silliness of his pointless argument, but he had a strange urge to express his fury — something that surprised Nissan.

"Excuse me, Your Excellency!" said Nissan, offering to win his friend over by joking. "Do I own this side of the wall or not? Of course I do. Am I allowed to scratch the wall on my side of the house? Of course I am. Go to work, have a good Shabbat and I assure you nothing will happen to this lousy, half-ruined wall."

To Nissan's utter astonishment, Ruben exploded. He slapped his chest with his fist and hollered, "At least you owe me the courtesy of asking my permission before ruining our joint wall. But what do you do instead? You make fun of me!"

"What's with you, Ruben? I can't believe you're making such a big fuss over such a trivial matter. Instead of reciting a fertility blessing over the vine, you are condemning it? All right," Nissan said in a low tone and began climbing down the ladder. "If it bothers you that much, I won't do it." He took the ladder and put it at the bottom of the wall and then, as he was walking away, he raised his head and said, "I owe everything I have to you, Ruben, and I'll be damned if I will put the bond with my best friend and our kadkhoda in jeopardy over a silly thing like this."

"Why is it that I always have to be the understanding one? Take my kadkhoda-hood and shove it up the ass of the Butcher's donkey."

"You won't fit there, my friend," Nissan laughed uproariously. "Take it easy, for goodness' sake."

"How do you want me to take it easy when you think I'm too big to fit in a donkey's ass?"

"I...was...joking," Nissan stressed, this time in a more serious tone. Then he lowered his voice and continued, "You know what, Ruben? I started to do this with so much happiness this morning and you've put such a bad taste in my mouth, I feel as if I've swallowed a mule-load of snake venom. Now, if you'll excuse me, I'm going in."

"No, I will *not* excuse you!" Ruben yelled in a ghastly tone. "You have to admit that this wall is *mine* and not yours. You remember when we were building these houses I lent you the money to construct this wall?"

"Ruben. Please calm down. I repeat: Everything I have belongs to you. Everything. My business, my house, I mean you've helped me every step of the way to get to where I am now and for that, I am extremely grateful to you. But let me assure you, I have kept a full accounting of all the money you've loaned me, and my repayments to you. You're most welcome to come and take a look at them."

But Ruben wasn't listening to Nissan. All he saw was the father of a boy who claimed his most precious asset—Rebecca. A voice from within was commanding him to crush the friendship with his best friend of many years. So he went on and on taunting Nissan, who eventually became so outraged that he went back to the wall, again put the ladder against it and began digging the hole in the wall as he shouted back at Ruben at the top of his lungs.

Hearing the two men quarrelling, their wives ran out of their adjacent kitchens, while Rebecca, Eli and his sisters came out of their rooms, all of them shaken.

Tuba was the first to speak. "*Agha jaan*—my dear master. What's the matter?"

"Shut up and go back to your kitchen."

Frightened at his harshness, Jewel stayed put.

On the other side of the wall, Zilfa stood at the bottom of the ladder and said to her husband, "May I go blind and not see you and Kadkhoda Ruben arguing and shouting at each other!"

"Before you go blind, I'm going to show you that this is not an argument," Nissan yelled as he stepped down the ladder, raising his voice higher at each step. At the last step he waved his fist in the air and shouted at Ruben, "It's a fight! If you are a man, come to the end of this rotten wall and we will settle this right now."

Zilfa threw herself at Nissan's feet. "Please don't, Agha. I beg you." But, like a warrior, Nissan marched towards the open end of the wall. At the same time, Ruben snarled at his wives and his daughter as he strode across the veranda and into the courtyard. "You are all my witness. He, this idiot whose head isn't worth the hat he's wearing, *he* started all this."

Rebecca chased her father, grabbed him by his sleeve and begged, "What has happened to you, Baba? Please don't fight Uncle Nissan."

"If I leave this man alone, he will steal you from me," he said to Rebecca, and then to Nissan, "You little, miserable thing. You want to fight with *me*?"

"Please, Baba…"

"Get away from me," he shouted at Rebecca, pushing her away.

Rebecca fell to the ground as Tuba and Jewel rushed to her help.

"Oh, neighbors!" Nissan shouted loudly. "Did you hear what he said? He calls me a thief. What have I stolen from you, kadkhoda?"

Rebecca stood up and followed her father as Tuba and Jewel chased her—the three of them begging Ruben to calm down. On the other side, Zilfa and her two daughters were pleading with Nissan not to fight. Eli, with his face turned as pale as gypsum and his hand over his open mouth, hung back watching the scene.

"Look at your poor boy," Zilfa begged Nissan. "Look how scared he is. Please Agha, calm yourself."

Hearing this, as if he had been waiting for an acknowledgement, Eli followed his father, tugging at his sleeve and begging him to stop. "Go away!" Nissan pushed Eli aside who turned around, went into his room and closed the door behind him. Outside, despite the pleas of their wives, the two men were now standing face to face. With everyone's breath held fast, Nissan looked at Ruben, and as if realizing for the first time how massive his opponent was, he simply turned around and walked away. "Fine," Nissan said to Zilfa as he headed back inside the house. "I know how to teach him the biggest lesson of his life."

Ruben followed Nissan into his house, but Zilfa stood in his way. "You come into this house to hurt your best friend, Kadkhoda Ruben ? Beat me instead!"

"This coward sends a *woman* to fight in his place?" Ruben was loud and malicious. "I am telling you and I am telling that ungrateful traitor who is hiding from me. I don't want you anywhere near my family, I don't want your son anywhere near my daughter and if I see him playing with Rebecca one more time," he raised his voice and shouted, "Do you hear me, Eli? If I ever catch you playing, or even talking to my daughter, you will have to deal with me!" Then, pointing at his wives, he continued, "And the same goes for you and this man's wife. No talking, no friendship, nothing, nothing, nothing!" he roared.

Tuba and Jewel looked at each other—a look that said, *Are you thinking what I am thinking? That our man is so attached to Rebecca that he wants her to himself and no one else? That despite his rhino-like figure, he is scared of timid, little Eli? That he feels insecure when he sees Rebecca and Eli together—afraid that he might lose his only child to someone else?"*

Ruben's wives took him by his hands and pulled him back to the other side of the wall, prodding him into Tuba's room. They sat him down and gave him tea, but his anger would not be assuaged. "He is ruining my wall?" he grunted. "For all the good that I have done him, *this* is my reward?"

His wives nodded dutifully until the Rhino wore himself out with grumbling. Then, just as he was about to leave, the hammering on the wall began again. He turned around and looked towards Nissan's house in disbelief. His wives and Rebecca froze. Ruben pursed his lips. *I could kill him*, he thought. But this time he stopped dead in his tracks. Was he really capable, he wondered, of killing his best friend? Had he reached the point, once again, when he could kill another human being? Had his soul finally become that depraved?

Within a few hours, numerous reports of the quarrel between Ruben and Nissan had spread throughout the ghetto. Tuti the Exfoliator knew from very, very reliable sources that Nissan had caught Ruben kissing Zilfa. "After all, Ruben had kissed his first wife, and goodness knows what else he had done before they were even married," she said, reviving the phantom of the old gossip, forever burned into the common memory of the Jewbarites.

"And then, our sultan married a second wife. Nothing seems to stop his appetite for women," said the Wartfaced Monir. But according to Nosrat the Lavender, the reverse had happened. Ruben had discovered that his friend Nissan, while pretending to serve as a mediator between Ruben's wives, had developed a secret affair with Jewel. "Certainly Nissan has had many opportunities to put himself in Jewel's favor," Nina the Singer whispered to Rana the Coyote. In addition to all these, there were half a dozen other stories, each a variation on those two supposedly clandestine relationships. And when the rumors and the gossip reached Ruben and Nissan, their resentment against each other soared.

A few days later, on the Tuesday following the confrontation between Ruben and Nissan, to be exact, Tuba brought Ruth her breakfast and found her on the floor, lying on her back, her eyes wide open as though staring at the ceiling. Dead. Ruth was dead. Tuba didn't cry. She put the tray aside and lay down next to her mother-in-law's body. Tuba didn't know how long she stayed there lying next to Ruth. How long did she lie there next to Ruth? She didn't know. But when she got up again, Ruth's eyes were closed, her face peaceful. Tuba came out of the dead woman's room, stood on the veranda and took a deep breath—a breath she had not taken with such tranquility in years. She tasted the air. It was sweet, wholesome. The green leaves of the berry tree were glittering, the walls of her house whiter than ever. Jewel, who was going back and forth to the kitchen, suddenly looked adoringly beautiful. Tuba felt light. The heavy weight of her hatred for Ruth had been taken off her heart. Tuba had no tears to shed for her husband's mother, no voice to mourn her passing. This horrid woman had tormented her for years. And now, finally, she was dead and would never insult and mock and belittle Tuba again. She called Jewel and whispered to her that their mother-in-law was dead. "At last," Jewel shrugged, as though hearing long-desired news. Tuba then told her havoo to take Rebecca to Gohar's house before the commotion began. Jewel complied and when she returned, the wives of Ruben the Rhino, the kadkhoda of Jewbareh, began screaming the loss of their dearest mother-in-law. They sat the seven days of *shiva* and the thirty days of mourning. Ruben refused to allow Nissan and his family to attend the funeral and the mourning rituals, for he believed that in her muteness, Ruth had heard them fight and that "the evil on the other side of the wall," as he put it, had killed his mother.

From this point on, every night Ruben came back home with news to support his growing hatred toward Nissan.

"Guess who came to visit me today?" Ruben asked his wives and Rebecca. Everyone sitting around the sofreh braced themselves, knowing where he was heading. "Haskell the Mayor," he said, answering his own question. "The same Haskell who, throughout many years of our joint community work, has been so respectful of me, the same Haskell who embraced me whenever we met, today he came into my shop and sat there like I didn't exist. 'What's the matter,' I asked him, but he remained mute. 'Talk to me!' I implored him, 'Are you upset with me?' He sat there sighing. 'No' was all he could say. I tried to get him to open up to me in every way, using the tongue of forty birds, as they say, to find out what was bothering him, but he refused to tell me. All he did was shake his head. To make a long story short, when he finally spoke, he said, 'I'm sorry kadkhoda. It's about the wounds that we inflict upon ourselves,' and saying this, he left. Now, you tell me. What does this mean?"

"I don't know. What does it mean, Agha?" Tuba asked, bouncing the question back at him.

"Poor Haskell," said Jewel, making the mistake of responding to the question Ruben had prepared himself to answer. "This morning, women at the Meat Market Alley were talking about his son-in-law. He has turned out to be a terribly unfit match for his daughter. Haskell's wife had begged him not to give his daughter's hand in marriage to this impostor, but Haskell refused to listen to her. The groom has already thrown the bride out of his house. 'Go and get money from your father and don't come back empty-handed,' this idiot has told his wife of only two months. The poor girl has gone back to her parents' home and no mediator has been successful in working anything out so far. I'm sure that's why..."

"Shut up!" Ruben blurted out. "Who asked *you*? How come women on the Meat Market Alley know this and I, the governor of Jewbareh, don't?"

Both of his wives, and in fact Ruben himself, had come to realize how people were gradually losing faith and confidence in him. Perhaps that was why Haskell hadn't shared his problem with him or asked for his help. "My master," Tuba said coolly, coming to Jewel's rescue. "Poor Jewel is just trying to answer your question and explain why the man is upset. It is clear that Haskell knows that he himself is to blame for the disaster that has befallen his daughter." Jewel was amazed that her havoo was standing up for her and taking her side. But she wasn't alone in her astonishment. Ruben raised his arms up to the heavens. "Has the Messiah come? Why all of a sudden has my second wife become 'a poor woman' to my first? Fine. I asked you a question and now I take it back. Neither one of you could possibly know what *I* know. Haskell's statement had everything to do with this..." He pointed his forefinger at Nissan's house to avoid mentioning his name, "this enemy next door, may his name be erased from the book of existence." Then he turned to Rebecca and continued, "You should listen to this carefully, my dear. What the poor Haskell meant was that the son of our next-door enemy is about to harm you."

"Who, Baba?" Rebecca said in a peaceful voice. "Eli? Eli is not even capable of killing a fly. Even when he walks, he makes sure not to step on any ants."

"My *aziz*—dearest. You are too young to understand what I am saying. So, just be a good girl and listen to your father."

On the other side of the wall, the mood was very much the same. Nissan was so upset that he had forbidden his family even to mention Ruben's name or to utter a word about the Rhino's clan. Over time, the women and children learned to squelch their opposition to the quarrel between the two men and to remain silent as Nissan and Ruben carried on with their hate-tainted lectures. Fearing Ruben's fury, his wives—who had always enjoyed their chats with Zilfa as they prepared lunch and dinner in their adjacent kitchens—no longer talked to her, and acted as though they had never known each other. As for the children of the two households, Eli spent most of his time alone, hidden in his room, whereas Rebecca complained passionately to her mothers that she missed playing with her friend.

Still, the most remarkable outcome of this conflict between Ruben and Nissan was the way it brought Tuba and Jewel somehow closer to each other. When they were busy cooking together in their kitchen, they shared their thoughts about their husband. They agreed that despite spreading gossip which was a pastime for Jewbarites, they respected their patriarch who at all times had served his community selflessly. They both knew him to be the most important man in Jewbareh, the governor who had been to Jerusalem, from whence he had come back, enriched with a wealth of knowledge and understanding of Jewish ethics.

"Even in my worst days of the ordeal of my barrenness," Tuba said to her havoo, "I could see that he did his utmost to be fair-minded and decent. He was truly torn."

"And to think of his people in the wisest way," Jewel added. "It's a shame that all this could be defeated because of his paranoia about losing Rebecca to another male—be it a man or a child like Eli."

Although Tuba didn't reject Jewel's assumption, she believed that someone must have cast an evil eye over the friendship between the two families, so she decided to consult a soothsayer to solve this calamity. During the time when she was trying to conceive a child, out of the many expert prognosticates and sorcerers she had visited outside Jewbareh, Tuba had been most impressed with Naji the Soothsayer. After only a few sessions he had claimed that a girl with a scar on her face, in collaboration with her mother, had put a permanent and irreversible curse on her womb. Years later, when Tuba resigned to the fact that she was never going to have a child, she remembered Naji's prophecy and concluded that this could only have been Nosrat the Lavender who, for years had tried to marry Batia, her scar-faced daughter, to Ruben. Then Naji had performed some acts of sorcery at the conclusion of which he had said, "A day will come when you will raise a child in your bosom. This child will make you very happy, but your happiness will be continually interrupted."

One morning, when Ruben had left for the day, Tuba took Jewel to Naji's tiny house near Juma Mosque, at the entrance to Jewbareh. It had been many years since Tuba had seen Naji. The man's long beard had turned gray, the wrinkles around his eyes had deepened and his saintly aura had grown. As Jewel looked on, Tuba told him why they had come and asked if evil eyes had caused the catastrophe between their husband and his friend. Hearing this, the Soothsayer walked out of his room and returned with a piece of charcoal and an egg on a napkin. "I'm sure you know that anyone, friend or foe, can cast the evil eye on people. So, you have to give me the names of all those around you. Anyone that you can remember."

"How about..." Jewel began, but Naji cut her short.

"How about starting with the two of you." He put the napkin on his crossed legs, then took the egg in his left hand, the piece of charcoal in his right hand and began. "Tuba, I know your name." Saying this, he drew a line on the egg. "And," he looked at Jewel, who said her name. "Jewel," he repeated, and drew the next line. They gave him the names of Jewbarites they recalled — Ruben, Nissan, Zilfa, Rebecca, Eli and his sisters, and many other names. As either Tuba or Jewel said a name, Naji would repeat it, drawing a line on the egg. When the egg was all blackened with the multitude of lines, Naji put the palms of his hands on the two sides of the egg and asked Tuba and Jewel to repeat the names they had said once again. With every name, the soothsayer pressed his palms against the two ends of the egg, which was supposed to break with the name of the evil-eyed person. Ruben! Naji pushed, but the egg didn't break. Tuba! He pushed and again it didn't break. Jewel! The same. They went on and on until Tuba said, Batia! And the egg exploded, making a messy mix of yoke and charcoal soot on the napkin.

"Who is this woman?" Naji asked.

"The woman who wanted to marry my husband. The woman who, as years ago you predicted quite rightly, cast a curse on me and made me childless. Don't you remember, Agha Naji?"

"Vaguely," Naji said, scratching his beard. "Very vaguely. Anyhow, look at the mess I see here," he added, pointing to the disgustingly soiled napkin. "This woman has a very, very powerful evil eye."

"So, what's to be done?" Jewel asked.

"I will recite the necessary incantations, which will take a long time to take effect. Unless, of course, a magical energy intervenes."

The person with magical energy turned out to be the Graceful Rebecca.

It was a hot summer afternoon in 1857. Six months had passed since the confrontation between the two heads of households. Rebecca was sitting on the edge of the small pool below the veranda, her little skirt rolled up as always, dangling her legs as the water rippled around them. Nissan and Ruben were at work and their wives were in their kitchens cooking dinner. Coming out of his parents' room, Eli went out to his own veranda to get some fresh air and saw Rebecca.

"Rebecca! Put down your skirt," Tuba shouted, emerging briefly from the kitchen. "How many times do I have to tell you? You are not a little girl any longer. You are *ten years old!* You have to cover yourself. God help us with this disobedient child!" Tuba grumbled as she disappeared back into the kitchen.

Rebecca looked at her mother and shrugged her shoulders. She turned her gaze from Tuba, and saw Eli looking at her and smiled as she motioned for him to come to the end of the veranda near her house, which he did cautiously. "Hey! I miss playing with you. Don't you?" she whispered. Eli's eyes widened with fear as he nodded.

"So, come over and let's play." She pointed to the basement of her house.

"I can't. My father will kill me," he whispered back, passing his hand rapidly across his neck.

"Then I will see you down there." This time she pointed to the basement of Eli's house.

The boy's knees began to shake as he saw Rebecca walking

toward the open end of the wall and entering Nissan's house. Tuba and Jewel ran out of the kitchen. "Where are you going, sweetheart?" asked Jewel. Ignoring the question, Rebecca kept on moving toward Nissan's house. Jewel shouted, "I'm talking to you, Rebecca! Where do you think you're going?"

"I'm going to play with Eli," she said, not turning around.

Zilfa heard Jewel and rushed out of her kitchen. Forgetting for the moment that they were not supposed to be talking to each other, Tuba asked Zilfa, "Do you see what I see?"

"Well. She is going to play with Eli," Zilfa said, smiling.

The three women looked at each other and froze. Then they threw themselves into each other's arms, laughing and crying at the same time. The bravery of the young girl had suddenly become contagious and given the women the courage to venture into what they had believed to be dangerous territory.

"Why don't you come into our kitchen, Zilfa, and taste the eggplant stew that this havoo of mine has cooked?" said Tuba, addressing her dear neighbor for the first time in months. "I think it needs a dash of saffron, but then this naughty woman never listens to me. Maybe she'll listen to you."

Zilfa was overjoyed to be talking with her neighbors once again and amazed at the friendly way in which Tuba talked about Jewel. In the kitchen, Tuba gave her a taste of the stew which she pronounced excellent. Then Zilfa shook her head and said, "What's with our men?"

"Call them children, not men," Tuba said.

"Don't insult children," Jewel chuckled. "Look how innocently real children disobey us and follow their own hearts."

"For all these years our husbands have been like brothers to one another, and now..." Zilfa sighed.

"To this very moment, as I stand here, I don't know why they went so crazy over this rotten, disintegrating wall. Do you?" Jewel added.

"The answer is simple," Tuba said laughing. "One was making a hole while the other made an ass out of himself."

The three women laughed loudly. "Maybe it's their age," Zilfa concluded. "The older they get, instead of acting like grownups, the more they revert back to their adolescence."

So, as of that moment, the wives and the children of the two households stealthily re-established their friendship. And in fact, it was Rebecca who—with her courage and her determination not to fight her parents' silly battles, and to be reunited with her playmate— had initiated it and made it happen. From that day on, whenever Ruben and Nissan left home, Rebecca and Eli went underground into the basement and their mothers talked, giggled and, in the privacy of their kitchens, hungrily resumed the exchange of gossip. In the meantime, as their families were clandestinely embracing each other, Ruben and Nissan worked on finding even more toxic news to bring home.

Under these circumstances, the long-standing grudge between Tuba and Jewel diminished further as they came to realize that though they might be rivals, they were most certainly no longer enemies.

The animosity between Ruben and Nissan and the clandestine friendship between their families continued until Rebecca and Eli entered into early adolescence. At thirteen, Rebecca looked like a cross between Jewel and her father. Her long hair was light. The hazel eyes she had been born with now tended toward a brilliant, gleaming green. Thin and shapely, she had the body of her mother and, under her fair skin, the firm muscles of the Rhino. Eli had inherited the slimness and fragility of his father, but very much like his late uncle Yehuda, said his mother, at fourteen he was taller than his father.

As Rebecca's breasts began to sprout, the Rhino's wives witnessed how his fear of losing his only child to someone else escalated. "Does she have to wear such tight shirts?" he questioned his wives scornfully. "She's only a child. Don't you think you two should be encouraging her to wear more modest dresses?"

"*Ghorbane shoma*, Agha—may my life be sacrificed for you, my master," Tuba said cheerfully. "Our daughter is almost fourteen."

"No she's not. She's twelve, turning thirteen. She's still a child."

"Thirteen, fourteen, whatever," said Jewel calmly. "May the evil eye be blind, our daughter is so tall, so slender and so beautiful, I'm sure, before we know, khastegar after khastegar will be knocking on our door."

"Khastegar after khastegar can go and piss on their fathers' graves. I'm warning the two of you—no one will take my daughter to the Meat Market when she is fourteen, and that is *two* years from now. She is mine and I will decide when. Do you understand?"

"Yes Agha," said both women simultaneously.

Ruben's concerns aside, his wives shared many fears about what was going on behind the back of their irrationally rigid husband. So far they had been very lucky in that their secret friendship with Nissan's family had not been betrayed, but with Rebecca's imminent puberty and the soft hair that showed itself on Eli's face, further bothersome concerns took shape in the minds of the Rhino's wives. As the mothers of a female child, they felt the heavy responsibility of keeping their daughter's virginity intact and in doing so, more and more they became convinced that they had to prevent her from seeing Eli. Jewel and Tuba agreed that it would be relatively easy to find some way to keep Eli from Rebecca, but it would be much more difficult to control the stubborn and single-minded Rebecca who was devoted to her friend. That was when they shared their concern with Zilfa, appealing to her for help. Zilfa was sympathetic with the two mothers and reassured them that she would help them accomplish what they requested. So, on the morning after Tuba and Jewel had spoken to her, as Zilfa was walking her son to Rabbi Shimon's *sheik* — where he studied Torah and Talmud — she spoke to Eli and told him of the hazards faced by young girls and boys who were exceptionally close to each other, and concluded that he should not see Rebecca any longer.

Eli turned sullen for a few minutes and then, to his mother's utter astonishment, he spoke. "But Rebecca and I have been friends and played together forever."

Zilfa stopped and stared at her son, obviously not believing what she was hearing. There was more than a trace of Rebecca's presence of mind and determination in the boy's voice. "Since when... I mean..." she threw her arms up in the air and continued, "Remember that poor Rebecca's name must not be tarnished," she said with emphasis to her son. "God forbid, if the news that you and she secretly get together leaked out, besides your father, can you imagine what Uncle Ruben would do to you? May my tongue stick to the roof of my mouth and may I not live to see that day, but he would slice you into pieces thinner than your ears." Zilfa slapped the back of her hand as though she were watching the scene. "Why don't you play with boys, my dear?"

"Because... because they say I'm timid like a stray dog and they throw me out of their games. But Rebecca plays with me."

"You see, my dear," Zilfa said, becoming sterner. "There's

playing and then there's *playing.* Until now you were a young boy and she was a little girl. Now you are a man and she is a becoming a woman. Children play, adults get married."

"But I don't want to get married." Eli tugged his hair.

"Of course not. You're only fourteen. You will wait until you are ready and I will find you the right match, my boy. Now, promise me!"

Eli agreed that he would no longer seek out his beloved friend, Rebecca, but he was not happy about it. He grumbled all the way to the *sheik,* "It's not fair. Who the hell has set this rule that at fourteen you lose your friends? It's so ridiculous..." He went on and on as Zilfa thought, not without pleasure, about the source of Eli's inspiration and the quiet inner courage he had began to muster. It had to be Rebecca. She was turning him into a man — a determined, honest, and decent man, strengthened by love for a remarkable girl.

The next day, when Eli didn't show up, Rebecca came to the kitchen and asked Zilfa where he was. "Haven't you told Rebecca?" Zilfa asked Jewel and Tuba. Rebecca was suddenly alarmed. "Has something happened to Eli?"

"Let me explain the situation to you, my dear," Tuba muttered. "You see, my child, you are a young woman now. So we," — she pointed at Jewel and herself — "and Auntie Zilfa, believe that you and Eli should no longer see each other, because..."

Rebecca was gone. She had dashed out of the kitchen and was flying toward Eli's room. She found Eli sitting on the ground, his back against the wall, with his legs lazily stretched out before him. She stood at the threshold and addressed him. "Have they told you not to play with me?"

"Yes," he murmured.

"And you agreed? Agreed not to see me?"

"What could I do? I mean, how could I not agree when our mothers want this?" he sighed.

Rebecca walked up to him and stood over his head, "You are not a stallion," she said. "You are no more than a little bunny."

"Please, don't call me that. It's *your* mothers who are afraid that... I don't know what they are afraid of. Go ask them!"

"Bunny, bunny, bunny!" she said laughing, pointing at him while turning to go.

"I cannot put up with your disdain, Rebecca!" said Eli who didn't know if he was sorrier to hear her make fun of him or to see that she was about to leave.

"Listen to my brave hero! I'm proud of you." Rebecca said in a comforting tone. "Wait for me and I will find the solution."

Chapter 17
A Jen Prodigy

Once upon a time, there was a young girl named The Graceful Rebecca who was foolish, headstrong, stubborn and brazen, and didn't listen to her parents…

This is how, for generations, the Jewbarite mothers began the stories they told their daughters about this girl, Rebecca by name, who, because she was so obstinate, must have been possessed by jens when she was very young. Jens, they explained, these gruesome living creatures that were half-man-half-demon, these fairy-like evil genies with long faces like goats, wide hooves like cows and hairy bodies like monkeys who lived in abandoned bathhouses, targeted young women who disobeyed their parents. Once they captured a girl, they used their wicked powers to make her numb, and then they crawled inside her while many other jens surrounded them, reciting chilling, ancient chants. The mothers pointed to Rebecca's early pattern of disobeying her parents as one sure sign that the jens had penetrated the girl's soul. Then, they said, late one night, these little demons had summoned Rebecca to an old dormant bathhouse near the eleventh twist of the Alley, which no longer existed, and she went there while sleepwalking. These small scary creatures opened the door for her. "Come in, come in," she heard them say, and the corrupted girl went in. Once she was inside, the door slammed shut behind her and they did many strange things to her. She was now their slave and did whatever they wanted her to do. Armed with the evil powers they had given her, she could do many things that others couldn't. For example, she was able to see through your mind, take it over and make you do whatever wicked act she wanted you to do. She did many ugly things also. She covered herself in a transparent chador and underneath that she wore sheer blouses, turning against each other two men of virtue who before then had been like brothers. And who were those two men? Her own father, the legendary Ruben the Rhino, and his best friend, Nissan the Fabricseller. And as if this weren't enough, she went on to bewitch Nissan's son, making him fall in love with her and transforming this shy kid into an unruly, hostile boy who did whatever evil act she wanted him to do.

One day, to the astonishment of her poor parents—mothers told their frightened daughters—Rebecca, who had never been schooled, began to recite the holy prayer book by heart. The whole book. Now even the rabbi was scared too. "It must be those demons," he concluded. Then he went to the synagogue, beat his chest and chanted, "Woe is upon us! A girl who knows the whole prayer book by heart! This can only be a bad omen!" But Rebecca's parents and indeed all the Jewbarites required more than chest-beating from their rabbi. They urged him to summon Rebecca and investigate himself the calamity that had befallen her.

So, one day, the girl's distraught parents called the rabbi to their house, then they called in Rebecca, and the rabbi questioned the poor jen-stricken soul.

"Where have you learned these prayers?" the rabbi asked her.

"I have heard my father recite them many times," the arrogant girl responded.

"And you have memorized them just by hearing them?"

"Just by listening!" she responded brazenly. "Anybody could learn them if they heard them as often as I have."

Infuriated by this shameless girl, the rabbi raised his voice on her and said, "Young lady! If what you are saying were right, then all Jewbarite girls would know as many prayers as you do. Besides, the holy words are meant to be spoken by men only. You are forbidden to recite them."

But if you think that this deceived, conceited girl—who, of course, was bewitched by the jens—would shut up, you are wrong. Instead of obeying the rabbi's instruction, she tartly asked, "And why is that?" Then—may she bear the requital of her sins—she said something that only Satan himself would say. "You are telling me," she said, "that only men's prayers are heard, not women's?"

Attempting to exorcise her, they took her to a famous sorcerer who recited many prescribed incantations over her, but to no avail and…

So, as generation after generation of Jewbarite mothers told these fables about the Graceful Rebecca to their daughters, each one of them added a touch of imagination here and a dose of fantasy there to the life story of a young woman who in reality must have been a prodigy and whose genius was nevertheless incomprehensible to the timid, conventional Jewbarites.

At thirteen, Rebecca did not as yet know very much about men and women. But this longing that she felt for Eli she knew to be something that was not entirely innocent. Unaware of her instinctive desires, she nevertheless felt an incessant urge to unearth this thrilling feeling and give it a name. All she knew was that she wanted to be with Eli for the rest of her life, especially since she was convinced that Eli had the same feelings for her. Unfortunately, Eli's affection for her was over-shadowed by his immaturity and timidity of spirit, so much so that he was willing to take the easy way out. The thing that even her genius couldn't comprehend was why she felt about Eli the way she did and why she was so attached to this naïve and fearful young man. Rebecca understood the challenge that lay before her—to once again regain Eli despite Tuba's, Jewel's, and Zilfa's prohibition against their seeing each other. Taking into account that she and Eli were both under their mothers' constant surveillance, Rebecca launched her long-contemplated plan in the early afternoon hours of a cold winter day in the winter of 1861. She was in the kitchen helping Jewel and Tuba when she heard Zilfa call for Eli to go and get some freshly baked bread. From the window she saw Eli leave the house for the street, and at that moment she slipped out and followed him. Covered in her white chador, Rebecca blended in with the heavy snow that had been falling for the last few days, and was virtually invisible to prying eyes. On the fourth turn of the Alley of Eleven Twists, under the darkness of the entrance to an abandoned house, she stopped and called his name. Eli turned around, looked at her and froze. She motioned to him to join her.

"What do you want?" Eli whispered as he approached her with hesitant steps.

"I want to see you again."

"But…"

"Listen to me Eli," she said as she put her finger to his lips, silencing him. "I have the solution. All we have to do is to be very careful and get together in our basement very late at night. I mean sometime after midnight when everybody is fast sleep. And, for God's sake, stop shaking!"

For Eli, the very thought of sneaking in the dark of night into a hideout that his father had decreed an enemy zone and to which his mother had forbidden him to go was just too frightening. "Are you crazy?" he told Rebecca and went on parroting his mother's dire warning that Ruben would kill them both if he found out. "He will slice me so thin that..."

"...that your ears will be the biggest part that remains," she cut in. "Don't worry. I will glue you back together," she added, laughing as she ran away, leaving the boy dumbfounded. But before disappearing to the next alley, Rebecca turned around and said, "Listen! Tonight, at the first toll of camel bells, I will see you in the basement of my house."

The toll of camel bells was a time-keeping device for Jewbarites. The camels in caravans that hauled provisions into the city of Esfahan had bells on their necks that could be heard from a long distance. They followed each other in a straight line, with the first one pacing behind the caravan leader, who held its leash, and the other animals walking behind it in harmony, creating a captivating symphony. Usually, the bells would start at about midnight, when they could be heard, at first faintly, in the distance. Jewbarites called this *zangeh aval*—the first ring. Then, as the caravans got closer to the ghetto, the chiming became louder and then quite clear in the earliest morning hours as the camel caravans passed by and headed to the nearby bazaar. This they called *zangeh dovom*—the second ring. Zangeh aval was the alarm clock for the earliest risers, while just before sunrise the zangeh dovom awoke the muezzin of the Juma Mosque, which was near Jewbareh. He would climb up the minaret of the mosque and cry loudly, *"Allah Akbar!"*—Allah is great. This called the Muslims to the mosque and signaled to the Jews that it was time to visit the synagogue.

Eli didn't sleep that night. Tossing in his bed, he was anticipating the bells whose ringing would herald the arrival of the camel caravans. To the young man, time seemed to have stopped. With every little sound, he jumped up, wondering whether he had just heard the bells or if there were someone lurking out there, waiting to catch him the moment he stepped out. Many times he ran to the window and looked outside, carefully viewing the courtyard of Rebecca's house in the bright moonlight and its reflection on the frozen snow. Despite the cold, he felt feverish. Ruben's threats aside, what would happen if his own parents caught him on his way to Rebecca's house? Waves of fear and the excitement inherent in the mesmerizing challenge of doing what Rebecca had dared him to do were turning around in his brain like a windmill.

And then, suddenly he heard the sound of camel bells from a far, far distance. Its resonance awakened a peculiar vigor in Eli. At once he was determined to prove to Rebecca that he was not a timid bunny, but a man deserving of his title, the Stallion. He wrapped himself in a white sheepskin coat his father had bought him from a tribesman and sneaked out of his room. The snow had blanketed the ground, trees, roofs and stairs. The surface of the small pool in the courtyard was frozen. The street dogs howled in languid harmony with the sound of the arriving caravan bells. Despite his determination, Eli felt his knees shaking as he came down to the veranda. He held tightly to the snow-covered banisters. At the bottom of the stairs he stopped and looked around, cautious lest someone see him. The shadows on the white snow of the trees in the courtyard looked like images of his parents, ready to ambush him. Ahead stood the gap between the two houses. He would go up to that point, turn around at the other end and enter Ruben's house. He would then go back the same distance on the other side of the wall to reach the stairs leading to the basement where Rebecca, the daughter of the hostile tribe's head, was awaiting him.

"Oh God, please protect me," he prayed, his eyes tearing in the cold breeze, perhaps weeping also. "I'm only fourteen."

The wetness of the tears made his cheeks even colder. He took a deep breath, mustered his energy, stood up straight, wiped his tears with the sleeve of his fur coat and began his precarious journey.

A new chapter had begun in the lives of Rebecca and Eli. They looked forward to the appointed nights, when, in the early morning hours, Eli would sneak into the basement of Ruben's house. There, as he held Rebecca in his arms, she would whisper sweet stories into his ears and give him courage to come back again despite the fear that never left him. Their pleasant visits would last only until they heard the muezzin's voice, reciting the morning prayer. Then, just before their parents awoke, Eli went back to his bed.

The winter snow melted, spring came and went, followed by hot summer nights, which brought with them a problem for the young lovers. To avoid the heat of the summer, it was customary for people to make their beds outdoors at night and sleep in the open where it was cooler. This made it more difficult for Eli and Rebecca to meet. Nevertheless, meet they did, but more cautiously than before, as they looked forward to the arrival of the cooler season, which would force the outdoor people back into their bedrooms. Although the thought of being caught during one of his nocturnal adventures still terrified Eli, Rebecca's love and her encouragements had emboldened him so much that, every morning when he left Rebecca, he couldn't wait until the next night to return, embrace her and listen to another one of her tales. These were the many bedtime stories her grandmother, Zari, had murmured into her ears when she was a child. Tales of A Thousand and One Nights that Shahrzad the Storyteller had recounted to the Sultan. Eli put his head on Rebecca's lap and listened to her soothing voice as she ran her fingers through his hair, down to his cheekbones and his lips.

"Once upon a time, there was a ruthless sultan who married a girl each evening and had her killed in the morning," Rebecca said, reciting the first story in this ancient group of tales to a rapt Eli. "With the Sultan intent on killing innocent women, the brave young Shahrzad decided to stop the brutal king and volunteered to marry him for one night. The first night she told the cruel sultan a charming story that went on to the early morning hours, but the insightful Shahrzad left the tale unfinished, promising the sultan that she would tell him the ending the following night. The next night, she finished the old story and began a new one, again leaving the ending open. With the trick she played on the coldblooded king and the magic of her stories, which lasted a thousand and one nights, Shahrzad ultimately encouraged him to give up the murdering of women."

Following the pattern of Shahrzad the storyteller, Rebecca left her tales unfinished until the next night, leaving Eli in almost unbearable suspense about what was going to happen next, so that he couldn't wait to see her again. Rebecca's skill in bringing these tales to life and making every incident in them as vivid as possible captured the imagination of the young boy. To Eli, the most astounding of all these tales was the one about the brave daughter of the farmer who led a revolutionary movement to save the emperor's throne. She fought her enemies and defeated them, after which the son of the emperor fell in love with this ordinary girl and chose her over all the aristocratic and royal women he could have had instead.

"The Prince is riding a milk-white horse, a stallion with golden hooves and silvery wings. His arms are graceful, his hands shapely, his face luminous, his eyes those of a gazelle and his soft hair, blowing in the air, like a field of un-harvested wheat in the autumn. The charming prince arrives looking for the girl of his dreams — the savior of his throne. He knows who she is, although he has never met her. He gallops through the swerving alleys of this far away small village where his beloved lives. People of the village are wearing their dark winter clothes, their heads submerged in their heavy jackets as they scurry around making their way through the passages that had been dug between the piles of snow. With the arrival of the prince also comes the spring. A warm breeze begins to blow, melting the snow. Now the village is reborn. The sun becomes kind and friendly and the skies celebrate the majesty of the prince. Men have no words of mockery to exchange and women's voices are void of gossip..."

"Allah Akbar, Allah Akbar!" Suddenly, with the hoarse cry of the muezzin's voice from the nearby mosque, Rebecca abruptly stopped, lifting Eli's head from her lap. "This is the end of the story for today. Get up! You should leave."

"Please don't stop," he begged, "Please go on."

"Didn't you hear the muezzin?" Rebecca asked coquettishly. "He has seen the morning star."

It was a despondent Eli who had to leave and wait for the next part of the story until they met again. And the next night, when they met in their hideout, Rebecca did indeed bring this long story that she had been telling now for many nights to its happy ending.

"Elegantly dressed girls line up along the twisted alleys and spread a carpet of flowers, soon to be smashed under the golden hooves of his stallion, as the prince floats by, heedless of their admiration. All the women reach out to touch him, envying the lucky girl he will choose." Rebecca paused. Then she brought her head close to Eli's and whispered, "Can you guess where the prince is headed?"

Eli smiled. "To the twin houses where *my* princess lives."

She giggled with satisfaction and went on, as if she hadn't heard him. "After the prince rides through all the alleys of the village, he suddenly stops at the two identical houses with a broken wall between them. He glides from his horse and goes to the house on his left. A tall girl with brilliant green eyes comes toward him. The girl is wearing a thin, white silk dress. Her head is down and she is holding a clover in her hand."

Eli sat up, held Rebecca's face in his hands and tenderly kissed her eyes. Rebecca's voice became quiet and she fingered Eli's shirt. "You come closer to me. You put your hand under my chin, raise my head, kiss my eyes gently and take my hand. Then you lead me to the horse, lift me up upon it, mount it yourself and ride off as the stallion spreads its silvery wings and the two of us fly off into the deep blue skies."

Rebecca searched Eli's face. "Will you take me there with you, to the faraway places?"

Eli nodded. "Yes. A thousand times yes."

When Rebecca turned sixteen, she received her first suitor, Yahya the Cobbler, who was in his late thirties. Panicked at the thought of what her parents had in store for her, she implored Eli, "You have to marry me right away, or they will give me away to this..." She threw her hands up, "this cobbler!"

"Marry? I'm only seventeen!" Eli was equally frightened.

"You're almost eighteen."

"Sixteen, seventeen, I'm certain my parents would laugh at me if I told them I wanted to get married. And if I told them the girl I wanted to marry was you, then only God knows what would happen."

"Won't you even try?" Rebecca begged. "Maybe they wouldn't mind. Ask them. Ask your father."

"As my father if he wouldn't mind me marrying you? The daughter of the man he considers his worst enemy?"

Rebecca explained to Eli that with only one child, a daughter, Ruben wanted very much to marry her off to somebody so that he could become a grandfather and have a grandson. She warned Eli that if he didn't marry her, they would force her to marry the Cobbler. But all Eli could do was beg Rebecca to send the suitor away and wait until he was at least twenty. Rebecca reasoned to Eli that her three parents would not allow her to send away a "suitable" suitor and wait another three or four years for an invisible one. And even if she managed to send this one away, another one would just take his place.

"But you can't marry these people," Eli exclaimed.

After this encounter, Rebecca was convinced that she had to wage this battle alone, carrying Eli's load as well. But when she mustered her courage and announced that she was not going to marry Yahya the Cobbler, to her utter surprise she found Ruben taking sides with her. "The Cobbler? That ugly monkey?" he shouted at his wives. "Can you imagine what their children would look like?"

"Don't be so upset, Agha Ruben," Tuba said, trying to placate him. "But you are aware, of course, that Rebecca is no longer a little girl."

"She is only a child, for Heaven's sake," he said, putting his large arm around Rebecca and pulling her to his side. "How old are you, my dearest?" he asked his daughter. "Fourteen?"

Rebecca nodded.

"She's sixteen," Tuba snapped. "You married me when I was fourteen, Agha!"

"No. It was your mother who... Don't get me started again, woman."

"Listen Rebecca jaan," Jewel said in a cajoling tone. "Soon we have to take you to the Meat Market Alley and..."

"Rebecca has to at least see her khastegar," Tuba resumed where Jewel had been interrupted. "Otherwise people will say things about her." And to Rebecca, "You will see him my dear, won't you?"

"No."

Tuba stared at her daughter and saw unyielding resolve in her eyes.

"You heard her," Ruben stressed, running his hand over Rebecca's head. "That is all there is to say."

"You know what," Tuba said to Jewel the next day after the Rhino had gone to work. "It's not that I am envious of our daughter, but Ruben has emptied his heart of all the love in the world—for you, for me, for anyone else—and filled it with crazy love for Rebecca alone."

"Good for him. Let him love her as much as he wants," said

Jewel. "What bothers me is the girl's future. Goodness knows what would happen if he came to know that the two kids played with each other until recently."

"And that despite his orders, we are friends with Zilfa."

At the end, the two wives of Ruben the Rhino concluded that, knowing their husband's attachment to her, she had rejected her first khastegar and that if this continued, Rebecca would never get married. They told Rebecca that, despite her rejection of her first khastegar, she had to get married to someone, that Yahya was an excellent suitor and that she should consider him seriously.

"On every other question, you two have so many disagreements," Rebecca responded to her mothers, slapping the back of her hand, "But when it comes to my destiny, you are like a couple of parrots."

Ignoring her comment, Tuba began counting Yahya's merits on her fingers. "He's only thirty-eight."

"Almost twice my age," Rebecca countered. "I bet his teeth are falling out already."

"And he is a hardworking man," Jewel said, picking up the litany where Tuba had left off. "Also, he makes good money. His father has set aside *two* rooms in his house for him and his lucky bride. So what's your problem, Rebecca? Is it because he's slightly shorter than you are? So what? He's a good man and he is neither blind nor bald."

Yahya is a very nice man... Yahya is the best chance you have... You can't find a better suitor and what's more you never will find a better... Rebecca's mothers took turns and went on and on until Rebecca couldn't take it anymore and walked away.

"What's with this young woman of ours?" Jewel asked Tuba after she left.

"I don't know. Perhaps she likes someone else," answered the more experienced of the two.

The mothers speculated, came up with some names, including Eli, and rejected them on the spot.

For the next four years, despite her mothers' constant efforts, with her father on her side, Rebecca was never taken to the Meat Market Alley to be presented to the community as "eligible for marriage." As far as the women who gathered daily at this alley were concerned, her absence was a major unresolved issue. How could her parents disregard the traditional practice which was such an integral part of their lives, especially since with each passing day, Rebecca became more attractive? To the Meat Market Alley morning crowd — both those of the older generation and the younger ones who were in line to replace their seniors — this situation was so unusual that they were determined to get to the bottom of it. They gathered at the house of Tannaz the Barrel and *twenty* was the magic word among this crowd.

"She's *twenty* and not initiated yet?" began Tannaz who had advanced both in age and size over the last twenty years.

"My cousin, Abba the Quiltmaker," Mehri the Tweezers exclaimed. "This handsome man who is only thirty-eight and his wife died last year, I'm sure you remember. Well he sends a message to Ruben that he wants to come to khastegari for Rebecca and guess what our kadkhoda says? 'It's been written that your wife's sister should marry you and you have one!' I mean, what does he want for this *old* daughter of his that he passes up such a good match?"

"Weird, weird, weird," said the old toothless, Tuti the Exfoliator, speaking through her bare gums. With each word that she uttered, it was as though she were swallowing her lips. "This is one weird family. First, he kissed — and who knows what else he did to Tuba — before he married her. Then he married a second wife. Then he was able to make one child only — a daughter. And then, he refuses to allow any khastegars near his house. What is it with this family?"

Thus went on the never-ending stories that had begun when Rebecca had turned fourteen and continued ever since. By now, Rebecca had rejected countless suitors, further diminishing her chances of getting married — each time shocking her mothers. Meanwhile, miraculously, her secret relationship with Eli had lasted through these years. However, the emergence of every new suitor amplified the pressure that Rebecca. Time was now against Rebecca, and that made her anxious because her persistent efforts to encourage Eli to marry her were going nowhere. As time went by, she feared that Tuba and Jewel would gradually convince Ruben to join forces with them and make her succumb to one of her khastegars. After all, little by little, she was reaching the frightening age of twenty-one!

At last, one day in the winter of 1866, as Tuba and Jewel went to the kitchen to start preparing lunch and dinner, Ruben asked Rebecca to stay back. The father and daughter sat facing each other in the living-room. "One day," Ruben began, "when the right man comes along, we—you and I, my princess—will say yes to him..." And as he spoke, the gifted girl could see signs of her mothers' influence on their husband and that the Rhino's determination to send her khastegars away had weakened. "You see," Ruben went on to tell his daughter, "I have only you as a child. I have always wanted many more, and you, my dearest, are going to bring to this world all the boys that I have longed for."

Rebecca was frightened. She looked out of the window and saw the heavy snow that had once again covered the branches of the pomegranate tree in the courtyard. Her heart was heavy. She had already spoken to Eli and pushed him to do something about this labyrinth she had been caught in. "I have waited for you so long that I have reached the age of spinsterhood," she had screamed at him. "It is time for you to take one, *only one* step and help us get married. You are twenty-one now, for God's sake."

But appealing to Eli had amounted to nothing. Given his fear and susceptibility to intimidation, Eli who worked for his father— whom he would one day succeed—did not dare tell Nissan that he was even contemplating marriage, let alone to his friend-turned-enemy's daughter.

That day, long after her father left, Rebecca sat pondering the situation she was in and finally realized that in this unfair battle that she had started, she was the lonely warrior. Determined to win, she arrived at a plan, and figured out a strategy to make it work. The first step, she decided, was to end the animosity between Ruben and Nissan and the best candidates for the job were Eli and her mothers.

"Tuba will persuade my father to reconcile with Uncle Nissan," Rebecca said, sharing the details of her scheme with Eli. "She will not do this on her own, but with the help of Auntie Zilfa, Mayor Haskell and later Mullah Shimon as mediators. Haskell is the perfect man for this. I know it because whenever my mothers had a serious fight, my father asked Haskell to mediate between them."

"It's a great plan!" Eli declared resolutely. And as he went on discussing, approving or questioning the details of her scheme,

Rebecca was delighted to notice that all these years of her continuous efforts to instill self-confidence in the man she loved had worked. He seemed to her unafraid, clear, and able to plan and act without timidity or nervousness.

"Wait a minute." Eli was curious. "You mentioned nothing about Auntie Jewel. Is she playing a part in this?" Eli asked, impressing Rebecca even more.

This was nothing that Rebecca had not thought about. For many days she had pondered which of her two mothers she should choose for this mission and with this question returned many bitter memories. Throughout her life she had been torn between Tuba and Jewel, who each claimed her as her own. One day the girl loved one and hated the other, the next day her feelings were just the opposite. Finally, because of Tuba's seniority, experience and, most important, her influence on Ruben, Rebecca had decided to ask her to be the one to begin negotiations with her father. Rebecca was sure, she told Eli, that if she asked either one of her mothers for help, she would do her best. But if she asked both of them, despite their seeming reconciliation, each would try to outdo the other and this would ruin everything. "But before we proceed," she cautioned Eli, "I have to try to soften my father's lingering resentment against Uncle Nissan, who I'm sure will embrace his old friend if my Baba relents."

So one night after dinner, Rebecca sat next to Ruben and began caressing his beard — something that she had done when she was a little girl and he loved. "May I ask you something, Baba?" she said in a soft voice as she wound her fingers through his beard.

"You can ask me as many questions as you want as long as you don't stop playing with my beard," he said, his voice relaxing and his face looking drowsy.

"You are a learned and experienced man, Baba. You have been all the way to Jerusalem, you have suffered countless calamities and learned numerous lessons, and I have been fortunate to benefit from this treasure."

"What do you want me to get you this time?" Ruben snorted, his eyes suddenly opening and looking right at her.

"Love," she said, smiling.

"Well. Say yes to your next khastegar and you'll have love!"

"Many times you have told me that when Evil settles in one's soul, hatred follows," she went on, ignoring his comment.

"You are killing me, Rebecca!" said Ruben. "What are you trying to say, for God's sake?"

"Do you remember you were talking to me about a verse in the Book of Job which said: *The fear of the Lord is wisdom and to shun evil is understanding?*" Don't you think that by shunning the evil of your hatred for Uncle Nissan, you will get closer to the Almighty?"

Ruben froze and stared at his daughter. He had no answer — neither for himself nor for his daughter. He turned pale, Rebecca noticed. Then he pushed her hands away, jumped up and left.

Had she finally made a dent in her father's unyielding hatred against Nissan? Rebecca wondered.

The next step was to persuade Tuba to implement her plan whose immediate reaction was, "Have you also told Jewel?" Rebecca wanted to scream: Is this the first thing you think about? Instead, she reassured Tuba that she had chosen her only. Then she told her that she had been seeing Eli behind her back. "Tell me, are you still a virgin? Think of this *madar ghahbeh!* – child of an indecent mother. I will kill him with my own hands if he has deflowered you. Has he?"

"No!" Rebecca cried in disgust. She was already sorry she hadn't told Jewel instead. Now the situation became even graver when she asked Tuba to reconcile Ruben with Nissan. Ultimately, Rebecca had to threaten that she would ask Jewel instead; that's what did it. Not only did Tuba calm down, but all of a sudden her entire demeanor changed. She had to succeed in the mission that her daughter had laid out for her. She had to prove her right of motherhood. She had to prevail over Jewel.

"I'm thinking," she said, nodding in a thoughtful manner. "I have to figure out how to approach this problem." As she looked at her daughter, she contemplated many other thoughts that she couldn't voice. Would this young man make Rebecca happy? Was he going to be a good husband for her? She had always pictured Rebecca with someone vibrant like herself, not with a quiet and perhaps even timid man like Eli. And as she was thinking, a fearful thought dawned on her. Would Jewel claim Rebecca's children as her own grandchildren, as she had claimed Rebecca? "This is a major task," she finally spoke. "Your father is not an easy man to persuade, neither is Nissan. And after all these years, their hatred and estrangement have only become more cemented."

"Eli and I have thought that Mayor Haskell can be of great help to you."

Eli and I? Tuba thought.

Eli was happy when he heard that Rebecca's first step in solving their problem had been successful. He reported that he had fulfilled his first assignment and told Zilfa he would marry only Rebecca at any cost. Zilfa had suspected her son's love for Rebecca and feared its consequences, but she had at least listened to him. It was at this point that Rebecca asked Tuba to get together with Zilfa and work out a joint plan of action.

On a Tuesday morning in the late winter of 1867, when the air was fresh, the sun warm, and Jewbareh was submerged in the aromas of various breakfasts cooked overnight, among them *adasi* – lentil soup and *halim* – barley soup. The mood in the households of Ruben the Rhino and Nissan the Fabricseller was tense as both patriarchs were being given shocking news by their wives. In Ruben's house, after Tuba had made sure that Jewel had gone out for her first round of shopping, she broke the news to Ruben. "WHAT?!" he bellowed. His body froze and his jaw locked. After a while, when he could finally speak, he shouted again, "WHAT?!" as though all the other words he knew had escaped him. Then he took the teacups from the tray in front of him and threw them one by one against the wall, shouting, "So all that blather about Job and evil speech was the first chapter of a larger plot!"

"What Job, Agha?" Tuba asked calmly.

"I'm talking about Haskell and don't you dare play innocent!" He kicked the samovar, and punched the wall. And then, as if suddenly exhausted, he sat down, put his head against the wall and began biting his forefinger. "You can talk until you choke on your own tombstone," he said after awhile, pointing his finger at Tuba. "My answer is no, regardless of what anyone says. A very big fat NO, the size of Jewbareh. The size of Esfahan. Water and fire don't mix. You expect me to accept this marriage? I will not sit back and watch my grandchildren be a mix of my blood and that of this next-door coyote. I am *not* giving my blessing. I will not, not now or ever. So don't waste your breath. I can't give what I don't have. It's not in me. I pledge to God..."

And as he went on demeaning his only daughter, citing her bad reputation, her possession by jens and her spinsterhood, suddenly what Ruben had just uttered, *"I pledge to God,"* struck a chord in the back of Tuba's memory. The day Rebecca was born. Why hadn't she thought of this before? "Are you finished?" she asked.

The Rhino turned around and looked out of the window, ignoring her.

"Good, because I am going to remind you of something," she said as she went to the window and stood in front of him. "Didn't you pledge to God that you would do whatever your child wanted, if God granted you one?"

Ruben sat straight up and looked at Tuba. His face was pale. "Bite your tongue. You are talking about the life of my only child, you idiot!"

Tuba knew that she had hit the mark. Ruben would now fear God's revenge for breaking his oath with Him.

Meanwhile, next door, as she was taking the plates away from the breakfast tray, Zilfa gave the news to Nissan cautiously and timidly, waiting for an outburst of anger and invective. But this time Nissan surprised his wife. When she was finished speaking, he remained mute for a few moments. Then, as if sleepwalking, he went out of his house and moved aimlessly along the alleys of Jewbareh with his head down. Hours later he looked about and realized that he was outside the ghetto, walking through a nearby farm Jewbarites called *Sahara* — paradoxically meaning both desert and farm. Sahara, with an area of one hundred acres, ran parallel to the east of Jewbareh. It was owned by a major landowner — Haj Mahmood — who had subdivided the land into a couple of acres apiece. Poor, hardworking peasants leased land from Haj Mohammad and planted fruits and vegetables which they sold at the local bazaar. In the hot summers and early falls days, when the crops ripened, Jewbarites gathered at Sahara to picnic and also buy fresh farm produce. Nissan sat on a rock and watched the strenuous work of a farmer plowing the land with the help of his ox. Observing the farmer's exhausting labor took Nissan back to his own past. Then he recalled his friendship with Ruben, which had been the first that had meant anything to him since his parents' death, but had also lasted only so long. Now he thought back on his life and saw it as nothing but a succession of losses. Surely, he thought, this ox he was watching had a better life than he had. It had an owner who took care of it, whereas all his life Nissan had taken care of his siblings and now his own family. And what had he gotten in return? Three daughters, a lost child and only one son, Eli, who obviously had been making a fool of him, seeing this girl behind his back, and despite his father's admonitions, was expecting Nissan to give his blessing to this crazy marriage.

Well, it was impossible. Simply impossible.

The first mediation session between the two men was held at the house of Mayor Haskell. Mullah Shimon, Tuba and Zilfa were also there. For a long time the only thing that could be heard was shouting, complaining and mutual accusations. Finally, at just the point where the two men were about to grab each other's throats, the mayor cancelled the meeting. The second meeting took place at the rabbi's house, and although the two adversaries had somewhat softened, no amicable conclusion was reached. Hearing the disappointing news, Rebecca decided that she should talk to Nissan. She told Eli that she needed his support in this formidable task. So, one cold afternoon, Nissan came home and was shocked to see Rebecca sitting in their living room with Eli and Zilfa.

"What is *she* doing here?" he asked in an astonished tone.

"She wants to talk to you and you will, please, listen to her," said Eli.

Rebecca leaped up from where she was sitting, threw her arms around Nissan and whispered in his ear, "Uncle Nissan... Uncle Nissan."

Twice Nissan brought his arms up as if to embrace Rebecca but held them back, Eli noticed. Then he untangled her arms from around his neck, gently pushed her back, looked into her eyes and smiled. "Ten years. It's been ten years since..." he choked.

Rebecca didn't waste any time. "As it is written in Psalms," she said, *"Let a righteous man strike me – it is a kindness; let him rebuke me – it is oil on my head. My head will not refuse it."* I'm here to beg you not to refuse me, Uncle Nissan."

With his palm to his forehead, Nissan said, "You have become such an eloquent speaker, little... Well, I guess you are no more 'little Rebecca.' You're Rebecca khanom who speaks like a fifty-year-old rabbi! Where have you learned all this?"

"A little bit here, a little bit there," she chuckled. "God knows how much I have missed you, Uncle Nissan."

"She is here to ask you to permit us to marry," Eli called unexpectedly. "Rebecca and I will marry even if our parents disagree."

Rebecca's jaw dropped. Certainly this unexpected announcement was not part of what she and Eli had planned. Suddenly she was afraid, for this abrupt declaration could agitate Nissan. But she was proud of Eli too, because he had spoken up for them like a man—a grown man.

Silence followed. Rebecca prepared herself to witness an outburst as Nissan stood up. "Zilfa is my witness, every time our joint friends persuade us to put our differences aside, it's your father who comes up with an excuse not to let this happen. My dear girl. It's your father who can't bury his anger. Was there any reason why he broke our friendship over something as petty as a trellis? No! Is he sincere in wanting the two of you to marry? I don't know. How you two young souls want to…" Nissan sighed, shaking his head.

"May I answer that question?" Zilfa asked calmly. "The trouble, Agha Nissan, if you don't get angry, is that you men, being men, have so much pride. So much vanity. Don't even ask me how much!" she said with a laugh, shaking her torso sideways.

"The two of you should meet halfway, Baba!" said Eli, again surprising Rebecca.

"When Jacob was dying," Rebecca now declared, "this is the message he sent to Joseph: 'I ask you to *forgive* your brothers, the sins and the wrongs they committed in treating you so badly.' And now, Uncle Nissan, I beg you to forgive my father. We all know that you and Baba Ruben love each other. All Eli and I are asking you is to give us your blessing. Can you do this for us? Please."

Nissan began laughing wildly. "Again, since when have you become such an articulate rabbi, you little girl?! How do you know all this?"

"If you promise that you will reconcile with my father, your best friend, I promise that I'll tell you."

"Well," Nissan said, squirming on the cushion he was sitting on. Then he groaned something unintelligible and finally said, "If he behaves, I will behave."

"Which means yes, my daughter-in-law," Zilfa said to Rebecca, putting her arms around her and kissing her roundly on the forehead. "Now, go home before your father gets back. I don't think I could survive another brawl."

The third meeting was held in Mullah Shimon's synagogue with only the rabbi, the mayor and the two men present. The rabbi, who had arranged this gathering, first asked the two men to stand in front of the Torah scrolls. "Actually, as your rabbi, I will not allow either of you to leave the House of God until you have buried your differences." Then he spoke. "The Talmud says, *"A person without friends is like a right hand without a left."* Ever since you fell into this evil trap of animosity, each of you has become an incomplete person—a right hand without a left. Hillel says, *"Love peace and pursue peace."* Instead of acting like children, think of your own children and celebrate their joy. End this ugly curse that God knows who has put upon you two best friends." He held them both by the hand and brought them close together. At that moment the two old friends embraced, kissed each other on both cheeks, hugged, and wept.

Had they overcome their deep-rooted anger or had demons taken shelter even more deeply within them? Only time would tell.

With both families now resigned to the marriage of their children, the time had come to make their betrothal official by the tradition of khastegari, whereby Eli's parents had to go to Ruben's house to ask them for Rebecca's hand in marriage to their son. But before khastegari, they had to break the news of the impending betrothal to Jewel. So, Ruben, Tuba and Rebecca went to Jewel's room and Ruben told her that because Eli wanted to marry Rebecca, he had reconciled his differences with Nissan, that he and Tuba, aided by Mayor Haskell and Mullah Shimon, had taken the initial steps toward reconciliation and that soon Nissan and Zilfa were going to come for khastegari.

Jewel froze. Her eyes widened, gazing into nowhere, unblinking. She was like a statue of fury about to come to life and explode.

"Aren't you happy?" Ruben muttered. "Don't you want to congratulate your daughter?"

"Mother!" Rebecca said softly.

Jewel turned her head and looked at Rebecca. She felt a deep chiseling sensation in her stomach. How long had these secret negotiations been going on behind her back to marry off her daughter while nobody had said even one single word to her? Then she pointed her shaking finger at Tuba, and said, choking on her words, "*She* is your mother, not me!"

"Mother, please, let me explain," Rebecca begged.

Now Jewel jumped up and screamed at her daughter, "Whatever you say, it will only bring shame on you, shame on your father and shame on this kidnapper who stole you from me at your birth. The three of you will get out of my room at once or I will leave this house and never come back."

Nobody moved. Rebecca could feel the fire of anger as her birth-mother's eyes burned her skin. "I promise you, Mani," she said, her voice shaking. "Without your blessing, I will not marry anyone."

Ruben noticed Jewel's agitation and was concerned. "Don't you feel well?"

Jewel raised her head, gazed at her husband and shouted, "Do I feel well? No, I don't! You want to know how I feel? I feel betrayed *again,* this time not by you and your wife who fettered me in this cage to make you children, but by our... no, *your* daughter." Suddenly she picked up the sugar bowl and threw it at Rebecca, who, luckily, dodged it. "This ungrateful, shameless child!"

"You have no shame," Ruben said as he bent to pick up the broken pieces of the bowl, which had landed against the wall. "Is this the best thing you can say on such a happy occasion?"

Jewel took a deep breath as if she were preparing to pour out a whole new stream of furious words, but pursed her lips. There was a choking silence in the room until Jewel's fury erupted again. "You want my blessing?" she screamed at Rebecca. "Then listen to what I have to say. Actually, I am talking to the three of you, three people who for years have put me through hell." She first pointed at Ruben. "You married me, impregnated me, stole my child and gave her to my havoo. For all these years, I have acted as my own child's nanny while your first wife has pretended—yes, *pretended*—to be her mother. I have been nothing to you but a concubine in a harem headed by Her Majesty Tuba, the Queen of Jewbareh. I have tolerated all the hardships that you have subjected me to, but not this one. This one I won't stand for. How dare you marry my daughter without telling me?"

"Jewel dear," said Tuba, "You have to understand..."

"Shut up, you childless, barren old monkey."

"Mother..."

"Don't you dare open your mouth until I'm done with these two wretched creatures. Then I will settle my accounts with you!"

Tuba screamed at Ruben, "Are you just going to stand there, as you've always done, and allow her to say whatever she wants?" "What do you want him to do? Beat me?" Jewel slapped her chest with her fist. "Go ahead Agha Ruben. Do what your queen tells you to do. Punish me!" Now she turned to Rebecca. "I can't deny you my blessing, for you are my child. As far as I am concerned, go and do whatever you want. Get married and live as you wish, but leave me out of it. Now I want all of you to get out of here and just leave me alone. Now! This instant! I mean it!"

"This is my house," cried Ruben, "and nobody can tell me when to leave any part of it!"

Hearing this, Jewel put on her chador, wrapped it around her waist, threw Tuba, Ruben and Rebecca a spiteful look and left the room. Ruben and Rebecca hurriedly followed her, but she had already left the house and was walking, in fact almost running away as fast as she could. Eventually Rebecca, followed by Ruben, caught up with her after the fourth twist of the Alley. Rebecca took her mother's arm and begged her not to go away. "*I* am to blame for this," she pleaded with her. "It was *my* stupid idea. Nobody else thought of this but me. I didn't involve you because I was afraid that you and Tuba would get into a quarrel and ruin everything." But seeing that Jewel just kept on running and paying no attention to her, Rebecca swiftly stepped in front of her mother, blocking her way. "Please forgive me, Mani."

Jewel stopped. "I'm not feeling well. They all told me that you would be *my* daughter." She was flushed now and sweating profusely. "But from the very beginning I knew this was nothing but a false prophecy." She was shaking as she went down on her knees. "I've been nothing but a housekeeper and a maid. Not even a concubine. I thought I would have other children. But your father has not touched me in... it's been so many years I don't even remember."

Rebecca knelt down and held on to her mother. People gathered around them. "What's the matter kadkhoda?" they asked Ruben.

"Nothing," he answered. "My wife has a high fever. We're just coming back from the Hakim's place. She..."

"She's the Queen's maid and the King's castoff baby-maker," Jewel hollered, interrupting her husband.

"She'll be fine," Rebecca said, coming to her father's rescue. Ruben helped Jewel stand up and lean against him, and then slowly and tenderly he and Rebecca walked her home. Rebecca put Jewel to bed, brought her tea with crystal sugar and lay down next to her, putting her hand on her breasts. "I have nursed from these breasts, not Tuba's," she whispered in her ear. "*You* are my mother and you will forgive me. Please tell me that you will."

Jewel opened her eyes to see Rebecca's beseeching expression and tears. Though she could no longer bear her daughter's misery, she still felt rage. "I will forget what you have done and I will forgive you if you promise me something. This is my will. This is my death wish. Write on my grave this epitaph. 'She came into this world alone, she lived a lonely life and she died alone.' Will you do this?"

"These are the happiest moments of my life and I have no intention of burying you," said Rebecca, wrapping her arms around Jewel's shaking shoulders and holding her tightly. "Let me repeat. *You* are my mother. I came out of *your* body. No matter how angry you are with me, if you only knew what I have gone through to bring these two stubborn men, my father and Uncle Nissan, together, you would be proud of me. Now, get up, freshen up and let's get ready for your daughter's wedding."

Chapter 18
At the Feast of the Stallion

At the appointed time on a Friday morning, a few weeks before the late autumn of 1867, Nissan and Zilfa went next door to officially ask Ruben and his wives for Rebecca's hand in marriage to Eli. Rebecca beckoned her Uncle Nissan and Auntie Zilfa inside and showed them up the stairs to the veranda and to the guestroom where Ruben, Tuba, Jewel and Mayor Haskell awaited them. Traditionally, Rebecca and Eli were not allowed to attend the khastegari; however, both of them had put their ears to the door between Rebecca's room and the guest room, and were eavesdropping anxiously. Haskell took Nissan's and Ruben's hands and brought them together.

"Before anything is said, kiss each other once again and forget the past," he instructed the men. "As they say, *'Be like a mill. Take coarse and give soft.'"*

The two men embraced, as did Tuba, Jewel and Zilfa. After tea was served and expected compliments exchanged, Nissan began the dialogue of traditional khastegari, words that had been repeated like a prayer over generations.

"We are here, Kadkhoda Ruben, to ask your kind permission in allowing our son, your humble servant, your slave child, to take shelter, firstly under the shadow of God Almighty and secondarily under your generous protection. He has seen the lovely bride and has chosen her. So, we humbly beg that you allow your beautiful and accomplished daughter, Rebecca, to shed her radiance on our lives by becoming the wife of our son. My son Eli is a hardworking young man—six days a week, long hours each and every day. In the morning he opens my shop and works straight through the late hours of the evening. Needless to say, he is a noble, honest and fine person who wants to start his own family. Blessed be His name, Eli makes good money and he saves it all. God willing, we are presently negotiating to buy the shop next door to the existing one that you, my dear friend Ruben, helped me buy and where I have established my business. We will tear down the wall in between the two shops and we will expand our business. As it has been said, when the destined day comes, each of us will have to go. So, once I'm gone, my son will be sole owner of this big business."

In the adjacent room, Rebecca and Eli laughed with joy. Ruben and Nissan turned their heads toward the door to Rebecca's room. Now it was Ruben's turn as father of the bride-to-be to respond in kind by first thanking the suitor's family and then, as convention required, postponing the time to answer this offer, so that the gossipmongers couldn't otherwise go around and say: *They couldn't wait to get rid of her!* "First of all," Ruben began, "it was God's will and your good heart that helped your business grow and not me. Secondly, I am humbled that you have considered my daughter worthy of your son. As I have always said, it will be a great honor to dignify myself to rise to the level of the dust of your footsteps. But, unfortunately, Rebecca, my only daughter, is very young. As they say, we have raised this child on a bed of swan feathers and a pillow of flower petals. We have taken excellent care of her and we are very concerned about her future. Your son, our dear Eli, is also very young, too young to be married. Let Rebecca and Eli grow a little bit older, and then let us sit down and talk about this again."

Having heard this, which was a customary first rejection of khastegari, Eli's parents were required to then leave and send an intermediary to finally receive the acceptance and close the deal. But, fearing further confrontations between Ruben and Nissan, the Mayor suggested—and it was agreed—to put off the negotiations on the terms of the marriage until the time of the wedding, and so finally Ruben and Nissan gave their blessing for Rebecca and Eli to become engaged. They consulted Rabbi Shimon, who recommended the third day of *Shavuot*, a day in the Jewish calendar traditionally associated with good omens—a day that not only signified God's giving of the Torah to the Jewish nation at Mount Sinai, but also the beginning of the grain harvest. "The day is good for their engagement ceremony," Mullah Shimon declared, "because it's symbolic of fertility."

And so this is how the ceremonies for the engagement of The Graceful Rebecca to Eli the Stallion began on a bright, warm day in the late autumn of 1867. That afternoon, the groom, his family and their guests, accompanied by a caravan of gift carriers and musicians—known as the caravan of joy—left Nissan's house. Keeping the tradition, this caravan in ordinary circumstances would have made its happy way from the groom's house to the bride's, but since the twin houses were adjoined, and as it was necessary that the ceremonies be visible throughout all the alleys of Jewbareh, they walked from Nissan's house toward *Sahara* at the bottom, southern end of the Alley of Eleven Twists. At that point the processional turned around and returned to Ruben's house. The musical band of Mansur, the son of David the Butcher, accompanied by Eli, his parents and other family members and friends, was followed by five strong men, each carrying over his head a *khoncheh*—a charmingly decorated large wooden tray, measuring almost six by three feet, filled with gifts from the groom for the bride. The khoncheh carriers had the unique skill of balancing these large trays on their turbaned heads—a skill mastered by only a few in Jewbareh. A tray that fell caused great worry, not because of the monetary loss, but because people considered it a catastrophic sign and an indication that the marriage would fail. And the main concern on this particular occasion was that the trays were much heavier than usual, for, in addition to his parents' gifts, Eli had spent most of his life savings on his own presents for Rebecca. And so, this unusual weight gave the carriers the much riskier task of balancing the extremely heavy trays on their heads.

The first tray held a Torah, a mirror, a pair of candlesticks and twelve porcelain bowls filled with crystal sugar, each bowl symbolizing a tribe of Israel and a wish that the newly betrothed couple would have twelve sons. On the next tray there was jewelry, hand-worked silk fabrics, silverware and clothing for the parents of the bride. The third tray contained a *kaseh nabat*—a bowl made of crystal sugar and decorated with colored papers—surrounded by various confections. In the fourth tray were mounds of *kolucheh*—homemade cookies, *gaz*—nougat, and various homemade cakes, all skillfully assembled in tall conical shapes with the use of honey as an adhesive. The last tray contained mostly off-season fruits such as apples and pears, kept in cool basements. These were also set up in mounds almost three feet tall and joined together with toothpick-like pieces of wood. All the trays were embellished with fresh flowers, colored papers and lit candles.

The long, flamboyant procession brought many Jewbarites to the alleys, where they lined up along the sides of the walkways and joined the singing and dancing and ululating, hugging Eli and wishing him well. Eli was ecstatic. Now *he* was the hero of Rebecca's stories, the prince who had come from his ivory palace to this far away village to claim his beloved. Along his path, for him and his bride and their future, Jewbareh had abandoned its rigid, everyday small-mindedness, and was breathing in joy. It seemed to him that even the heavy old thick walls of the Alley of Eleven Twists were dancing, that in fact the whole world was dancing as well.

By the time the caravan of joy arrived at the nearby farm, the setting sun had been blissfully watching over the festivities, just as it had done during all the centuries that Jewbarites had been living in their small ghetto. From *Sahara*, the procession re-entered the northern end of the Alley of Eleven Twists. Throughout this procession, all that was on Eli's mind was Rebecca. When would they arrive at her house? "Can't we move a little bit faster?" he whispered to his father impatiently. Nissan roared laughing, "You'll have the rest of your life, my son, to see her very close, every day, every minute. Be patient and enjoy the ceremonies. Look back and watch the cheerful people who follow you." Eli turned around and saw the lit candles on the khoncheh trays that shone much brighter and the caravan of joy that looked like a stream of lights flowing through the deepening darkness of the alleys of Jewbareh. Finally, the procession came to Rebecca's house where the musicians and the crowd following them raised their voices, announcing the arrival of the groom with a folksong, old as the Jews of Persia:

You've become the groom
Let His blessings be with you
So that you'll be the head and the patron
Of the tribes of Israel

Here again Eli had to wait, because it was considered bad luck to knock on the door and so they waited for the door to be opened from within to the sounds of jubilation.

The singing crowd asked, "Is there anybody home?"

"It all depends on who wants to know!" came voices from inside Rebecca's house.

"Your groom, who is as tall and slender as a cypress tree."

"It depends on who the groom is!"

To lengthen the fun — which was torturous for poor Eli — before opening the door on the groom and his entourage, the bride's family repeated the questions and the groom's family and friends responded, singing more folksongs praising him and not asking for the door to be opened until, suddenly, at last Ruben *did* open it, at which point Eli rushed in and to the Rhino's utter astonishment, embraced him. "Uncle Ruben, Uncle Ruben," he whispered weeping. And people saw the Rhino's eyes glazed with tears as he bit his lips. Unable to restrain himself, Nissan joined his son holding both of them in his arms. "My brother," he said to Ruben. "My savior." Watching this scene, women wept silently with joy and men swallowed, their mouths dry. After a long silence, Jewel began with a shaky voice: *May... this...* at which point the singing crowd on both sides joined in the same chorus and everybody together sang:

May this majestic union be blessed

May this auspicious feast of the noblemen be blessed

From this point, the street crowd who had followed the caravan disbursed, leaving the groom's family and the engagement party guests to enter Ruben's courtyard. The musicians played and the tray carriers entertained, showing their mastery as they spun around themselves while balancing the heavy trays on their heads. Eli, however, wasn't watching the performance. He was looking anxiously into the crowd of women where he should have found Rebecca. He didn't see her. Where was she? Was she playing her favorite game with him, hiding herself? Was she watching him, enjoying his confusion, as he looked for her in distress? Then Nissan approached his son and pointing to the veranda, whispered to him, "Looking for somebody? She's up there." And there indeed she was.

"Rebecca," murmured Eli under his breath, savoring the sweet taste of every syllable of her name. She wore a long, tight, sheer silk dress that shimmered gold in the afternoon light. It outlined her voluptuous breasts and showed her narrow waist. Eli's eyes slid down the curves of Rebecca's body, so well defined. Her long hair flowed down over her shoulders under a scarf woven with gold threads. Her beauty was tantalizing and her features flawless. Eli felt light, weightless, as if he were being carried to another realm of existence. The voices of the crowd and the sounds of the musicians faded away. He saw everything in slow motion—the tray-bearers rotating, the movements and gestures of the guests, all lost in Rebecca's magnificence. He saw everyone else become paler slowly as his beloved's presence took over the house of the Rhino, swelled over its walls into the alleys of Jewbareh and beyond until the voice of his father broke into his revery and tumbled him back down to earth.

"Why is she dressed like this?" Nissan grunted.

"Baba!" Eli snapped. "Enough before you turn this happy time into a catastrophe."

Mullah Shimon, who had overheard the conversation, prodded the musicians, "Come on. Play! Play!" as he put a hand behind Eli and showed him to the staircase with the other. Eli's knees were shaking and he had to hold onto the banister not to lose his balance. When he eventually joined Rebecca at the veranda, Ruben, Tuba and Jewel invited the bride and the groom and all the guests into the *panj-dari*—the five-door room—a large guest room with three full-length windows opening onto the veranda and two doors to the adjacent rooms. Rebecca and Eli entered and took their assigned seats below the mantelpiece on Persian silk cushions designed with butterflies over candles against a background of roses, red and pink. A few small pillows separated the cushions on which they were sitting into two adjoining seats, creating a barrier so that the unmarried couple would not touch. Now the guests entered, and along with the musicians and the hosts, they sang and drank to the health of the engaged couple as they enjoyed their dinner, throughout which Eli fixed his eyes on Rebecca. She smiled and returned his look of love as she inched closer to him and he inched away. One by one, Rebecca began to remove the pillows that were between them, putting each behind her except for the last one that she put on her lap. "What are you doing?" whispered Eli nervously. "Don't move," she said under her breath and slid closer to him until their legs—which she had covered with the pillow on her lap— touched. Then she rubbed her thigh against his knee. It was as if a stream of hot melted lead was flowing from her thigh into his body. "People are watching us," Eli gasped as drops of sweat began to form on his face and his ears became hot and red. He was breathing heavily. Rebecca was overwhelmed with joy as she watched his reactions. Then he felt Rebecca's hand moving up his thigh. Now, with his head down in embarrassment, Eli's whole body was shaking.

"I've never seen such a shy groom in my life," said one guest.

Hearing this only frightened Eli more. Inundated with the sensation of Rebecca's touch as her hand moved ever higher on his thigh, Eli closed his eyes and for a moment he surrendered himself to the waves of immense pleasure going through his body.

"Ouch!" an excruciating pain in his thigh made Eli jump. Rebecca, who was uncontrollably excited, had purposely pinched his thigh. All the attention was drawn to Eli and his bride-to-be.

"Bless you," said Rebecca in a low, innocent voice.

"What happened?" asked a few guests.

"Nothing," responded Rebecca calmly. "The groom sneezed."

Within weeks of the engagement ceremonies, preparations for the wedding started with *ejazeh-giran*—asking permission for marriage. The groom and his family visited the bride's family to make the necessary arrangements for the wedding. Unlike the khastegari, the bride and the groom were allowed to be present at this meeting. The most important issue at hand was determining the marriage terms, which had been put off at the time of the engagement. What had to be decided was the value of *jahiziyeh*—the dowry—that the bride would bring to her husband's home. Of equal importance to the bride's family was her *mehrieh*—the marriage portion. This was the amount payable by the husband to his wife in the event he should die or divorce her.

"With the permission of God," Nissan said to Ruben, "we are here to set a date and sign the marriage contract for our children. May the shadow of, first and foremost, God, and then you, Tuba khanom and Jewel khanom, be over their heads and protect them and their children for the blessings of your good acts, past and present. As I was saying to my wife Zilfa last night, we feel very honored and proud to become relatives of your esteemed family. It goes without saying how very dear to us Rebecca is."

"We feel the same way about Eli," said Tuba. "Look at them," she pointed at Rebecca and Eli, who were sitting silent but obviously gleeful. "I swear they have been made for each other."

"We love Eli as our own child," Jewel echoed Tuba.

"You are really and truly so kind," said Zilfa.

"Let's turn to the business at hand," Ruben, whose silence so far had begun to make everyone nervous, finally spoke in a serious tone. "As the saying goes, 'Let's go easy with the compliments and get to the tangibles.' As you know, both the amount of the marriage portion and the value of the dowry have to be recorded in our children's marriage contract."

"You're quite right," Nissan responded. "But Rebecca is so dear and precious to us that we," he pointed to Zilfa and then himself, "wish to welcome her to our family without any dowry."

Hearing the words, *"welcome to our family,"* the reality that he was about to lose Rebecca to another man, dawned on Ruben. He heard voices in his head. *They are taking your daughter away from you. Rebecca. The woman who is different, very different, from Tuba, Jewel or anyone else. Your prize for years of waiting. Your only child.* He simply could not let go of his daughter, and for that reason he twisted Nissan's sincere gesture into an insult. "You know something, my friend," he said, "You talk as if my precious Rebecca is worth nothing." With his brows puckered, he pointed at Nissan and continued, "We are here to follow all the customary rules in accordance with what is common in the community, and what do you do? You undermine our traditions."

Nissan opened his mouth to respond, but Zilfa jumped in, "Please Agha Ruben."

"The poor man is praising your daughter," Tuba interrupted her.

"Don't you dare start another brawl," Jewel said to Ruben, surprising everyone. "We have had enough of this."

"I have a duty that I am well aware of," Ruben said, ignoring Zilfa and his wives. "I will not be sending my daughter to her husband's home empty-handed and without jahiziyeh. And like any other respectable girl, I expect a mehrieh for her."

"Whatever makes you happy," said Nissan calmly.

"Yes?" Ruben asked in a tone that revealed his disgruntlement at failing to instigate a quarrel. But the Rhino was not about to give up. "All right," he snarled. "This is what makes me happy. As you yourself said, Rebecca is a gem of a girl, and so I'm sure you will agree with me that it is only fair for us to expect to get her mothers' *Shirbaha*—milk money. Jewel who has nursed and Tuba who has raised such a bundle of roses are inevitably entitled to fair compensation for that. I have been thinking that twenty-six gold coins for each of them would be fair."

Rebecca, Eli and their mothers were stunned. No one had a clue where that idea had come from and which demon had penetrated Ruben's soul this time. All eyes turned on Nissan to see his reaction. Looking into his son's pleading face, he smiled. "May health and happiness be your fair share in life," he said blithely, "but you must be joking. Shirbaha? Shirbaha, my dear friend Kadkhoda Ruben, is something in fairy tales, given for princesses and royalty, not for us Jewbarites!"

"It is not," Ruben hollered as he shook his head adamantly. "All deserving girls have gotten it in Jewbareh and there's no reason why Rebecca should be an exception."

"All right," said Zilfa, jumping into this precarious exchange. "All the gold coins that I have been given for my dowry, they're all Rebecca's. Please, let's not talk about jahiziyeh, mehrieh or Shirbaha and get to the auspicious part of setting a date for the wedding."

"In Jewbareh?" Nissan asked Ruben half-jokingly, as if he hadn't heard Zilfa. "In Jewbareh people have given Shirbaha to the mothers of their brides? Can you name me one please? If so, you name Rebecca's milk money and I will pay it."

"It is no time to be playful or funny, Baba!" Eli begged. "This is not a game of cat and mouse, for God's sake."

"It's *my* Shirbaha" Rebecca exclaimed beating her chest. "I don't want it!"

"Calm down," Ruben ordered, but Rebecca roared, "I WILL KILL MYSELF! I will kill myself and I want all of you to know that you," she pointed at her father, "Yes, *you* will have been the cause of my death."

Everybody jumped up. Ruben opened his mouth to say something, but he just stood there, unable to utter a sound. He tried to reach for Rebecca, but began staggering. Nissan was the first to catch him. "Everything will be fine. Calm yourself my friend." Observing that his father seemed to be losing his grip on the Rhino's huge and heavy body, Eli rushed to help him. As he lay there, Ruben heard mix of voices. Tuba: Are you all right? Nissan: What happened? Jewel: Listen to his heart! Zilfa: He's fainting. Eli: Uncle Ruben! But in all of these, Rebecca's voice he did not hear. His eyelids fell like a drunkard's and as Nissan, Zilfa and the Rhino's wives were running back and forth in panic, shaking him, rubbing his arms, shouting, crying and begging one another to do something. Ruben was in another world. It was as though someone were holding his hand and walking him through the turns and twists of his life with no specific order. He saw the innocence of his childhood that had culminated in the respect and reverence with which he was regarded as the leader of his community, interrupted by the dreadful incident when he had killed the nomad. The lonely, estranged life he had lived in the glory of Jerusalem and then his return to Jewbareh and a life of work and selfless service to the ghetto whirled and swirled in his head. He had been so selfless that he had killed someone defending one of his own. His brotherly friendship with Nissan had been destroyed and he had no one but himself to blame. He, Ruben the Rhino, had been overwhelmed by pathetic animosity. He thought of his noble love for Tuba and the grief he had caused both her and Jewel, making them share the same man. And he had done all this because of his need to have an heir. An heir he had wanted to be a boy, when in fact the child had turned out to be a creature of lesser value, a mere girl. But Rebecca herself, he had seen that she was intelligent and resourceful and strong like himself. Now the cruel reality of what he was doing to Rebecca struck him. Rebecca, his only child, who loved Eli, a decent young man he had known since childhood. Rebecca's voice resonated in his head. In so many words she had asked him, "Don't you think that your hatred of Uncle Nissan has something to do with the Evil that's lurking somewhere within you?" Then there was what Mullah Ahmad had said: "You're lost and worse than damned when Evil penetrates your spirit." Lost within himself he wondered now whether all the evils in the world had conspired and triumphed over his soul.

Ruben opened his eyes. Everyone in the room had surrounded him, his wives and Rebecca on one side, Eli and his parents on the other. As he sat up, all present noticed something enigmatic about him. His face was glowing. His imposing posture was like that of a prophet about to reveal a message from beyond. His aura seemed to be a reflection of the image hanging on the wall over his head— King Solomon, sitting on his crown, mighty and determined. "I have something to say!" Ruben proclaimed in a voice not his own. "Please sit down and listen to me." There was a mysterious supremacy in his words. Rebecca reached for Eli's shaky hand and Tuba for Jewel's and Zilfa's. Nissan held his hand in front of his open jaw. "I beg you all to forgive me. I don't know what's happening to me. All I know is that even *I* can't bear myself anymore and it is, therefore, not fair that you should put up with my nonsense." The whites of his eyes were red and the red of his cheeks pale. "My skull is flooded with so many thoughts that I can no longer tell right from wrong. Like shattered glass, my whole being has fallen apart in thousand-and-one pieces. But I can put it back together. I will."

There was silence in the room. Everyone's eyes were fixed on Ruben, the rhino he had always been, but also a baffled, detached human being, who was confessing that he was undergoing a reckoning with himself, with the man he had been for a long time now and perhaps since he had killed the nomad. "In search of my unblemished self—the man that I had always been," Ruben continued, "I can see myself going into the depths of far, faraway lands." He paused, staring into nowhere like a dazed child. Then suddenly he stood up and declared, "In fact I will go to Jerusalem. Yes, I will. I need to go and stay there until I have regained the knowledge and wisdom I found there. I will go and try to rid myself of whatever evil has possessed me all these years that makes me ruin the happiness of those closest to me—my wives, my daughter, my friend Nissan and his loving family. I will stay there until I have expiated my sin."

Tuba cried, "Oh my God. You're not leaving for another two years!"

"I will leave enough money for each one of you," he pointed at Tuba, Jewel and Rebecca.

"But Baba," Rebecca pleaded as she stood up and stretched her arms. "What happens to Eli and me?" she said, her face pale, her voice shaking. "If you think we belong to each other, why do you want to go away and why now?" she broke down.

The Rhino embraced his daughter and whispered in her ear, "Sorry. I'm not myself. I'm someone else. Once I'm back from this journey, I'll make sure that you will be fine, Eli will be fine, Nissan will be fine and the whole world will be fine."

When Ruben refused to hear the pleas of his wives and his daughter, they sent for the rabbi and the mayor, who came later that afternoon and questioned their kadkhoda's abrupt decision to go to Jerusalem again. Back and forth the two men took turns interrogating Ruben's mystifying decision and all they heard was that he had to go. "Help me understand this," the rabbi finally said in a defiant tone. "You want meat, you go to the Butcher. You want fish, you go to the Fishmonger. You want, let's say, a wash, you go to the communal bathhouse. For a seasoned man of your standing, the governor of our ghetto, what puzzles me is that you don't seem to know what Jerusalem can offer you beyond what you learned in your first trip."

"*Want*, Rabbi, *want*—that's where I'm lost. I want meat, but I have lost my way to the butcher. I want fish but don't know how to get to the fishmonger. After all that I have gone through, I have come to realize that although I am not a perfect person, I'm convinced that at the core I am not evil. To wash away layer after layer of guilt that has scabbed my soul, I want to go to Jerusalem — to cleanse my spirit, to purify my soul. It is not that Jerusalem has something more to give me, but that perhaps I lost what I found there so long ago and must return to seek it once again."

There was silence for a few long minutes before the rabbi spoke. "Why don't you come to the synagogue and let us pray together?"

"Because there are times that you have to give the Almighty a break and go after the answer yourself. Thirty-four years ago, when I was forced to flee Jewbareh to Jerusalem, many of my questions — be it by dervishes or by rabbis — were answered. But I feel that since my return, my soul has been tainted. Just let me go, my friends. Let me go."

The next day Ruben packed a bundle of clothes, said farewell to his tearful family and left for the caravansary at the entrance of Jewbareh. The owner of the caravansary, Ali, who was the grandson of Gholam Ali, Naphtali's friend, was sitting with one of his caravan leaders in the shade on a worn-out carpet, drinking tea. Ali, who had known Ruben for years, asked what had brought him there. Ruben told him that he wanted to go away.

"Where to?" Ali asked

"Kermanshah and beyond."

Ali pointed to the a sturdy man whose face was sun burnt and dark as his beard and said, "This is Masha the Black Leopard," Ali introduced him. "His carriage leaves shortly for '*Kermanshah and beyond*' as you call it. Actually for Baghdad."

Now Ruben was convinced that going to Jerusalem through Baghdad, as in his previous journey, was meant to be. "Then I will go with him," he said.

"But Agha Masha," Ali said, with a sly laugh, "is not taking any passengers with him. He's going alone. And why Baghdad?" He turned to Masha as though waiting for his permission to answer the question. But Masha shook his head in disapproval.

"Come on Masha! Kadkhoda Ruben is one of us. He's a nice Jew. Let's tell him why you're going to Baghdad alone."

"No, Ali Agha, No! I know Haji Ruben and I will be happy to take him with me. All right?" the Leopard asserted to the custodian of his apparent secret.

"Fine, fine!" said Ali, raising his hands in surrender. "I won't say anything."

So that afternoon, in the summer of 1867, Ruben the Rhino began the second journey of his life to Jerusalem. This time he was not escaping the ghost of a man he had killed, he was running in search of himself. In the days that followed, the carriage passed through Bisotoon and Ruben remembered the enigmatic Deyr of Dervishes and in Kermanshah the caring people who had helped him escape over three decades ago. Masha the Leopard drove the carriage relentlessly, stopping only occasionally for short breaks in either a teahouse to eat or a caravansary to rest. One late night at a caravansary near Kermanshah, the two men were so tired that they had to stay for the night. They sat down on an old carpet in the middle of the room they were sharing, and as they were having dinner, Masha spoke.

"You may not know me," he said, "but I have known of you for a long time, Kadkhoda Ruben. I also know many Jewbarites who think very highly of you. 'A man that all of us trust,' Abba the Quiltmaker has told me often. Joshua the Aragh-Kesh considers you a master problem-solver. But more than anyone else, believe it or not, Nachamia the Baker..."

"Wait a minute," Ruben chuckled. "You seem to know all of my people!"

"Not all, but quite a few. You see, kadkhoda, unlike many other Muslims, I have always been fascinated by Jews and that has subjected me to a lot of contempt and ridicule." He paused, looked at the Rhino curiously and continued, "Haven't you heard of '*Haji Jew*'?"

"Oh my God!" Ruben cried. "It's you they call Haji Jew? Of

course I have heard about you and your kindness to my people."

"Let those who mock the Jews say whatever makes them happy and, at the same time, furthers their own stupidity."

Ruben was startled, for his companion was only a carriage driver and presumably illiterate. "How come we haven't met before?" he asked.

"I believe getting to meet and know people has a destined time of its own. Like the miracle of birth, it happens when it is supposed to happen. Like this girl I met..." and he went on telling his love story, the one he had refused to let Ali talk about. "A few months ago, I took a group of pilgrims to Najaf to visit the shrine of Imam Ali. I had all twenty of my passengers on board and we were ready to leave when this middle-aged Arab man stood in front of my carriage and yelled, 'What's your destination?' 'Baghdad,' I said. 'Can you take us with you?' he asked, and pointed to a woman standing behind him, firmly wrapped in her chador. 'Sorry pilgrim, I have no room.' 'But the coach that brought my daughter and me from Baghdad left us behind.' The old man began begging me. 'I told you' I said. 'There's no room in the back. Why don't you go and see for yourself?' But when I said this, my passengers began showing sympathy for the stranded travelers. 'They're pilgrims, Allah-loving Muslims,' they said. 'We will squeeze together and make room for them. Let them up.' 'Suit yourselves,' I said and the man and his daughter climbed into the back of my carriage. So, I drove them to Baghdad and when we got there in the late afternoon, the man insisted that I should be his guest for the night. 'For you have been so kind to us,' he said. I thanked him and told him that I would be going to the caravansary I always stay at when I come to Baghdad.

"Then," Masha went on, "It happened! The fated time to meet my beloved! Suddenly, his daughter spoke. No. Before she spoke, she opened her chador wide and I could see her face." Saying this, Masha slapped his knees with both hands, then reached for the opium pipe on the brazier in front of him, inhaled deeply, held his breath until his eyes were reddened and then blew the smoke out of his nostrils. "She was so beautiful! Her face like the moon. Her tall and slender unveiled figure like a cypress of Shiraz. And when she spoke and said, 'This is the least my father and I can do to return your kindness,' her voice was as soothing as the song of nightingales. You had to be there and hear her, Haji Ruben, and see those voluptuous lips beckoning me to their house. Allah Akbar!" Masha sighed, slapping his forehead this time. "She was prettier than colorful butterflies, dazzling like the paintings of Reza Abbasi."

It was obvious to Ruben that the Black Leopard was madly in love with this girl, whom he likened to the paintings of a peerless Persian artist of centuries ago. He was much more than an ordinary carriage driver. His broadmindedness towards Jews, his genuine belief in fate, his determination and selfless love for this woman, revealed a person of exceptional kindness, intelligence and sensitivity.

"Look at these," he said, holding his shaking hands before Ruben. "Even talking about her makes me shiver. So, I went to their house. With Asad, the father, Zainab, his wife, and their lovely daughter, Jamileh, we sat around their dinner sofreh. But who could eat? Not me! No matter how embarrassed I was, I couldn't take my eyes away from Jamileh. How can I describe it to you, kadkhoda? I simply cannot! And what's more was that every time I turned my head to look at her, she looked directly into my eyes. What made things worse was that no matter how much we tried, we could not conceal our constant glances at each other. At that moment, I was certain that this girl and I belonged to each other."

"How come you are so sure?" Ruben wanted to go on but stopped short of telling the carriage driver that his belief in destiny was frankly beyond reason.

"I'm sure," Masha responded as though he had read the Rhino's mind. "Because after dinner, as Asad was showing me to my room, you won't believe what happened. I was dumbfounded as he said, 'I noticed how you were looking at my daughter!' Kadkhoda Ruben, I've been traveling between Esfahan and Najaf for many years, I can speak Arabic and I could detect the rage in his voice. Honor killing being common among Arabs, I thought he would pull his dagger and decapitate me. I was about to throw myself at his feet and beg for mercy when he surprised me. 'If you want Jamileh, I can carry out a short sigheh ceremony, declare her your temporary wife for the night and have her come to your bed.'"

Ruben's eyes widened. "He said that? He really said that?"

"What a night! What a girl!" Masha sighed as the Rhino stared at him in disbelief. "But I didn't fall in love with her only because of her beauty. I was stunned when she opened her heart to me. 'I want to have a real life,' she said. 'I'm sick of being this man's sigheh one night and that man's the next.' It turned out that her father took money for these temporary marriages and that made my heart bleed for this statue of beauty. She begged me to marry her and, I'm telling you kadkhoda, there was transparent sincerity in her pleas. 'I know you are a good man and I would go wherever you take me,' she sobbed. But unfortunately, I had to leave in the morning. I promised that I would soon come back to Baghdad and marry her. All the way back to Esfahan, I cursed myself for having left Jamileh behind. When I arrived, Ali had another group of pilgrims for Najaf. 'I will take them,' I offered. But he refused. 'You have just arrived and are too tired. I will not risk the lives of my passengers in the hand of a tired opium addict like you.' I insisted. He refused. Then I begged him and that got him curious. 'What's the hurry?' he asked. 'If you need money, I can lend you some.' And when he said no again, like an idiot, I told him why."

"But Ali is a nice man. I knew his father and I know him," Ruben said.

"Of course he is. His problem is that he enjoys teasing people in love mercilessly. As soon as I told him about Jamileh, first he began mocking and embarrassing me in front of all my colleagues until he had tired himself. Then he allowed me to take off the next day."

"Which you did?" Ruben asked. "Another five weeks of this precarious journey?"

"Three!" Masha showed three fingers. "I did it in three weeks. I made my horses gallop so fast that my poor passengers were scared to death. 'Slow down, Haji Masha,' they begged me. But the only thing I could think about was Jamileh. All the way to Baghdad I kept saying to myself, 'As soon as we arrive in Baghdad and my passengers are settled in a caravansary for the night, I will go to her house, I will ask her parents to let me marry her and I will bring Jamileh to Esfahan with me.' And if they didn't want to give their daughter away, I would stay there, in Baghdad, and find myself a job. I didn't care. I loved her so much. I had to be with her. Jamileh—that superbly beautiful woman—was the one who would mother my children."

Invigorated by the opium, the Black Leopard talked ceaselessly. Based on what Ruben had heard so far, it was obvious that the carriage driver's wish had not come true. "My brother Ruben!" Masha went on as he shook his head. "When I finally got to

Jamileh's, the house was there, but there was no Jamileh, no Asad, no Zainab. They were gone. 'Where are they?' I asked the man who opened the door. He just stood there, frowning and shrugging, saying nothing. 'Tell me where they are!' I begged him, and then this chimpanzee howled, 'Are you a Shiite also?' This time I took a good look at his outfit and realized that he was a Sunni Ottoman officer. 'I sent the bastards to hell and this is my house now,' he said as he slammed the door in my face."

Once again Masha reached for the opium pipe, but Ruben held his hand and said, "I'm sorry. You have had enough. Don't smoke. Tell me what happened next."

"Well," Masha said, putting the pipe back on the brazier. "I began running towards the Shiite mosque where I go for my prayers whenever I am in Baghdad and asked its custodian, Mullah Bagher, about Asad's family. The news was bad. Apparently this Ottoman officer—who now lived in Jamileh's house—had asked to marry her, but because he was a Sunni, Asad had refused his proposal. Angered by the rejection, the officer and his soldiers had raided the house and killed Asad and his wife. Somehow Jamileh had escaped."

"She was lucky, Masha!" Ruben said.

"Lucky, yes. But where was she? First the mullah wouldn't divulge her whereabouts, but when I told him that she had been my sigheh and that I knew her parents, he loosened up. All he knew was that he had helped Jamileh escape to a nearby village where her aunt lived, but he did not know where the village was. 'What do you mean you don't know?' I howled. 'Well, I don't know, but I can find out and takes time,' he said. 'I'm a mullah and I have to put bread on the table for three wives and eight children.' Then it dawned on me that this clergyman, who struck me as lazy and ignorant and almost dim-witted, was after money. 'Tell me her exact address and I will make a generous donation to your mosque.' 'No gifts—money only!' said the greedy Mullah Bagher. 'How much?' I said, 'If I can afford it, I will be happy to pay you.' He suggested Ten Tugra gold coins and we settled on five."

Saying this, Masha now brought a small leather pouch out of his pocket and dangled it in front of Ruben's eyes. "Five Tugras," he said. "I sold a Persian carpet and some silverware I inherited from my father to buy this in Esfahan bazaar."

There was an air of sincerity about this fellow, Ruben thought, similar to that of Ardalan the Eagle, the Kurdish Sunni carriage driver who had first taken him to Jerusalem. He even talked and acted like Ardalan, so much so, in fact, that Ruben had the eerie feeling that he was traveling back in time. Was there a message in this coincidence? Ruben wondered.

"Are you sure you are doing the right thing?" Ruben asked. "I mean, after all, this girl you've spent only one night with her. How do you know...?"

"I know because it was destined to happen!" Then he turned to Ruben and continued, "Now you know my story. I am sure that something more than a visit has brought you this way. I see the aura of sadness that surrounds you and I can feel that you are looking for a place to lay it to rest."

"Here is why I am traveling away from Esfahan," Ruben began.

Masha held his palm in front of the Rhino and said, "Really, you don't have to tell me why. You know what, Haji? It is late and we are both tired. After I have found Jamileh, I will wait for you in Baghdad until you have done whatever you are here to do, and then on our way back to Esfahan, we will have ample time for you to tell me your story."

But I'm going to Jerusalem, Ruben wanted to cry out.

So, the next day, the two travel companions continued their journey towards Baghdad. They passed through the cities and crossed the Zagros Mountains Ruben had traveled in during the winter of 1834, except that this time, the freezing weather had given place to the torching heat of summer. On his previous expedition, besides the guilt that had afflicted Ruben for having killed Zain, his greatest concern had been the future of his family and his people. But this time, all he could think about was the abomination that had overshadowed his spirit, for the further he rode away from Jewbareh, the more he came to realize how much suffering he had caused those dearest and nearest to him. At last, three weeks after they left Esfahan, they arrived in Baghdad on a hot and sand-stormy day. Masha drove directly to Mullah Bagher's mosque. "Have a rest and I'll be back soon," he said, taking the pouch of gold coins out of his pocket, jingling it in front of Ruben's face, and then dashing off toward the mosque.

For as long as Masha was away, Ruben could not rest. He couldn't take his mind off this selfless and caring lover. He himself had been married to Tuba thirty-two years and to Jewel twenty-two. How could he compare himself with a man like Masha who had given up everything he had to get the woman he loved and make her happy? A woman with whom he had spent only one night. Yet, ironically, he actually saw himself in Masha. Both of them were on a quest—one in search of the woman he loved and the other seeking his lost self after a host of misfortunes—many of his own doing. Ruben was lost in these thoughts when an ecstatic Masha emerged from the mosque and hurried to the carriage. The pouch that contained the worth of all his worldly belongings and life savings had been exchanged for a piece of paper. *"This,"* Masha said, slapping the paper with the back of his hand. "This is where she lives and this is where I shall go," he said. As if his companion's exuberance were contagious, Ruben cried, "Let's get moving!"

Masha turned silent.

"What?" Ruben asked curiously.

"No, my friend," he said with his hand on the Rhino's shoulder. "I know you are as excited as I am and want to help me, but Jamileh is in Karbala and I would be crazy if I took a Jew to the holiest of Shiite cities. My dear Haji Ruben, I don't want to risk your life. If you need another carriage to take you back to Esfahan, I can arrange for that. There is a caravansary in Baghdad that belongs to my friend, Muhammad-al-Jabbar. We will hire you a carriage there to take you wherever you want to go."

Ruben was at a crossroad, wondering whether he should continue his journey to Jerusalem or remain in Baghdad and wait for Masha. He had the peculiar feeling that this carriage driver had been placed in his way as a medium. How could he go to Jerusalem, closing his eyes to this dear man's destiny?

"I will go nowhere before you have found your wife and returned to Baghdad," Ruben said firmly. "I will stay at Jabbar's caravansary until you have come back."

Masha went on his way and Ruben remained in Baghdad, staying at the caravansary of Muhammad-al-Jabbar. During the day he strolled through the city of Baghdad, seeing places and killing time while he waited for Masha to return. On his last journey, Ruben had not stopped in Baghdad. At the time, under the rule of a cruel Ottoman Sultan, the city looked like a ghost town—a larger Jewbareh at best. And now, thirty-four years later, as he walked the streets, he noticed that thanks to a more compassionate Sultan, it had grown into a real city. Many new homes and wide streets had been built since his last visit. For the first time in his life, Ruben saw steamships on the Tigris and from a distance, the glittering dome and minarets of mosques.

A week had gone by with no news from Masha, leaving Ruben worried about what might have happened to his friend. It was a hot summer day and the skies were covered with a thin film of desert sand. Scattered rays of sun made their way through the hazy skies and settled on the domes of the Kadhimain Mosque. Ruben was walking along the shores of the Tigris River that roared mightily through the city of Baghdad. This great flowing body of water, Ruben thought, was nothing but the tears of his forefathers, whom Cyrus the Great had saved from captivity as recorded in Psalms.

By the rivers of Babylon, there we sat, sat and wept, as we thought of Zion.

There on the willows we hung up our lyres,

For our captors asked us there for songs, our tormentors, for amusement,

"Sing us one of the songs of Zion."

How can we sing a song of the Lord on alien soil?

And there, more than two thousand years later, on the very shores of the river that ran through Babylon, Ruben the Rhino, the son of Naphtali the Tailor, sat down and as he sewed his eyes to the roiling foam of the river, he wondered why his people had gone through so much hardship and whether they had been chosen by God only to suffer. Deep in contemplating, he lost track of time until he noticed the sun melting into the horizon beyond the Tigris at the point where the sky and the desert met. That was when he stood up and looked around. Aware that he had to return before it got dark, Ruben began striding toward his caravansary. He walked a long way before he realized that he was lost. The night fell and a cloud of sand covered the moonlight. Now, all he could see was the desert on his right the Tigris on his left and some tiny scattered shacks by the river.

He knocked on a door and asked for directions to the caravansary of Muhammad-al-Jabbar. The Bedouin who had opened the door motioned him to enter and, according to Arab tradition, received him as his guest. *Shokran*, Ruben murmured, thanking him with what little Arabic that he knew, repeating it again, and then insisting nevertheless on directions to Jabbar's caravansary and the man pointed in the same direction Ruben was heading. An hour passed and there was still no sign of Jabbar's place in sight. Ruben was not particularly concerned because, after all, this was not the frozen desert he had traveled across many years ago. If he didn't find his way, he could go back to the kind Bedouin and sleep in his small shack for the night. So, he marched ahead. He had a peculiar feeling that he was surrounded by the spirits of his ancestors who had died here before Cyrus the Great had conquered Babylon. It felt to him as if they were looking after him, protecting him. He was of the seed of a lucky soul who had survived the slavery of the Babylonians and had made it to Persia. This was where he had come from. *"You must know where you came from in order to know where you are going to,"* he said to himself, recalling this quotation from Mishnah—one of Rabbi Shimon's favorite lines. Ruben knew where he had come from, but where was he going?

Just when the Rhino was seriously thinking of going back to the Bedouin's shack, he saw a huge house. In fact it was a mansion, perhaps even a palace, fortified by tall terracotta walls and illuminated by torchlights attached to long columns that rose to the roof. Ruben closed and rubbed his eyes, and when he opened them he realized that what he was looking at was real and not a mirage. Beyond this building there was nothing else but the river and the desert. Perhaps someone in this house could help him find his caravansary, he thought, lifting the large brass knocker and clang it against the door. It opened to reveal an Abyssinian servant in a long black jacket and baggy trousers. Ruben asked the man if he knew of Jabbar's place. The servant raised his palms in a sign telling Ruben to wait and suddenly disappeared, leaving the Rhino standing there by the open door. Moments later he returned with another man, pointed at Ruben and walked away. "You're looking for a caravansary?" he asked in Persian, with an Arabic accent. This was a young man in his twenties whose outfit, unlike the Abyssinian's black clothing, was all white, from turban to shoes.

"Oh, you speak my language," Ruben said excitedly.

"Jabbar's Caravansary," the second servant said, narrowing his eyes as if searching for something in Ruben's face. "I don't know, but I can't send you away. You're a *mehman- habib-Allah—a* guest loved by Allah—and if a guest knocks on his door and I send him away, my master, His Highness Prince Muhebbedin Mamluki, will punish me. You *have to* come in. Please follow me in and I will inform His Highness of your arrival." Saying this, the man took two steps, stared straight into Ruben's eyes, then turned around and went away.

"Didn't I tell you?" said the young man when he returned. "His Highness has asked you to bless his home with your auspicious steps. He wants you to come in and be his guest. Now, follow me."

"But I don't want to be a burden."

"*Ya seyedi* – my dear sir," said the young man in an assertive tone. "I'm not permitted to let you go even if I have to force you to stay. So please come in."

Ruben followed the young man into the courtyard of the mansion where statues of naked women, at least six feet tall, stood in the middle of a round pool surrounded by flowerbeds. Planted in immaculate order, there was circle after circle of petunias, pansies, irises, lilies and sage. Behind the fountain, built on a raised foundation, sat the mansion, glowing in the light of many torches. The man opened the door, which was fancifully carved with birds and branches, bowed to Ruben and motioned him to go in.

"Thanks. What's your name, brother?" Ruben asked the servant as he entered the foyer and raised his head, marveling at a painted scene of men and women drinking wine together, situated beneath the ceiling of the entrance dome.

The man bowed his head. "Abbas, *seyedi* – my mater."

"I am Mustafa," said Ruben, "And I'm grateful for..."

"Don't thank me, seyedi. I'm only a servant here."

"Bring our guest, habib-Allah, up here and show him to his room." The voice issuing that order in broken Persian from the top of the stairs could only belong to the master of the house, thought Ruben, glancing upward to perceive a short man with a bulging belly, a full, nicely trimmed beard and unusually thick eyebrows. He wore a green, domelike felt hat and a long, light brown robe.

"*Salam alikom* – greetings to you – Your Highness. May Allah bless you for your kind hospitality," said Ruben as Abbas translated his every word. The prince nodded and then motioned Abbas to lead Ruben to his room, while he himself turned and disappeared into his own. Once ushered into his chamber, Ruben stood in shock. Never in his life had he beheld such luxury. There was a carved oak bed with a shiny silk red bedcover embroidered with peacocks, a rare Persian carpet on the floor and a window that opened to the courtyard. The scent of frankincense hovered in the air. Abbas bowed and went out. Now alone, Ruben wanted to pinch himself. Was he still in the trance in which he had passed out arguing over Rebecca's dowry? Or was it like that time, so long ago, when he had entered the house of the Dervishes. Certainly it seemed to him now as if he were in another world altogether.

"Since dinner will be served in a few hours," Abbas's voice brought him back, "my master has asked me to bring you something to eat. Right now, at the kitchen we have lamb kabob, pheasant and chicken kabob."

"I hope you have something lighter, like eggs," Ruben said, trying to avoid eating non-Kosher food.

Abbas came closer and stared into his eyes. "You're not a Jew, are you?"

Ruben was breathless. *Not another teahouse debacle*, he thought. But before he was able to react, came the next blow. "And you are from Jewbareh!" Abbas said firmly.

"Not Jewbareh," Ruben jumped. "I come from Esfahan but not Jewbareh."

Abbas rushed to the door, closed it firmly, came back and, to Ruben's utter surprise, took Ruben's face in his palms, kissed him on his cheeks and his forehead and whispered, "The color of your eyes, the tone of your voice—how can I ever forget my Uncle Ruben?"

Ruben stared at the young man's face. "Who are you?" he demanded.

"One day," Abbas sighed, "Yes. One day, right in front of your shop, when I was only seven, they kidnapped me…"

"Aa… Aa… Aaron?" Ruben choked as his hair stood on end. The young man standing in front of him threw his arms around the Rhino's neck and burst into tears. Ruben gradually loosened the grip of the young man's arms, pushed him gently back and looked into his tearful eyes. He was Aaron all right. Nothing except for his size had changed—his jet-black eyes, the crack right in the middle of his lower lip, his abundant hair that grew very close to his eyebrows, giving him a short forehead.

"Remember what your father called you?" Ruben was not sure why he was asking this question. Perhaps to reassure himself that the man's claim was genuine.

"My little monkey," he sighed, tears welling up again.

"You've been missing for such a long time, little monkey," Ruben said wiping the young man's tears.

"Twenty-four years, Uncle Ruben. It was twenty-four years ago. I have counted each and every day." And Aaron began to recount what had happened to him since he had been kidnapped. First he had been taken to a mullah who had ordered him to say something in a tongue he hadn't understood then, though now he knew they were Arabic words that meant, "I testify that there's no god but Allah, that Mohammad is his prophet and Ali His guardian." By saying that, he had been converted to Islam and renamed Abbas. Then he had been sold as a slave to a sheik from the Persian Gulf who had taken him to his palace where little Aaron had worked as a cleaning boy. As he had grown, Aaron had shown talent in fixing whatever needed repair. But when he had grown and passed puberty, the old sheik suspected that one of his young concubines had fallen in love with the young man. So the sheik had sold him to a slave dealer from Baghdad who in turn had sold him to Prince Mamluki.

Listening intently to Aaron's story, Ruben remembered Talmudic words: *"Everything is decreed in our destiny as a divine plan for each and every person in the Heavenly records,"* and thought, it's destiny, sheer destiny, that he had come here, to this no man's land where he had found the son of his best friend — the very one whom he had hurt so deeply. Now he felt himself beginning to climb the steps of the dungeon of his inexcusable acts toward the light of tranquility, purging himself of the evil that had bit-by-bit poisoned his soul.

"During these years," Ruben asked gently, "you didn't even make an effort to escape?"

"I was seven, for God's sake." He looked at Ruben with such apprehension that the Rhino was shaken.

"I'm sorry. You're absolutely right," Ruben said. "But that was then. Now that you are thirty something, don't you miss your parents and don't you think they deserve to have their missing son back? Why have you remained here? Why haven't you run away?"

"You know something, Uncle Ruben?" Aaron sighed. "I *have* thought a lot about this. As a child, I was too scared to escape. I had no idea where I was and where I would escape to. After awhile Jewbareh began to fade in my mind and with the passage of time, I wondered whether it even existed. In my memory, our ghetto turned into a place in a fantastic tale, a place to which I could only return on a magic carpet. Then, later, when I became a man, I felt anger. At my mother who was so busy gossiping with her friends that she didn't notice when they kidnapped me, and at Jewbarites and at myself too for no good reason." Aaron walked to the window and continued, as if talking to someone outside, "And now, who remembers me anymore? Who wants me?" He stayed silent for a while, then he turned to Ruben and said, "Here, I am doing fine. I have a roof above my head, food to eat and most importantly, the prince is very kind to me. No lashes like my previous owner, no cruelty. If I return to Jewbareh, what is there for me? Who will rejoice at my return?"

"My dear little monkey," said Ruben, walking up to Aaron and pressing his finger to the young man's chest. "You have an entire world waiting for you and it's not in a fantastic tale, either. Your parents, your sisters and Eli—your brother whom you have never seen—would die of joy to see you."

"I have a brother?" Aaron gasped.

Ruben nodded and continued, "And believe me, Jewbareh has a long, long memory. You've not been forgotten nor would you ever be."

"How's my Auntie Tuba doing?" Aaron asked unexpectedly.

"She... She's... fine." Something—perhaps his shame—refrained Ruben from admitting that his "Auntie Tuba" was now living with a havoo.

"And you, yourself Uncle Ruben?"

"Ah, that's a very long story. It can wait."

Ruben yearned to open his heart to Aaron and tell him that ever since the killing of Zain, his life had been far from easy. That he had lived with an empty heart, hanging from one side of a steelyard with no weights on the other side to keep his balance. That in the immensity of this emptiness, he had been constantly sinking deeper and deeper into a terrifying void. What Ruben did not say was that finding Aaron was, even as the two of them stood there, talking to each other, like the shining of an immeasurable light of hope on the pitch-black shadow that had eclipsed his heart and his mind. What Ruben did not say to Aaron was that with this sudden meeting, this bringing together the broken pieces of the past, he felt now—after all these years—that his hands were washed clean of the blood of the nomad.

A life lost. A life found.

Ruben, who had realized that ahead of him lay the task of taking Aaron back home, began to work on a plan he had immediately contemplated. "I have traveled a great deal," he said to Aaron, "But I have never eaten non-Kosher, and here I'm not going to make an exception."

"You have to make an exception here, Uncle Ruben."

"Listen, my dear boy. If you do what I tell you, not only will I not have to make an exception, but before the prince knows, *I* will be out of here." Ruben intentionally stressed the word "I" and noticed a sudden change of expression on Aaron's face — an expression of disappointment. Nevertheless, he went on immediately to tell the young man what to say to his boss.

"Your mehman has a bad cold — let it be far from the health of Your Highness," Aaron began to tell the prince, to whose chamber he had just returned. "And since he is a descent person and doesn't want to give his ailment to Your Highness, I hope you will allow me to bring his food to his room tonight. Then let us hope that by tomorrow, when he has recovered, he will come to kiss your gracious hands, have breakfast with you and of course thank you in person for your hospitality."

Having secured his master's permission, Aaron rushed to the kitchen and brought Ruben a tray of boiled eggs, bread and tea. Together they sat down and had their dinner as Ruben talked passionately with Aaron for hours into the night, undoing not only his own knots of rage, but unraveling the intricate web of fury that over time had spun over this deprived young man's mind against his family and the rest of the Jewbareh until Aaron had calmed down. The Rhino's next mission was to encourage Aaron — this lost treasure, the way he saw it — to escape and return to his parents. Ruben realized that it would be a major undertaking to free this feeble caged slave. He had to both encourage and help Aaron to flee. At this moment, with the thought of Masha's setting out to find his beloved Jamileh flickering through his mind, Ruben the Rhino, the son of Naphtali the Tailor, and kadkhoda of Jewbareh, had a revelation. Now he could feel, think and even believe that this was a destined mission, as his carriage driver had told him. He realized that God had filled his heart with concern about Masha in order to make him stay in Baghdad, and lead him to this young man, whom he now realized was his destiny to take back to Jewbareh and his parents. That was when Ruben decided that he was going to Jewbareh and not to Jerusalem. "For Jerusalem," he reasoned to himself, "is wherever one is at peace with oneself and God."

It was before daybreak when Ruben and Aaron slipped out of the mansion of Prince Mamluki through an underground escape canal that all the Ottoman rulers and royalty dug under their palaces for their own safety. From behind the walls of Mamluki's palace, they ran to Jabbar's caravansary, where another surprise was waiting for the Rhino. "I looked every-where for you, Kadkhoda Ruben. Were it not because of my concern for you," said a euphoric Masha who had arrived the night before, "Jamileh and I would have left for Esfahan last night."

Ruben looked at Jamileh who stood next to her husband with her head down.

"Salam, *khahareh-man—Greetings, my sister*" Ruben said to Jamileh. She raised her head and Ruben saw the truth of every word in praise of this woman's beauty that he had heard from the carriage driver.

"And who is this young man?" Masha asked.

"A friend who is coming with us to Esfahan. We will talk about him on our way back home. Now, are we ready to leave?" asked Ruben, who was anxious to smuggle Aaron out of Baghdad before the Ottoman soldiers caught up with them.

"As I said, we were only waiting for you, Kadkhoda Ruben."

It took the carriage several weeks to get from Baghdad to Jew-bareh. On their way home, the passengers—Ruben, Aaron, Masha and Jamileh—had plenty of stories to exchange. In the privacy of the rooms Ruben and Aaron shared in different caravansaries, the Rhino told the son of his best friend everything that had happened since the kidnapping. He gave an account of all the additions to the two families since his disappearance. He told Aaron that Eli and Rebecca were in love and that he, Ruben, had foolishly refused to consent to the marriage. Ruben told Masha and his wife about Aaron's life story and that now, after twenty-four years, he was escaping captivity and was going back to his family.

"May Allah protect this coach," Masha laughed loudly, "in which I am carrying a load of escapees!" Then he pointed to the back where Jamileh was sitting and said, "God bless Mullah

Bagher's soul. The address he gave me was right. But Jamileh's aunt and her husband wouldn't let her go. She said, 'My slain sister never, ever told me that you were married,' and her husband accused me of having had immoral relations outside the confines of the faith of Muhammad with a virgin girl." Exhilarated, Masha turned around and told Jamileh, "Do you want to tell them the rest of the story?" Embarrassed, the girl brought her head down and shook it.

"What is it? You're shy, little angel?" the carriage driver sounded euphoric. "She's the bravest of all women I have known, Kadkhoda Ruben!"

"So, what happened next?" Ruben demanded.

"As I was telling you," Masha resumed, "no matter how much we argued with her custodians, they refused to believe that we were married according to Islamic law. So finally, one day I kept watch on their house, and when they both left, I went in, took my precious jewel and — here we are!"

"Now that we are talking about a jewel," Ruben asked Masha, "Where is the best place to buy good quality jewelry?"

"Had I called her a rose," the jubilant carriage driver teased the Rhino, "then would you have wanted rosebushes?"

"Tell me, you crazy man," Ruben laughed.

"On our way to Kermanshah, there's a jewelry shop in this small Kurdish village. Mohsen, the owner, is a friend of mine. Don't ask me where he gets his magnificent Russian bracelets and necklaces from. You won't believe what masterpieces he carries in his little shop."

Two identical gold enameled bracelets adorned with sapphires and diamonds, one gold necklace embellished with strands of diamonds, opals, turquoises and many other precious stones that Ruben had never even heard of were what he bought from Mohsen at his "little shop."

On a late afternoon early in the autumn of 1867, Ruben and Aaron passed through the gates of the city of Esfahan. At Ali's caravansary, Masha embraced Ruben and thanked him for his support as he bid farewell to the Rhino and Aaron. "I will miss you," he said.

"We will be seeing each other soon because in a little while I will invite you and your lovely bride to a feast," the Rhino replied.

"A feast to celebrate many happy occasions—finding this young man," he pointed to Aaron, "your reunion with Sister Jamileh *and* another major celebration that you will see for yourself."

From there, Ruben and Aaron headed to Jewbareh. As they walked the turns of the Alley of Eleven Twists, in a shaky voice, Aaron whispered, "Please tell me that this is not a dream, Uncle Ruben. In my imagination, I have been here so many times throughout the years. Tell me that I will not wake up to find myself in the same spot at Mamluki's palace."

Ruben put his arm around Aaron's shoulder, looked into his eyes and smiled. "You are not dreaming! Now, let's move fast. I don't want anybody to see you. We are going to overwhelm this ghetto with such a surprise, they will never forget it. Beside your parents, can you imagine how happy all the Jewbarites will be?"

When Ruben entered his house with Aaron, it was Rebecca they saw first. She stood there mute—neither happy, nor sad. Her eyes were sunken, her face pale. He ran to his daughter, his arms open and for the first time that anyone in Jewbareh could remember, Ruben the Rhino wept, sobbed, and begged Rebecca to forgive him for all the suffering he had caused her and the man she loved. Rebecca raised her head and looked at this mountain of a man falling apart in front of her. Astonished, dazed even, she could not help but open her arms and embrace her father. Now Ruben lifted her up into the air just as he'd done on the day she'd been born. As always, the smell of her father's neck intoxicated Rebecca. She put her head on his shoulder and father and daughter shed tears together.

"Who's there?" Tuba called from the kitchen. "I said: Who's there?" Then, as she came out of the kitchen, she saw Rebecca and her father embracing. "Agha is back!" she yelled. Jewel rushed out of her room and froze at the scene in front of her. Tuba clapped and ululated, "Time to rejoice!" she cried. Then she noticed Aaron. "Who are you?" she said, eyeing the young man with curiosity. Before Aaron could open his mouth, Ruben put his forefinger of the tip of his nose. "Hush," he said. "He is a friend from faraway lands and he won't be staying long. Just..." But before Ruben could finish what he was saying, Aaron ran to Tuba, embraced her and whispered, "Auntie Tuba, it's me. Aaron!"

Tuba pulled herself back from his grip, looked into the young man's eyes, cupped her opened jaw and groaned in a shaky voice,

"It can't be." Then she took one step forward, narrowed her eyes and repeated, "No. It can't be." She stepped back again, inspected him from head to toe and said, "Heavens. It's you. Aaron!"

"Who is he?" Jewel said to Tuba and Rebecca asked her father the same question, for neither of the two women had ever seen Aaron before.

After he told them who the stranger was, Ruben said, "I don't want his parents to know yet. I want to surprise them." Then he added in a whisper, "So please lower your voices, let's go inside and I'll tell you the whole story."

They went into the guestroom where the women of Rhino's household surrounded Aaron. It wasn't until dinner that they learned from Ruben the details of how he had found Aaron. Then Ruben brought out his gifts and put the bracelets on his wives' wrists and the necklace around Rebecca's neck. That evening, after dinner, Ruben sent for the rabbi and the mayor, both of whom were excited to see their friend again and thrilled to notice that he was far more composed than before he had left. "Who's this young man?" Haskell asked, pointing at Aaron. "We haven't seen him before," the rabbi added and the Rhino promised that he would tell them in time. Then, Ruben the Rhino spoke.

"For a long time, I have done terrible things, insane things, things that have caused nothing but grief and anguish to those who are dear to me. I apologize to you, my wives, for all the distress that I have caused you. I regret the way I have treated you, my beloved daughter, Rebecca. I am shamed by my uncivil acts to my wonderfully patient friend Nissan, who tolerated my ill manners and in time, I will extend my regrets to him also and beg his forgiveness."

Mullah Shimon put his hand on Ruben's head and blessed him. "It is written in Mishnah Torah," he said, "*When asked by an offender for forgiveness, one should forgive with a sincere mind and a willing spirit.*' And so we do, Kadkhoda Ruben. Now, tell us. Where have you been and why don't you introduce your guest?"

"I have told my family where I have been and I will tell you in time. All that matters is that I have come back with a gift that no money could buy and no miracle could grant. And that gift is this young man." Ruben put his large warm hand on Aaron's shoulder and looked directly at Mullah Shimon and Mayor Haskell. "He is a native of our ghetto who has been away for many years and I want the two of you to take a good look at him and see if you can remember him."The two men now looked at Aaron, who sat there patiently enduring their scrutiny. "Is he... No!" said the rabbi. "It can't be...." The mayor too shook his head. Aaron smiled, for he remembered them both even after so many years. Ruben looked at Aaron, who was sitting back, enjoying the game, and said, "Give your word that this will remain a secret between us," he pointed at the two men.

"Promise," said Haskell. "I promise, Rabbi Shimon promises, we both promise. You're killing us, Ruben. Will you tell us who he is?"

"Ready?" Ruben whispered. And he did at last tell them.

"*Elohim gadol*" — Devine is the Almighty — said the rabbi, raising his arms skyward. And Haskell slapped his cheek and exclaimed, "No!"

"Yes. It is he, Aaron himself. Take a good look at him. This is the man who was once the child we all loved. It is he and no one else. And here's what I suggest we do. All of us will go next door now. It's time for a celebration, for I have brought Nissan his lost son. I will give him this precious gift in exchange for his other son, Eli, who will marry my beloved daughter."

The three women in the room were crying silently. Ruben stood up. So did everyone else. The young man came up to Ruben. "Thanks for saving me, Uncle Ruben," he said. Then Ruben's wives, Rebecca, the mayor and the rabbi surrounded Ruben and touched him, as if he were a divine pillar.

Eli opened the door and was shocked to see Rebecca and others standing in front of him. As planned, Mullah Shimon and Mayor Haskell entered the house, leaving the rest of the group behind. The rabbi calmly went up to Nissan and Zilfa. "That man," he said, pointing through the open door at Ruben, "has just returned from a long journey, and has brought you a most precious gift. Now, invite him into your home!"

Aaron, who had been hiding nervously and impatiently behind Ruben's long robe, stepped forward and over the threshold into the interior of his childhood home. He ran toward his mother and took her in his arms, roaring "Mani!"

For Zilfa, time stopped. At first she simply sensed, and then in an instant perceived a familiar way of running — shoulders relaxed, arms stretched, palms held forward and slack dark hair that waved like willows in the wind. Then she took in the adult version of the child she had known—wide chest, strong torso, long legs. As he came nearer, again in just a flash, a mere instant, she looked at the hazel brown eyes of the infant boy whom she had nursed so long ago. "Aaron," she whispered as she yielded to her son's embrace.

"What? Who? What's *this* trick now?" Nissan yelled at Ruben. "Who is this man?" he shouted, turning to Zilfa, "And what gives him the right to embrace you?"

Heedless of Nissan, Zilfa whispered to her son, "I knew you would come back one day. No mother loses faith in the return of her lost child." Then she held his face in her palms and staring into his eyes, said loudly, "You don't recognize your own son, Nissan? Our Aaron is back!"

Nissan tore Aaron out of Zilfa's embrace. Holding the young man at arm's length, he stared at him with a look of the utmost suspicion, coldness and hostility. Aaron did not resist, but gazed unblinkingly into Nissan's eyes. "Don't you remember me, Baba?" Nissan took deep breaths. "Baba," said Aaron, now with a look of infinite patience, with a sweet, sad smile on his face. Everyone was now in the house—Zilfa, the mayor, the rabbi, Ruben, Jewel, Tuba, Rebecca and Eli. They all remained silent. Zilfa came up and stood beside her son. Nissan's eyes remained on Aaron. He looked at Zilfa, who nodded. Then he again looked at Aaron. With a sob, Nissan fell into the arms of his son, who, catching him, embraced and led him gently to the flowerbed in the courtyard where they sank down together and wept.

The following day, the ejazeh-giran ceremonies—which had been so unpleasantly interrupted a few months ago—were resumed at Ruben's house. This time everyone was jubilant and there were no arguments about mehrieh, jahiziyeh or Shirbaha. Tuba talked about her niece, Hannah, as the best possible match for Aaron. Jewel suggested her cousin, Rana, and Zilfa ended the discussion by announcing that for her beloved first son, Aaron, she had the perfect match in mind, whose identity, however, she refused to divulge, since, she said, she had a more immediate matter at hand— the forthcoming marriage of her second son to his lovely bride-to-be. Nissan suggested to Ruben that it was time to rebuild the dividing wall between the two houses and Ruben replied with a laugh, "No my friend. It's time to bring it down. I want to have easy access to my grandchildren."

And so, on that sunny day in the summer of 1868, as their fathers once again renewed the friendship once so dear to them both, The Graceful Rebecca and Eli the Stallion held hands and looked forward to their marriage.

Chapter 19
The Ways of Destiny

After they were married, Rebecca moved to Nissan's house and in less than a year, she gave birth to a boy. On the infant's Brit Mila—covenant of circumcision—Ruben sat on a special chair called the Chair of Elijah for the prophet is thought to be the child's guardian, with the baby on a white pillow over his knees, his eyes fixed on the infant, waiting for Rabbi Shimon to perform the prescribed rituals and circumcise the boy. Gazing at the baby, Ruben thought that he looked more like Rebecca than Eli. And he contemplated the ways of destiny and how amazing it was that he had had to wait for what he had so long desired until he was over sixty.

At the ceremonies, Tuba had been honored with the ritual of bringing the baby from his room to be circumcised and Jewel with the privilege of taking the newborn back to his cradle afterwards. "And he will be named Naphtali, after his grandfather," the rabbi intoned. "Naphtali, the Hebrew word for 'my struggle.' And didn't our friend Ruben struggle to have this boy," he said cheerfully waving his right arm in the air, inviting women guests to ululate. "Naphtali, the founder of one of the Twelve Tribes of Israel," he said, resuming his sermon after the crowd had become quiet.

After Naphtali, Rebecca gave birth to three more boys and two girls. Ruben the Rhino lived long enough to see all his grandchildren and entrust his duties as the kadkhoda of Jewbareh to his grandson, Naphtali, to live a peaceful life with his wives and his best friend, Nissan the Fabricseller, his wife Zilfa, and the grandchildren they shared.